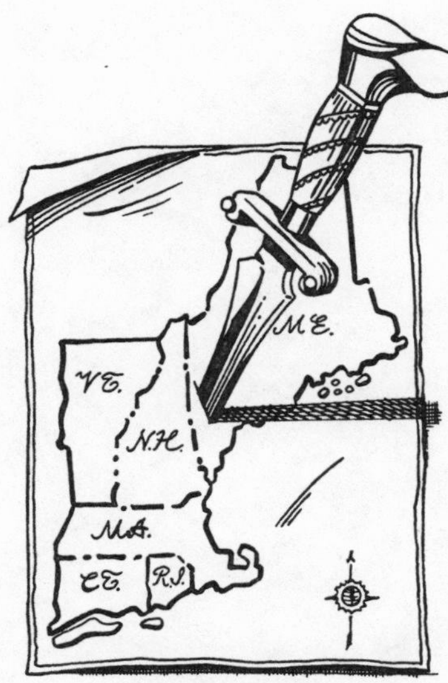
M.E.
V.T.
N.H.
M.A.
C.T.
R.I.

NEW ENGLAND CRIME CHOWDER

Prepared and edited by
Cynthia Manson and Charles Ardai

LIBRARY OF CRIME CLASSICS®

MISTER E'S™

INTERNATIONAL POLYGONICS, LTD.
NEW YORK CITY

In memory of Eleanor Sullivan, a New Englander by birth and at heart.

Grateful acknowledgment is made to the following for permission to reprint their copyrighted material:

I.O.U.—ONE LIFE by Marjorie Carleton, copyright ©1960 by E.J. Carleton, reprinted by permission of Harold Ober Associates, Inc.; UNACCEPTABLE PROCEDURES by Stanley Ellin, copyright ©1985 by Davis Publications, Inc., reprinted by permission of Curtis Brown, Ltd.; LIZZIE BORDEN IN THE P.M. by Robert Henson, copyright ©1980 by Robert Henson, reprinted by permission of the author; SOMETHING YOU HAVE TO LIVE WITH by Patricia Highsmith, copyright ©1976 by Davis Publications, Inc., reprinted by permission of McIntosh & Otis, Inc.; A BORDERLINE CASE by Rufus King, copyright ©1959 by Rufus King, reprinted by permission of Rogers Terrill Literary Agency; MIFFLIN MUST GO by Shannon OCork, copyright ©1986 by Davis Publications, Inc., reprinted by permission of the Ann Elmo Agency; THE DAY THE CHILDREN VANISHED by Hugh Pentecost, copyright ©1958 by United Newspapers Magazine Corporation, reprinted by permission of Brandt & Brandt Literary Agency; OLD KILLEEN'S PROMISE by Thomas Walsh, copyright ©1979 by Davis Publications, Inc., reprinted by permission of the author; NICE, WELL-MEANING FOLK by N. Scott Warner, copyright ©1986 by Davis Publications, Inc., reprinted by permission of the author; all stories previously appeared in ELLERY QUEEN'S MYSTERY MAGAZINE, published by Davis Publications, Inc. PAID IN FULL by W. W. Fredericks, copyright ©1989 by Davis Publications, Inc., reprinted by permission of the author; A SOUL TO TELL by Jeremiah Healy, copyright ©1989 by Davis Publications, Inc., reprinted by permission of Jed Mattes, Inc.; LIEUTENANT HARALD AND THE *TREASURE ISLAND* TREASURE by Margaret Maron, copyright ©1989 by Davis Publications, Inc., reprinted by permission of the author; THE GOLDEN PARACHUTE by Martin N. Meyer, copyright ©1990 by Davis Publications, Inc., reprinted by permission of the author; THINGS THAT GO BUMP AND GRIND IN THE NIGHT by S. S. Rafferty, copyright ©1976 by Davis Publications, Inc., reprinted by permission of the author; all stories previously appeared in ALFRED HITCHCOCK'S MYSTERY MAGAZINE, published by Davis Publications, Inc.

Library of Congress Cataloging-in-Publication Data

New England crime chowder / prepared and edited by Cynthia Manson and Charles Ardai.
p. cm. — (Library of Crime Classics)
ISBN 1-55882-127-9 : $12.95
1. Detective and mystery stories, American, New England. 2. New England—Fiction. I. Manson, Cynthia.
II. Ardai, Charles. III. Series.
PS648.D4N54 1992
813'.0872083274—dc20 92-52741
CIP

Library of Congress Card Catalog No. 92-52741
ISBN 1-55882-127-9

Printed and manufactured in the United States of America
First IPL printing April 1992
10 9 8 7 6 5 4 3 2 1

NEW ENGLAND CRIME CHOWDER

List of Ingredients

Introduction

There are two images of New England that people carry with them.

There is the New England of picture-postcard villages, houses with gabled roofs and churches with tall steeples, and tightly knit, intensely private communities. This is a New England of history, tradition, and upright morality.

Then there is the New England of Lizzie Borden and the Salem witch trials, cold nights during long winters, brisk winds carrying whispered secrets, and dark deeds done behind closed doors. Which New England one sees depends on the light in which one looks at it . . . or the darkness.

Neither image is false. New England is both an inviting and a forbidding place, and it is this combination that has proven irresistible to mystery writers. Crime in New England can seem a strange and violent intruder, disrupting lives that are otherwise notoriously placid; yet crime can also seem strangely at home here, lodging deep in stubborn hearts and exploding within closed ranks. The stories in this collection show both sides.

Hugh Pentecost's "The Day the Children Vanished" considers an impossible crime committed against innocents: a carload of school children disappears—car, driver, and all. The entire town, not just the children, is the victim of this crime—and it takes action by the entire town to solve the mystery. On the other side, Stanley Ellin's "Unacceptable Procedures" portrays a gallery of apparently upstanding citizens who are really nothing of the sort. From the sheriff on down to the town mechanic, everyone has a secret agenda and a way of implementing it at other people's expense.

Other authors in the book explore the levels of moral ambiguity in between, from Shannon OCork, who deftly satirizes Connecticut high society in "Mifflin Must Go," to Patricia Highsmith, who tells a subtle tale of guilt and penance in "Something You Have to Live With." S. S. Rafferty tackles false morality in "Things That Go Bump and Grind in the Night"; Thomas Walsh explores broken commitments in "Old Killeen's Promise"; and Marjorie Carleton illustrates the problems of medical confidentiality in "I.O.U.—One Life." Even Rufus King, whose villain in "A Borderline Case" is as unambiguously hateful as a villain can be, raises a serious moral problem in his story: why is it that the same crime receives a harsher punishment on one side of a border than on the other?

These stories give their authors a chance to investigate the subtleties of morality and immorality, and in this the New England settings play a crucial role. Robert Henson's award-winning "Lizzie Borden in the P.M." would not have the same impact if the Borden family scandal had been played out against a different backdrop. Nor would Jeremiah Healy's "A Soul to Tell," in which a veil of polite lies covers up some brutal truths, or W. W. Fredericks's "Paid in Full," in which brutal truths (in this case, scrupulously candid theater reviews) are a catalyst for a more violent form of brutality.

And throughout, the authors present a variety of New England scenery as a backdrop for their mysteries. The description of the Connecticut woods in Margaret Maron's "Lieutenant Harald and the *Treasure Island* Treasure" offers a special pleasure for New England readers, as does the portrait of suburban New England in N. Scott Warner's "Nice, Well-Meaning Folk" and urban New England in Martin N. Meyer's "The Golden Parachute."

Any reader can enjoy the mysteries in this anthology, which run the gamut from the classic puzzle to the chilling suspense story. But readers who love New England are in for a double treat, since all the stories are set in their neck of the woods. For them, the mysteries literally take place in their own backyard—or living room, barroom, or bedroom, as the case may be.

To one and all we say: dig in and enjoy. Have an exciting visit to New England.

And please remember to keep a weather eye out . . . there is trouble brewing.

Next stop, the Connecticut shoreline.

—Charles Ardai
June 24, 1991

About the editors:

CYNTHIA MANSON is the Director of Marketing at Davis Publications, publishers of *Ellery Queen* and *Alfred Hitchcock's Mystery Magazines.* She has also edited several anthologies, including the bestselling *Mystery for Christmas* and *Mystery Cats* series.

CHARLES ARDAI's writing has appeared in numerous magazines and anthologies, including *The Year's Best Horror Stories* and *Best Mystery of the Year*. In 1991 he received the Pearlman Prize for his fiction. Among the anthologies he has edited are *Great Tales of Madness and the Macabre* and *Great Tales of Crime and Detection.*

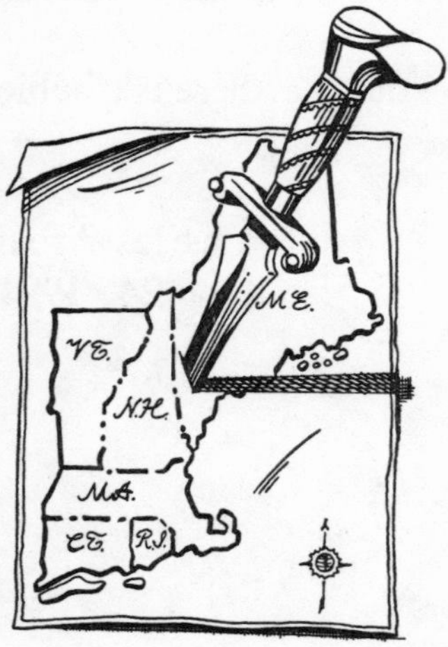

MIFFLIN MUST GO

by Shannon OCork

Shannon OCork is the author of several novels including Hell Bent for Heaven, *set in a marvelously evoked New York City. She lives in Connecticut, however, and her short stories are more often set in equally well-evoked New England settings. In "Mifflin Must Go," she illustrates why it is wise not to judge people too quickly.*

Mifflin hiccuped. It was a small, involuntary hiccup and he swallowed it immediately, but he was bending over his elder mistress's left elbow at the time, offering the dinner fish. Miss Marianne Wycliffe, seventy-one, pretended not to hear. And she kept her nose from wrinkling at the butler's moist, alcoholic breath. But her eyes blinked rapidly in maidenly alarm as she reached for the serving fork. The Crown Derbyshire platter dipped toward her as it should not have done, the sauce hollandaise pooled dangerously upon the beveled rim. With a hand that trembled, Miss Marianne served herself a portion of poached salmon.

"Thank you, Mifflin," she said with a faint voice. But firmly she replaced the serving fork. And firmly she tilted up the platter.

Mifflin lurched back, straightened almost to his full height, and, listing slightly to starboard, shuffled down the Kilim carpet the length of the satinwood table to his other employer, Miss Violet Wycliffe, sixty-nine.

The younger of the two spinster sisters warily watched him approach. For a moment she thought the better thing would be to refuse the salmon entirely. But she was keen for cook's fish. Mrs. Perez was new to the Wycliffe house. She had studied in New York under Monsieur Claré and had come highly recommended by the late Mrs. Lockholm. Fish dishes were Mrs. Perez's specialty. Miss Violet decided she would emulate her sister's bravery.

The platter swayed at her left side now. To reassure herself, she looked up at the once-elegant figure who had been in their service for forty years. He had come into the house at nineteen as underbutler, straight off the boat from London, where he had apprenticed to Lord and Lady Arleigh of Kent.

He had been tall and solid then, and, from the first, the paradigm of the perfect butler. He was always correct in manner, always fastidious in dress and impeccable in service. Among their set Mifflin had been, and still was as far as the Wycliffe sisters knew, the envy of the Connecticut shoreline.

Now as Mifflin in his cups bowed over the salmon salver, Miss Violet saw how sadly he had fallen off the mark. He had lost his paunch in the last six months and had not had his uniform refitted. His hair, two regal silver wings, was parted in the center of his head as usual. But the part was crooked. And dandruff—yes, it *was* dandruff—littered what once had been pristine shoulders of moss-green livery. His shirt was misbuttoned, too, and there was a faint brown stain on the front just where the left lapel of the jacket crossed his heart.

She must have stared too long, for when she lowered her lavender eyes and reached for the silver fork she saw that the lake of hollandaise was overflowing the platter and the baby salmon was swimming toward her lap.

With a deftness she was later to congratulate herself upon, Miss Violet deflected the catastrophe. She rose from her eighteenth-century dining chair quicker than she thought she could with her weak ankles. She righted the platter with both hands and saved the fish. But a few drops of hollandaise yellowed the table linen.

"Mifflin," she said in her tiny lilt. "Kindly watch yourself. The sauce has splattered on the cloth."

Incredibly, Mifflin hiccuped again, a loud hiccup he was unable to defeat. He tripped backward, red-faced, red-eyed. "Madam," he said when he could, "madam, please forgive me." Recklessly, he balanced the precious platter in one unsteady hand. With the other he flicked at the droplets of sauce with his service towel. Then, inexplicably, he set the fish plate upon the soiled spot and bowed ineptly. "Please excuse me," he said in his British baritone and turned his back to his mistresses. Drifting toward the double sliding doors, he missed the hand inset by several inches, but corrected himself and disappeared in an outbreak of hiccups and nasty chuckles. From the drawing-room side, the door slammed shut.

Miss Violet spoke down the table to her sister. "Whatever shall we do, Marianne?" Her sister, being the older, took the lead in such matters.

Miss Marianne had frozen in position with a forkful of salmon halfway to her quivering lips. Still in shock, she completed her gesture, swallowed the fish without chewing, and allowed herself a little shiver. "It's gotten too much," she said. "Much too much. We've closed our eyes too long for old time's sake. He'll have to go, that's all. You know it as well as I do."

"We could lock up the liquor cabinet again," suggested Miss Violet.

"That didn't do a speck of good last time we tried it. And it's not the sherry he's drinking, Violet, it's the brandy. I'm sure he's bringing in his own so we can't measure his intake. It's some of ours one time, some of his the next. Whatever's close to hand."

"Brandy!" breathed Miss Violet. Still on her feet, she limped to the sideboard and brought the vegetable dish to her sister. She lifted the cover and sighed.

Miss Marianne dutifully spooned herself three brussels sprouts. "I caught him at it this afternoon," she said. "He had one of the crystal goblets almost full of our apricot cordial. He drank it down like that—" she snapped her fingers "—when I asked what he was drinking, he told me it was apple juice. As if I don't know brandy when I smell it."

"He does have his good days still," said Miss Violet. She carried the vegetable dish to her own place and sat down.

"Oh, it's no good pretending, dear," said her sister. "These last weeks have been a nightmare. Mifflin's out of control and there's no getting him back. And he'll only get worse. Forget about our reputation—think of his. He may have slipped badly, very badly, but we're the only ones to know it. And the party we're giving in, what is it, ten days? I shudder at the thought, Violet. I truly shudder."

Miss Violet cut herself a little salmon and gave her plate the smallest brussels sprout. "It's true," she said. "Even on his good days he's not what he used to be." At last she tasted the fish. It was wonderfully good. She had another bite and another and then the brussels sprout.

It really was too bad, she thought. Mifflin had begun drinking in the afternoons last year after their mother died and Marianne had the hip operation and had had to give up her golf. And with the golf gone, so had the socializing and the dinner parties Mifflin loved so much.

Alone in the world, the two sisters grew closer and more reclusive. Older. And as a result Mifflin's duties shrank to almost nothing. He was bored, she supposed. That was it. He hadn't, of course, asked to leave. How could he? The Wycliffe family had been his whole life. It was understood he would be with them until the end.

"When Mama died," Miss Violet said, "do you remember how he cried?"

"He was devoted to Mama," said Miss Marianne. "Well, to Daddy, too. He's been really devoted to us all."

"And we've been devoted to him in return, haven't we? I'm sure we have."

"Well, not so much these last few months, dear."

"Poor Mifflin," said Miss Violet. "We'll have to give him his stipend all at once if we dismiss him. All at once and right away."

"Let's give him the choice," said Miss Marianne. "However he wants it is the way it will be."

"What a nice thought," said Miss Violet. "But how will we tell him?"

"Together," said her sister, finishing her lemonade. "We'll sit on the sofa together very close, holding hands. We'll tell him tonight."

"After the toddies?"

"Oh, yes, decidedly after the toddies. For the courage." And Miss Marianne tried to smile away the tremor in her breast.

"For the courage," agreed Miss Violet. She arranged her knife and fork on her plate. "But what about the party, Marianne? If he could only stay sober for that, it would be the perfect finale for him, don't you think? Going out in glory?"

Miss Marianne patted her lips with damask. "I think the party would be quite impossible without him. Anyone new in the house would be lost at such an elaborate affair so early on. And our friends expect Mifflin," she said. "It would ruin everything to have to explain his absence over and over." Her flat little bosom heaved. "If only he's able."

"Perhaps we could dangle a carrot," said Miss Violet, "and suggest that his pension depended upon it."

"Yes," said Miss Marianne, "we could give that a try."

The two spinsters, last of the Wycliffe line, rose from their great chairs in somber decision, leaving their napkins to the left of their places as they had done from childhood. They passed, one stiff and straight as though the rod in her hip extended up her spine, the other stooped with arthritis, into the library across the hall where their bedtime toddies awaited.

Cook did not live in as Mifflin did. There was no need. After dinner was prepared, Mrs. Perez left in her sensible Datsun for her little home the other side of Stormfork, on the New Haven side. She drove back mornings at eleven with the daily provisions for luncheon and dinner. She had Sundays off, as did Mifflin. On Sundays the Wycliffe sisters subsisted on crackers and milk.

It was Mifflin's duty to clear the table, Mifflin's duty to handwash the dishes and flatware, Mifflin's duty to dry each piece and put it away. It was Mifflin's duty to undress the table of its dinner cloth and candelabra and redress it for breakfast in cheerful pastel, with the flowers which three times a week the florist delivered at eight. Once the flowers had come from the Wycliffe garden, but that was long ago.

Mifflin did these final chores after making up the sisters' toddies and setting the tray in the library while they were still at table. At their leisure, they poured their own water from the hot pot—the brandy and sugar and cinnamon pre-mixed in the snifters by Mifflin in the kitchen. When the sisters were ready for bed, they rang for Mifflin, discussed the next day's schedule, and dismissed him for the night. This was their long-established and invariable routine.

In the library, the sisters settled themselves before the April fire. Miss Violet made up the drinks. As it was Miss Marianne's turn, she read aloud a chapter from the spy novel they were reading. Miss Violet thrilled to the chase while she longed for the persimmon pudding they had been denied by Mifflin's excusing himself. They both so loved persimmon pudding, but to go to the kitchen for it themselves would have been an unthinkable insult to their butler.

It was going on nine o'clock when Miss Marianne rang the service bell.

Mifflin was slow in coming, but when he came he seemed much his better self. Gone were the bumbling and the shuffle, gone the red in his eye and the hiccups. His hair was beautifully parted. His jacket shoulders were spotless. He stood before the sisters with immaculate white-gloved hands.

Miss Violet, so close to her sister their dresses intermingled cream and rose, had a tear in her eye. We just can't do it, she thought. No matter what he's come to, he's *ours*. But even as she thought it, she heard her sister say, "Mifflin, dear," and knew retreat was impossible.

Mifflin bowed. "Mesdames," he rumbled.

Miss Marianne told him of their decision in the sweet, direct way that had always been her advantage. She told him of the pension they had established in his name immediately following their mother's death. She told him of their deep affection, great respect, and lifelong gratitude. Mifflin paled as she spoke—paled and paled. Miss Violet listened with chin down and averted eyes. When Miss Marianne had said her piece, she asked Mifflin to remain in service through the dinner party they were giving for their new neighbors; that is, she said, if he thought he could recapture his former standard for one last evening. "It will be a lovely swan-song for you, Mifflin dear, and a courtesy to us."

Miss Marianne ceased speaking. Miss Violet squeezed her sister's hand for comfort. Mifflin was still as a grave and white as wax. Finally he bowed as beautifully as he had in his prime and said, "It has only been my object to comply with your every wish. I shall, when the time comes, try to do you proud. Will that be all, then, for tonight?"

Miss Marianne nodded. Miss Violet nodded. "Thank you, Mifflin, good night, Mifflin," they said for almost the last time.

"Good night, mesdames." Mifflin picked up the cloisonné tray from the Phyfe table and backed from the room with a grace they'd thought never to see in him again.

There was only a little moon when, late that night, Mifflin rose from his bed at the other side of the kitchen and crept through the garden to the shed. Vines of rambling rose which had not been cut back for years snagged at his pajama legs and long grass dampened his velvet slippers. But he was not deterred.

He pushed open the shed door with a hand protected by a rubber working glove. By a dim yellow light he searched the shelves for the weed killer. He found it in a corner of the second shelf, a rusty tin with a rose on the face and a small skull and crossbones in the upper right-hand edge.

Mifflin consulted the ingredients, peering close at the small type.

Arsenic, the list began, 42%. He read no further. With a screwdriver, he pried up the oval top. With a kitchen spoon, he scooped the grey powder into a sugar dish in the shape of a child's red wagon. It was a cracked piece, disposed of by the family and kept by him, with their permission, in his room. He liked the workmanship, the charm, the insouciance of the thing.

The sugar wagon comfortably full, Mifflin tamped back down the oval top and returned the tin to its position, setting it, as best he could, into the dust lines where it had waited, untouched, season after season.

He turned out the light, closed the shed door, and slipped back to the house, one gloved hand over the top of the wagon to keep the poison from spilling.

Back in his room, Mifflin got down on his knees. Under his bed was a cache of brandy, nine bottles in a small wine cage turned on their sides. They were all apricot cordial—an inexpensive brand, but good enough, he'd thought, for him. He drank the brandy to ease the pain of the cancer. "An operation won't help you," Dr. Dunbar had said. "There's not much to be done at this late date, old boy." The doctor had written him a prescription for Nembutal, but so far Mifflin had not used it. As long as he didn't use it, he could pretend there was nothing wrong and rampant in his stomach.

He had never, despite what the sisters thought, helped himself to their fine stores unless invited to, as he had been on special occasions in happier days.

With hands that shook a little, Mifflin carefully cut away the bottle's seal with a single slice of a paring knife. Putting the seal aside, he poured half the contents of the dark-brown bottle into his teapot, then he added all the weed killer he had to the bottle, spooning it in through a funnel. Then he refilled the bottle as much as he could and screwed back the top. Tight, tight. He shook the bottle hard, back and forth, up and down, around and around. When he was satisfied that the powder was dissolved, he wrapped the seal around the top again and secured it with transparent tape. Then he tore away a corner of the bottle label as an identifying mark and put the bottle back among its brothers.

He cleaned up everything, brushed up his slippers, changed his pajamas, and went to bed. He was almost instantly asleep.

The night of the party Mifflin was magnificent, virtually his glorious self of old. The guests-of-honor were the nouveau riche Trenton-Wests, and the Wycliffe sisters' party was their grand entrance into Stormfork society. The beautiful couple had begun life in Stormfork as poor Amy Trenton and plain Arnold West. But as Aimee and Arnie Trenton-West, they had risen, through clever real-estate manipulations and public charities, to become Stormfork's richest and most civically generous couple. Yet perhaps their riches were too quickly amassed and their donations too publicized, for society was slow to open its arms to them. They began their campaign to change this upon the Wycliffe sisters, long Stormfork's social arbiters. They purchased the Hemphill estate next to the Wycliffe house as their residence and named a geriatric wing they'd donated to the hospital the Wycliffe Wing. The sisters were forced to capitulate.

But as Miss Marianne said to Miss Violet after the party was over and they sat in their library among the remnants of lavish desserts, this was the last party the sisters would give. "We're too old to do this again," she said, dipping a spoon into a melted ice-cream bombe.

"And we've retired Mifflin," said Miss Violet. "It would never be the same." She was sampling almond cheesecake.

"It's better to stop now. It was a triumph, but I'm exhausted—not exhilarated the way I used to be."

"And we eat too many sweets at our parties," said Miss Violet, biting into a strawberry glacé petit four.

"Yes." Miss Marianne cut herself a tiny bit of rum-butterscotch pie. "And wasn't Mifflin fine?"

"I was so proud of him!" said Miss Violet with her hand on her heart. "Aimee couldn't sing his praises enough."

"Well," said Miss Marianne, "shall we forego our toddies tonight? We've had so many other sumptuous things already."

"Nevertheless, I think I'll have mine," said Miss Violet. "I want to sleep well and my ankles hurt." Mifflin was in the other rooms directing the hired crew in the cleanup but, as ever, he had set out their toddy tray.

Miss Violet poured hot water into a snifter and stirred the drink with a glass stick.

"Well, I'll join you," said Miss Marianne. "I don't want to be a stick-in-the-mud in my old age."

They laughed together like young girls, drank the toddies, and picked again and again at the desserts. They sat up late, until almost one, talking about other parties in days gone by.

Just as they started to go upstairs to their beds, Miss Violet felt a sharp stomach pain. "Oh, dear," she said, gasping at the strength of it. "I hope I don't get sick."

Miss Marianne was holding onto the back of the Sheraton loveseat. "I'm not feeling well, either, Violet, my dear."

"As you say," said Miss Violet, "we're too old, Marianne. That's our problem. We'll feel better in the morning."

They helped each other up the broad steps to the second floor. Miss Marianne was able to undress and slip into her nightshift, but Miss Violet lay down in her crepe de chine.

"If you need me during the night you must wake me, do you promise?" Miss Marianne said, breathing rapidly through her nose.

"If you promise the same," said Miss Violet with an effort.

They slept a while. But a second pang came to each of them and then a third, and after that the pain stayed. Doubled and tripled. Each in her turn stumbled to the bath and vomited, but still the pain stayed —and spread.

When they could no longer endure it, they rang for Mifflin. Miss Marianne couldn't remember ever ringing for Mifflin so late or ever before ringing for him from their bedroom.

He did not come at once.

Miss Marianne managed to say, "Perhaps he can't hear it or doesn't understand the bell so late at night."

Miss Violet only moaned weakly in her bed.

Miss Marianne rang for Mifflin again and again. Faintly, she could hear the bell buzzing far away in his room. She thought he must have already left them or that he must be sick himself. But at last she heard a shuffling tread on the staircase.

The light flashed on in the hall. Mifflin, in pajamas and bathrobe, swayed drunkenly in the doorway. He held himself erect by a hand against the doorjamb. Seeing his mistresses in distress, his eyes widened. He looked ready to faint.

"Dr. Dunbar," croaked Miss Marianne. "Tell him it's an emer—" The pain took her voice.

Mifflin backed from the room. "Yes, madam—right away, madam." He fled, a-tilt, down the stairs.

Miss Marianne glanced at the turquoise-and-silver clock on her side table. The hands read 3:15. Miss Violet had lost consciousness. She was curled around her stomach, breathing slow, ragged breaths.

Dr. Dunbar arrived at the Wycliffe house at about 5:30 A.M., having received an emergency call from his telephone service at 4:42. When he arrived, a sober, correct Mifflin apologized for taking so long to summon him. He couldn't find the doctor's home telephone number, he said, and he had had difficulty convincing the answering service to put the call through. Then Mifflin showed him to the sisters' room.

Both women were delirious with pain and beyond help. Dr. Dunbar did what he could to make them comfortable, but they died within an hour of his coming. Miss Violet went first. Within minutes, Miss Marianne followed.

Dr. Dunbar telephoned the police and the bodies were removed for autopsy.

The police questioned Mifflin immediately. He told them about the dinner party the evening before. "Mesdames were usually restricted in their diets," Mifflin said. "But they imbibed freely of the champagne last night and of the different desserts. They were up later than usual. I heard them mount the stairs about one. I did not see them after the guests departed, as I was cleaning up and they did not ring. Until much later, that is." That was all Mifflin could tell them. He had, he said, been in Wycliffe employ all his adult life, and other than a few broken bones, some mild colds, and Miss Violet's arthritis, the two sisters had enjoyed an exemplary health.

As the day was Sunday and cook's day off, Mrs. Perez was summoned by the police. Told of the sisters' deaths, she sat down with a thump on a kitchen chair and fanned herself. "Wouldn'tcha know it," she said. "I was so happy in this job. Lovely ladies, the two of them. Real appreciators. Let me cook for them any way I wanted, anything I wanted, and then thanked me for it." She rapped the kitchen table with her knuckles. "It's us who're the losers, mister. We, the living. We've lost more'n them."

"What have we lost, Mrs. Perez?" inquired Lieutenant Axelrod.

The cook raised her chin and looked him in the eye. “Why, we’ve lost grace,” she said. “Why, grace and genteel ways. Sweet little voices and the most lovely manners you ever saw. Angels, that’s what we’ve lost, mister. Angels. Don’t tell me no.”

Lieutenant Axelrod was silent for several seconds as Mrs. Perez nodded her head and rapped her knuckles. Then he said, “Could you tell me about the food served last night? What you cooked?”

Mrs. Perez drew herself up. “Are you insinuating anything about *my* food? I’ll have you know I’ve worked for the best families in Stormfork. Five years with Mrs. Lockholm, may she rest in peace, and before that eight years with Mrs. Melody Combes. Not Cora. Melody. How’s that for proper credentials?” She rapped her knuckles on the metal table so hard it echoed. “There has never, *never* been any question about *my* food, mister. Why, I do everything myself. Ground up. I choose my own ingredients, skin every onion. I studied under Monsieur Claré, you know. You’ll find no flies on me. No, sir.”

It took some time to calm her, but Lieutenant Axelrod with a gentle voice and great patience gradually induced Mrs. Perez to give him the menu for Saturday night.

There had been cocktails and appetizers, with which the cook was not concerned. The appetizers had been catered by Sarton’s and delivered hot, straight to the drawing room, which adjoined the dining room where dinner was laid. The two rooms were Mifflin’s territory. He had made the cocktails. He had served the hors d’oeuvres.

Dinner had been, first, a crab bisque. “Rose-beige my bisque is, and you won’t find the like of it anywhere else this side of the Atlantic. I’m famous for my bisques. It’s cayenne gives the lovely pink color.” Then had come broiled tomato cups filled with grilled mushroom caps and minced bacon. The main course was breast of chicken Florentine. “That’s flattened chicken breast rolled around sautéed spinach and garlic in my secret spiced oil.” And glazed baby carrots and Caesar salad. A pear sherbet had completed the meal, and Spanish coffee. Champagne had been the dinner wine. “Not strictly legit, okay, but champagne, mister, is never wrong, no time. And it was a party, doncha see. Festive.”

Desserts had been supplied by the different guests. There had been twenty at table and everyone had eaten heartily and well. “And no one else got sick I heard of." Mrs. Perez had left the house at 10:30 with a small bottle of champagne given her by the sisters and a bonus check for her extra work. Mrs. Perez still had the champagne in her pocketbook. She took it out and waved it under Lieutenant Axelrod's nose. "And the check for fifty dollars goes into the bank on Monday," she said and banged on the kitchen table.

"I cooked it, he served it." She gestured toward Mifflin. "I went home, he stayed. And there you are, that's all I know." Her nostrils flared. "Only maybe a little more." She leaned close. "He musta done it. In pique, ya see. He's just been—" she put her mouth very close to the lieutenant's ear "—bumped. *Dismissed* for cause." She pantomimed drinking with an upraised hand, thumb moving back toward her open mouth.

Mifflin denied his dismissal and denied harming his mistresses. Their love of him was such, he said, he thought he had been mentioned in their wills.

While the police waited out the autopsy report, both cook and butler were retained in the house. Mifflin kept to his room, drinking steadily. Mrs. Perez made lunch for Lieutenant Axelrod and Officer Duff: tomato-and-cheese omelettes and watercress salad.

A copy of the sisters' joint will was found in Miss Marianne's Louis XIV escritoire. The trust established for Mifflin was there. It gave him a generous stipend for the rest of his life. The sisters' checkbook was also brought forth. In it was the stub for check #4309: $25,000 in cash to Mr. Bernard Milcox Mifflin for severance pay. The check stub was seven days old.

Confronted, Mifflin admitted there had been a "misunderstanding." The sisters had dismissed him and paid him off, but they had not meant it. He had been derelict in duty and they had punished him, but he had reformed, he said, and they had rescinded the discharging. He had not cashed the severance check. He showed it to Lieutenant Axelrod with fingers that shook.

Dr. Dunbar called the Wycliffe house with the autopsy results. Miss Marianne and Miss Violet had died from arsenic poisoning. A massive amount.

Mifflin was arrested, formally charged, and booked. His bail was set at $50,000.

In the early evening, Mifflin's bail was posted and he was released. He returned to the Wycliffe house. Mrs. Perez and the police were gone and the house was empty.

The telephone rang. Mifflin answered it, wondering. It was Mrs. Trenton-West. She offered him immediate employment and told him it was she and her husband who had posted his bail. They would also assume his court costs.

Mifflin wept. "This is so kind of you," he said, "to open your house to me when I might be a monstrous murderer. I am overcome."

Mrs. Trenton-West minimized her efforts on Mifflin's behalf. "Your room is ready here," she said. "I shall expect you tomorrow morning."

The next day, still weeping, Mifflin packed his things. With several belts of brandy to brace himself and with his two valises on a rolling rack, he walked the half mile to the old Hemphill estate and presented himself at the side door.

Mrs. Trenton-West opened the door to him. She was wearing an apron over a tennis dress of linen lace. She appeared to be making brunch—a bowl of batter and a portable mixer stood on the tiled island in the middle of the enormous kitchen.

"As you can see," she said, cocking her handsome head, "I haven't got a steady cook yet. But I've got you. Come in."

Mifflin left his bags outside, entered, and stood respectfully before her. He had his speech all ready. "I came," he said, "to thank you personally for all you've done for me. But I cannot work for you, dear lady. I shall never work in service again. I am not well enough. I shall stand my trial and take my punishment if convicted or retire if they let me go. I came to assure you the monies you posted in my behalf will not be lost and to kiss your hand for your lovely kindness."

Aimee Trenton-West thrilled at Mifflin's dignity of bearing. "Let's understand each other, Mifflin," she said, staring at him as at a prized antique. "I know very well you're no murderer. What do you take me for? But even if you were, that wouldn't stand in my way one bit. I didn't get to where I am without risk. Do you understand? I'd do anything, *anything*—now do you understand?—for the perfect butler."

Mifflin bowed. He was remembering the dessert of Aimee Trenton-

West. Persimmon pudding, the Wycliffe sisters' favorite. She had sent it over early in the afternoon. There had been only the two cups, pretty *muguet des bois* cache pots of Sèvres porcelain rimmed in royal blue. They were signed only, "with delicious thanks."

Miss Marianne and Miss Violet had eaten the puddings in the quiet of the library before the party began. After they had finished, they asked Mifflin to fill the cups with little flowers and set them on the table at dinner.

So now Mifflin did understand. But no longer did he pale when struck by thunderbolts. Mifflin had toughened.

He straightened. "In that case," he said in his peerless British mumble, "perhaps you will allow me, this one time, to finish preparing luncheon for you and Mr. Arnold. I could serve in, let us say, an hour?"

"Delighted!" said Mrs. Trenton-West. Here was a butler she could live with. She whipped off her apron and handed it over to him and fluffed out her tawny hair. "Arnie's down at the stable. I'll run and tell him—he'll be as excited as I am. But first I'll show you to your room."

The room was large and wood-paneled. There were horse prints on the wall, Stubbs's reproductions. A wide window looked in the direction of the Wycliffe house. It was a handsome room for an Englishman, but Mifflin barely noticed. He unpacked quickly, only his uniform and toilet articles and the unopened bottle of arsenic-full brandy he had mixed last week with the intention of ending it all when he left the Wycliffe employ.

He shaved for the second time that morning. He scented. He brushed up his uniform and shined his shoes. Then he split the seal on the brandy and poured half of it into a silver pocket flask he then tucked into his jacket pocket.

He checked the dining room. The table had already been laid. He went to the kitchen. It was surrounded by windows. Looking out, he saw Mr. Trenton-West on a great chestnut hunter cantering around the lawn in riding coat and jodhpurs. The man did not ride well. He rocked in the saddle like a cowboy and drummed the horse's sides with his stirrups. Mrs. Trenton-West was watching her husband, laughing and flicking a black buggy whip whenever the chestnut swung within its reach.

Mifflin put on the apron, picked up the portable mixer, and set the batter spinning. Chutney crepes, he thought. They'll like that. And green beans almondine. He pulled out the silver flask and poured in the tainted brandy. Golden-brown lines whirled into thick yellow. The batter warmed to the color of eggshell.

In all probity, he thought, it was the least he could do for his mistresses. He knew he was no longer what he used to be. But Miss Marianne and Miss Violet had been right. Standards. One had to try to live up to them. To the end.

And, after all, he smiled to himself thinking ahead to his trial, he might as well be hung for a horse as a hare. The mixer sang under his hand.

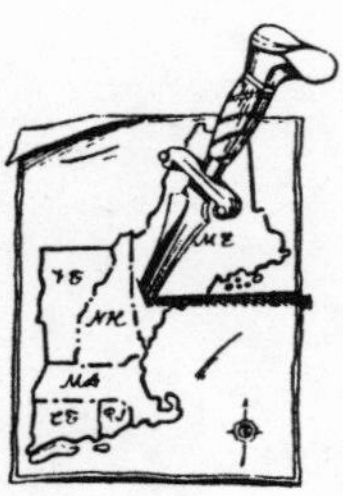

THINGS THAT GO BUMP AND GRIND IN THE NIGHT

by S. S. Rafferty

S. S. Rafferty is the best-known pseudonym of Jack Hurley, whose series of stories about Captain Jeremy Cork (set largely in Colonial New England) has been collected in Cork of the Colonies, *available through IPL. Here, he trades the eighteenth century for the twentieth in a tale about the conflict between modern pleasures and Victorian attitudes.*

Finding Rooney's is always difficult once the sun punches out for the day, but after 2A.M., it's next to impossible. Since state law says all bars must close at 2 A.M., Rooney dutifully turns off the red neon sign that says BAR AND GRILL and pulls down the window shades. Of course, the place is still open for business, but Rooney justifies bending the law with what he calls the Littoral Responsibility Rule. He claims the rule is a bona fide part of seventeenth-century maritime law which says, "The failure to maintain a lighthouse on dangerous shores puts the responsibility for wreck survivors squarely on the lighthouse keeper."

It makes a certain amount of sense, when you consider that the back alley to Rooney's is undeniably dangerous without the sign on, and most of the people in Rooney's are wrecks of one kind or another; mostly newspapermen from one of the two competing dailies and the one Sunday rag in the neighborhood.

At the stroke of two, when the sign goes out, you're on your own getting up that alley, brother. Everybody has his own guidance system which he swears by. Mine is a little unique in that it incorporates some elements of braille with a few tricks I once learned from an Iroquois I used to drink with up in Buffalo. This particular evening, my system worked like it had a Swiss movement, and I thumped on Rooney's door.

"Another survivor," the host says, extending a hand somberly, the way I imagined the old monks did at monastery gates during the plagues and Italian ducal wars. The comparison ends there, however, for the monks gave the travelers bowls of hot thick soup called *minestra* —Rooney does not serve food. "Tough passage?" he asked, closing the door behind me.

"Some rocks, a few shoals," I said, walking into the barroom. I spotted my group in the usual back booth, and started for them, after saying hello to a county sheriff and an alderman drinking at the bar.

At the table, Sid Genderman, the sportswriter, gave me a toast. "Esteemed colleague, it's your round."

"No, it's mine," Opie Hooter, an ancient wire editor, protested, moving over to make room for me. "Drinking has to be systematic and disciplined to remain a science. You wouldn't want it to become an art form, would you?"

Buzzy Lang, a rewrite man on the *Blade,* was sitting in the corner opposite me. "Why not an art form?" he asked, with some confusion.

"Because, Buzzy," Opie said, giving a finger wave to a waiter, "anyone can call himself an artist, but a scientist has to have credentials. Like Doc West here. He can *practice* medicine, but we can only fake it."

I didn't want to quarrel with Opie's point, but Doc West doesn't exactly practice medicine. Since he's one of the city's medical examiners, it's obvious that his skills aren't going to do anyone any therapeutic good. The Doc covers the west side of town, so that's how he got the moniker. His real name is Richard Sparks.

"Let's ask the esteemed colleauge," Genderman said, nodding at me. "When you walked in, I was saying a good reporter can cover any town on ten minutes' notice."

"And I say baloney." Opie disagreed like a batter over a close call.

"You mean walk into a town cold and start digging up news?" I asked. "Impossible. It would take at least half an hour to learn the street map and the paper's style book."

"You see, Opie," Genderman was smirking, "I told you so."

"You think that way, Sid, because you're a sportswriter," Opie told him. "You cover the game, which is always the same from one town to another. A *real* reporter covers people, and all the cozy little places they stuff things they don't want anyone to know."

"What do you mean, a *real* reporter?" Genderman tossed his chin out.

"Like someone who writes in English, for openers. But you're missing my point. For instance, how do you pronounce C-A-I-R-O?"

"Cairo, like in Egypt." Genderman was looking for a prize.

"Not if you were covering the state of Illinois. It's pronounced Kayrow out there, but spelled C-A-I-R-O. If you asked some yokel how to get to Cairo, you'd end up on a boat."

"I see what you mean, Opie," I said, recalling a similar problem. "I was working on a paper up in Bridgeport, Connecticut, back in 'thirty-eight. Been on the job for two days, and I get a bulletin over the police teletype that details a homicide on Iranistan Avenue. Drove around for four hours asking people where the bloody street was and missed the scoop. In Bridgeport, they pronounce Iranistan 'Ironsten.' Figure that one out."

"Local pronunciations grow out of regional accents," Doc West chimed in.

"Baloney," Opie said. "It's a plot to keep things secret from outsiders. Like you doctors writing things in Latin. It's an inside lingo."

"Like argot," I said.

"Huh? You got what?"

"Genderman." I shook my head. "Don't you know anything but the names of outfielders? Argot was the idiomatic language of the French underworld."

"You'd make some French correspondent," Buzzy Lang said incredulously. "It's pronounced ar-go, not ar-got. Some police reporter you'd make around the Sureté." There is no arguing with Buzzy about French. He was with the AEF in the first scuffle overseas. He's our house Balzac by default.

"I say it's more than pronunciation, it's a plot to foil outsiders," Opie went on. "I once saw a murder case that almost went unsolved because no one kept their ears open, and their eyes as well."

"Well, go on," I said.

"Esteemed colleague, a machine needs oil to run smoothly."

I ordered my round and Opie started in—on both the booze and the story.

"You can look through a lot of back issues and it would be hard to find a trace of this yarn, even though it was sensational. The only trouble was that it had competition from the war news. In a sense, the war was the cause of the whole thing, or at least an accessory.

"This took place in a small town up on the Massachusetts coast called Boker's Bay. Since the good Pilgrims stepped off the Mayflower, Boker's Bay had been a quiet little port that had three industries: fishing, shipbuilding, and Puritanism. I took a job on a small daily to get in out of the Depression, and found myself more depressed than ever. Do you know how depressing the clean and wholesome life can be? Righteous piety covered the town like a halo. Even stray cats in alleys were dutifully chaste and abstemious. About the juiciest piece of scandal ever had occurred a hundred years ago, when some milkmaid ran off with a one-eyed gypsy, and, even a hundred years later, no one would talk about it. Entertainment, I mean Saturday night wild stuff, was going to the public library to read Cotton Mather. They had forty copies of *Memorable Providences* to accommodate a rush crowd."

Doc West said, tamping his pipe, "Didn't someone once define a Puritan as 'a person who lives with the nagging fear that someone, somewhere, is having fun'?"

"That's Mencken. Not exact, but close enough," Opie said, "and right on the head, in fact, because when the war broke out, that nagging fear came home to roost. Overnight, Boker's Bay was turned into a shipbuilding port. Not the handcrafted ships of the past, but tankers and transports of hard metal built by hard men. And with the shipbuilders, the riggers, welders, and boilermakers, came fun. Yes sir, the Main Street area turned into a honky-tonk, with bar after bar of watered booze and bad women. Now most of the townfolk were horrified until they found out that the burg was booming, and they were making money on property rentals and such. All except a hard-core group that called itself the Bay Protective League."

"There's always people like that," Genderman said. "You know, there was a town down south that wanted to do away with night baseball."

"From what I've seen of southern teams," Opie said, "they should have considered day games as well. Well, the Bay Protective League was a formidable array of pistols. It was headed by the Reverend Amos Fornone himself. Fornone could not only trace his lineage back to Plymouth Rock, but beyond the low tide mark as well. I mean, he was the *first* of the first. His only indiscretion in life had been to marry a woman from Boston, but then I'm sure Boston wasn't any too happy about one of its women being carried off to Boker's Bay. About the biggest mouth in the league was an old war horse named Phoebe Hackler. Her only indiscretion, legal though it was, was giving birth to Percy Hackler the Fourth."

"The fourth? Four Percys?"

"Yes, Genderman. But if you ever met Percy the Fourth, you would be assured that there would never be a fifth. He was the spinster of the parish, as they say. To round out the team, they had Dr. Marcus Quibbs, who practiced medicine by divine right. No offense, Doc West."

"None taken, Opie. I've known some newsmen who couldn't spell or punctuate."

"That's only to keep editors in work, Doc," I corrected him. "What did this league do, Opie, close up the town?"

"They tried real hard, but liquor was legal and ladies of the evening are cleverly elusive. They went from one court to another, and kept getting turned down like a poverty-stricken debutante at an opportunist's ball.

"Hell, the country was up to its scuppers in war problems, and didn't have time for a pack of do-gooders. They just put their respective tails between their legs and went home to ignore the evil taking place downtown on the waterfront. Everything was quiet until the strippers showed up and the murders began."

"Strippers? Coochie dancers?" Genderman showed renewed interest. "Why didn't you start out with them instead of this Puritan stuff?"

"Because you have to know the lineup before you report the game, don't you?" I put in. "That's the trouble with sportswriters, Sid. You guys write the story for yourselves, the managers, and the players."

"I deny it. What about the strippers, Opie?"

"They came to town in late spring to work at a joint called the Golden Hoist. Five of 'em. Now, don't go thinking like a rube, Genderman. These were professionals. Real artists, not hookers. But their naked presence was more a punch in the nose to the Protective League than anything since the British imposed the tea tax. I had seen the show at the Hoist and there was nothing lewd about it. Just five well-constructed ladies undraping themselves to music. But that tore it as far as Mrs. Phoebe Hackler was concerned. She called a council of war at the parson's house and my editor sent me along to see what was cooking.

"It was some meeting, I'll tell you. I'll bet Lucifer wasn't within five miles of the fumes of righteous indignation that poured out of the place.

With the exception of Dr. Marcus Quibbs, it was the first time I had met the salvation crew, but most of them lived up to their billing.

"Old Phoebe looked like she couldn't bear to toss out her grandma's dresses, so she put them to use. She looked like a Gibson Girl who had lost three straight to the Manassas Mauler. Percy boy must have taken after his dear departed papa. I assumed Papa Hackler had been a nervous midget who had been weaned on lemons, or maybe fuzzy quinces.

"As far as the Reverend and his missus, they were plain, quiet people who seemed to be caught up in Hackler's maelstrom. The Reverend was a bald guy with a pince-nez that made him look fifty instead of the forty that he was. His missus, Amy, was living proof that they feed people better in Boston. Not that she was fat, just round and healthy. Her only weak points were that she was very plain, walked like a duck, and listened to every word that Phoebe Hackler said. I was sitting on a davenport next to the police chief and one of the town selectmen who had been invited to watch the fireworks.

" 'I'm sure you gentlemen will agree,' Phoebe said in an irritating contralto, 'that these women will have to be told to leave town. Gambling and drinking are sin enough, but naked women will not be tolerated.'

"The Chief of Police, whose name was Corky Ryan, swiggled in his seat. 'They aren't exactly naked, ma'am,' he said. 'More in a state of undress, you might say. We wouldn't allow them to take off all their clothes.'

"That was not entirely correct in Corky's case. Since the strippers' arrival, he had made what the French call a liaison with one of the girls, who billed herself as Non Non LaTouche—an appellation that didn't apply to Chief Ryan.

" 'There's very little that we can do.' Selectman Gus Kreeger threw up his hands. 'We're the victims of state law, madam. There is nothing lewd or lascivious about the performances. Believe me, I have checked with my brother, the state senator, and there is absolutely nothing we can do.'

"Actually, his performance was a bit above Ryan's, when you considered that his brother, the august senator, owned the Golden Hoist through a holding company that was supposed to be in the sand-and-gravel business.

" 'And what about your newspaper, Mr. Hooter? Where is its moral fiber, its duty to the people?'

"I told her it wasn't *my* newspaper. I didn't tell her it didn't have much moral fiber–only circulation. As far as duty, that was to the advertisers.

" 'Then you leave us no choice,' Phoebe said in exasperation. 'We will have to go down there and take care of the matter ourselves this very evening.'

" 'Now wait a minute, Mrs. Hackler.' Kreeger was on his feet with visions of a Carry Nation ax party wrecking his brother's joint. 'That's private property, ma'am.'

" 'It's a public place, is it not?' Dr. Quibbs spoke for the first time. His pan would have gone great on Mount Rushmore. 'Then we demand admission. Let these hussies perform their Delilah dances in front of God-fearing people, if they can.'

" 'You mean you're going down there and sit and watch?' Ryan was more than appalled, he was apoplectic.

" 'I see our plan makes sense, Chief,' the Reverend said. 'Face ye the sinner and he will repent.'

" 'Look, Reverend,' I said, 'you have as much chance of converting those girls as I have of winning the Irish sweeps.'

" 'Mr. Hooter, I do not condone gambling, but since you make the comparison, I suggest you buy a ticket immediately. The power of good shall not fail. Shall we go, ladies and gentlemen?'

"Percy Hackler looked sick, and tried to excuse himself from the expedition.

" 'Nonsense, Percy,' his mother chastised, 'they shall not bother you, because you have inner good.'

" 'I don't think I want to go either, Amos,' the Reverend's wife said softly. 'I know, dear, it's in a good cause, but I must . . . well . . . be weak, because I can't bring myself to do it.'

" 'I heartily agree,' Percy said, happy to find an ally.

" 'Well, I don't,' Phoebe routed her son. 'It's time for all good Christians to stand against the tide.'

" 'Please, Amos,' Amy Fornone was blushing. 'How could you ask me to go among those sinful Sallys? I don't think I could ever face you again.'

"Well, she got out of it, but not Percy. His mama dragged him out of there and down to the Golden Hoist along with the Reverend and Dr. Quibbs. They sat through the entire show like prunes in sour milk. Phoebe and the Reverend cornered one redhead who worked under the name of Dirty Gerty from Albuquerque and read her the riot act on what happens in the land of fire and brimstone. Gerty, it seems, was from East St. Louis, and had already been through hell. What can you do with a sophisticate?

"One by one, they appealed to the performers. The Back Bay Butterball said missionaries were pikers, and Non Non LaTouche said she didn't speak English. She didn't speak French, either. For a few minutes, it looked as if they were getting through to Jezebel Jones, but it turned out that she wasn't entranced by the sermon, she was schnockered. A brassy type named Flambé, who did her act with fiery tongs, told them to see her agent in Boston.

"They left in a huff around midnight, threatening to write to Mrs. Roosevelt, despite the fact that the First Lady was a Democrat. Things went back to normal for a week, and then the murders began."

"The strippers got knocked off?" Genderman asked, regretfully.

"Three of them, one right after another. The girls didn't have dressing rooms at the Hoist, so they changed into their costumes at a small house they rented a few blocks away. On her way to the Hoist, Dirty Gerty got her throat cut in an alley. She wasn't molested, but there was an element of mystery in that the killer carefully took off the girl's outer costume—they call them break-away gowns—and slashed it to threads."

"Maniac," I said.

"Obviously. Nuttier than a walnut grove. Well, Chief Ryan puts on his Sherlock cap and goes to work. The first suspects were the men who work in the shipyard, but those that weren't working the night shift were all accounted for in one bar or bed or another. Hell, why would those guys want to do away with a source of entertainment?

"A week later, Flambé goes to the Happy Hunting Ground in the same fashion."

"Same all the way, Opie?" Buzzy Lang had a notebook out and was writing down some points.

"To a tee. Slashed costume and all."

"It's like Jack the Ripper all over again," Genderman said with creative insight. "Jack the Stripper Ripper."

"Or costume ripper," Opie corrected him.

"Was she killed in the same way, Opie? Throat slashed?" Doc West asked.

Opie nodded and went on. "Exactly. Believe me, the women in that town were as frightened as a fish on Friday. Ryan set up extra street patrols and the remaining strippers were escorted to and from work every night. Didn't do much good, though, because a week later the Back Bay Butterball was found dead in her bed, her costume slashed to pieces on the floor."

"So that left two strippers," Buzzy read from his notes. "Jezebel Jones and Non Non LaTouche."

"It left nobody, because the other two girls got out of town like a shot. Much to the chief's chagrin."

"That was a mistake," I put in. "They were prime suspects."

"How do you figure that?" Genderman smirked. "Looks to me like the Bay Protective League was in it, and my money is on the battleaxe."

I couldn't disagree, but I had reservations. "You have to consider that the last one was killed in her bed. How would an outsider get into the house?"

"Opie said it was rented," Buzzy said. "Who owned the house, Opie?"

"Good point. The owner would have a set of keys. Ready for this, fellas? The house had been owned by Dr. Quibbs. He had sold it to a realty company before the war, but the locks hadn't been changed after the transfer."

Doc West took his pipe from his mouth, smiled, and shook his head. "The old surgeon-knows-how-to-kill-quickly ploy, huh? Anyone can slit a throat. You're dwelling on opportunity to murder, not motive."

"You don't have to prove motive, Doc," I cautioned him.

"Of course, but before we go off on a tangent, let me ask Opie something. You said the case almost went unsolved because no one kept their eyes and ears open. It was solved satisfactorily, then?"

"Not in a court of law, Doc, but satisfactorily."

"All right, then we have a puzzle and you have a solution. Let's examine motive. Our esteemed colleague has a point about letting the two remaining strippers leave town. One of them could have held a grudge against the others."

"They never met each other before in their lives. Some agent in Boston put together a show package and sent them down to Boker's Bay. They got along fine. No petty fights like women can get into."

"If you guys are looking for motive, I'm still backing the battleaxe," Genderman persisted. "She saw these broads as carriers of sin and degradation. Did she have an alibi for the times of the killings?"

"Mrs. Hackler and her son were at dinner with Dr. Quibbs when the first two went. Of course, everyone was home asleep during the third killing, or said they were."

"That's not much of an alibi. Maybe all three of them were in it together, the doctor and the old lady and Percy."

"It's unlikely, Genderman," I said. "Not with the slashed costumes. One maniac, okay, but three?"

"The costumes could have been slashed to make it look like a maniac."

He had a point, and I considered it while Buzzy went over his notes again and asked, "We can't discount the Reverend and his wife, you know."

"Chief Ryan did," Opie said, "because the preacher wasn't that all fired up about the girls. He was being prodded more by Phoebe Hackler than heavenly zeal. The enlightened sort, despite his pious exterior. His wife wasn't involved at all. She didn't even know what the girls looked like."

"Hey, wait a minute!" Genderman had an idea. "One of the theories in the Jack the Ripper case was that the killer had to be a policeman, because he could get through police cordons, strike, and get back out unnoticed. How about Chief Ryan? He was real cozy with this French dame."

"He was drinking with me when the first one was killed in the alley and on duty at headquarters in full view when the other cases occurred."

"Damnit, Opie," Genderman said, "this had better not be one of those trick deals where the killer is some drummer passing through town."

"It isn't, Sid. That wouldn't be fair. You've been keeping notes, Buzzy, so you can back me up."

"How about this agent in Boston?" Buzzy asked him. "He knew the girls before he sent them down there."

"Not really, he just managed the Back Bay Butterball. The others he recruited."

"Well, the Butterball was murdered, wasn't she?"

"But so were two other women, Sid, two women he had met for about an hour or so in his office before he booked them into Boker's Bay."

"Don't brush that aside so lightly, Opie," I cautioned. "It wouldn't be the first time that several people were murdered to make it seem like a nut was on the loose, when the rest were actually a cover-up for one rational murder. Did the cops question the agent?"

"No, but not because they didn't want to. He fell out of his office window right after the last girl was killed."

"Fell?"

"Or jumped. The police bought suicide, and tagged the poor guy with the murders. They dreamed up a motive that made sense. They figured that he was cheating on the strippers' salaries and got caught, so he knocked the squawkers off."

"And that was the solution?" I was incensed. "Why, that's a load of claptrap. Why would a guy kill off three sources of income over nickels and dimes?"

"Esteemed colleague," Opie said, "that was the *official* story. I didn't buy it any more than you did. It was a convenient way to clear the books and not uncover something that might stink to high heaven."

"The Protective League again," I said.

"Yep."

"I knew it." Genderman was smiling. "Enter Mrs. Hackler."

"You're getting psychotic over her," I informed him. "Opie told us she was with her son and the doctor at dinner when the first two got it."

"Collusion." Genderman used one of his big words.

"The Hacklers had money, didn't they, Opie?" I asked.

"Scads."

"So they had a maid?"

"And a cook and a butler."

"Witnesses that they were at dinner."

"Check."

"So that leaves us with the parson and his wife," I said.

"Guilt by elimination isn't strong evidence," Opie reminded me. "But the Doc is grinning like a Cheshire cat, so maybe he's got something."

I looked at the medico and said, "Well, this is one case you're not going to solve with inside medical knowledge."

"Not inside medical knowledge, but science does have a bearing. You said earlier, Opie, that Chief Ryan had put on his Sherlock cap. I know you were striving for imagery, but it's too bad he didn't do it literally. The Holmes technique could have helped him."

"But that was fiction," Genderman offered another observation. "This is real life."

"Well, Conan Doyle was real, and he was Holmes' creator. He was also a doctor, and you can see the doctor's training in observing habitus in his work."

"What do you mean, *habitus?*"

"The physical characteristics and constitutional tendencies of a person. In medicine, it's tied to a person's disposition to disease. However, Doyle used it to determine a person's occupation, where he had been, all the social trappings. When you walk into a doctor's office, he doesn't start his examination when you lie down on his table. He starts the minute you walk into the room. He's looking at your gait, skin tone, eyes, everything."

"That's very informative, Doc," I said, "but what's it got to do with this case?"

"Well, while Opie was relating the facts, I took his warning and kept my eyes and ears open. I also kept in mind that we started off talking about argot and local speech patterns. Where are the Reverend Fornone and his wife now, Opie?"

"Last I heard, they were missionaries in South America."

"The Fornones did it?" Genderman was astounded. "A preacher?"

"No, Sid," Doc said. "His wife Amy. Correct, Opie?"

"Maybe, but let's hear how you pinned it down."

"Surely. If Buzzy's notes are correct, I think you said Mrs. Fornone was an ample woman who walked like a duck."

"You're right, Doc," Buzzy said, checking his notes.

"I get it," Genderman said. "She was strong enough to overpower the strippers. But so was the battleaxe and Dr. Quibbs."

"Strength is not the factor. Now, along with being ample and walking like a duck, she was either a better student of the bible than Dr. Quibbs or she was something else."

"Being a student of the bible isn't so strange in a parson's wife, Doc," I said.

"True. But Quibbs described the strippers as 'Delilahs,' which doesn't make sense because she wasn't a dancer. But when Mrs. Fornone said she didn't want to join the party going to the Golden Hoist, she called them 'sinful Sallys.' Salome was a dancer, gentlemen. But leave that for a moment. Let's get back to the duck walk. Did she waddle, Opie?"

"No, stiff legged, with her feet out at forty-five-degree angles."

"I thought so. You see, gentlemen, Mrs. Amy Fornone was an ex-stripper, protecting herself from exposure."

"How's that again, Doc?" I said."

"The stiff-legged walk with the feet at forty-five-degree angles is the classic gait of the dancer, especially someone who has either danced ballet or used ballet exercises to stay in shape. I thought it odd that a puritanical minister should marry a performer. But when Opie reported that she said 'sinful Sallys,' I was sure she knew more about the striptease business than anyone in the room. Strippers don't refer to themselves as such, and they would no more call themselves coochie dancers than I would call myself a sawbones. But 'Sally' is a carney term for exotic dancers, a derivative of Salome. Today, they call themselves ecdysiasts, I believe."

"So you think she had been a stripper because she was well built and knew a few trade terms."

"Yes, Sid, when you couple it to some other telling points. The strippers were all unknown to each other before they came to Boker's Bay. Some even used origin names in their professional names—Dirty Gerty from Albuquerque and the Back Bay Butterball. Back Bay's in Boston, isn't it?"

"Sure," I said. "And Mrs. Fornone was from Boston."

"So there could be a connection between them. She wouldn't go to the Golden Hoist that night because she didn't want to be recognized by the Butterball. Who could blame her? She had gotten out of that garish world and found peace and respectability as a parson's wife in a small town."

"How about a stronger motive than just being exposed by the Butterball?" Buzzy Lang asked, looking up from his notebook. "How about blackmail, or the fear of it?"

"Check," I said. "The agent's convenient suicide points to that. I'll bet there weren't any old pictures of Amy in his office files."

Genderman frowned. "But the Butterball wasn't the first one to get knocked off. Dirty Gerty was. The Butterball was the last one killed. And after Flambé went, she'd be on her guard, even in her room."

"You want me to field that one, Doc?" I asked.

"Be my guest," he invited.

"Butterball was the target victim all the time, but Amy was smart enough not to kill her first. There was no connection between her and any of the other girls, and she used the first two killings to create the maniac theory. Of course she had no trouble getting into the Butterball's room at night. They knew each other. A tap at the window, entry, and then, murder. But that killing would be seen as part of the Ripper pattern."

"And the fourth killing of the agent put the frosting on the cake," the Doc said. "Damn clever woman, that Amy."

"You know, Opie," Genderman said, "I have renewed respect for you, figuring it out the way Doc did."

"Oh, I didn't do it that way. Nothing that fancy. You see, I used to be in love from afar with a stripper named 'Amy the Amazon' when she was at the Chicago Minsky's."

"You mean you knew all the time that she was an ex-stripper, and you didn't tell Ryan?"

"Not *all* the time. It was about a year after the case was closed, just before the Fornones became missionaries. I was covering a kids' swimming race out at the beach, and I saw her in a bathing suit. I recognized her immediately. I just hadn't recognized her with all her clothes on. Like Doc says, when I saw her at Minsky's, I was concentrating on her habitus."

That set off a round of guffaws and several rounds of drinks. Then Genderman said that the agent reminded him of a manager of a girls' softball team who mysteriously disappeared from the team bus between Chicago and Peoria, and how he was found dead two days later on a 'gator farm in Fort Lauderdale. But it's late and that's another story. Drop in when you get a chance, but make it before 2 A.M. so you can travel safely up the alley.

THE GOLDEN PARACHUTE
by Martin N. Meyer

Martin N. Meyer is a fairly new writer, having started writing mysteries after encountering the novels of Dashiell Hammett and Raymond Chandler. When he isn't writing, he repairs and restores clocks. Both sides of Mr. Meyer's background come through in his writing, which is a blend of razor-sharp prose and finely tuned plotting.

The clatter of metal against porcelain roused me from a trance. I stretched my arms over my head and called down the hallway toward Maggie's sculpture studio. "What's going on in there, hon?"

"Just banging pots and pans together," came the predictable reply. It was a ritual of ours, one of those marital dialogues that couples recite to reassure each other that all is as it should be, that the grounding is still firm. I smiled and saw, in my mind, Maggie smiling back.

Beyond the Venetian blinds was a late November day, but in my study the air was warm and thick, and a latticework of sunbeams shimmered on the hardwood floor. My computer screen taunted me with last year's notes for "Intro to the Metaphysical Poets," but I couldn't coax a new idea from my mind. The telephone's ring offered a diversion from my torpor.

"I say, old boy, how are things behind the ivy-colored walls?" I never knew quite how to respond to the phony British accent; was it to be taken seriously, was it a joke, was it some eccentric idea of panache? It was Harry Simmons, a voice from the past that never seemed to stay there.

"Very well, thank you," I answered icily. "Look, Harry, I don't imagine you're calling to pass the time of day after . . . what is it, two, three years?"

"Two years and more, old friend. I say, you don't sound very professorial, you know. Do you talk to your students like that?"

"No, Harry, I guess you just bring it out in me. So let's skip the Rudyard Kipling act and get to the point."

"Righto. You know, prof, in some ways you haven't changed . . . still all business. Well, certain channels have put me in contact with an individual who requires some discreet assistance which you may be able to provide." Oh, I sighed, the self-importance of this fellow

"Listen to me, Harry. I'm an English teacher, I'm a professor, I have a wife and a house and two cats. And what's more, I have tenure. And I'm not going to jeopardize any of it. Past is past, Harry."

"This is a high-level individual, prof." Harry went on as if I had never spoken. "He came to me in a very roundabout way, you know. I was recommended to him as a person who knows people who can be relied upon for a high degree of confidentiality." In translation, I thought, Harry was a sleaze broker. He did nothing himself, he merely linked up desperate people with shady characters who would do just about anything. And I resented being included in that group.

As he spoke faster, his accent began to fade. "Well, this individual is in need of someone who can do a little . . . poking around . . . and be absolutely trustworthy, 'incorruptible,' he said, because the stakes are very high, he said, and someone who can work with high-level business types, 'move within executive circles,' he said. I thought of you right away. I told him you're a prof, and that was all he needed to hear. I don't know any more about it; he refused to tell me a thing about what the 'high stakes' were." Whoever this person was, he seemed at least to be a fair judge of character.

"Tell him to hire a P.I. There are about fifty of them in the phone book. I have a class to prepare for, and I'm looking at a pile of year-old notes. And what's more, Maggie would kill me if she knew I was talking to you. Remember the last time I helped you out? She nearly left me after that fiasco. And I'm not an investigator. You know, Harry, a person needs a license to do that kind of 'poking around.' I don't see anything I could do for this guy."

"Oh, but you do, prof. And you can do it better than any P.I. for sure." The accent had disappeared entirely now. "You won't be investigating, you'll just be . . . analyzing the situation. Just like way back when." "Way back when" was during the war, when I had first met Harry, when we were in Joint Services C.I.D. together. I had been picked for it because I spoke French, the second language of Southeast Asia. Harry had been selected for somewhat less respectable skills. For two years that seemed like a lifetime we had been partners, shuttling to Bangkok or Singapore, Saigon or Tokyo in search of deserters, drug smugglers, and, occasionally, murderers. One day I found myself back in the States beginning my first teaching job, and for a while I didn't know which world seemed more like a dream. But reality finally returned, and I'd been trying to put the C.I.D., and Harry, behind me ever since.

". . . just like way back when. It's like riding a bicycle, prof, you know that."

I leaned back in my office chair and its springs creaked. The office felt even warmer and stuffier than before, the latticework of sunlight had moved another inch across the floor, and the computer screen still flickered with last year's notes. I watched a leaf float listlessly to the ground outside my window.

"Okay," I capitulated. "Just a meeting, Harry, just a conversation. No obligation, no investigating, just a little advice. The Shop. Twelve-thirty. *Hamlet.* And Harry . . ."

"Anything you want, old boy."

"Don't call me again."

Winston Atwater was a man out of his milieu. Even without a description, I recognized him immediately. I let him flounder for a few moments as he entered the diner. The Shop is a dumpy hole-in-the-wall in the commercial no-man's land between the university district and the city's freshly rehabbed North Side. I was sitting in a booth at the back near the kitchen door. It was a noisy spot, but it gave me a good view of the entrance. Atwater stepped timidly inside, stopped, and the door swung shut behind him, hitting him in the shoulder. Shrugging off the blow or the embarrassment, he looked over the crowded room. I watched his technique, such as it was, as he studied each face at each table, arousing the hostile interest of several diners. This was a man who knew how to maintain eye contact but had never learned how to avoid it.

He was overweight but he carried it well, and I suspected that others described him as "portly." His complexion was florid, and he wore the round horn-rimmed glasses currently popular with executives and attorneys. He was dressed in a dark blue suit with a red silk tie just wide enough to be complacently out of style, and he carried a very thin alligator attaché case.

His eyes finally met mine, but still he hesitated. I picked up the dogeared paperback copy of *Hamlet* from the table and stood it on end momentarily so that he could see the title. He exhaled visibly, made his way to me through the closely arranged tables as if walking through a minefield, and settled gratefully into the booth.

"How do you do, Dr. Rhodes," he gasped. His forehead sparkled with perspiration.

"Noah will be fine, thanks," I answered. "But if you insist on formality, it's Mr. Rhodes. I'm not the kind of doctor who takes your blood pressure." The way he looked, I thought, that might not be a bad idea. "So, our mutual friend Harry tells me you have a problem. Fill me in."

Atwater's eyes bulged in his red face. His lips twitched as if he were trying to form words in an unfamiliar language. Finally the words burst forth.

"I've received a note, a threat, not a threat actually, but an implication. An intimidating implication, connecting me with a murder."

They always begin at the ending. "Who was murdered, Mr. Atwater?"

"Well, no one actually. I'm the president of Dichron Industries. My plant manager, Ed Reilly, was killed last night, but it was an accident. He fell from a scaffold while he was repairing a compressor at the plant."

"So have you been implicated in a murder or in an accident?" I knew the man was distraught, but his confusion irritated me to sarcasm. I softened my tone. "Look, I know you're upset. Just tell me what the note said."

He leaned toward me across the Formica tabletop, his eyes darting from side to side. "My name was on the outside. Inside it said, 'I know you killed Reilly, and I'm going to call the police.' I found it under my office door when I got to work this morning."

"So it was some crank with a sick sense of humor pulling your chain." I was thinking about Harry. Why did he bother me with this nonsense, with this nervous little man? Maybe he was pulling my chain. "You said it was an accident, you've got nothing to fear. So what's the problem?"

Atwater rested his arms on the table, palms down as if bracing himself in a heavy sea. His cuff caught some sticky residue on the table and he jerked his arm up, wiping at the stain with the heel of his hand. He looked back at me and blinked, his train of thought momentarily lost.

"There was an argument. Yesterday afternoon. The whole plant saw it. Ed's always been a friend, a good friend, but I was furious with him. We got into a shouting match in his office. I knew everyone in the production floor could hear it through the glass, that was bad enough. But he stormed out of his office and I followed him, still shouting. His office is up on the second level, overlooking the production area. I was yelling at him and suddenly I looked down at the floor, and everyone had stopped working. It was humiliating."

I sat silently for a moment, not so much to reflect as to give Atwater time to calm down. I spoke in a soothing tone. "What exactly did you say? What was the most incriminating thing you said to him?"

Atwater must have asked himself that question already because he responded quickly. "I said, 'If you don't back me up on this, you're through.' "

I raised my eyebrows involuntarily. "Nonetheless, he died in an accident. How did it happen?"

"It happened last night after everyone had gone home. Ed was working late, repairing a compressor that had been acting up all day. The switchbox that supplies power to the compressor is on an overhead, a steel catwalk running along the wall way above the production floor. Apparently he climbed up there to turn the power off. He touched the wrong wire, I guess. The compressor runs on a 440–volt line. He got a shock and must have lost his balance and fallen. It's probably fifty feet down to the floor. The medical examiner who came to the plant said it looked like the fall killed him rather than the shock." Atwater settled back into his seat with a long exhalation, his hands resting lightly now on the edge of the table.

"So that's it?" I asked.

"What do you mean?"

"I mean you've left something out, haven't you? What was the argument about?"

"Oh. Yes." He paused, looked absently toward the front door and the street outside. "Dichron is fighting a takeover attempt. The three managers—Ed Reilly, Gene, the R&D director, and myself—are at odds on how to respond. I'm flatly against it, this company is my life.

Gene's in favor of it, thinks it would be good for the company and for us. Ed has been undecided. Yesterday afternoon he said he thought Gene might be right. I couldn't believe it. I felt personally betrayed, and I let him know it. That was the argument."

They always begin at the ending.

Leaving the commercial strip, I wandered down treelined North Side streets past garreted Victorian mansions and trendy shops, drifting unconsciously toward the campus. Atwater had a problem, all right, but I didn't know if he needed me or a prescription for tranquilizers. About all I could do for him was try to find out who had written the note. If Reilly's death was indeed an accident, he had nothing to fear in the way of either blackmail or extortion. Nothing, that is, except someone out there who didn't like him. And we all have a few of those in our lives. I was kicking myself for not sending him packing. But I hadn't. Something was nagging at me, an ungrounded suspicion that I couldn't shake. Whether Reilly's death was an accident or not, a corporate takeover play spelled trouble. The stakes are high and the players are ruthless. Corporate raiders, arbitrageurs, call them what you will, they're sleight of hand experts playing a shell game for enormous stakes, and all you can count on is that everything is not as it seems.

From my campus office I phoned Jack Kilbourne, an investment counselor and old friend of mine, and asked him what he knew about Atwater's company.

"Hmmm. Dichron. Not too big a company. Electronics, control systems, some defense work. New York exchange. Pretty active lately. Lots of takeover rumors, but I don't know if there's any substance to them. The company's solid enough but nothing special, nothing that would inspire a takeover. Rumor also has it that Randall Crown is the would-be buyer. But he's a hit-and-run man; even if he is buying stock, that wouldn't necessarily mean he's looking to take over the company."

"How about management? Would it be a hostile takeover?"

"Very interesting question. I have a feeling you already know the answer. Unusual management. The CEO is Winston Atwater, one of the wimpiest-looking guys I've ever seen, but don't let him fool you. He's been in the business for thirty years, and he knows the ropes. But he's not the whole story. There's an operations manager named

Ed Reilly, and a research and development director, Eugene Salzman. Ordinarily, they'd be subordinate to the CEO. But the Board of Directors listens to all three of them, pretty much equally. They've all been together since the vacuum tube days, and they bang their heads together and come up with the decisions. They call them the Triumvirate. As long as they're in accord, the board rubber-stamps their recommendations. How am I doing?"

"Great, Jack, thanks. There's just one thing you should know about the Triumvirate. . . ."

Maggie met me at the door with fire in her eyes. "Noah, where have you been?" She wasn't waiting for an answer. "Some man has been calling every fifteen minutes. He's hysterical, says it's urgent that he talk to you right away." She stopped speaking and stared at me long and hard, a practiced expression that never failed to wither me. "He's no student and he doesn't sound like a professor. Noah, we talked about this." Another long pause. "You promised me. You could get into trouble, acting like some dime-novel detective. Or you could get hurt." The worry in her voice turned to anger. "And the caller didn't have a tinplate British accent, but I'll bet Harry Simmons is mixed up in this somehow."

I shrugged and edged past her in the doorway. "Did he leave a number?"

"Where on earth have you been, Rhodes?"

Atwater was a basket case. "You've got to help me. They're saying it's murder. You've got to do something, Noah." From "Dr." to "Rhodes" to "Noah" in four hours; by tomorrow I'd be a close relation.

"Who's they?"

"What?"

"Winston, who are 'they' who are saying it's murder?" I was speaking calmly, hoping it would rub off.

"Oh. The detectives. The detectives came to the plant while we were at that horrible diner. One of them climbed up on the catwalk and examined the switchbox. He said it had been tampered with. He said there had been 'foul play.' I couldn't believe it, he actually said 'foul play,' like in some old movie."

"Winston, listen to me." I spoke to him as to a child. "Calm down, take a few deep breaths. I'll see what I can find out. Did you get the detectives' names?"

"Yes. My secretary wrote them down for me." There was a pause as he shuffled through the papers. "Here it is. Kozlowski and Williams. Sergeant Kozlowski and Detective Williams."

"That's good. I know Kozlowski. He's okay. Did they talk to you?"

"Yes. They asked me a lot of questions. Do you think they'd tell me if they suspected me?"

"Count on it." Right before they put the cuffs on, I thought. But Atwater was in no condition to hear hard truths right now. "Where were you last night?"

The pause on the other end was longer this time. "I was out, I was alone. I went to a movie. By myself. I had an argument with my wife."

"No one saw you, no one who could identify you?"

"No. No one. No one at all." No pause this time.

"Did the detectives ask you the same question?"

"Yes. I told them what I told you."

"Great, that's great, Winston." I sighed, then hoped he hadn't heard it.

After dinner and an unsuccessful effort at appeasing Maggie, I retreated to the study, dug up Leo Kozlowski's business card, and called him at his home number.

"Hello, Leo, it's Noah Rhodes. How have you been?"

"Who?" I waited for the shoe to drop. "Rhodes . . . oh yeah, I remember you. Listen, this had better be about enrolling me in night school or I'm gonna pull you in for operating without a license. I haven't forgotten the last time, you know."

Good old Leo. He wasn't really a bad guy, but he didn't appreciate interference from amateurs. A couple of years ago Harry Simmons had persuaded me to help out a woman who was suspected of killing her husband. At the same moment that Leo was booking the wife, I was meeting with the victim's business partner, the real killer. The meeting received quite a bit of publicity, as the partner was shooting at me at the time, and Leo found it all rather embarrassing.

"I'm trying to reassure a friend, a real nervous type. I thought you might be able to help. Winston Atwater."

"Oh, brother." Leo's voice was half laughter, half annoyance. "He's the nervous type, all right. He ought to be, considering."

He was going to make me draw it out of him. "What do you mean? Considering what?"

"I mean considering his plant manager couldn't fly and didn't bounce." Leo loved to talk tough. "Considering it wasn't an accident and the whole plant heard Atwater arguing with Reilly yesterday afternoon, and considering he topped it off with a death threat."

"Come on, Leo. He didn't threaten to kill him, he threatened to fire him. These guys are executives, they're under a lot of pressure. They probably argue like that all the time. How did it happen, anyway? I understand the wiring had been tampered with."

Leo didn't answer right away. He disliked being probed for information, but he loved playing the expert and he loved an opportunity to talk like Mike Hammer. Eventually his ego got the best of him. "Yeah. Very smooth. The perp switched the wires on the power box. Three wires: hot black, hot white, green for ground. Only, the green wire should've been black and Reilly didn't know it. Dirt had been rubbed on the thumb nuts so they didn't look tampered with. And just for insurance, the killer smeared some grease on the catwalk to make it nice and slippery near the box. Reilly touched the hot wire thinking it was safe, and got a 440–volt zap. His fingers looked like french fries." Kozlowski paused to savor his metaphor. "Apparently the shock didn't kill him, but he lost his balance, slipped on the grease, and did a triple gainer onto the concrete floor fifty feet below. The M.E. established the time of death as between nine P.M. and midnight."

Leo was enjoying himself now. I took a breath and went for the big one. "Winston went to a movie alone last night. I understand he wasn't getting along with his wife. He's afraid you don't believe him."

"Right. We talked to him. Three times he told us he was alone. Absolutely sure no one saw him. You know, I've seen plenty of jumpy suspects, and they grab at straws. There's always a ticket girl or a waitress or a bus driver who they at least hope might remember them. He had a spat with the little woman all right, we checked it out, but the rest of that story's a ringer."

I wasn't about to argue the point. "Any other suspects? You must have heard there's a takeover attempt in the works; that ought to get lots of people nervous."

"Yeah, we know about it. I'm wondering how come you do. There's the third manager . . . these guys were a trio, you know . . . Eugene Salzman. He was there during the argument, but he wasn't really involved. Anyway, he doesn't have a motive; he's in favor of the buyout, and Reilly was coming around to his point of view when he was killed. The last thing he needed was Reilly dead."

"Did you check for an alibi, just in case?"

"Sure we did. He was at a party all evening. A 'black tie affair.' " Leo gave the words sarcastic emphasis.

"What about the other possibility?"

"What other possibility?" There was irritation in Leo's voice at my suggestion that he had missed something.

"The money man. The buyer in this takeover bid. Whoever he might be."

Leo growled. "If you find out, make sure you give me a call."

"You'll be the first to know," I said.

I slipped out the door and eased it shut behind me. Going out again, at eleven o'clock at night and without explanation, was not the way to get back in Maggie's good graces. But telling her where I was going would have been worse.

I stopped briefly at Atwater's house, then drove to Dichron Industries' headquarters and plant. The complex, a newly constructed office building attached to a refurbished old foundry, sat atop a low grassy rise at the end of a winding driveway. The moonlight revealed the office first, a long, angular structure made of the gray stony stuff that looks like granite block but is really smeared on like plaster over construction panels. Its broad, low configuration, beveled roofline, and smoked glass windows made it look like a gigantic version of one of its own computer chips. As I drew closer I could see the plant, a towering skeleton of steel I-beams and sheet metal, flat black, peak-roofed, and hovering like a stormcloud behind the spiffy new offices.

I parked at the side of the building to avoid the attention of passing patrol cars and walked to the main entrance. I slid Atwater's employee I.D. card through the security terminal, and its magnetic strip electronically unlocked the door. With the aid of a pocket flashlight, I threaded my way through dark hallways looking for the crossover to the plant building. Eventually I found the double doors Atwater had described to me, a sign on the left one reading PRODUCTION FACILITY and on the right WATCH YOUR STEP.

Through the doors, my flashlight beam dissipated into empty blackness. I stepped forward tentatively, heard my foot strike metal flooring, groped ahead until my hand felt a railing. Running my other hand along the wall behind me, I found a light switch and flicked it on. I was standing on a railinged walkway, a sort of gallery running along two sides of the plant building perhaps twenty-five feet above the production floor. The plant floor spread out below me, one huge open space divided into work stations by head-height partitions. All along the wall behind me were glass-windowed doors, where foremen and managers could work while observing their staffs on the floor below. The third door down bore a plaque that read EDWARD REILLY, OPERATIONS MANAGER. This must be where the unfortunate argument took place, I thought. I imagined Atwater's shouts echoing through the building, his round red face, and his embarrassment as he realized what he was doing and looked down at the plant floor to see employees' astonished faces staring up at him.

I looked toward the roof, a vaulted framework of metal dotted with skylights. Along one side, where wall and roof met, was a gray steel catwalk with conduits, pipes, and cables running beside it. It was a good twenty feet higher than the walkway I was standing on. My eyes found the switchbox, big as a refrigerator, its door left open by the detectives. Inside it was a maze of heavy electrical wiring of different colors. I looked down from it to the concrete floor below and saw an area roped off by bright yellow plastic ribbon with POLICE LINE: DO NOT CROSS printed repeatedly across it. In the center of the area was a smeary red stain. I shuddered and felt suddenly cold in the huge empty space. I flicked off the lights and stepped back through the double doors.

A few yards down the corridor, a red sign on a door caught my eye: RESTRICTED AREA: NO ADMITTANCE. Below the sign a brass plate read RESEARCH & DEVELOPMENT: EUGENE SALZMAN. I tried Atwater's I.D. card in the door's security terminal, but it didn't work. An ordinary credit card between the door and the frame was more successful. The latch clicked and the door slipped open.

Playing my flashlight around the room, I found mazes of equipment carefully arranged on the lab tables. Along the back wall was an especially large assemblage of electronic devices, meters, wiring, and tubing, with a sign on the table saying DO NOT TOUCH! In the middle of the setup were two heavy stainless steel boxes, each about a foot square. One of them had tubing running out of it and over the side of the table, while the other was connected only to electrical wiring. The box with the tubes felt cold. I turned my light underneath the table and saw that the source of the tubing was a white steel tank labeled LIQUID NITROGEN. No wonder the box was cold.

I directed the light across the floor and into the corners, found the wastebasket, dumped its contents onto the floow, and quickly browsed through them. A sheet of crumpled paper caught my eye. I examined it, touched it, smelled it, put it in my pocket. I aimed my light at the telephone. It was a computerized model with an LCD display that printed out the number you were dialing.

On my way out of the building, I stopped at the office manager's computer terminal. I selected "Main Menu" and studied the screen. A box in the center listed five options: Word-processor, D-Base, Security Log, Calling Record, Employee Schedule. I selected "Calling Record," punched in responses to several inquiries, and waited as the screen flashed "Searching." In a few seconds a list of phone numbers was printed in columns beneath two-digit extension numbers. I pressed "Print." Next I selected "Security Log" from the Main Menu. I typed in yesterday's and today's dates and waited. The screen printed out names and times. I hit "Print" a second time, and tore off the copy.

I poured my coffee and shrugged off a chill, but Maggie's icy gaze would not release me. Yesterday's anger had congealed into this morning's silent resignation, and my seven A.M. call to Winston Atwater hadn't helped a bit. I told him we needed to meet first thing at his office, but he was reluctant. An emergency Board of Directors meeting had been called for tomorrow morning, and he was frantically preparing for it. I reminded him that he couldn't run Dichron from a prison cell, and he acquiesced.

I gulped down my coffee and escaped to my study. Randall Crown's secretary wouldn't give me the time of day, much less an appointment with her boss. I told her it was a confidential matter regarding Dichron Industries, and she put me on hold. She came back in about thirty seconds and told me Mr. Crown had had a cancellation and would fit me in at eleven-thirty. I checked my watch, pulled on my overcoat, and hurried out the door, attempting a casual "See you later, hon" on the way out. It didn't take. I had just enough time for a quick stop at the physics department on campus and a chat with Professor George Atkins, a friend and colleague of mine.

Atwater instructed his secretary to hold his calls and leaned back in his chair, hands folded across his stomach. "All right, Noah. You have my attention." He was a different person in his environment.

"Look, I've got to be straight with you, Winston. You're the prime suspect, and I need a few answers if I'm going to have a shot at helping you out. First of all, cut out the dancing on this alibi. You weren't straight with me, and you weren't straight with the police. And the police know it. Do you have an alibi or not?"

Silence hung in the room for moments. I listened to the air conditioning humming through the ventilator grate. Finally Atwater spoke, his voice faltering. "Yes. No. I mean yes, but I can't use it."

"Let me help. You had a fight with the wife, so you went to visit the girlfriend, right?" Atwater wore an expression like a small boy caught pulling the cat's tail.

"It's my wife. I can't let her find out. It may sound old-fashioned to you, Noah, but she means the world to me. I've made mistakes and I've jeopardized my marriage, but I can't lose her. Especially now."

I thought of Maggie's smile, and realized I hadn't seen it in two days. "No," I answered, "it doesn't sound old-fashioned to me at all." I was going to have to solve this one the hard way.

The intercom buzzed and we both started. "Excuse me, Mr. Atwater. Mr. Salzman is here with some papers that he says can't wait."

Atwater nervously straightened his tie. "Send him in, Miriam."

Eugene Salzman was tall and skeletal with high cheekbones and an arching nose. He wore a tie but no suit coat, and his sleeves were rolled up to his elbows. The pocket of his white shirt held a row of pens.

"Sorry to interrupt, Winston." He glanced at me and paused.

"Gene, this is Noah Rhodes, an old friend of mine from college. We're fraternity brothers. Noah's a professor at State." I was amazed at wimpy Atwater's facility at lying. I stood and shook hands with Salzman. He had a firm, easy handshake and a friendly smile.

"State University? What's your field, Mr. Rhodes? Or is it Dr. Rhodes?"

"English literature. My specialty is the metaphysical poets. You know, Donne, Wyatt, those boys." I always felt awkward about it. No one knew, or cared particularly, who the metaphysical poets were anyway. It sounded moldy and boring, and it seemed only I saw their poems as intricate puzzles daring me to solve them.

"Really. Yes." He turned to Atwater. "Well, Winston, these are the papers for the meeting tomorrow. Please look them over, make sure you approve." He looked at me and nodded. "Sorry again to interrupt. Nice meeting you, Dr. Rhodes." He ambled out of the office like a gangly schoolboy.

"He's really a decent fellow," Atwater said when the door had closed. "It's too bad we don't see eye to eye on the takeover. It's tearing this company apart, and it hasn't even happened yet. Maybe I should just go along with it. But I can't, this company means too much to me." He seemed to be talking more to himself than to me. "Where were we?"

"You were just giving up the alibi that might keep you out of prison. Look, just a couple more questions and I'll be on my way. What are your communications with prospective buyers?"

He looked mystified. "What do you mean?"

"I mean who from Dichron is negotiating with them?"

"Why, no one. There are no negotiations. This is a hostile takeover attempt, we're not even positive who's behind it. We assume it's Randall Crown, but we don't know for sure. And we're not interested in communicating with him, in any case. When he's ready, he'll contact us. Why do you ask?"

I ignored his question. "One more thing. Liquid nitrogen. What do you use it for?"

"I don't think we do. Not in any quantity, anyway, or I'd be aware of it. I really don't understand these questions, Noah."

I shrugged indifferently. "Just covering all the bases. Would you mind if I come to the board meeting tomorrow?"

He looked surprised. "It's rather irregular, but I don't think anyone will mind. I don't see what good it will do, though."

"Like I said, just covering the bases." I headed toward the door.

"Say." I turned back to Atwater. "What were those papers Salzman brought in?" I saw resistance in his eyes. "Trust me. What are they?"

"All right, but this is corporate business, no one outside Dichron must know about it. It's a golden parachute."

"A golden parachute?" I hesitated. "Ah, a bailout arrangement for the executives, right? You're afraid you'll all lose your jobs in a buyout, so you write yourselves a contract; Dichron pays you the equivalent of the treasury of a small nation if you get axed. If you win you win, and if you lose you win, right?"

Atwater didn't like my explanation, but he nodded. "Yes, for the three managers and the board members. We have to protect ourselves."

"So why is Salzman giving it to you?"

"For me to check over and approve, make any adjustments that might be necessary."

"Yes, I know. What I mean is, why aren't you giving it to him to look over? You're the business manager, he's the scientist."

"Oh." Atwater nodded. "I see what you mean. I don't want this buyout at all, golden parachute or no. Gene offered to draw it up, partly because the task would be distasteful to me and partly, I suppose, because he felt he could do a better job since his heart is in it. I'll approve the wording, but I'm not giving up my fight." I saw a determination in his eyes that I hadn't noticed before, and I remembered Jack's warning not to mistake this man for a wimp.

Randall Crown was a man who loved wealth for what it gave him, and loved power for itself. His secretary had directed me into his office, and as I sat waiting for him to enter, I looked over my surroundings. The room was as big as the first floor of my house, but sparsely furnished: a mahogany conference table and six chairs along one wall, a built-in bar along another, a grouping of low-backed armchairs around a glass cocktail table. The far wall was a panorama of floor-to-ceiling windows overlooking a picture postcard view of the city. Centered in front of the windows was an enormous oval desk made of a tropical wood which I couldn't identify and topped with plate glass. It was covered with sheafs of papers, all meticulously ordered and symmetrically arranged. Glass shelves on the wall behind the bar displayed Crown's collections: blown-glass vases, pre-Columbian pottery, Renaissance salt cellars of silver and gold. Paintings hung on all the walls, but no photographs were visible anywhere, no family snapshots on his desk. My observations were interrupted by the sound of the door opening.

"Good afternoon, Dr. Rhodes. Sorry to keep you waiting." His tone of voice said he wasn't, and I hadn't identified myself as "doctor" to his secretary.

He was of average height and build, clean-shaven, and combed his hair, thinning at the temples, straight back. He wore a gray English suit and a gray silk tie. His features were ordinary except for a strong jaw and unnervingly intense dark eyes. He settled into his desk chair with a sigh, in the manner of a busy man who finds little opportunity for rest. He fixed his eyes on me and didn't speak for what seemed like a long time. He picked up a small glass paperweight from his desk and peered into it as if it were a crystal ball. He looked back at me.

"So, Dr. Rhodes, what could an English professor from State University possibly have to tell me about Dichron Industries?" I wasn't surprised that he had taken the trouble to learn who I was.

"You've been on the telephone with Eugene Salzman several times in the past few days. I was wondering what you had discussed." There was no point in wasting time with preliminaries.

His gaze didn't waver. "Your information, wherever it may have come from, is in error, Dr. Rhodes." I noticed a trace of accent, unidentifiable but definitely there. "But even if it were accurate, why would I be disposed to discuss it with you? Perhaps you should explain your interest in the matter. You are a stockholder in Dichron?"

He knew perfectly well I wasn't. "No, I'm not. I'm sure you've heard about Ed Reilly's murder. No arrests have been made yet, but there are several suspects. The other two managers are among them."

He leaned toward me, his disinterested stare transforming to hostility. "So what, Dr. Rhodes? This is not of interest to me."

"But you may be of interest to the police. You might even be considered a suspect. This publicity about Dichron is bad enough, given the delicate stage of your dealings. Certainly you wouldn't want the spotlight focused on you personally."

He sat back in his chair again. "So what would you suggest?"

"Just answer a few questions. Believe me, it could be beneficial to you; there may be variables in the Dichron buyout of which even you are not aware."

"All right. What do you want to know?" I was getting his interest.

"So you have been discussing the takeover with Salzman?"

"Yes. He's in favor of it. He has been assisting me in persuading the rest of the Triumvirate and the Board of Directors to cooperate, and I have suggested that there will be a place for him in the company when I control it."

"And what place is that?" Crown glared at me, but answered.

"CEO. Head of the company." Half my mind was with Crown, formulating my next question, but the other half was trying to fit pieces together. That half was telling me something was wrong. But for now I had to concentrate on Crown.

"From R&D director to president of the company. That's an impressive promotion for a scientific man, a man without a business background. A bit too much reward for greasing some wheels with the board. I wonder why?" It was time to play my hole card. "A new development perhaps, an invention, a scientific advance."

Suddenly Crown was on his feet, leaning toward me, his knuckles braced on his desk, his face reddening. "Understand this, Rhodes." He spit his words through clenched teeth. "I am not a man you should fence with. If you try, I will run you through. I don't know why you're involved in this matter at all, but I suggest you get out while you still can." His voice was rising. "There is no new development, and your suggestion that there is is pure fantasy. You have been in your little literary world too long, Dr. Rhodes!"

The more he leaned toward me, the more I relaxed back into my chair. When he was done I waited a moment. I smiled. "To paraphrase a quote from my little literary world, 'you do protest too much,' Mr. Crown. I'm not making wild guesses. I've seen the evidence . . . the equipment, the liquid nitrogen. It's thought-provoking: you, Salzman, and a new development that Dichron itself doesn't know about. I'd say we have fraud and conspiracy, and whatever the Securities and Exchange Commission boys come up with. They're really feeling their oats since they put Ivan Boesky away."

Crown deflated back into his chair. His face was ashen. He looked at me with his still-intense eyes. "Salzman approached me, not the other way around. The buyout was his idea. He had the invention, and he wanted to be appropriately rewarded for it. He offered to railroad the buyout through the board if I'd make him president. Without the invention, the company is a turkey. With it, well, that's a different story. He wanted to be CEO, nothing less, and you know what the invention is worth. I couldn't turn him down."

Suddenly the piece that hadn't fit fell into place in my mind. "Quite a scheme, Mr. Crown. But there's more to it than you realize. Tell me, are you free tomorrow morning?"

I stepped out into a late fall morning of bright sun, leafless tress, and my breath steaming in the air before me. I felt invigorated, but the feeling was marred by the thought that Maggie was still angry with me. What was worse, the very thing that made me feel so alive, my investigation into the Atwater affair, was the source of Maggie's anger. Life is never simple, I thought, and turned my attention to the day's work. After my meeting with Crown I had stopped at Atwater's office. Over his protestations, I had read through a copy of the golden parachute and confirmed my suspicions. We had then enlisted Miriam's secretarial skills in preparation for today's meeting.

The chairman of the board, a very old man with silver hair and prunish features, rapped his gavel weakly. He was looking at Randall Crown and me, as was everyone else in the room. "Winston, I'm not sure how to conduct the meeting under these . . . circumstances."

Atwater stood. "Perhaps a word of explanation is in order. I've invited Dr. Rhodes because he may be able to help us out of our dilemma. I've also granted his request to bring along Mr. Crown, although we all realize it is a rather . . . unconventional procedure."

"Unconventional?" It was Salzman, his birdlike visage exaggerated by anger. "This isn't unconventional, it's unprecedented. It's outrageous! We cannot conduct a board meeting in the presence of the very individual whose takeover attempt is its subject. Winston, your judgment in allowing him here is irresponsible. Not to mention the fact that you're the prime suspect in Ed's murder."

Atwater rested his hands on the papers before him, a calmness coming over his face. "At the moment, I'm still the president of this company, Gene. You may change that if you all see fit." He looked disdainfully at the faces at the table. "But first, we will conduct this meeting." His demeanor was utterly different in this one place where he felt supremely in control.

"So now I'll turn the meeting over to Dr. Rhodes. Following that, he and Mr. Crown will leave us to our privacy. Dr. Rhodes, you have the floor."

I stood and surveyed the field of skeptical faces: seven men and three women, in addition to Atwater and Salzman. Atwater was to my left at the foot of the table, and Crown was at my right. Salzman, across from us, was peering suspiciously at Crown, who was looking at no one in particular. The chairman of the board was at the head of the table. I picked up a copy from the stack of stapled papers before me and cleared my throat, but I was interrupted before I could speak.

"Excuse me, Dr. Rhodes," croaked the old chairman. "May I ask what you are a doctor of?" He sounded more like an eccentric old man than a chairman of the board.

"English literature, Mr. Chairman." I smiled as the room gasped in unison. "But I can assure you that I will not let it affect my judgment . . . if you will promise the same for your judgment of me." A few restrained laughs could be heard.

"I'm aware that the directors and three managers of this company have been at loggerheads over how to respond to a takeover attempt. I'm not here to offer an opinion on the advisability of such a buyout, but rather to forge a compromise that will be agreeable to all.

"My proposal is as follows. First, Mr. Crown has agreed to buy your stock at a price of forty-five dollars a share." Positive "hmms" ran through the room. Salzman looked warily at Atwater, then Crown, then me.

I picked up the pile of papers and circulated copies down the table. "Second, I've developed a golden parachute plan acceptable to Mr. Atwater. If you approve it, he will recommend that you cooperate with Mr. Crown's purchase offer." Atwater nodded in assent. "It is, essentially, the plan prepared by Mr. Salzman." Salzman's eyes were fixed on the stack of copies moving toward him along the table. "My revision simply increases the bonuses to the officers and the board—I think you'll be pleased at the figures—and makes a few minor non-monetary changes." Salzman grabbed wildly for a copy. Throughout the rest of the room, smiles were popping up like spring flowers as the board members read their proposed bonuses.

Salzman was riffling frantically through his copy while the rest of the board silently awaited his reaction. He stopped and read one passage intently. He leaned closer and reread it. Finally he looked up, the color drained from his face, his lips tight. He looked more birdlike than ever.

"Winston, you cheat!" He stood up and his chair nearly toppled over behind him. He was trembling visibly. "And you . . . he turned toward me. "Who are you, anyway? What are you doing here?" Back toward Atwater. "Never! I will not accept this agreement!" He threw his copy onto the table. The rest of the room was staring at him in amazement.

The old chairman rose reluctantly to his office. "Gene, I don't understand. This is a very good offer. Very good indeed. What, exactly, is your objection? It is your own plan, isn't it?"

Salzman was attempting to compose himself. He breathed deeply, blinked and looked around. "No, this is not my plan. It's been changed. The R&D rights. They've been taken away from me." Crown, who had been sitting impassively throughout, sat up straighter in his seat, his burning eyes riveted on Salzman.

"Ah," said Winston, as if on cue. What Gene is referring to," he spoke patronizingly to the board, "is Paragraph 16, Subheading c. A very minor item, really. Gene had specified that the rights for any new technical developments, anything not previously patented by Dichron, would revert to him if he left the company or was terminated." Crown leaned forward on the table, listening intently, his eyes frozen on Salzman. Atwater continued. "It's a perfectly understandable error; he is the R&D director, and those are his creations, so to speak." Now he looked at Gene. "But of course, the company always retains the rights to employees' inventions; it's the only way it's done." He spoke in a matter-of-fact tone. "I simply corrected a standard clause."

The chairman spoke. "Gene, Winston's correct. It's perfectly routine, you mustn't take it personally. And what is there to lose? As of your last R&D report there wasn't anything earthshaking in the works." He looked slightly embarrassed. "I don't mean that critically, of course," he added.

I stood and looked toward Salzman. "Perhaps you do need to explain,

Mr. Salzman." He was sitting perfectly still, looking off toward the far wall at nothing in particular. "You could explain to us about the experiment that's set up in your laboratory, the one with the liquid nitrogen." He turned toward me slowly, looking at me with tired eyes.

"Mr. Salzman did have something earthshaking in the works," I went on. "So earthshaking, in fact, that he chose not to share it with the board or anyone else at Dichron. Liquid nitrogen is used, among other things, for cooling electronic circuits to extremely low temperatures. As you ladies and gentlemen know, there are certain substances which, when very cold, conduct electricity with extraordinary efficiency. I'm told by a physicist friend, a colleague of mine, that they're called 'supercooled superconductors.' Eugene developed a practical application of these superconductors which can be used at room temperatures in ordinary electronic devices, computers, and such." The members of the board sat open-mouthed. "I see from your expressions that you appreciate the significance: he found the Holy Grail of electronics, the invention that will revolutionize the microchip industry." Salzman's expression was vacant now, dreamy-eyed and distant.

"He knew his discovery was priceless, and he knew he wouldn't be fairly rewarded for it. There was a clause in his employment contract with Dichron . . . perfectly routine . . ." I nodded to the chairman, "providing that any of his developments would become the company's property. Fame he would certainly get, but fortune . . . no reward that Dichron could give him would be enough."

I turned to Randall Crown. "So he approached Mr. Crown with an offer; he would help him take over the company in return for its leadership."

Salzman seemed to be waking slowly, like a child. He spoke in a quiet voice. "That's absurd. Dichron would have given me the presidency in a minute for a development like that."

"Yes," I said, "it would have. But you had no interest in being president of Dichron. You persuaded Randall Crown to take over the company while, unknown to him, you drafted a golden parachute agreement that would give you the invention as soon as he did. You didn't think Winston would notice the clause because he didn't want anything to do with the agreement anyway, and the rest of the board was only interested in their own compensation, not in a quiescent R&D department. And as for Crown," I turned to him, but his cauterizing gaze was fixed on Salzman, his hands grasping the edge of the table as if to restrain himself from attacking. "The value of the superconductor is so great that it clouded even Randall Crown's judgment. All he could think of was owning it. He didn't realize that you would never settle for such a paltry reward as the presidency of Dichron. With ownership of the patent, you could have started ten Dichrons."

"This is nonsense." Salzman was fully awake. "It's all your fabrication, and Atwater brought you in. Right after he killed Ed Reilly."

"But he didn't kill Reilly, did he, Eugene? You of all people ought to know that."

He stood up abruptly and leaned toward me across the table. "Are you saying I did?" he snarled.

"Not at all. You had plenty of witnesses for your whereabouts that night. No, you never set foot in the plant till you arrived at work the next morning. What time was that, Eugene?"

"Around six-thirty. I come to work early, everyone knows that."

"And so you did on Tuesday. You were the first one in the building. You went into the plant area for something . . . a tool, a part, it doesn't really matter. And you found Ed Reilly's body where he had fallen—accidentally—while working at the switchbox. You saw your hopes to sway the Triumvirate in favor of the buyout dashed along with Ed's life and you were desperate.

"So you made a silk purse out of a sow's ear. You reversed the wires at the switchbox to make the shock look arranged, smudged some dirt over the nuts to simulate a coverup, and spread a little grease on the catwalk. I found the paper that you used to wipe your hand with in your laboratory wastebasket; it had heavy machine grease on it, but there's no heavy machinery in your lab. You just worked as usual in your lab until the plant workers arrived and 'discovered' the body."

A silence had fallen over the room. The board members were staring down at the table or resting their heads in their hands. Crown glared at Salzman, who was again staring absently at the ceiling. Atwater looked more relaxed than he had since I'd met him. The old chairman was smiling broadly, looking around at everyone as if this were the best time he'd had in a decade.

I broke the silence. "Tell me one thing, Eugene." He turned a weary face toward me. "Why the note, why to Atwater? If you'd sent it to the police, it might have helped frame him. But you couldn't have expected him to reveal it. "

Salzman smiled sadly and shook his head. "I couldn't chance sending it to the police; for all I knew, he had an alibi. The best I could do was make it look like a murder and hope the argument with Ed would be enough to implicate him. I knew it was thin. So I wrote the note to panic him. I hoped I could scare him into resigning or even running away. I've known Winston for years, and he's a tiger in the boardroom but a child everywhere else. I knew I couldn't compete with him here," he looked around at the wainscoted walls, "but in the outside world I had a chance. All I needed was an edge, and the edge was his own panic." Salzman laughed. "And it would have worked. Except for one thing."

I raised my eyebrows questioningly. "What was that, Eugene?"

"He found you first."

I sat in the kitchen sipping my coffee. It was no longer fall outside, and a white wintry sun glistened over frost on the lawn. Maggie was putting the breakfast dishes away.

Reflecting on the past few days, I was quietly satisfied. Atwater was back in the saddle at Dichron, and Dichron was soon to be the biggest game in town. Randall Crown, of course, had withdrawn his takeover bid. An indictment was expected, said the papers, but I supposed he'd rather go to jail than get suckered on a deal. Eugene Salzman was out on bail, thinking about what might have been. He had his fame, but fortune still eluded him. I hadn't heard from Harry, and that was well and good. I suppose.

Maggie banged a pan against the faucet. "What are you doing there, hon?" I asked.

"Just banging pots and pans together," she said. I looked up and Maggie smiled.

UNACCEPTABLE PROCEDURES

by Stanley Ellin

Stanley Ellin is generally considered one of the field's greatest short story writers. His first story, "Specialty of the House," appeared in Ellery Queen's Mystery Magazine *in 1948. Two of his stories and one of his novels received the genre's highest honor, the Edgar Allan Poe Award. In "Unacceptable Procedures," he explores the subtle moral ambiguities of crime in the way only he can.*

The meeting, surprisingly summoned on only one day's notice, was held in the Chief Selectman's office at the far end of the upstairs corridor of the town hall. Not much of an office for size and thriftily furnished with essentials acquired cheaply over the past century, it still provided sufficient accommodation for the Board of Selectmen around the well-worn oak table there.

Of course, since the room was at the rear of the building, it did offer to anyone with an eye for that sort of thing the view of a vast rolling woodland extending to the faraway horizon. A spectacular view especially this mid-autumn time of year, what with those hills showing as much scarlet and gold as evergreen. And even more so at this hour of day, when the star-spangled darkness already shadowing Maine to the east could almost perceptibly be seen flowing westward toward Vermont to dim the flaming sunset there.

However, the gathering around the table took no notice of this familiar scene: it was the ancient Naval Observatory clock ticking away on the wall between the windows that engaged its interest. Five selectmen, all greyhaired, thin-lipped men of substance. Chief Selectman Samuel Sprague, president of the Merchants Bank. Jacob Sprague, younger brother to Samuel and the bank's treasurer. Abner Perkins, real-estate sales, rentals, and property maintenance. Benjamin Starr, Starr's Cars—Sales and Service. Fraser Smith, Smith's Market—Quality Meats and Groceries. All five of them done up neatly in jacket and necktie as was the tradition at selectmen's meetings, they sat silently with eyes fixed on the clock. The meeting had been called for six. The clock now plainly marked three minutes past the hour.

It was Fraser Smith who broke the silence. He cleared his throat and addressed Chief Selectman Samuel Sprague. "You said special meeting, Sam. Special how? Not getting started on time?"

"Seems so," admitted Samuel Sprague. "But what we're waiting for is our police chief. Told me last night to get us all together so we could meet with him in strict private. Make it for when the building's cleared out, said he, so there wouldn't be any ears at the door."

Benjamin Starr raised an eyebrow. "Considering that Chief Ralph Gibbs has the biggest and busiest ears in town—"

"And worse than ever these last few months," put in Abner Perkins. "Matter of fact, he's getting downright peculiar. Could be that what we just gab about now and then—I mean, after going on thirty years maybe he's been on the job a mite too long—well, could be time we do something about it."

"He works cheap," Samuel Sprague pointed out.

"Can't much call it work," said Abner Perkins, "in any town peaceable as this."

"Except," said Benjamin Starr, "for them high-school kids using my car lot nights for rumpus-raising and playing them stereo machines to all hours. I tell Ralph about it, and what's he say? He says to me, 'Well, they're young and full of oats the way we once was. We grew out of it and so will they.' That's our police chief talking, mind you."

"Talking about what?" said a voice from the doorway, and the selectmen all swiveled heads to coldly regard their police chief. Unlike the company he was joining, Ralph Gibbs was exceedingly well fleshed, his double chin draped over his shirt collar, his belly overlapping his belt. His uniform—the town's choice of grey with brown piping—needed pressing; when he removed his cap the white hairs fringing his shining pate indicated that he had been a long time away from any barber chair. To add to this study in dishevelment he was clutching a large, dingy plastic bag bulging with papers and cardboard folders. On the bag was inscribed in red lettering *Smith's Market—Quality Meats and Groceries.* He smiled at the company. "And just what was your police chief talking about?"

"More to the point," said Samuel Sprague, "you asked for this meeting, and seems like you're the one late to it."

"Few minutes at most," said Ralph Gibbs. "Had to get a man to take over my desk. Ain't easy when the department's this shorthanded."

"Shorthanded?" snorted Benjamin Starr. "With four men on days—"

"That includes me," said Ralph Gibbs, seating himself at the foot of the table with the plastic bag on what there was of his lap.

"Including you," said Benjamin Starr. "For this size town to have as much as four paid police for days and two for nights—"

Samuel Sprague rapped his knuckles on the table. "Ben, pipe down. Ralph told me this business we're here for is real important, so let's get to it. I therefore call to order this confidential meeting—"

"Meeting in executive session," corrected Jacob Sprague.

"—meeting in executive session—meaning strictly confidential—of this Board of Selectmen of the township of Huxtable Falls. Go on, Ralph, speak your piece."

"Thank you kindly, Sam," said Ralph Gibbs. He spilled the contents of the shopping bag on the table and stacked them into an untidy heap.

"What's all this?" asked Abner Perkins.

"Four months of police work, Abner," said Ralph Gibbs. "Real fine big-city police work, if I do say so myself." He sat back and eased open the remaining closed button of his jacket. "Well then, gentlemen, all this starts with some disappearances in these parts."

"Disappearances?" said Fraser Smith. "Of what?"

"People, Fraser. Folks heading up the road towards Huxtable Falls here but never made it. Never made it anywhere, far as some of these records in front of me shows. First was summertime three years ago. Two high-school boys from Antico town went bicycling off to get a look at Canada. Never heard of again."

"Stale news, Ralph," remarked Benjamin Starr. "Them Antico people made a considerable fuss about it at the time."

"Fact," said Ralph Gibbs. "Then two years ago, also summertime, there was that young Greendale couple, fellow and girl, headed Canada way on their motorbike, and, far as anyone yet knows, rode right off into limbo, so to speak."

"Not married neither," said Fraser Smith. "So I heard."

"Not married neither," agreed Ralph Gibbs. "Just young, healthy, and sinful. And now among the missing. Then last summer there was that young married couple set off from Inchester, backpacking up to the north woods, and that was the last seen of them. Nobody outside of Inchester recollects getting even a look at them going by. And the girl was mighty pretty, judging from her picture. Not the kind to be overlooked that easy."

"Maybe not," said Fraser Smith. "Saw that picture on the TV news when she was first suspected missing. Real handsome leggy girl all right."

"But out of Inchester," protested Benjamin Starr. "And those others were out of Antico and Greendale. So except for those towns being in the same county as us, I don't see what this has to do with Huxtable Falls."

"Which," said Ralph Gibbs, "was my line of thought, too, up to last Fourth of July. Tourist party stopped by headquarters that day to ask directions. So I took out the old state map to point them right, and whilst at it my eye was caught by something there,"

"Do tell," said Benjamin Starr drily.

"Like, for instance, all three of them towns is southward of us, oh, maybe seven, eight miles away. Now squint your eyes and picture it. Antico's right there on the main highway and Inchester and Greendale ain't that far away on each side of it on them county blacktops. Antico folks going north just use the highway right through here. Those from Inchester and Greendale, well, their blacktops join up with the highway from each side at Piney Junction a mile south of our town limits."

"Real keen police work, Ralph," said Fraser Smith. "So you know the county map, do you?"

"Fact, Fraser. But the worrisome part is that every one of them young folks that disappeared had to pass right through town here to wherever they was headed. And for not one single soul in Huxtable Falls to ever get a glimpse of them? Makes you wonder if any of them got this far at all, don't it?"

"You mean," said Samuel Sprague, "if anything did happen to them, you're pinning it down to around the Junction?

"Closer than that, Sam. Just take notice that right inside our town limits near the Junction is the old Samson estate. Right?"

"Wrong," put in Abner Perkins. "That property hasn't rightly been the Samson estate for quite a spell now."

"Good point, Abner," said Ralph Gibbs. "Since you got them outsiders to take a five-year lease on it—and four years are already used up—maybe we should call it the Dr. Karl Jodl estate. Especially with all that work the Doctor's paying you to fix it up. Looks sure he'll pick up that option to buy next year, don't it?"

"My business," said Abner Perkins. " And the Doctor's. Not yours. And if you—"

"Hush up, Abner," said Samuel Sprague. He aimed his jaw at Ralph Gibbs. "What about Dr. Karl Jodl, Ralph? Seems to be a nice fellow, far as anyone knows. A little stand-offish maybe, but respectable, him and that whole crew he moved in with him on the estate."

"Seems to be," agreed Ralph Gibbs. "Anyhow, what it comes to is sort of a problem that's too much for me. So before I work out the bottom line I'd like the opinion of you folks here. And before you provide that opinion just listen close."

"About Dr. Jodl?" said Samuel Sprague.

"That's right, Sam. Like, to start with, the fact that him and his crew settled four years ago for a five-year lease on the Samson estate, lease money to apply to purchase price if and when there was a sale. True, Abner? You made the deal, so you'd know."

"It was a fair deal," said Abner Perkins shortly.

"Kind of a happy surprise, too, wasn't it? That big old mansion and them outbuildings rotting away, twenty acres of ground overgrown, that swamp in back oozing right up to the buildings. Didn't look like you'd ever get rid of that property. Then all of a sudden—"

"It was a fair deal all around," Abner Perkins said.

"—and all of a sudden along comes this Mr. Thomas from the Doctor—"

"Tomas," said Abner Perkins. "Toe-mass. Tomas."

"Beg pardon, Abner. Mr. Toe-mass. Along he comes, the Doctor's check in hand, to sign the papers, and next thing you look to have struck gold in that property. I mean, what with all that contract work to bring it back to shape, buildings and grounds. Swamp's all drained now except for its far end, ain't it? Place does look pretty all right."

"Honest work, every inch," said Abner Perkins. "Buildings and grounds."

"That's your style, Abner, no denying it. Then one night before work's hardly got started, along comes this fleet of hired haulage vans, all doing business out of California, and quite a lineup of fancy cars with

California plates, and next morning the Doctor and his people are settled in snug as can be. Maybe twenty of them by my count."

"Twenty?" said Samuel Sprague.

"Well, figuring in the Doctor and his lady—that Madam Solange—and what looks to be assistant doctors and house help and security men, somewhat around twenty." Ralph Gibbs nodded toward Fraser Smith. "Seems they do all their marketing at Fraser's place, too. His books ought to show enough to back that figure up."

"You looking to be my bookkeeper now, Ralph?" said Fraser Smith.

"Not likely, Fraser. Anyhow, gentlemen, there we have a whole new community, so to speak, hitched onto Huxtable Falls. Stand-offish and highly prosperous. And not far from the Junction, where it seems young healthy folks have a way of disappearing now and then."

"And you are soured on the Doctor for living there?" asked Abner Perkins coldly.

"You're rushing me out of turn, Abner," said Ralph Gibbs. "I was just getting around to asking how much anybody here ever sees of them folks close up. Aside from that Mr. Tomas who looks to be sort of manager of the works, and shows up all sunshine and smiles around town. Anybody here ever get a real close look at the Doctor and that Madam Solange?"

"Well," said Samuel Sprague. "I've seen them waiting in that limo in town square a couple of times. What's more, I give them a nod, they give me a nod. Nothing mysterious about it."

"Seen them, too," said Fraser Smith. "Nice-looking couple. High-toned. Old-fashioned mannerly. They just don't want their feet stepped on by busybodies, that's my guess."

"And mine, " said Benjamin Starr. "They're in the limo now and then when it gasses up. Never argue price for repairs or for any of them new cars they order. And those cars are always top dollar. And they pay all bills on the dot. Stand-offish? Why not? Maybe they've got more important business in mind than some."

"You mean like medical business, Ben?" asked Ralph Gibbs.

"That's what I mean."

"Ralph," said Samuel Sprague impatiently, "you know as well as us it's medical business. That Mr. Tomas never made any secret of it. Dr. Jodl's a heart man, top rank. Doing some big research for the government. With a fat grant from Washington, D.C. to pay for it. Can't say I truckle to public money going that direction, but there's nothing unlawful about it, is there?"

"Well, maybe just a mite, Sam. Like, for instance, Dr. Karl Jodl is not on any government grant at all. And he is not a heart man, any rank."

The selectmen gaped. Finally Samuel Sprague said, "Not doing heart research? No grant?"

"Neither," said Ralph Gibbs.

"But from what I heard—"

"Same as we all heard, Sam, from that Mr. Tomas. However" —Ralph Gibbs dug into the pile of papers on the table and came up with a well stuffed folder. He slid it across the table to Samuel Sprague—"however, what you've got there, Sam, is some letters between me and the government people in Washington. And the state people in California. Read 'em close. Take your time about it."

The selectmen kept eyes on Samuel Sprague as he took his time about it, his brow furrowing. Then he looked up at them. "No grant," he said. "No heart man. Leastways, that's what I make of it." He looked at Ralph Gibbs. "What I can't make of it is this medical stuff. This hemodynamics talk. What's it mean?"

"Blood," said Ralph Gibbs.

"Come again?"

"Blood, Sam. That red stuff that leaks out when you cut yourself shaving." Ralph Gibbs tapped the stack of papers before him. "It's all here. Seems that's where the Doctor's an expert. On the Coast he had those two outfits: the Jodl Institute for Hemodynamic Research and the Jodl Clinic for Rejuvenation, both tied tight together. And you saw those figures there for his last ten years' profits, didn't you? Money coming in by the barrel. All that part is from the private investigation agency I hired out there. Private but reliable."

"Hired?" said Abner Perkins. "Out of the police budget?"

"Worth it, Abner. Especially if Sam here tells you about that letter from the state of California itself saying why that institute and that clinic were all of a sudden shut up."

"Well, Sam?" said Abner Perkins.

"It's down here in black and white, Abner. Just two words is all.

'Unacceptable procedures.' "

"Meaning?"

"Meaning," said Ralph Gibbs, "that a lot of beat-up old millionaires around the world were getting themselves rejuvenated some way the state of California didn't truckle to."

"Without saying why it didn't, more than this?"

"Nary a hint, Abner. When I pushed them on it all I could get was goodbye and good luck."

"And goodbye's the right word, Ralph,"said Abner Perkins. "All right, so the Doctor's living on his own money, not any government handout. All the better. And that institute and clinic could have bent some California rules, but what about it? He didn't open them up again here, did he? You don't mind me saying it, Ralph, but you have gone so far off the track that you want to lay everybody missing from the county on that man just because he's new to these parts."

"Didn't want to, Abner. Just couldn't help it, once I got to the Europe part of it."

"Now it's Europe?" Abner Perkins rose abruptly. "Look, I have got a hot supper waiting for me at seven, and I don't—"

"Abner," said Samuel Sprague, "hush up and sit down." He addressed Ralph Gibbs. "And don't you play games, Ralph. What's Europe got to do with this?"

"Ever hear of Interpol, Sam?"

"I might have. Some kind of international police, right?"

"Well, more like an information place to help police in one country get lined up with those elsewhere. Help make connections, so to speak."

"And how come Huxtable Falls needs any such connections?"

"Well," said Ralph Gibbs, "according to these California documents, Dr. Karl Jodl landed there from Switzerland where he used to have another such institute and clinic. And the Switzerland government people told me they was just shut up tight one day. Want to guess why?"

"Unacceptable procedures?" said Samuel Sprague.

"You get the cigar, Sam. So then I got in touch with Interpol and had them look up Dr. Jodl. Didn't get much from them really, but did get friendly with one of their men over the phone."

"Our headquarters phone?" said Benjamin Starr. "To Europe?"

"We'll get to that later, Ben. Right now the point is that this fellow steered me to a private agency in Switzerland that would look real close into people's private business, for a price. And yes, Ben, before you come out with it, it cost money signing up that outfit. But, as duly noted before, it was worth every cent."

"Worth it?" said Fraser Smith. "Lord almighty, you must have run right through your whole department budget already."

"Pretty near, Fraser. And even gone into my own pocket. But here and now"—Ralph Gibbs detached several folders from the stack—"is what you could call the history of Dr. Karl Jodl in Europe from way back when. Copies of everything that agency sent, along with old photos from magazines and newspapers there. There's a set for each of you gents so as not to waste time." He passed the folders around the table, then sat back comfortably in his chair. "Just say the word when you're ready."

For fifteen minutes by the Naval Observatory clock there was intense concentration around the table on the contents of the folders. Samuel Sprague finally closed his folder very gently. He waited until the laggards had finished their reading and a frowning examination of the photographs. All faces around the table, excluding the police chief's, reflected bewilderment.

"Well?" said Ralph Gibbs.

"There's something crazy here, Ralph," said Samuel Sprague.

"My thought, too, Sam, when I plowed through that mess first time around."

"It was?"

"Had to be. After all, here was all that Europe information put together. The whole works. Birth certificate from Austria, schooling, medical training, marriage, that rejuvenation clinic up in the mountains there, then Italy right across the border and another clinic, then Switzerland and still another, and those dates just didn't make sense. And those photos even less. Had to be at least three different people here, I told myself, not one Dr. Karl Jodl. Except, however you add it up, it comes out only one."

"Lord almighty, Ralph," said Fraser Smith, "it can't be. It makes that man a hundred years old. And that woman—that Madam Solange—near as much. I've seen them this close. I'd figure him to be maybe forty, if that much. And she don't go much over thirty by any reckoning."

"That's how it looks, Fraser, not how it is. The dates on these papers and pictures are all truthful. Allowing for the old-fashioned clothes and hairdos, can you tell me that those aren't photos of Dr. Karl Jodl and his wife and nobody else? Fact is, she's the clincher. Maybe the original Karl Jodl would have had a son and grandson and great-grandson who was every one in turn his spitting image and for some reason wanted to make out they themselves was all the original when they grew up. But we know each of them did not marry women who one and all just happened to be the spitting image of Mrs. Dr. Karl Jodl. No way could that happen. So that leaves just one answer that makes sense. And it's all down in those papers, like it or not."

"The clinics," said Samuel Sprague heavily. "Hemodynamics. Total transfusion."

"Total's the payoff word, Sam," said Ralph Gibbs. "Take a few quarts of fresh young blood, add a dab of some secret chemicals, pump out all the old stuff, pump in all new, and look what you've got. Why, it could be the biggest thing any doctor ever come up with—except it might be a little too total for some people's good. Specially some healthy young folks who wouldn't be offered any vote in the matter, would they?"

"Not much," said Samuel Sprague. "But I still can't get it into my head that a man like that— "

"Right," Abner Perkins cut in. "Because this whole thing is wild-eyed speculation, that's all. That man never set up any such clinic here, did he? There's no reason in the world to think what you all look like you're thinking."

"Just one, Abner," said Ralph Gibbs. "He and his wife do look mighty spry for their age. And there's something more to take into account. Kind of touching, too, in a way."

"Touching?" said Samuel Sprague. "What's that supposed to mean?"

"Means I put in a stretch a few times this summer up in the brush in Samson's Hill with the binoculars. Couldn't see inside the main house that way, but could get a good look at the grounds roundabout."

"Why?" said Samuel Sprague. "Trying to find out if any customers in Rolls-Royces were sneaking in to get rejuvenated?"

"You are sharp, Sam, that I'll give you. That's why, all right. And never did see any such customers. What I did see was the Doctor and his lady doing a slow ramble through those fancy gardens up to what's left of the old swamp. Just walking along slow and easy, talking to each other and mostly holding hands. Sometimes they'd set themselves down on one of them ironwork benches and have a kissing party. Those are high-powered binoculars all right. And one thing came clear through them. I figure that man's a little crazy more ways than one, but one way I know for sure. He is crazy in love with that woman. Easy to see why, too, with her looks and style. And that's what it's all about. Whatever it takes, he is going to keep her just the way she is for as long as he can. And himself right there along with her."

"Whatever it takes," said Samuel Sprague.

"Afraid so, Sam. That's the catch."

"Only if you buy all this foolishness," said Abner Perkins.

"Abner," said Samuel Sprague, "you know that what we've got here is no foolishness, so quit trying to make it sound that way." He turned to Ralph Gibbs. "Now what? You aim to get out a warrant against the Doctor?"

"Lord almighty," said Fraser Smith.

"But there's no bodies," said Benjamin Starr. "Only some people missing."

"Just the same, Ben," said Ralph Gibbs, "there's enough here to make quite a case. And whether Dr. Karl Jodl wins it or loses it, he's a marked man afterwards. How do you think the newspapers and TV will handle this right across the country? Still and all— "

"Yes?" said Samuel Sprague.

"Still and all, Sam, I can see two directions to move. This thing's too big for me anyhow. Best to go down to Concord and lay it all out for the state people. Let them take over. After all, it covers more than Huxtable Falls, don't it? There's three other towns nearby with what you might call a vested interest in it."

Samuel Sprague considered this. "That's one direction, Ralph. "What's the other?"

"Well now, Sam, one thing is pretty sure. We cut loose on Dr. Karl Jodl and company, they'll take off from these parts quick as they can. Fact. So putting myself in your place— "

"My place?"

"Yours and Jacob's, what with you two owning our good old Merchants Bank. I was thinking of you two waving goodbye to the biggest customer the bank's got. A six-figure depositor no less."

"Who told you about that?" demanded Samuel Sprague.

"Don't matter who, Sam. What matters is it's the truth. As for Abner there and his real-estate business, well, he stands to have that white elephant Samson estate dumped right back in his hands. No closing the sale for it, no fat contract afterwards to keep the place in shape. Same for Ben there and his car business. No more Dr. Jodl for luxury buys, no more high-price repairs on that whole fleet the Doctor's lined up for his kind services. And I guess I don't have to remind Fraser that the Doctor and his crowd have to be the market's number-one customers for sure. I mean, what with those loads of fancy meat and trimmings being trucked out there every few days. Am I making myself clear?"

"Some," said Samuel Sprague. "Not all. What's on your mind, Ralph?"

"Well now, what's on my mind is that all this started because some folks turned up missing from towns roundabout. But let's look at it this way. That's not my business, is it? They want the answers I got, let them go hunt them up like I did. Get the point now, Sam?"

"Except for what you left out. What makes you so sure that next summertime, let's say, a couple of our own young folks won't turn up missing from right here in Huxtable Falls?"

"Fair question, Sam. But I guarantee nobody as smart as Dr. Karl Jodl looks to make waves right here in home port. No chance of that. That's how it's been since he settled down here; that's how it'll keep on."

"All the same, Ralph– "

"So I could just tuck all these papers here back in this shopping bag and lock it up nice and tight in my house. Which, for that matter, is where it's been kept all along. Strictly my own private business so far. Nobody else's."

"Even so, Ralph," said Abner Perkins, "if you'd just heave all that stuff in the fire– "

"No; don't see it quite that way, Abner," said Ralph Gibbs. "And there's still some items on the agenda."

"Such as?" said Samuel Sprague.

"Well, for one thing, seems there's been talk amongst you gentlemen that after me holding down my desk for nigh thirty years, it's time to put the old horse out to pasture. Fact is, I like my job. It'll do my morale a lot of good to know I'm set in it until I say otherwise."

"What else?" said Samuel Sprague.

"Matter of repayment, Sam. That Europe agency cost me cash out of my pocket. Can't see making repayment a town budget item, so best way to handle it, I figure, is for each of you gents to make out a check for one thousand Yankee dollars, payable to cash, and hand it over to Jacob here at the bank first thing tomorrow. He puts it all straight into my account, and there we are, no fuss, no big noise about it."

"Maybe not," said Jacob Sprague, "but that kind of transaction by the whole Board of Selectmen– "

"I didn't finish yet, Jacob," said Ralph Gibbs. "Didn't mention that I have already set up a meeting with the state people down to Concord three P.M. tomorrow. I figure around noon tomorrow I'll know whether to call it off or drive down there."

"Noon tomorrow," said Samuel Sprague. "And that finishes the agenda?"

"Not yet, Sam. There's them pay raises that keep getting left out of the budget every year. What I see for next year is a twenty percent raise across the board. That's for everybody in my department, including me. And two shiny new police cars with all extras, because them heaps we have now got were due for the scrap pile long ago. And that is the whole agenda." Ralph Gibbs rose and dumped the papers and folders before him into the shopping bag. He made a circuit around the table, sweeping the rest of the documents into it. He planted his cap squarely on his head. "Shouldn't rightly be here when the vote's taken, so I'll get along home now. Anyhow," he said from the door, "hate to miss the TV news any night. Never know what'll show up on it."

All eyes were on the door as it very gently closed behind him. The sound of footsteps down the corridor faded away.

"Lord almighty," whispered Fraser Smith.

The Naval Observatory clock on the wall ticked loudly, marking off a minute and then some.

"Well," said Samuel Sprague, "it looks like Ralph left us a motion here to vote on. No need to spell it out again, line for line. Anybody stand against it?" He waited a seemly time, then rapped his knuckles on the table. "The motion is adopted unanimously."

Benjamin Starr raised his hand.

"Yes, Ben?" said Samuel Sprague.

"Well, it's about the new police cars, Sam. Looks to me that Starr's Cars could get a special discount from the manufacturer that'll–"

"No way." Samuel Sprague shook his head in reproach. "That is a conflict of interest for you, Ben, and you know it. Anything else?"

"That was it," said Benjamin Starr sadly.

"Then this meeting is herewith adjourned," said Samuel Sprague.

A SOUL TO TELL

by Jeremiah Healy

In addition to being a professor at Boston's New England School of Law, Jeremiah Healy is the Shamus Award-winning author of several mystery novels and the creator of private eye John Francis Cuddy. In the following story, Cuddy takes on an unusual assignment and an unusual role. Is a P.I. really just a detached observer of the scenes he investigates? Or is he sometimes a participant . . . ?

"May I have your attention. The Delta Connection, Business Express Flight 3557, with direct service to Nantucket and continuing service to Martha's Vineyard, is now ready for passengers through Gate 15. All rows may now board the aircraft."

I hefted my duffel bag and joined the line of folks handing little passes to the uniformed smile. An hour before, I'd locked "John Francis Cuddy, Confidential Investigations," and hailed a Boston cab to Logan Airport. It's cheaper to drive to Cape Cod and take the ferry to Nantucket, but I was on expenses, and the client on the phone had said the sooner the better. She also said I wouldn't be needing a firearm or dress clothes, just a camera and lots of film.

We made our way down a flight of stairs and onto a jitney bus with deep leatherette seats. Gas tankers, Marriott food service trucks, and baggage shuttles made for heavy traffic on the macadam. The bus driver pulled up to our plane, a twin-prop Shorts 360 that looked a lot like our jitney with wings. I heaved my duffel into the open baggage hold near the tail. The maybe thirty of us filled most of the seats in the cabin, the takeoff reminding me of walking through a machine shop going full blast. When the pilot reached cruising altitude, the stewardess began pouring soft drinks.

The plastic cups were barely on the trays before we began our descent into Nantucket, the "Faraway Isle" of whalers. Gentle hills and moors, sporting a dozen shades of yellow, brown, and orange in the clear October air. My wife Beth and I used to talk about taking a getaway weekend to the island. Before the cancer took her.

On the ground, a guy wearing sonic earmuffs unloaded the baggage hold onto a cart and wheeled the cart to a glassless service window, through which he passed our luggage. Following the client's suggestion, I signed for a Jeep Cherokee at one of the rental counters and got a map and finger-traced directions to 76 Main Street, the bed and breakfast the client named.

There was only one architectural style on the drive from the airport, even the gas stations done in silver cedar-shake siding. The predominant trim color was white, a few nonconformists daring powder blue and even dull red. Once in town, however, there was a Federalist flavor to things, including a number of brick or clapboard mansions and cottages.

The inn turned out to be one of the white clapboard places, a friendly woman named Shirley registering me and asking what I wanted from my time on the island. When I said I wasn't sure, she rattled off ten or twelve spots I could visit, with brochures on what to look for when I arrived at each. After I was shown to my room and oriented on breakfast and next morning, Shirley wished me a good dinner and a good night.

Unpacking took only until four o'clock. Since the weather was clear and I didn't know what the client had in mind for my time, I decided to walk the town and harbor. Main Street angled downhill past quaint shops, spreading and petering out at wharves that held tiny shacks dolled up as art and crafts galleries. Not too many pleasure craft so late in the season, but still a lot of scallopers and charter boats.

At the sound of a hooting horn, people who had been lounging on benches or curbs suddenly gathered themselves and rushed toward a docking ferry. One couple doggy-walked a sea-kayak on its two-wheeled trailer, him at the bow, her at the stern, smiling tolerantly at the odd looks and snapshots being taken of them.

Leaving the harbor, I crisscrossed the streets, noticing the police station on South Water only by the one black and white Ford patrol car parked in front of it. As the sun set, I joined the rest of the tourists in what seemed to be the major preoccupation: reading menus posted outside restaurants and shaking heads at the high prices listed. I eventually settled on a reasonable place called Obadiah's, an old-fashioned basement dining room on India Street. The wide-board pine benches were laquered, the clam chowder and swordfish magnificent. I added a bottle of sauvignon blanc to the bill.

Upstairs, the sidewalks were rolling up. I walked off dinner for twenty minutes or so, appreciating the charm of the town in the afterglow of the wine. Climbing back up Main, I nearly broke my ankle twice on the cobblestone street, the stones themselves rounded but hummocky above the old cement.

At the inn, an equally friendly man named Mitch welcomed me all over again. After a few minutes of small talk, I went up to my room. In the spirit of the island, I went to sleep with the windows open and the door to the corridor unlocked.

"I'd rather hoped to go deaf first, you see."

Eleanor Ware sat across from me, sipping herb tea from a delicate china cup. The cup was the only delicate thing about her. High forehead, broad nose, strong jaw. A whisper of makeup around the eyes, and black hair generously streaked with gray. The hair was pulled back and caught in a ponytail, as though she did that just once each day and undid it just once each night. The kind of clothes you see in a Talbot's window, all earth colors. Fifty-plus, and not the least bit afraid to show it.

Ware received me on a wicker settee in the solarium of a traditional Cape Cod, a railed wood deck visible through the sliding glass doors behind her. She already had asked me if I'd enjoyed the inn, and I already had told her that breakfast on the patio there had been great except for the yellow jackets. Apparently, the beautiful weather brought them out, wasps being "a small price to pay for sunshine in October." I'd just managed to get us onto why she wanted to hire me, but I was having trouble understanding her.

"Let me get this straight, Mrs. Ware. You want me to follow your husband around?"

"Yes, yes, but not for some—what do you detectives call it, 'ulterior motive'?"

"Investigator."

"Excuse me?"

"I'm an investigator. Detectives are on police forces."

"Yes, yes. Tell me, Mr. Cuddy. Are you married?"

"Widower."

"Oh. Oh, I am sorry." Her eyes blurred as she set the cup in a matching saucer. "Forgive me, Mr. Cuddy. And please forgive me too my joke about going deaf. You see, my husband Mycah has been in real estate ever since he came to the island—his office is just off Main Street. He turns fifty-five next February and he's always promised to retire then. Mycah certainly deserves it, the man has worked day and night for decades and has always been a fine provider. But, with the boom in housing the last few years, he's scarcely had any time to spend with me. And I'm afraid, frankly, that in maintaining and expanding my own circle of friends . . . I'm just afraid that Mycah and I have rather lost touch with one another, that we won't have much in common once he retires."

"So you want me to follow him around?"

"Yes. To see what he does, how he spends his day. Then report back to me so that I can learn more about his interests and at least have topics of conversation when we begin spending more time together in a few months."

I shifted in my wicker chair. "Couldn't you just sort of ask him about that?"

Ware blushed. "Ask Mycah about what he does, you mean?"

"Yes."

"Oh, no. No, that would be . . . inappropriate. He'd feel that I didn't love him enough to have kept up with him."

I thought about Beth, all the time I spent away from her before knowing she was sick. Eleanor Ware's sentiment was a little corny, but I could understand it.

I said, "You want pictures of him?"

"Pictures?"

"Photographs. All the camera equipment I bought."

"Oh. Oh, I see. No, the island attracts a lot of naturalists, you see. When I suggested camera gear on the phone I meant for it to give you —do detec—sorry, in*vest*igators, call it 'cover'?"

"Close enough. I follow him around pretending to take pictures of the birds and the bushes."

"Precisely."

"You don't think he'll notice that?"

"Mycah? No. No, everyone who visits Nantucket and rents a Jeep is sightseeing, and this is a small island with only so many roads. Even if he saw you more than once, he wouldn't give it a second thought."

"Do you want pictures of any of the people he meets?"

"No. Thank you, but no. Mycah must spend a good deal of his time showing properties to prospective buyers from away. From off-island, that is. I wouldn't be needing to meet or talk to any of them. I just want you to trail after him for, oh, say, three days? Then report back to me. Would that be satisfactory?"

"Three days at four hundred a day added onto my time to get here and get back, plus expenses."

"I assure you that I can afford it."

I looked around at the elaborate furniture, adjoining a living room with a baby grand piano but without a television. People who don't have a TV in their living room usually can afford it.

"What I meant, Mrs. Ware, is that you might not be getting much value for your money."

"I'm a fair judge of value, Mr. Cuddy. And besides, even if this is just a whim, I'd like to know. It will help me be a better helpmate to Mycah during his transitions from active professional to retired husband."

"You have a recent picture of him?"

She frowned. "Can't you just–what, 'pick him up' outside the house here?"

I gestured toward the front door. "Your house sits on this little knoll with a meadow in front of it. There's no place for me to conceal the Jeep, and even your husband would wonder about a car that picked him up right outside his driveway."

"Yes. Yes, I see your point."

"It would be a lot easier for me to latch onto him at his real estate office, and that way I could start this afternoon."

"Just a moment."

Ware rose and strode purposefully to the piano. She came back carrying a large photo, holding the frame at northwest and southeast corners like an auctioneer's assistant. "This is a portrait we had done at Bachrach's in Boston." The woman couldn't quite keep the pride from her voice. "I'm told they even had it displayed in their glass case on Boylston Street."

The photo showed Mrs. Ware sitting and a bold, assured man with auburn hair standing halfway behind her. His right hand rested on her shoulder, her left hand bent upward to touch his.

"You make a striking couple."

She blushed again and replaced the frame on the piano. Her sentimentality and strength made an attractive combination, and I found myself envying husband Mycah just a bit.

Resuming her seat, Eleanor Ware asked if there was anything else.

"What kind of car does your husband drive?"

"Cadillac."

"Model and color."

"Coupe de Ville, rather a burgundy. With all the dirt roads on the island, a Jeep would be more practical, but Mycah has always loved his Cadillacs."

"You know anyone on the local police force?"

My questions seemed to throw her. "The police?"

"Yes."

"What do they have to do with our arrangement?"

"Hopefully nothing. It's just standard procedure to check in with them when I start working in a new town."

"Is it . . . some kind of law or regulation?"

"No. Just good business practice."

"I see. Well, I have a problem with that."

"What is it?"

"On the telephone, when I called, you said that your licensing statute would keep everything between us confidential."

"That's right."

"Confidential even from the police?"

"I don't read the statute every week, but it just says I might have to reveal to a court, not the cops. Why?"

"Well, you see, I'm an islander. I was raised here, with the chief of police, among others. I would . . . It would be embarrassing to me for them to know that I'd hired you to follow Mycah."

"That's understandable. Tell you what. I'll just let the police know I'm down here on business, not what the business is or who it's for. Would that be all right?"

Ware seemed to think about it. "Yes. Yes, that would be fine." She reached down next to her chair and brought up a handbag from which she coaxed a fat envelope. "I'd like to pay you a retainer in advance."

As she counted fifties from the envelope, I said, "A check would be fine."

Ware stopped counting for a minute, weighing the bills in her palm as though that would somehow be a quality control on her tally. "No. No, I got the cash for this, and frankly, it makes it better."

"Better?"

"This is a small island, Mr. Cuddy. It's hard to have secrets, even harder to share them. That's why I wanted someone from away —someone like you—to help me. Paying you in cash means no snoopy bank teller will know my personal business."

Eleanor Ware finished counting and handed me the bills, being careful, I thought not to let our fingers touch.

"Kate Hearn."

"John Cuddy, sergeant."

"Kate, please."

I released her hand. She sat back down behind a cluttered desk, me taking one of the metal chairs in front of it. The biggish patrol officer who had brought me into her office closed the door as he left.

Hearn said, "Chief's on vacation, off-island."

Mrs. Ware would be pleased.

Hearn inclined her head toward the door. "Ben said you're a private investigator."

"Yes."

"From Boston?"

"My accent gave me away?"

Hearn laughed, one sharp bray. "No, it's just there aren't so many from the Cape, and I thought I knew most of the operatives from New Bedford and Fall River."

Her hair on the sides and back touched the collar of her shirt. The bangs in front were just past her brow. Any longer and she'd have to blow out a breath to keep them off her eyes, which were blue and steady. "So, what brings you to Nantucket?"

"I'm going to be driving around with a camera, and I thought I ought to check in with you first."

"Uh-huh." The steady eyes never left me. "You're going to be driving around a lot."

"Right."

"Make, model, and plate?"

I told her. She wrote them down.

"Where are you staying?"

"Seventy-six Main Street."

"Good choice."

"I'm comfortable."

Hearn waited me out, then said, "Am I going to get a real answer to my question about what brought you here?"

"Confidential."

"Confidential."

"Sorry."

Hearn puffed out a breath, flipping the bangs. "Okay. Consider yourself checked in, then. But don't expect any favors without doing some yourself."

When I got up, we shook hands anyway.

High noon, but not much happening in downtown Nantucket. Three elderly women were window-shopping, pointing politely and nodding at everything each one said. A hard-faced guy in a blue jogging suit was loafing on the hood of his car, arms and ankles crossed. He looked like he'd made his money young. Some kids of college age were camped on a curb, knapsacks as backrests, eating ice cream.

I could see the doorway to Ware Realty through the driver's side mirror. I studied a map of the island and fiddled with my camera like a tourist about to strike off for the afternoon. A burgundy Coupe de Ville occupied a parking space three down from mine. A tweedy middle-aged couple had gone into the realty office about fifteen minutes before, he seeming less enthusiastic than she did.

I was down to counting the number of ponds on my map when Mycah Ware came out holding a clipboard in his right hand. In tow were the middle-aged couple and a stunning redhead in a bottle-green dress that I would bet complemented her eyes. The quartet crossed to the Cadillac, the men taking the front seats, the women the rear, the redhead showing some leg as she climbed in. Even the guy in the jogging suit seemed to sit up straighter. Waiting until Ware passed me, I started up and after them.

I should have had ice cream with the knapsackers.

Ware took his customers to three houses, all indistinguishable to me under weathered shingles and white picket widow's walks. At each stop, Ware sashayed the woman in the couple all over the grounds, tapping and then holding a pen to the clipboard in his hands. The redhead tagged behind with the man in the couple, seemingly doing the same things with her pen and clipboard. Then everybody went into the house for half an hour or so.

The only change in the routine was the part of the island we visited. First west to the Dionis Beach area, then south to Cisco Beach, then east past the airport toward Low Beach.

While Ware and the redhead hucked, and the couple absorbed, I took photos. Of everything. Kids windsurfing in striped wetsuits, a woman in a straw hat painting a seascape on an easel, tufted grasses at the base of dunes. Double-rung fences of gray split rails, country mailboxes with little red flags, kaleidoscopic fields of wildflowers. Estuaries with small sailboats, moors of pumpkin-hued heather. Small trees bent over from the prevailing wind, briar patches even Br'er Rabbit wouldn't call home. You name it, I shot it, my eyes blearing and my back creaking.

At house number three, a blue Thunderbird with classical music wafting from the radio pulled even with me. Bent over my umpteenth wildflower, I looked up at the driver. Preppy face, short blond hair, the kind of guy who wouldn't look quite thirty until he was well past forty.

He said, "You okay?"

"Fine, thanks."

"Saw your car on my way into town, then saw you still here. Thought you might be broken down."

"No. Just taking pictures. Thanks, though."

"Any time." He waved and accelerated slowly away.

I wondered if I had just met one of Kate Hearn's officers out of uniform.

The Thunderbird was barely out of sight when Ware and the others left the house and piled into the Caddy. We drove back toward town, stopping at a classy private clubhouse set a hundred feet from its driveway. I stole the spirits from some more flora, trying not to notice the rabbit squashed flat near the entrance or the ravens licking their chops on the power lines. An hour later, the Coupe de Ville pulled back onto the road and went the rest of the way into Nantucket. The fabulous foursome disappeared into the realty office for half an hour more, then reappeared with vigorous handshakes and polite kisses all around. The wife in the couple was clutching a big manila envelope and beaming ecstatically; the husband was missing a shirt pocket with his pen and wearing an expression like he'd just been in a train crash.

Once the couple was out of sight, Ware and the redhead smiled at each other and went to the Cadillac. Off we went, this time toward the east along Milestone Road. I checked a couple of times for the Thunderbird but didn't see it.

When we got to the village of Siasconset, Ware and the redhead started house-hopping again. They'd circle around a place, clipboards in hand, Ware apparently giving her some tips as he pointed at exterior features, then to a form on her clipboard. At each house they'd go insided for half an hour or so, then come back out. These times I shot a towering, red-banded lighthouse; gray, dumpy hens that looked wild; and larger silver-shake mansions with English hedges and gardens.

After the third house, we again returned to town, dusk and a little fog heavy on the moors along the road. A block from the realty office, Ware came to a stop. The redhead and he shook hands theatrically, a pronounced "We-did-it" pantomime, then laughed. She got out of the Caddy and into a Mercedes convertible, the only one I'd seen on the island so far. Ware waited until she started up before he put his car in gear.

I followed Ware back to his own house, continuing on as he slewed into his driveway and put the Caddy in the garage via some kind of electronic door-opener. Figuring he was through for the night, I drove back to the inn, thinking over dinner that old Mycah had probably turned a tad more than four hundred for his day's work with the middle-aged couple.

I was getting better at keeping the yellow jackets out of my Wheat Chex.

On the patio in the backyard of 76 Main Street, I read the local newspaper and tossed sugar cubes to the sparrows. Past the overhanging branches, there wasn't a cloud in the sky, temperature at eight A.M. in the low sixties. Sweater weather. Mycah Ware might lead a boring life, but I could see why people would want to live their only one on Nantucket.

Reluctantly, I folded the paper and went around front to the Cherokee.

There were two sets of different elderly ladies window-shopping, three male knapsackers who spoke in German or Dutch to each other while they ate croissants and slurped coffee, and the same rough-faced guy in a different jogging outfit. The redhead's Mercedes was already on the street. I didn't see Ware's Cadillac, but I wasn't worried.

Just after nine, the redhead came out of the realty office. She was dressed in a conservative gray suit today, talking and nodding a lot to a short, squat, older woman who appeared to be calling the shots for a taller, younger woman from the same gene pool.

The threesome moved on foot toward my car, the jogging suit guy swiveling around, following the redhead with his eyes and sighing. I realized it might be a daily ritual for him, watching the best-looking woman on the island. As the redhead drew even with my car, she squeezed a smile at me into her nodding at everything the squat woman said. Up close, the redhead's face looked carefully maintained, and I bumped her age up toward forty. The squat woman's voice was raspy and commanding, and I decided I didn't envy the redhead her next few hours.

Hearing a car door slam, I looked back up the street. Mycah Ware, in rose slacks and a teal sweater, was crossing to his office. He went inside, staying maybe fifteen minutes before emerging, going to his Caddy, and taking off. I started up and followed him eastward to the Sankatay Head Golf Club, near the lighthouse from the day before. He pulled into the driveway. I stayed at the edge of the road and got out. I walked until I could see Ware at the trunk of his car, yanking out a bag of golf clubs and waving to a kid who hustled over to help him with it.

For the next six and a half hours, I counted four-wheel drive vehicles (fifty-one, but some of them were doubles), species of birds (seven, with only the sparrows, seagulls, and starlings sure I.D.'s), and finally kinds of flowers (I quit at thirty). I even got cruel, snapping candids of overweight tourists on mopeds. They wore helmets at all the wrong angles and silently screamed through open mouths as they careened down the hill.

The Cadillac finally reappeared at the mouth of the driveway. On the way to town, Ware stopped for a couple of belts at the same private club, then continued home, putting his car to sleep again in the garage.

As I drove back to town, I thought it looked like a long thirty years in front of wife Eleanor.

It was just dark when I parked half a block from 76 Main Street. Before I could get out, a tall guy in a Mets baseball cap and sunglasses limped over to my driver's side with a map in his hands.

"I wonder if you can help me?"

My hand on the door handle, I said, "Sorry. I don't know the island too well."

The passenger's side door rocked open and the guy in the jogging suit got in, a Smith & Wesson Bodyguard revolver almost lost in his fist. "That's okay. We do."

The guy with the Mets cap lowered his shades. The preppy blond from the Thunderbird. I didn't like his smile much.

"Okay, now pull over against that log there."

We were in the parking area for Dionis Beach. There was a big house with two peaked gables and a couple of smaller ones on the bluff, but all looked closed up for the season.

Jogging Suit said, "Turn off the engine."

I did.

"Put the keys on the dashboard."

Same.

"Now play statue for a minute."

Jogging Suit stayed where he was while Preppy got out from behind me. Preppy pointed a little automatic at my face while Jogging Suit opened the passenger's side and came around. Both leveled on me from ten feet away and at different angles as I got out of the car. Very professional and not a good sign.

"Assume the position on the hood."

I complied. They didn't bother with my wallet. Another bad sign.

Preppy said, "We're going to take a walk on the beach. You go first. Turn when we say. Don't do anything stupid."

I led them up the sandpath and over the cliff, sidewinding to the beach below.

Nobody around.

"Turn right and walk east, up the beach."

I started east, them clumping and squeaking in the sand behind me. It was a lot colder right along the water, the moonlight dancing off the waves. The beach stretched into the distance, but was only twenty yards wide before it abutted the cliff. Nowhere to run.

We'd scuffed about a quarter mile along the bowed lines of flotsam when I asked, "Much farther?"

Jogging Suit's voice said, "Keep walking."

Before long, I heard the clattering of wheels on what must have been a boardwalked path. There was also a high-pitched but muted whine that took me a minute to place.

A man in a motorized wheelchair came onto the beach, the tires doing surprisingly well in the sand. He wore a Kangol cap low over his eyes and a muffler over his throat and under a heavy corduroy Norfolk jacket. The muffler was the same dark color as his sweater. He had what looked like calfskin driving gloves on both hands, one cradling a liquor bottle.

The Kangol Cap didn't speak for a good minute after we were close to him, probably to give me a chance to talk my way out of whatever I'd gotten into. I kept my own counsel.

Finally he said, "You know me?"

"I can't even see you."

Somebody kicked me behind the right knee. Cramping, I went down.

"View any better from there, Cuddy?"

I looked up and under the cap. Handsome face, youngish but strained from the chair. Something familiar.

"I've seen your picture."

"The name's Branca. Victor Branca."

Branca. A rising wiseguy in the Boston-to-Providence axis. Then a skiing accident, a total accident, if you could believe the papers, and he'd left the slope paralyzed from the waist down. Six, seven years ago.

"Now you know my name, you know you answer my questions straight when I ask them."

I said, "How come you know my name?"

A kick to the right kidney. I sagged onto that side and choked back what was rising in my throat.

Branca said, "I ask, you answer. Got it?"

I tried nodding this time.

Seeming satisfied, Branca said, "You camp outside the real estate office there. We figure, maybe you're tailing my wife. So we check with the car rental at the airport and run you with some people we know up to Boston. Turns out you're a P.I. Also turns out you look to be on Mycah Ware, not my wife. How come?"

There wasn't any good way to say it. "Sorry. Confidential."

A shot to the other kidney. Felt like a different kind of shoe.

"These guys, they can do this kind of thing till you're just jelly inside. How come you're tailing Ware?"

I shook my head and took a pointed toe just under the left shoulder blade that had me twisting in the sand next to a pink tampon applicator.

Branca said, "This Ware, he's clean. We checked him out quiet but good before I let my wife go to work for him. He don't juggle the books there, he don't even have a partner he could be shorting on the take. So, how come you're on him?"

I didn't bother to shake my head this time. One of the boys grabbed me by the hair and pulled me up to my knees.

Branca motioned toward the sea. "You know, even when it's this cold, them crabs out there like to eat." He waggled a finger at me. "Why're you tailing Ware?"

"No."

Somebody remembered they hadn't whacked me behind the left knee and let fly there.

Branca said, "Only one possibility. His own wife put a tail on him. Only one reason for that, too. She thinks he's stepping out on her."

Through clenched teeth, I said, "No."

"Stepping out with my wife."

I got past the cramp. "That's not it."

"It's not?"

"No. His wife just wanted me to find out what he does."

"Why?"

I tried Mrs. Ware's retirement theory on him. It sounded lame even to me, and Branca didn't buy it. Then nobody said anything for a while.

Branca's voice came back, but different in tone. "When I had my accident, that was one thing that didn't get broken, you know? I thought Cynthia was still happy with me. I wanted to live as far away from a mountain as I could get, and this place suited me just fine. But without her, it wouldn't be so good."

If Branca were trying to sound wistful, he needed a little more practice.

"The people up to Boston there told me you were a stand-up guy, Cuddy. I ain't seen nothing different." Branca tapped the liquor bottle. "Boys?"

I got a whiff of the chloroform before one of them clamped the rag over my mouth and nose, but there wasn't much I could have done about it.

"Hey, Cuddy? Wake up. Come on. Up, up."

A strong arm was tugging on my left side. If I could have gotten to my feet, the smell of scotch would have knocked me back down. I wanted to crawl away from the man's voice with the scotch. I cracked my eyes open. The sunlight hurt, but I realized that the man was in uniform, the officer named Ben from the town police. And I was the one who stank of scotch.

Ben helped me up, snatching the empty Johnnie Walker Black bottle from next to where I'd been in the sand. Ben waved to someone on the cliff who waved back. The lady in the straw hat at her easel.

I said, "What time is it?"

"Eleven fifteen."

My head was pounding as Ben made me start to shuffle up the beach.

Kate Hearn blew at her bangs and said, "So you drive out to Dionis Beach last night, tie one on, and sleep it off at the tideline."

"Like I said. I don't remember much."

"You look like you hit the ground without a parachute."

"I haven't slept on the beach for a while. Cold sand takes it out of you."

"So does a liter of scotch. You want more water?"

"Please."

I was handed another paper cup.

"This has been an exciting morning for us, John Cuddy."

"Wish I could say the same."

"Lost one of our stellar citizens to a terrible accident."

Finishing the water just kept me from gagging. "Sorry to hear it."

"Yeah. Mycah Ware, real estate broker. Know him?"

"We never met."

"His office is just a little ways from where you're staying. Or where you had been staying before you decided to bed down on the beach instead. Ben here couldn't find you at Seventy-six Main. Shirley and Mitch were some worried about you. One of the patrol cars spotted your Jeep at Dionis and routined it in to us. That was when we went out looking for you."

"I appreciate it."

"Back to this Ware? Terrible situation. Fell down a flight of stairs this morning at a house he was sizing. Witness, one Cynthia Branca, saw him take the tumble. Frightened her near to death. Broke his neck, he did."

"Tragedy."

"Yeah, sure it is. But since the witness is wife to somebody who's no stranger to violence, and since you checked in with me just two days before the accident, I though you might have something to tell us."

I crumpled the cup. "I don't."

"Nothing at all?"

"Sorry."

"I'm sorry, too. I really am."

Hearn turned away and said, "You're free to go, Cuddy. But not to come back."

At the inn, I thanked Shirley for her concern. Cleaned up and changed, I packed my duffel bag, got into the Cherokee, and started out.

There were two other cars in the driveway of the Ware house, so I edged the Jeep into the bushes on the shoulder of the road and walked up to the front door. A solemn woman of about fifty ushered me inside. There were three other similar women looking sympathetic in the living room and two older men looking useless and restless. Eleanor Ware was sitting on the couch, the centerpiece of the tableau.

She rose when she saw me, a handkerchief to her nose and mouth. "Thank you for coming."

"I know this is a difficult time for you, Mrs. Ware, but could I see you for just a few minutes?"

"Certainly." Turning to the others, she engaged each in eye contact. "We'll be on the deck. Please help yourselves to the refrigerator, and thank you again for coming."

Once outside, she slid the glass door shut in its track and joined me at the railing overlooking the moor below the knoll.

I said, "I have something you need to know about your husband's death."

"Go on."

I told her about Branca and the boys, that I thought they killed her husband in front of Cynthia to whipsaw her back into line.

Eleanor Ware let me finish before arching an eyebrow and allowing a twinkle into her eye. "Clever, killing two birds with one stone like that."

I was afraid she was losing her grip.

"Mrs. Ware, I don't think you understand. Branca thought—"

"That I believed my husband was having it on with his wife when they 'inspected' those houses. I may have been—is the word 'adultered,' Mr. Cuddy?—but I'm not stupid. That's exactly what Mycah was doing."

I had to hold onto the railing. "He was seeing Cynthia Branca, and you knew it?"

"Of course. Oh, Mycah was *ever* so discreet. No lipstick on the collar. I assume he stripped before he even touched her each time. But he'd grown so . . . inattentive. A wife really can sense these things."

"Then why did you have me follow him?"

"Now why do you think?"

"Jesus Christ."

A wry smile. "You see, Mr. Cuddy, Mycah wasn't just unfaithful. He wasn't even just inattentive. He was boring. God, I can't begin to tell you how unbearable it is to be on an island you love with a man who bores you to tears. I dreaded his retirement. A few hours a day with Mycah was one thing. But the rest of my waking hours for the rest of my life? Inconceivable."

"You set him up."

"I did not. And neither did you. In any way. I'm sure Mr. Branca's reputation is known to you. I know it wasn't to Mycah, or frankly even to me until I did some rather thorough research. But that research convinced me that Mr. Branca would deal with Mycah because of what Mycah had done to him, not because of what Mycah had done to me. And you and I had virtually no role in that."

"Wait a minute. You flew me down here just to get Branca's attention?"

Ware looked at me. "I researched you, too, Mr. Cuddy. You'd lost your wife young. I thought you'd find my desire to be closer to Mycah in his retirement . . . admirable. I felt it would work. And it did."

"Why not just tell him yourself?"

"Tell Branca? Speak to a mobster and inform on Mycah? Just what sort of woman do you think I am, Mr. Cuddy?"

"The sort who'd pull the switch on her own husband rather than just divorce him."

"Divorce would have been too . . . public. Besides, Mycah made his own bier and shortly will lie on it. I am sorry that you were—is it 'roughed up'?"

"Yeah. I still don't see why you needed me, though. You didn't want to talk to Branca, fine. Send him a note, an anonymous tip."

She looked out over the moor, the breeze ruffling the heather in a wave pattern like an ocean of iced tea. "No. No, you don't see it at all. It's as I said to you when we first met. This is a small island, and therefore secrets are very dear. If I'd done everything myself, I wouldn't dare share it with anyone here." She gestured back at the living room. "With anyone in there."

Mrs. Ware turned to me. "I needed somebody bound by confidentiality, but I could hardly hire a lawyer to follow Mycah about. You see, Mr. Cuddy, I needed *you.* Otherwise, I wouldn't have had a soul to tell."

I.O.U.—ONE LIFE

by Marjorie Carleton

Marjorie Carleton did not write often in the mystery field, but when she did she received high praise from no less than Ellery Queen (Fred Dannay), who called her writing "distinguished," "sensitive," and "beautiful." In the following story she tackles the especially sensitive issue of medical ethics: where does a doctor's responsibility to a patient end? And how far must a doctor go to keep a patient's secrets confidential?

The train whistled petulantly at the three passengers running down the ramp. But it waited, for these days the 11:08 was the only morning train to Boston.

George Potts, proprietor of the Edgeville Pharmacy, lowered his paper and watched from his seat by the car window. He was playing hookey from the drug store for the first time in twenty-five years, so everything about the week-day morning was slightly outsized and tinged with importance. The first two late-comers were the Henty sisters, schoolteachers. Bel-Airs and incredible quantities of Alka-Seltzer. He suspected that they drank on week-ends. But who wouldn't, teaching school in Edgeville?

His tolerant glance hurried by them and fastened on the third late-comer, Mattie Blanchard. She had changed a lot recently, though she was only fifty-one, a year younger than George. For decades she had maintained the slim little figure, the round rosy little face. Now, almost overnight, the figure had blurred, the face had become drawn and worried. Of course, George admitted, Nick Blanchard was a terrible loud-mouth. Still, she had put up with him for a quarter of a century, so more likely it was just physical—her time of life.

But George was sad about it because she had been the prettiest girl in town and he had been a little in love with her, though he had married someone else. He was a widower now, with no romantic yearnings; but Mattie had been part of his youth. She was still part of it in a way, since he had bought her father's drug store when Mr. Stanley retired. Perhaps in those days George had hoped he was taking over Mattie too. But it hadn't happened. The pharmacy was his whole life now, and Mattie just a small ghost flickering around its edges.

After a while he rose ponderously and walked down the aisle toward her. They had known each other since they were children but he could see he wasn't welcome now—her face had turned toward the window. It didn't stop George Potts. He reversed the empty seat in front of her and sat down.

"Hi, Mattie."

"Oh, hello, George. How are you? How's your daughter?"

"Fine."

"When you going to be a grandpa? Nice big girl like your Elsie ought to have half a dozen."

"She can't have any," he said.

"That so? I'm sorry." She didn't look sorry. She was wearing what George always thought of as "Mattie's selfish face"—turned inward, rejecting. He sighed to himself but picked up her casual tone.

"Doing some last-minute shopping?"

"No—doctor's appointment."

"Lotion didn't help the rash?"

"Not much." She glanced down at her gloved wrist. "But I'm not seeing him about that. Anyway, what does a gynecologist know about dermatology? Dad's lotion would have cleared it up in twelve hours."

George nodded admiringly. "I remember Mr. Stanley always had a run on that special of his, particularly during summer camp season—impetigo and all that. He'd have such a rush you'd always have to chase down there and help him." His eyes twinkled. "Maybe that's why I developed such a yen to own a pharmacy."

"Well, you have it now." Her tone was indifferent.

He persisted gallantly. "Seemed natural to see you bustling around the dispensary the other day when Jim was sick and I had to take over the fountain. Hey, that reminds me, you didn't leave the prescription on my desk."

For the first time she came alert. "Sorry, George." She began riffling through her purse, then looked up and smiled ruefully. "Must have mislaid it or left it at home. But just to keep you on the safe side, I'll get another prescription from Dr. Franz today and leave it with you on my way home."

"Just to make things look good," he agreed comfortably. "Things are different from what they were thirty years ago. Not that I say they're *better*—just different. Your pa could let you help in the dispensary then, without your having a degree and still a youngster. Now the government has so many rules a man don't dare lose an aspirin. But are any fewer people killed? No. The hoodlums beat up the old punks, husbands go after their wives with guns, and wives—"

"Use rolling pins and skillets, as usual," Mattie said with a flicker of humor.

"As usual," George sighed. "Not a mite of progress . . . How's Nick these days? And when do you take off for warmer climes?"

Mattie swallowed, and he could see for the first time that she must have lost a molar recently, for the dimple in her left cheek had become a hollow. "Nick is more impossible than ever—if *that's* possible. But you knew him before I did, so that won't be any news."

He was soothing. "Change of scene does everyone good. Edgeville will miss you, but if you're going to pull up stakes, now's the time."

"That's just it. There isn't going to be any change of scene."

"But you're all set. You're all—"

"Organized? Exactly. That's what Nick loves. To have everything organized—and then to upset it. Gives him a real excuse for yelling."

She rattled on, looking at George but not seeing him. He had always been someone for her to talk at, saying anything that came into her head. Once he had been flattered to be made so familiar with her private thoughts—until he had realized it was not a compliment, that he was merely a sounding board, a mirror, a hassock to be used or kicked aside. It didn't hurt any longer—at least, not much.

". . . and our things are packed right down to the suitcases," she was saying with a hostility that embraced the whole fleeing landscape beyond the train windows. "The furniture is sold and is going to be picked up Monday. Transfer of the house deed only needs Nick's signature—I've already signed. Yet this morning, this very morning, Nick said to me that he wasn't sure we were smart giving up a good home in a place where everyone knows us! A place where everyone knows us—ha! I'll say they do. Never occurs to him that I'd give my right arm to live in a place where *no one* knows Nick." She paused and said almost inconsequentially, "Maybe then I could do some real yelling myself."

They were clattering over a bridge into Boston now. For an instant there was a glimpse of its gnarled, rose-brick fingers clutching the diminished hills, splaying into the Atlantic. Then they were hurtling toward the station.

George ventured, "Oh, Nick will come around. Probably just his digestion." He paused and added mildly, "You ought to be careful what he eats, Mattie. Real careful."

She checked the clasp on her purse. "He's a born glutton, but I'd better phone and tell him not to get into the mince pie." She flushed suddenly, as though for some reason she had been disconcerted by her own innocent remark. Then she blurted, "Anyway, I made it for the Ladies Aid Bazaar." Her mouth snapped shut; she glared at George as she would have glared at an impertinent questioner.

But he wasn't perturbed. He had known Mattie and her moods since she had been a five-year-old; and he could always find a compliment for her. "Real good of you," he approved, "particularly since your cupboards are all cleaned out. But give me apple every time. You never used to like mince either."

"Still don't," she said shortly. "But it's Nick's favorite, and anything for peace." Her tone dismissed a boresome culinary subject.

"Well, not anything," he qualified for her, smiling. "Got to draw the line somewheres." There was a little silence. She looked at him, making a visible effort to be sociable, even a bit coquettish.

"That's good, coming from you, George. You always get your way sooner or later."

"Not always. Not twenty-five years ago. But about Nick—with his type indigestion, it's not how *much* he eats but *what* he eats."

"Oh, so you're a doctor now as well as a pharmacist," she said coolly.

He chuckled. "Well, as the only druggist in Edgeville, I know a lot about the town's innards. Too much, sometimes... When is your appointment with Dr. Franz?"

"Two o'clock, but don't ask me to lunch with you, George, because I have a few errands."

"Just wanted to be sure Doc would be back at the office in time. I'm having lunch with him at one."

"You know Dr. Franz *personally?*" She wasn't cool any more.

"Sure do. We were in North Africa together."

"But he was a captain—"

"And I was a non-com. Yep, but I was able to do him a little favor once and—well, we see each other once or twice a year."

"I suppose the little favor was the one that earned you the medal—and the limp," Mattie said softly. Then her voice changed suddenly. "But I don't want you two he-men discussing me. Understand?"

"Now, Mattie, doctors don't talk about their patients." Though this time will be an exception, he added to himself. It almost seemed that she had read his thoughts, for her color was high and for an instant she was the young, imperious, beautiful Mattie Stanley.

"Don't you even dare mention my name, George Potts!" Fortunately he didn't have to answer that, for the train had jolted to a stop. Mattie pulled her coat around her and marched down the aisle without a backward look or a goodbye.

Well, George reflected unhappily, it wasn't a goodbye. He was very much afraid he would have to see Mattie again, and soon. In the meantime, perhaps he had given her something to think about.

He had. In the station she went directly to a phone booth and dialed the house. Nick would almost certainly be there because he hated to eat out, even for lunch. The loud, hectoring voice answered and she said instantly, "Nick, I called about your lunch."

"I'm just fixing it."

"But I forgot to tell you not to touch the mince pie. Have an apple or banana instead."

"I'd rather have the pie."

"Nick, I'm taking it over to the Ladies Aid Bazaar later today. If you eat it, I'll have to buy one for them. You want me to spend a dollar and a half on a boughten pie?"

"Well, all right."

"Nick, *promise* not to touch it?"

"I just said I won't. What'd the doctor say?"

"Pity's sake, I just landed in the station."

"Mattie, I wish I'd told you something this morning before you left in such a huff and puff."

"You told me plenty."

"But you didn't give me time to finish—you just beat it out the door. I was sort of—well, I have a surprise for you, Mattie."

"I'll bet! One more of your surprises will finish me. It might finish you too."

"Please listen—" The argumentative voice blundered along, gathering a few more decibels. Mattie held the receiver at a distance from her ear. But she listened. Suddenly she forgot Nick as her eyes widened and her free hand pressed against her midriff. The disturbance was unmistakable.

"I'll be right home," she whispered.

Dr. Franz pushed his coffee cup away. "Damn it, George, you could lose your license for this. Letting a layman mess around in the dispensary." He shook his head.

"I know," George said unhappily, "but can't you see how natural it was to let her do it? Why, Doc, while I was still studying for my degree, she was helping her father in the pharmacy, measuring, weighing—all the rest. I was only getting theory while she was getting the real know-how."

"She knew your fountain boy was down with flu."

"Everybody knew it."

"And she'd know that three thirty in the afternoon was your busiest time, what with the high school letting out and shoppers coming in. She'd know it would be a good time to offer to put up the lotion herself. And if you *hadn't* been busy that afternoon, George, she'd have waited." Mr. Potts didn't say anything and the doctor went on abruptly, "What made you think of the arsenic?"

"When I looked for the prescription she ought to have left—and couldn't find it. But she'd said it was a lotion for a rash on her wrist. And that made me think of the special prescription her pa used to make up. Besides, if it wasn't a serious rash, you'd probably recommend a good proprietary. If you thought it might be serious, you'd send her to a dermatologist."

Dr. Franz said unsmilingly, "George, stop figuring what I or my colleagues would do. You're not a physician." He relented. "Anyway, we ran into some rather weird skin diseases in Africa, as you ought to remember. But what about the arsenic?"

"Well, like I said, I got to thinking about her pa's lotion. I still have his files, so I looked it up and it did call for potassium arsenite. He called it 'Stanley's Special' but basically it was just Fowler's solution—a sort of weak version with a frill or two added. So I checked supplies and sure enough—three grains of potassium arsenite was missing."

Dr. Franz thought that over. "About enough to cover a dime. You'd have to be looking for it, wouldn't you?"

George nodded. "Yep. But it comes one-eighth of an ounce to the bottle—and sealed. The seal was broken. Ought to have been a bit over fifty-four and a half grains in that bottle. It was three grains short."

Dr. Franz rubbed his chin and finally said, "You're jumping to a lot of conclusions about my patient. What makes you think the prescription *didn't* call for arsenic? Since," he added with deceptive mildness, "you didn't even ask to see it before you turned her loose."

George turned red but his voice remained defiant. "Okay, but a pharmacist does know a few things, Doc. Who prescribes that stuff these days? In two years I've only had three calls for it—one of 'em from a dentist who must have blown the cobwebs off an old manual." He was warming up now. "I don't believe your prescription called for it. In fact, I'm wondering if you wrote her a lotion prescription at all!"

In a sudden reversal of tone Dr. Franz said lightly, "I must consult counsel. At the moment, the only proven crime is yours, George. You permitted a layman to use your dispensary. You've mislaid a certain amount of potassium arsenite. Also, there's your negligence. Now you're asking me to see a connection between these things—at the expense of my patient. And solely on the grounds that you think she's fed up with her husband—a very biased conclusion which you have no way of proving—and a bit suspect, in view of the fact that she turned you down once."

George was visibly deflated. "Sorry I said anything, Captain."

"Nonsense, Sergeant. I was just indulging in a bit of relaxing sadism before returning to my ladies, bless their pelvic little hearts. Of course you should have told me. Equally, I had to chew you out. Now let's forget it. What's wrong with this fellow Blanchard, anyway?"

"Nothing a woman could take to court," George admitted. "That's the trouble. He's a good provider—on the thrifty side, maybe, but then so is Mattie. He's never looked at another woman. Don't smoke or drink," he added reluctantly.

"There must be *something.*" Dr. Franz was impatient.

"Look, Doc, he's just a complete stinker to live with. Always making scenes about nothing at all, throwing tantrums like a three-year-old. And he's got one of those noisy quarrelsome voices like a foghorn. Men won't play golf or bridge with him—"

"Ah-ha!"

"—and they'd never get invited anywhere if the women weren't sorry for Mattie. And he always picks a fight or argues or gets slighted about something and stalks out. I bet Nick has broken up more picnics and parties than anyone in Edgeville except the Fire Department. He hasn't a solitary friend but it doesn't bother him. He'd rather enjoy his tantrums."

"Why'd she ever marry him?"

"He's still one of the handsomest male critters the Lord ever made." George sighed down at his paunch. "When Mattie married him she thought she could do something about his temper. I warned her but she said I was jealous—and I was." He threw out his hands. "I told you it was hard to explain unless you know Nick. Honest, Doc, I'd rather have a hyena for a pet myself. Or turning it the other way round, I'd rather have a wife who was unfaithful or alcoholic than one who nagged and shouted at me twenty-four hours of the day."

"Keep your wife pregnant and your liquor at the club," Dr. Franz murmured, then said quickly, "Sorry. The situation isn't funny. Lots of wives have been liquidated for nothing worse than incessant nagging—if there *is* anything worse. Now here's where I join the ranks of the unethical: we have a problem, George, aside from the fact that Blanchard may be ingesting a bit of arsenic with his meals. He may deserve it but we can't allow it to continue. That's point one. Point two is the fact that Mrs. Blanchard is pregnant—and I've always thought it unseemly for infants to be born while their mothers were in custody."

George's head shot up, his jaw dropped. "Pregnant? She's fifty-one and she's never had any children!"

"Unusual but not unheard-of," Dr. Franz assured him. "She doesn't know it yet." He glanced at his watch. "The official announcement takes place at two o'clock. I didn't dare tell her until the results of certain other tests had come through. If there was no chance of her coming to term—she had to know that too."

"Is there that chance?"

"A good one. I've had a couple of other opinions and they agree with mine—that she's in better shape physically than most women fifteen years younger. Her mental state is something else again and I'll admit she had me fooled. Seemed well-adjusted, didn't mention moving away from New England, spoke pleasantly enough of her husband. But you see the problem. We have to think of *three* people now."

He shrugged into his topcoat, signaled for the check. He grinned down at George. "A primipara at fifty-one! And she thinks *I* think it's menopause—"

"You should have told her." George's worry was even more obvious.

"You haven't minded your own business very well, so stop minding mine. I had good reason for keeping mum until all the reports came in. Tell a woman her age that she's in a first pregnancy?—then turn around and tell her she'll never have the baby? Not I. Now I'll have really good news. So don't you upset the apple cart, George. I won't allow it. I'll throw you to the wolves if I have to."

George said flatly, "When you sail off the cloud, Doc, remember there's another little matter—some missing arsenic."

"Oh, yes, that reminds me. Surely you keep poisons under key?"

"Narcotics, but not the poisons," George said glumly. "And that's usual with most pharmacists, not a little notion of my own." He rose now too, and put on his coat. "You go have your big announcement scene but remember I've got to do something about Nick Blanchard's indigestion. I'll be at the store from six on. Will you call me? I'd kind of like to know what Mattie says about the baby *and* the arsenic," he added dryly.

Walking out of the restaurant he did not limp. It was painful not to limp but he managed it. Evidently it wasn't too convincing, for Dr. Franz poked his head from the taxi as it moved away and called back, "Better have someone take a look at those ingrowing toenails, Sergeant!"

George couldn't help grinning at the receding car. One foot would never have any toenails again. He had booted the grenade from the operating tent, but, unfortunately had tripped while pursuing it.

Now, a good many years later and watching the taxi disappear down Boylston Street, George rubbed his nose. At least, that was still there—the ample, alert Potts nose. His smile widened. Captain Franz was also still there, with his German name and his dyed-in-the-wool Vermont accent. He might not have been, so George's toes were a minor loss.

"George," Dr. Franz said over the telephone some hours later, "Mrs. Blanchard didn't show up for her two o'clock appointment."

"I know, Doc. I've been snooping around town. Seems Nick bought an Imperator Caravan two weeks ago. Chartreuse and black job, twenty-six thousand dollars. Sun deck, portable swimming pool—the works. He's been hiding it in his barn. Salesman told me he was planning a surprise for Mattie—it's their anniversary today."

"Very touching," Dr. Franz snarled.

"Well, they took off this afternoon but Mattie left a note at the store for me. Want I should read it to you? She says, 'Dear George, Nick really surprised me. We're leaving today to roam around the country in a trailer, of all things! Enclosed is house key. Please check doors and windows, we left in such a hurry. There's a note for you on kitchen table.' "

"You haven't been out there yet?" Dr. Franz asked sharply.

"No, I was waiting for your call."

"You can wait for *me*. I'll be there around nine, at your store. Blanchard may be traveling in a murder wagon and you're still in a bad spot, George. I wouldn't want you to walk into that house or touch anything without a witness."

"Okay, Doc. I'll be waiting."

The scent of beef stew was still new on the air, and the odor only pointed up the echoing rooms from which the last Blanchards had departed. Not that the furniture was gone as yet. But whatever had not been crated, had been shrouded. Plaster cupids leered coldly from the ceilings, fireplaces were bare and unfriendly. Only in the kitchen some sense of humanity still lingered: flowering plants on window sills; a battered alarm clock ticking as erratically as a battered heart.

There was a note on the counter, addressed to George. He opened it, pulled out a sheet of paper and a tiny folded packet. "That will be the potassium arsenite," he prophesied, unfolding the letter.

Mattie had written: "Dear George, I swiped some potassium arsenite but enclose same. Wouldn't want to get you in trouble if rules are stricter now. To tell the truth, I didn't see how I could put up with Nick any longer, so I was going to kill myself. Then I suspected I was pregnant and now I'm sure of it, though *no* thanks to Dr. Franz. Between you and me, a gynecologist who doesn't know the difference between pregnancy and menopausal symptoms should have stuck to carving up G.I.'s, so I don't feel too bad about breaking appointment. Did try to phone but his line was busy and I had to catch 1:03 back to Edgeville. I'm so old the baby may not live, but it's something to look forward to and I promise I'll never do anything silly again like the arsenic. Honest, George, you can believe me. Nick doesn't know about the baby yet —he'd have fits about taking me on caravan trip. You know how he goes to pieces if I even have a headache because after all I'm all he has. He's always been scared of everything and everybody, so it was really a big thing for him to plan the caravan surprise and I don't want to spoil it. Real estate man has General Delivery address in case of emergency. Yours, Mattie. P.S. Read and *burn*."

George handed the letter to Dr. Franz. He himself opened the packet very delicately and stirred its contents with the point of a pencil. Dr. Franz tossed the letter down with a snort. "I read it and I'm burning," he acknowledged. "Arsenic?"

"It's not gypsum." George refolded the packet, rinsed the pencil, and thrust it into the earth of the geranium on the sill. Then he washed his hands.

"You believe the letter?" Dr. Franz demanded.

"Why not?" George was shaken, though. It was one thing to put motive and opportunity together and come up with a shrewd guess. It was quite another thing to have that guess confirmed so baldly.

Dr. Franz had been bumped from his cloud too. "She's a reckless, irresponsible woman and I'm not sure *I* believe her—"

"And of course she's no longer your patient." George's face was innocent.

"That has nothing to do with it." The doctor paced the floor, his scowl formidable. "Arsenic is a murder weapon, painful, unpleasant. Definitely not a suicide choice. Why didn't she take one of the narcotics?"

"Locked up," George reminded him.

"Well, strychnine or cyanide then. Hell of a lot quicker. Wham! —and it's over."

"Sure, and with an autopsy following just as wham," George pointed out. "She wouldn't want Nick to know she'd killed herself. Or get him into trouble. And you can't die wham, without people asking questions. But arsenic—you can string that out. And at her age—and pregnant—well, she might have gotten away with it, without Nick or a strange doctor guessing a thing."

Dr. Franz said sourly, "Our lab routines are very thorough these days—"

"Rural doctors too?" But George went on very hastily, "Okay, Doc, okay. But Mattie took this stuff and returned it. So what do we do now? Have the police haul her back and put her in the jug for stealing it? Even if they believe her letter, there's the intent to commit suicide. That's a crime too, isn't it? Well, it's up to you to decide. I let her use the pharmacy, so I can't be on the jury."

The doctor's anger was cooling and he had turned hesitant. "You know her, George, I don't. You honestly think it was just a crazy suicide notion that she snapped out of?"

George shrugged. "Mattie's the kind who can do something wicked if she can do it quick. But she couldn't keep it up. She hasn't the meanness or the guts. She hasn't—" He groped helplessly.

"The cold malice of the slow poisoner?"

"That's it." George missed the sarcasm, or chose to ignore it. "Did you read that somewheres or make it up? Honest, Doc, I don't get you. Lunch today, you're beating my ears off. Only thing that matters, you say, is the baby. Now you're willing to believe anything about Mattie. But she's still having the baby, isn't she?"

He turned his back and walked across the wide expanse of kitchen floor to pull the window shades down again. His shoulders were very square but he limped heavily, blatantly. The doctor's mouth twisted as he observed that limp. Sooner or later a man has to pay; and there was no one so righteous as a sergeant for keeping the score. George was presenting the score now: To Captain Franz, one life. Please make payment to Martha Stanley Blanchard and family.

"Oh, hell," the doctor capitulated. "Why whip a dead horse?" It was, perhaps, an unfortunate figure of speech in the circumstances, but he didn't care. He was querulous, now that he had given in and authority was seeping from him. "I still don't like it."

"It's always sad to lose an interesting patient," George sympathized blandly, "especially if she kicks you in the face while saying goodbye. Especially if you're a physician *and* a captain."

"George, sometimes you're intolerable. Go to hell."

"Yes, sir, at once, sir."

But Mr. Potts did not immediately descend to the nether regions. After Dr. Franz had departed, he went around the Blanchard house checking doors and windows. Then he returned to the kitchen and paused there a moment. There was a small matter in the back of his mind.

Before supper he had dropped in to make a casual inquiry at the Ladies Aid Bazaar, with negative results. Now he sauntered out to the back porch. The rubbish pail held a few last odds and ends but the garbage container glistened pristinely. It was quite empty—except for a mince pie neatly wrapped in newspapers.

It was whole but it had suffered in transit. Mr. Potts thoughtfully removed it to his car. This time of year, no telling when there would be sudden hot weather; and the new owners weren't due until next week. Just a small neighborliness. Mattie set a lot of store by her housekeeping.

In the quiet back room of his pharmacy that night, he typed a laborious letter:

Dear Mattie, Am writing late from store where I been doing some food analysis for a friend. Happy about your good news. Checked house from attic right to garbage pail. All is okay now, though you forgot one or two things. Women mostly do when they go at things in a hurry. Take care of yourself, see doctors regular. Tell Nick to drop me post card at least once a month about his own health. Strong man like him shouldn't have indigestion, so I'll send out the bloodhounds if I don't hear from him often, ha, ha. Things are tough sometimes but all in all you been lucky, Mattie. You're pretty smart and mostly a good woman, but don't be so quick to think that doctors and pharmacists are dumb bunnies. Maybe we just care about you—like your pa did, and Dr. Franz, and

Yours truly, George Potts

He hesitated, then added grudgingly above his signature: "and Nick too." It spoiled the appearance of the letter but at least kept it truthful.

Other things were spoiled also—the neatness of his dispensary, for one. Crumpled newspapers lay on the floor and the remains of a pie cluttered old Mr. Stanley's cherished marble counter. There was a faint odor from a cooling retort.

Mr. Potts rose from the desk and began to tidy up. A nursery rhyme popped into his head. "When the pie was opened, the birds began to sing—" So who knows how a pie will turn out? And babies are more important than a pie that was never eaten. Mattie scared easy—and for keeps. After that talk on the train, Nick was safe as a church. Mr. Potts had known that, still knew it. But Dr. Franz couldn't have been so sure.

George's analysis had shown a small but appreciable amount of arsenic in the pie. Not enough to kill a man or to turn a woman into a murderer. But enough to remove Mr. Potts's last romantic illusions—enough, perhaps, to make Mattie Blanchard as frightened and remorseful a wife as she would be a devoted mother.

The room was now immaculate again, but Mr. Potts still teetered on his heels, consulting his conscience.

Was it necessary to tell Dr. Franz the result of his tests? No. A sergeant has to make many quick decisions—in order to spare his superiors the mental and moral anguish for which their more delicate natures are not equipped. Otherwise, he is a very poor sergeant indeed.

George locked up and left the pharmacy without giving it a backward glance. He was a dutiful man, but never obsessed by a duty after it had been discharged. His footsteps, despite the limp, marched down the night-silent street with a rhythm that had once been all too clearly familiar to the men of his platoon.

Behind him a faint but pervading blue light bloomed throughout the reaches of the drug store, warning all malefactors that George Potts, Pharmacist and Sergeant, would tolerate no nonsense—none whatever.

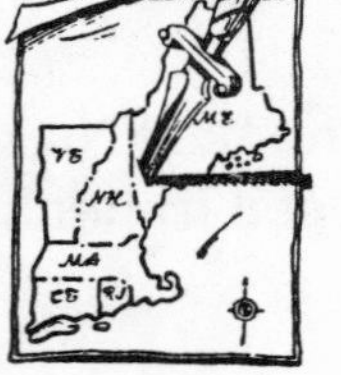

A BORDERLINE CASE

by Rufus King

Rufus King was born at the end of the nineteenth century and made a name for himself as a crime writer in the first half of the twentieth. His short stories were so successful that they were collected in four volumes. In "A Borderline Case," *Mr. King explores a question as old as Heinrich Von Kleist's great novel,* Michael Kohlhaas, *and as current as today's headlines. How do geographic boundaries relate to moral boundaries? Can crossing an external border free one to cross an internal border as well? Read on . . .*

That was what Dr. Williamson, in his capacity as county psychiatrist, labeled Jackson—"a borderline case." Not quite psychopathic and not quite sane but then, as the psychiatrist pointed out, who is?—and aren't we all?

Naturally, there was a modest touch of hindsight in the diagnosis because Jackson, by then, had been extradited from Florida and was under indictment up north for homicide in the first degree.

"You'd have to know him," Dr. Williamson said, acknowledging his manservant's murmur that dinner was served, "know him clinically before you could appreciate the emotional complexities that led to his murder of the old blister. He's a killer and must be considered a serious danger to society and still—still I liked him."

Everybody liked Jackson.

This wasn't a generality, it was literally true. Absurdly so, because he was far from being an attractive young man (age twenty-four) in the classic sense, his face having the storm lowerings of a fullback about to lunge and his body being a throwback to his grandfather Jason's, a bull of a man who had been a lumberjack before migrating to Florida after the turn of the century possessing only a head cold, $700 in gold coin, and a gutful of rum.

It was Jackson's sudden smile more than anything else that accounted for his universal popularity. It transfigured him from a brooding and hefty piece of sculpture by Gutzon Borglum into a body warmed by humor and the goodness of friendship. Dr. Williamson, who is funny that way, said the smile gave Jackson an ozone smell. Which is awfully near, he added, to the smell of brimstone.

"He is innately ruthless, but you would never suspect it. His surface magnetism, which is mostly animal, accounts for that. You would think him fearless and you would be right. With the exception," Dr. Williamson qualified, "of one overpowering dread—an absolute terror of death. Not other peoples' deaths—they are negligible to him—but his own death."

This was true. The details of dying, when Jackson applied them to himself, were an unwashed and horrible form of morbidity. That his mouth, for example, into which he could put such interesting things to eat, should be clamped shut by an undertaker. Such melancholy and unappetizing trivia would seize him whenever he was alone, and they gripped him on that Sunday afternoon of this year when a television series began its fall and winter season.

The telecast dealt with the theme of capital punishment, tracing the fascinating art from the days when a condemned felon was strapped down flat and a succession of lead blocks were arranged on his body until, in a state of helpless exasperation, he was crushed to death.

A variety of other methods followed—hanging, the guillotine, the gas chamber, and the now fashionable use of electricity to parboil the brain.

One detail of the broadcast impacted itself with the power of a revelation on Jackson's mind: seven of our United States did not have the death penalty. The more convenient of these to Florida were Rhode Island and Maine, both of which meted out to a convicted murderer the comparatively agreeable severity of imprisonment for the balance of his natural life.

This enticingly left open to the convicted wretch the hopeful vista of ultimate parole, or the more immediate possibility of escape contrived through heavy money properly placed in bribes.

Why, Jackson wondered, did not a man who intended to commit a murder seize upon this inestimable advantage of eliminating the electric chair (the shadow of which had so far proved an unsurmountable deterrent to his own wishful plans) and arrange his killing in one of those seven enlightened states?

Well, why didn't he—?

It attracted Jackson as the perfect form of life insurance.

"That broadcast," Dr. Williamson said, "was the spark that started the powder train of Jackson's conscienceless and foolishly complicated murder plot. He knew nothing whatever about the topography of Rhode Island or Maine, so he went about getting this information in the most reasonable way, straight from the horse's mouth . . ."

The Chamber of Commerce building in Halcyon (a domesticated township lying on the Gold Coast of Florida, between the theatrical splendors of Miami Beach and the more coupon-clipping solidity of Fort Lauderdale) is located in a meager park and affords among its other admirable activities a registration service for tourists who plan to settle during a short vacation or for the season. Their home town and state are listed, as well as their Halcyon address.

Jackson strolled there from the bank which his grandfather Jason had founded, after the old gentleman had cured his head cold and pyramided his 700 bucks, during the sucker-laden boom, into a fortune. Among the arrivals of the past couple of weeks Jackson found no one who was registered from Maine, but there was a Mr. Herkimer Smith from a place called Foster in Rhode Island. Mr. Smith listed his Halcyon residence as the Silver Lining Motel.

After banking hours Jackson called on Mr. Smith who was of retirement age, a widower, still friendless as far as Florida was concerned, and in such a state of homesick loneliness that he would have fervently welcomed the handclasp of a door-to-door salesman.

"I noticed your name on the tourist register," Jackson said with his electrifying smile, "and dropped by to say hello."

"Now don't tell me you're from Rhode Island, too," Smith said, growing warmly delighted.

"No, but I have a distant cousin who used to live in that town you come from—Foster—and I thought you might have known Charley. Charley Whipple."

"Whipple?" Smith would have given a lot to say yes, not to have to disturb this connecting link with a companionable stranger, but he could not. "No, seems as though I don't recollect any Whipples, and Foster's population is only around two thousand, so it's likely I'd have heard the name. Of course, I only lived there for the past five years."

"That accounts for it," Jackson said glibly. "Charley left Foster eight or nine years ago and where he is now I haven't the faintest idea. I hoped you might be able to give me a clue."

But Charley or no Charley, the ice was broken, and two hours and three obscure taverns later Jackson had a photographic picture of the village of Foster—of how to get there and (of primary importance) the nearby waters.

The only sizeable body of water, Smith told him, was Killingsby Pond which lay roughly twenty miles to the northwest of the village. "It's named a pond," Smith said, "but it's really a lake—sort of long and narrow, and pretty big at that."

Homicidal drownings, Jackson recalled from his research into an authoritative work, *are rare, comprising about 0.4 percent of all homicides in New York City.*

"Lonely sort of spot, Killingsby Pond," Smith went on, "but beautiful. Lets a man be alone with nature."

The circumstances of death are usually not ascertainable, for the chances are that the drowning occurred in the absence of eyewitnesses. Subsequent investigation may fail to elicit evidence which would justify classifying the drowning specifically as homicidal, suicidal, or accidental.

Unless, Jackson reasoned, specific indications were arranged to point strongly to one of the three—as in his proposed plan of the old blister's suicide. "Not many people around?" he asked. "Campers, things like that?"

"No," Smith said with the precise diction of six snorts and six beer chasers, "there are not. As I say, Killingsby Pond is a spot where a man can commune. When I think back on it, it makes me want to cry."

Smith did cry, and Jackson returned him to the Silver Lining Motel where he felt reasonably assured Smith would wake up in the morning with a terrifying hangover, a wrecked stomach, and with any memories of the past moist evening a convenient blur.

"So we know," Dr. Williamson explained, signaling his manservant to bring in the next course, "that the first emotional block was removed—Jackson's overpowering dread of death by the electric chair, should he be caught and brought to justice. Naturally he had no intention of being caught, but even if by the millionth chance he should

be, the State of Rhode Island would not, could not, take
he had plenty of loot to try and bribe his escape out of prison. His defalcations, as you know, were considerable . . .

The Halcyon Bank and Trust is a handsome stone-faced building on the boulevard leading to the beach, and its lobby contains, among gracious pillars, potted palms and urns of deceitful plastic flowers, a portrait of the founder. This insult to the name of Art depicts Grandfather Jason as the lumberjack he had been, but stiltedly glacéd with the habiliments of wealth and position. It is a thorough deletion of basic character, even to what had been the rumpot color of the old gentleman's powerful nose.

The assets of the bank are impressive, and Jackson in his sinecure as Assistant Manager in Charge of New Accounts had had little difficulty in absorbing into his own pockets (actually a pigskin suitcase stashed among stored luggage in his pseudo-Moorish homestead) some $230,000 in cash and negotiable securities.

"You must keep in mind," Dr. Williamson insisted, "that Jackson is the last of the line. His mother died shortly following his birth, and about a year ago his father exited in a blaze of glory when his cruiser *Saffron III* blew up in Biscayne Bay. The popular fiction of great family wealth, incidentally, blew up with it because the estate after probate yielded mostly debts, and certainly not enough to keep young Jackson even in his Sulka ties. His father with consummate skill had squandered old Jason's pile in a surreptitious carnival of gambling—in foreign casinos because of his position as president of the bank—as well as in a costly style of living and a succession of three jewel-happy mistresses, who subscribed wholeheartedly to the cliché that diamonds are a girl's best friend."

Dr. Williamson paused to squeeze a shot of key lime onto the tender flesh of a stone crab's claw. "If it seems to you that I am relating these odds and ends out of their chronological order," he said, "you are quite right. Jackson's intention—his necessity, really—to murder old Parker was born several nights previous to the television broadcast I've just mentioned, and it happened like this . . ."

The large staff of servants that had served the ancestral home were, after *Saffron III* ballooned in flame, a luxury of the past, and Jackson, who lived there in solitary bachelorhood, was sketchily taken care of by a minimum-wage Haitian couple who would drift in around eight in the morning and hustle out at five when Jackson either suppered at a tavern or in company of one of the few friends left him.

This night, when he got home after dining, he found Parker, known at the bank as "the old blister," seated in a wicker chair on the porch and puffing away on his putrid pipe.

"Well, good evening, Mr. Parker," Jackson said.

Parker made no effort toward uplifting his delicate bones from the chair. In the moon-faded darkness his black, beady eyes gave out onyx glints under their canopy of lemon-gray hairs.

"Sit down, Jackson," he said. "I've come to talk to you."

Jackson experienced a complex wave of reactions at this gently mouthed but peremptory command. Dominant among them was a sense of alarm—faint but as insistent as a warning bell.

"Delighted that you did," he said. "I'm always glad to see you."

"Well, you won't be this time, Jackson."

"No?"

"No. I've got you dead to rights."

"That has always struck me as an ambiguous expression," Jackson said with barely contrived pleasantness. "I don't know what it means in a literal sense."

"In my sense, Jackson, it means I've uncovered the fact that you've been robbing the bank blind."

One odd, and in an oblique way, admirable trait about Jackson was his habit of never sidestepping what he felt to be a demonstrable truth. Instead, he would not only face it but he would attack it head on. Now that he knew the worst—he brushed aside as stupid any doubts that Parker had the necessary proof of his larceny—he congealed into an efficient, clear-headed fighting machine to probe and pierce the core of his opponent's weakness. For there was a weakness, otherwise Parker would have taken his knowledge directly to the Board of Directors instead of coming to Jackson himself.

"What put you on?" he asked with honest curiosity.

Parker evidently got a shock of surprise at this certainly unexpected admission of Jackson's guilt. He wasn't prepared for it, having looked forward to an enjoyable hour of devious denials.

"Your vacation," he said, "last month."

"What of it?"

"They had me fill in for you while you were gone."

"I know they did. So what? All you had to do was sit on your rump and interview some tourist with a bundle every other day or so."

Parker sighed with the effect of a long-pent disgust. "You never did give a damn about the Bulletins that come in now and then, did you?"

"What about them?"

"I refer specifically to the most recent Loss Prevention Bulletin issued by the Bank-Share Owners Advisory League. I take it you didn't even bother to read it?"

"Good Lord, no."

"A pity. To paraphrase the section that pertains to your case, one of the first recommendations made by the F.B.I. to circumvent defaulters is that each bank employee have a two-week vacation every year."

"They always do have."

"Usually, yes, and while this might appear to be a purely humanitarian suggestion on the part of the F.B.I. it is actually directed at a very basic problem."

"I don't get it."

"I know you don't—and didn't. As the F.B.I. so kindly pointed out, it is relatively easy for anyone to juggle his books and records without detection—if he continues to be the *only* one to handle them. But if someone else must take them over for a couple of weeks, any falsifications run an excellent chance of being found out."

Jackson was coldly outraged at this uncalled for and, to him, presumptuous nosiness. "You had no legitimate reason for going back through my records. You're not an auditor or an examiner."

"The fact remains," Parker said smugly, "that I did."

"But why?"

"You."

"Me? Just because I'm me?"

"Not entirely, and this will seem strange to you, Jackson, but I've been interested in you ever since your father's death. Because, you see, the two of us are birds of a feather."

This stumped Jackson by its very absurdity, until the simple basis for the comparison struck him—each, given the urgency, had larceny in his soul. He knew why he himself had stolen. He had no curiosity as to what Parker's motive would have been had not he, Jackson, already amassed the loot. It was easy to appreciate Parker's intention—to suppress his knowledge of the damning evidence and, instead, to blackmail Jackson for as much as the pressure would bear.

Jackson's smile was different from his usual one. "How much do you want?" he asked.

"Naturally," Dr. Williamson said, "the one thing that Jackson needed at that instant was time. He was quite ready to buy it. He was prepared to concede to any demand Parker might make, no matter how drastic. To promise anything. Not that he had the remotest intention of keeping his word, but he could not at the moment determine any safe method for crushing this willowy vampire who was prepared to suck him dry, and who certainly held the equipment to do so.

"All Jackson was certain of was that he wanted to kill Parker, and the only thing that stopped him from braining the old goat on the spot was the devastating dread that possessed him of his own death—which would be an accomplished fact were he to be found guilty of Murder One in Florida."

Dr. Williamson turned his attention to the wet and intricate process of paring and eating a mango. "You might care to know," he said, wishing he had a bath towel, "what started Jackson off on his desperate looting. It was a girl, of course . . ."

People occasionally and rather snobbishly point out that Florida's Gold Coast society can best be described by saying it isn't. Not in the Palm Beach, Newport, or Bar Harbor sense of the meaning. Money apparently forms its basis—large industrial and trade fortunes which permit membership in all three of the ultra-ultra clubs.

Until his father was uncomfortably devoured by flames, Jackson had all his life had enough of a financial standing to be "accepted." It was the life he had been brought up in and the only one he knew. He had missed the leavening process of war, knew little of the country outside of Florida, and his standards were from habit those of the set in which he moved.

Some time before the *Saffron III* disaster Jackson had become engaged to Miss Manessa Lou Stotes whose family were in rubber. He had thought it love and so, at the time, had Miss Stotes. But after the probate of the father's will had made the ridiculousness of her fiancé's inheritance a matter of public knowledge, Miss Stotes changed her sharp little mind.

Later, Jackson attempted to explain the original love sensation to Dr. Williamson—the blinding effect Miss Stotes had first had on him. It was, he said, like all the five senses being rolled together—not cancelling, but augmenting each other into one intolerable blast of fierce pleasure. Actually, pain and pleasure. He had fumbled between the two words with an earnest intensity—as if they held the explanation, as if any juggling of words could hold a convincing explanation of love.

This triple shock—the breaking off of the engagement by Miss Stotes, the wiping out of easy affluence, and the burden of his father's concealed debts—these blows were, to put it mildly, rough. Nothing but the inherited lumberjack stamina of Grandfather Jason helped Jackson from becoming a punch-drunk bum.

Two things alone seemed clear to him: he still had his job at the bank and he was off all women for life.

This blanket decision about the perfidy of womankind was, Dr. Williamson feels, the crucial factor in shoving Jackson into his fling at crime. Jackson considered quite naturally that Miss Stotes had acted callously, brutally, and unforgivably in chucking him the minute his financial rating dropped to that of an ordinary bank employee.

She had explained her stand in the tenderest and most sensible manner—"Honestly, darling, it simply never works out. Just take a look at the cases around you—Wally Hazelton practically has to crawl to Estelle for cigarette money. I certainly don't intend to give up my little necessities like Biarritz and the yacht and a new Jag every year and what would you feel like, darling?"

Miss Stotes had herself supplied the answer: simply a sort of half-baked gigolo. Jackson's courtly reaction to her kindly meant effort was a hot impulse to squeeze the pulp out of her once-beloved swanlike neck.

He did go silly for a time, giving up his membership in three expensive clubs and eliminating all social contacts beyond unavoidable business encounters at the bank.

He did so because, as he explained to Dr. Williamson, if he continued the usual social rounds of night-club and general lushings without carrying his own weight with the tabs, he would have felt akin to any of the numerous muscular young men who studded the beach set's lavender fringe—the ones whose cachet-of-arrival was usually conventionalized by the fond gift of a star sapphire ring and charge accounts on Lincoln Road.

Following this give-it-all-up interlude, Jackson cooled off to the extent of becoming steel-cold. He clothed himself in the camouflage of being a fine, upstanding young banker who in spite of adversity could keep his tough chin up and could take it. He resumed contact with a few friends, accepting their casual hospitality, but never becoming overly indebted.

Then he really went to work on looting the bank.

"Jackson's purpose," Dr. Williamson conceded, "was quite understandable when you take into consideration the fact that his whole comfortable and happy concept of existence had suddenly been ripped from beneath him like a rug, and through absolutely no fault of his own. That's the important point—he'd had no finger in it, had no faintest advance indication that a cataclysmic pratfall was coming. Of course it warped him and turned him bitter. It brought to the surface all the dormant bad traits that admittedly must have lain subconsciously in his character. As they lie in most of us, I'm afraid."

Dr. Williamson thought coffee would be more agreeable on the patio and told his manservant so.

"What Jackson had in mind," the psychiatrist expanded, "was a new identity, a new life, and money enough to live comfortably for the extent of it. An absolute divorce from everyone and everything he had ever known, and a swift escape from the intolerable situation he considered fate had plunged him in. It's possible that in his youthful fashion he had a naive and romantic idea of a tropical islet where he would be born afresh to take up whatever work or hobby might appeal to him when the boredom of doing nothing began to irritate. And perhaps he might have done just that—if Parker hadn't thrown in his monkey wrench and thus elected himself to the role of an essential corpse . . ."

For the couple of days that intervened between Parker's ultimatum (one half of the loot as payment for his silence) and the television broadcast on capital punishment, Jackson blanked himself within a mental wall where every thought revolved cold-bloodedly and with intensive concentration on the safe accomplishment of murder.

He had been able to convince Parker that the securities and cash had been carefully concealed by him "outside of Florida" during his recent vacation. He refused to disclose the location of the cache, but agreed to meet Parker's demands as soon as he would have completed arrangements for his own disappearance.

This had appeared satisfactory to Parker because, perhaps, it had to be. Nevertheless, Jackson was aware that Parker did his best to watch him like a molting hawk.

Jackson evaded the jejune surveillance and spent some hours in a public library absorbing several standard works on criminology. He used the Miami library intstead of Halcyon's, where he would have been recognized and his unusual interest in the technicalities of crime noticed.

And still no satisfactory answer came to him until the television telecast hit with the effect of a long, cool drink of water. In the State of Rhode Island he could kill, and even if he were stupid enough to get caught the law could not kill him.

There was the problem to be faced of not only getting himself but of getting Parker to Rhode Island.

Haste seemed not only desirable but advisable now that Parker had brought the matter to a head. So the coming week-end became the target. With his detailed information gleaned from the garrulous tourist Herkimer Smith, Jackson figured he would catch a flight after banking hours on Friday for Boston.

He would arrange at the terminal to have a rental car waiting for him and would drive at once to his destination. He plotted his route from an automobile association's route maps. Massachusetts into Rhode Island to Woonsocket, on to Pascoag, then down to Herkimer Smith's village of Foster. Then the last lap—the twenty-odd miles northwestward to Killingsby Pond where, before the exposing light of dawn, he would polish off the job. He would be back in Halcyon by Saturday night, certainly by early Sunday morning. In time for church.

The biggest hurdle lay in devising a method for putting Parker on the spot at Killingsby Pond.

"I've already admitted," Dr. Williamson continued, "that the whole plot was a foolishly complicated one; but Jackson was forced to make it so because nothing on earth could have tempted him to commit murder except the fact that the crime would take place in a state that had abolished capital punishment. Never lose sight of that point—it is crucial."

Dr. Williamson thanked his manservant for the tray of bourbon and branch water, and said there would be nothing further for the night.

"The problem of getting Parker to Killingsby Pond actually was a simple one—just a case of good psychology on Jackson's part. He was satisfied that Parker was breaking his neck trying to keep him under surveillance, and he was equally satisfied that Parker would do his best to trail him when he would leave town, supposedly to recover the hidden securities and cash. To prevent a double-cross. So he made things almost childishly simple for Parker . . ."

Jackson drove at a conservative speed south on the Federal Highway toward Miami. He drove conservatively out of consideration for Parker who he knew was tailing him with the doubtful virtuosity of a late-show dick. At 36th he turned west and after a dowager-paced drive past drab reaches of shops, bars, and billboards Jackson parked at the airport.

He slowed down his movements in order to give Parker time to park and then slither into the tourist-spattered terminal after him. Under the alias of Jasper Morton, Jackson bought space for Boston on a flight late the following afternoon. Taking care to be completely unaware of Parker, he moved to another counter to arrange for a rental car to be awaiting his arrival.

While attending to this he obliquely kept an eye on Parker who spoke to the reservations clerk and himself bought flight space which he shoved into his pocket in a commendably furtive fashion. Jackson paused at the exit doors to light a cigarette and to watch, under cover of the movement, Parker heading for and stopping at the car rental counter, too.

"And so," Dr. Williamson said smugly, "the hook was baited. Jackson was as certain as sunrise that Parker, unquestionably in some abortive attempt at disguise, would accompany him aboard the plane and then trail him like a bloodhound in his own rental car. What he failed to suspect, and the thing that proved his ultimate downfall, was the fact that Parker would have with him . . ."

Jackson, carrying an outsize brief case, walked with other passengers toward the boarding ramp, having first unobservedly spotted his intended victim behind a family group of voluble South Americans.

Parker, who had once played the role of Polonius in a Halcyon Little Theater Group production, had spirit-gummed on his chin a lemon-gray crepe-hair Vandyke beard. It was a passable job and undetectable unless you looked twice, and nobody ever looked twice at Parker. Dark glasses and a shielding homburg completed the masquerade.

After they were airborne Jackson sat at ease gazing at banks of cumulus beyond the window and consciously exuding an impression of complete satisfaction that he had evaded being followed. Parker was seated, he knew, across the aisle and a good many rows behind him.

A stewardess moved leisurely about gathering coats, carried against the coming northern chill after Miami's sun, and hanging them in the rear of the plane. Jackson decided to catch several hours sleep. He hoped that Parker would also get some sleep. It was going to be a long, tough night.

Tougher than he knew.

The trouble didn't start until shortly before dawn when they reached Killingsby Pond, which lay, as Herkimer Smith had stated, some twenty miles to the northwest of Foster. It had been a more rugged and endless-seeming drive for Jackson than it had for Parker, because Jackson had had to make sure that Parker was following him without letting on to Parker that he knew he was being tailed. It was a queer sort of situation that became a greater and greater strain on Jackson's nerves, like the cautious playing of a delicately hooked fish.

The village of Foster was little more than that—a meagerly lighted main street, then the dark of the night and the silent, empty road to the lake. Beyond what was focused in the headlights, Jackson retained no impression of the countryside. His energies were beginning to fade. His arms felt heavy and tired, and his hands were weights of unleavened dough on the wheel; so he swallowed a capsule that a friend had given him and was becoming exhilarated in a small measure by the time he caught sight of the water—a dark, quiet sheen silvered in patches by a waning moon.

Slowly, aware that Parker now with his lights out had closed in on him, Jackson followed the shoreline of Killingsby Pond as though searching for identification guides that would lead him to the mythical cache.

The stillness, except for the sound of the car motor, was a breathing thing and Jackson experienced a surge of impatience to get the job over with. He had no idea how far they had driven parallel with the lakeshore nor had he the slightest knowledge of what this particular location was like; but he pulled off the road, doused his lights, and parked.

He got out and stood perfectly still, the brief case in one hand, a small flashlight in readiness in the other. He had not long to wait.

Hurrying, fluttering almost, toward him through the mock pallor of false dawn came Parker, and Jackson flashed the torch full on him. Parker stopped, a theatrical character in his silly false beard and tired-out old face, and it took a moment for Jackson to realize that the nickel-plated object in Parker's delicate hand was a revolver.

There was an undertone of laughter, of condescension in his voice, as Jackson said, "I see that you're taking no chances, Mr. Parker."

Parker held the gun aimed dead-center on Jackson's stomach. "Did you expect me to?"

"No, not really."

"You knew I was following you?"

"Of course."

"I wondered. I began to appreciate the care you took not to lose me."

"Thank you. Were the false whiskers for my benefit?"

"Not entirely. Rather as a protection against any chance recognition at the airport by someone else. My friends believe that I am spending the week-end at Key West."

Jackson was growing tired again, even a little bored. He considered the chances were negligible that Parker would shoot until after the supposed cache would be disclosed, unless he, Jackson, were to attempt some inimical move. He wondered idly, still faintly amused with the situation, whether the old scorpion's dream-cloud intention was to hijack the non-existent cache and then kill *him.*

"Let's get on with it," he said.

He turned his back on Parker and walked at a fair pace to the shore of the lake; then he continued along it in the direction they had been driving. Parker did not lag, and it was like having a venomous wraith breathing on his neck and holding a gun aimed at his back.

Jackson was glad of it. The fact of Parker being armed effaced the gap between his powerful strength and Parker's physical weakness. It altered the job in Jackson's mind from a one-sided murder into a duel where the antagonists were equalized. The victim now had a sporting chance.

It was no longer his muscle that counted against Parker. It would have to be his wits and the deadly value of surprise.

"Is it much farther?" Parker asked.

"Not much."

"We're over a mile at least from the cars."

"That's right."

"Why didn't you drive nearer?"

"Road turns inland from the lake." Jackson had no idea whether the road did so or not.

"What's the name of this lake?"

"Killingsby Pond."

Then Jackson found what he wanted, what he had been waiting for—the low-hanging, long, supple branch of a pine. He slowed his next few steps until he sensed Parker closing in on his back. Then he released the branch.

The backlash whipsnap caught Parker across the chest, knocking him flat, and Jackson leaped for the revolver still gripped in Parker's hand.

It was amazing how the old bromide sprang to life—how a man locked in a death struggle could be possessed with the strength of ten. An exaggeration, of course, for Jackson shortly wrenched and twisted the revolver from Parker's grip and tossed it out of reach.

After that it was quite easy.

He lugged Parker to the water's edge and held his old skull-feeling head under until he drowned. He got a razor blade from his brief case and carefully incised several parallel cuts across the body's dead wrist and neck.

Some suicidal cases [of drowning] *reveal characteristic parallel cuts on wrist and neck, strongly suggesting suicidal nature* [of the drowning].

Jackson then removed six negotiable securities from the brief case and stuffed them in Parker's inner coat pocket. He felt fine. He felt clever as hell.

In a few minutes he started back for Halcyon, wondering about the odd sound that reached him faintly across the waters of the lake. The cry, the sob of a loon.

"They say that the gods on Olympus used to laugh," Dr. Williamson said, adding a splash of branch water to the bourbon, "whenever a mortal touched the peaks of success. They would have been convulsed over Jackson. You can understand the sense of confidence that filled him, because he was so blindly satisfied with his own smartness. In fact, he couldn't resist improving upon it, with frills . . ."

The first thing Jackson attended to on Monday morning after reaching the bank was a partial doctoring of the records that Parker had examined. He made several rather obvious erasures of numerals at certain points of falsification and then re-entered exactly the same numerals.

He felt terribly clever about this, reasoning that Parker's fingerprints would be on the suspect pages (as indeed they were) and that Parker would be presumed to have made the false entries while he had taken over during Jackson's vacation—Parker's purpose being to make Jackson Suspect One when the bank examiners discovered the embezzlement.

This would, Jackson reasoned to his own satisfaction, tie in perfectly with the disclosure of Parker's "suicide-from-remorse," while on flight, with several of the stolen securities on his body, with the planted alibi among his friends that he was "spending the weekend at Key West," and—a perfect clincher—with the disguise of a crepe-hair beard still glued on his chin. What else would the guy be doing, except taking it on the lam?

As for the bulk of the plunder, the authorities could figure that Parker either had hidden it before remorse suddenly drove him to kill himself, or that an initial chance discoverer of the body had made off with the remainder of the securities and cash, leaving the body for somebody else to discover.

As a final precaution against any eventuality, no matter how improbable, Jackson removed the pigskin suitcase from the stored-luggage room and concealed in it an unused stone smokehouse in the rear of the estate, a small structure almost smothered through the years with tropical vegetation.

It was all very reassuring, and Jackson hadn't a shred of doubt but that he could sail through the upcoming investigation with flying, if hypocritically shocked, colors. He would not now have to disappear. He could take his time in clearing up the meager remnants of the estate and then with an honorable name, plus the pigskin suitcase stuffed with a fortune, take an orderly leave from Halcyon. Because of its no longer bearable tragic associations.

Yes, he was truly on top of the world.

"So that was Jackson's frame of mind," Dr. Williamson said, "when the news broke. It broke not only at the bank but in the Halcyon, Miami, and Fort Lauderdale papers and on the networks. Few people failed to hear or read about it. Among them, Mr. Herkimer Smith. Smith felt, after a few hours cogitation, that it was his duty as a now Florida citizen and a once-resident of Foster, Rhode Island, to put in his two cents' worth of obliquely peculiar but possibly pertinent information . . ."

The man, when Jackson answered the door chime, was a stranger. He was of Jackson's own age, well knit and quietly dressed, with an intellectual face unsmiling in the evening shadows.

"My name is Fillmore," he said in a mannerly voice. "With the F.B.I."

"Come in, Mr. Fillmore."

They went into an oppresively appointed study, heavy with mahogany and wine-colored brocade curtains, and Fillmore politely refused a drink.

"It's about the bank," he said.

"Yes?"

"Yes."

The silence held. The disproportionately loud sound of a tree frog outside an open jalousie broke it.

"Is there," Jackson asked, "any particular reason why you've come to see me?"

"There are several. We first became interested in you because of certain information volunteered to us by a Mr. Herkimer Smith. You do know Mr. Smith?"

"Smith?" *Keep the smile lazy, Jackson.* "Herkimer Smith?"

"He moved down here from Foster, Rhode Island. Where," Fillmore himself smiled faintly, "your distant cousin Charley Whipple once lived."

"Of course. That Smith. We downed a couple of brews together. What about him?"

"Well, when he heard the news about Mr. Parker, about the body being found at Killingsby Pond, he was reminded of your somewhat excessive questions about that particular locality. He remembered your name, although he wasn't aware that you were connected with the bank. We, of course, knew that you were. It interested us."

"Coincidence."

Fillmore raised polite eyebrows. "Isn't that rather far-fetched?"

"No. I remember now telling Mr. Parker about the place."

"Why would you?"

"Because of Smith. A newcomer. The possibility of his becoming a new account. It must have stuck in Mr. Parker's mind—possibly as a good place to vanish to, to take on a new identity."

"That's reasonable." Fillmore's voice hardened. "But it doesn't gibe."

"Gibe with what?"

"With your having been there with him at Killingsby Pond," Fillmore said.

It was a longer silence this time, and even the tree frog respected it.

"Just what makes you think so, Mr. Fillmore?"

"Any number of proofs." Fillmore's voice sounded tired with the ineptitude, the stupidities, the amateur complications of the plot that Jackson had woven, the wide open trail he had blazed for the state police and for the F.B.I. to follow.

"A set of fingerprints other than those of Mr. Parker," he said, "were on the nickel-plated revolver found near the body. As soon as Mr. Smith told us of your excessive interest in the locality we compared them with your prints on file with the bank's bonding company. Our conclusion was that the embezzlement had been a conspiracy between yourself and Mr. Parker. From the location of your prints on the gun we believed that you forced the gun out of his hand and tossed it to where the troopers found it. Then you killed him."

"It was suicide." *Keep pitching, Jackson.* "He slashed his wrist, his throat, then had some sort of seizure and fell down by the water's edge with his face in the water–"

"And you?"

"I–ran."

"The securities found in his pocket had *your* fingerprints on them–*but none of his.* So you put them there. What have you done with the rest?"

That's what he's been shadow boxing for, Jackson thought. To recover the plunder. His, Jackson's, solid ace in the hole.

"I told you," he said steadily. "I ran. I left everything there. It's a silly thing to admit, but the sight of blood unnerves me."

Fillmore, after a while, said, "There was no blood."

"I'm telling you I saw him slice his wrist and throat."

"Mr. Parker was dead when that was done. By you. One of the cuts on the wrist had severed an artery. Had he been living, had his heart been pumping when the cuts were made, there would have been blood–plenty of blood. Except for any small seepage caused by gravitation, the dead do not bleed."

Hold it tight, hold it tighter than you ever have before, Jackson. Even at the worst never lose sight of one blessed fact—the State of Rhode Island can't kill you.

"They'll want you here in Florida for grand larceny," Fillmore was saying. "But Connecticut will have precedence. They'll extradite you and indict you for murder in the first degree."

It took a moment for Fillmore's words to register–especially one word.

Then–

"You're all fouled up, Mr. Fillmore. What's Connecticut got to do with it?"

"Just a question of geography," Fillmore said with patience. "Rhode Island is bordered on the west by Connecticut, and the village of Foster is right by the state line. As for Killingsby Pond, it *straddles* the borderline and the murder was committed on the Connecticut side."

Fillmore added impersonally as he stood up, "So that's where you'll fry—in Connecticut."

Dr. Williamson led the way, continuing to talk as he went.

"Of course it smashed Jackson completely," he said. "He went utterly to pieces, and babbled out a detailed confession. Carried on like a maniac. That's why they called me in—to take a look at him before the Governor decided on extradition."

Dr. Williamson's smile was half apologetic as he added, "That's why, in all senses of the word, I call it a borderline case."

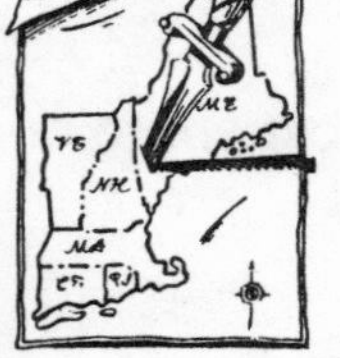

LIEUTENANT HARALD AND THE *TREASURE ISLAND* TREASURE

by Margaret Maron

Margaret Maron has written for Redbook, McCall's, *and* Reader's Digest, *as well as for mystery magazines. She is the author of several novels about Lt. Sigrid Harald of the NYPD who, in this story, travels to Connecticut to solve a puzzle in the tradition of Poe's "pure ratiocination."*

"I thought you liked puzzles," argued Oscar Nauman's disembodied voice.

"I do," Lieutenant Sigrid Harald answered, balancing the telephone receiver on her shoulder as she struggled with a balky can opener. "That's one of the reasons I joined the NYPD. I get paid for it, Nauman. I don't have to waste a free weekend."

"But this is a real buried treasure. One of my former students is going to lose her inheritance if it isn't found soon, and I told her we'd help."

As one of America's leading abstract artists, Oscar Nauman could have sold one or two paintings a year and lived in comfortable retirement on some Mediterranean island. Instead, he continued to chair the art department at Vanderlyn College over on the East River where Sigrid first met him during a homicide investigation. The end of the case hadn't been the end of their acquaintance, though. He kept walking in and out of her life as if he had a right there, lecturing, bullying, and keeping her off balance. Her prickly nature seemed to amuse him, and Sigrid had quit trying to analyze why he persisted.

Or why she allowed it.

"We can drive up tonight," said Nauman. "Unless," he added craftily, knowing her aversion to sunrises, "you'd rather leave around six tomorrow morning?"

"Now listen, Nauman, I don't—" The can opener slipped. "Oh, damn! I just dumped soup all over the blasted stove."

"Throw it out. I'll pick you up in thirty minutes and we'll have dinner on the way."

"I am *not* going to Connecticut," she said firmly, but he had already hung up.

Fourteen hours later, she sat on the terrace of Nauman's Connecticut house and placidly bit into a second Danish. A good night's sleep had removed most of her annoyance at being dragged from the city and hurtled through the night at Nauman's usual speed-of-sound driving. The sun was shining, the air was warm, and she had found an unworked double-crostic in an elderly issue of the New York *Times*.

She looked contented as a cat, thought Nauman. Her long dark hair was pinned at the nape more loosely than usual, and her faded jeans and cream-colored knit shirt were more becoming than those shapeless pantsuits she wore in town. Thin to the point of skinniness, with a mouth too wide for conventional beauty and a neck too long, her cool gray eyes were her best feature, but these were presently engrossed in her paper.

He'd been up for hours and was so impatient to be off that he swept cups, carafe, and the remaining sweet rolls back onto the large brass tray and carted it all away without asking Sigrid if she'd finished.

"I thought your friend wasn't expecting us before ten," she said, following Nauman to the kitchen where she retrieved her cup and refilled it while he loaded the dishwasher.

"It'll take us about that long to walk over." He took her cup and poured it in the sink.

"*Walk?*" Sigrid was appalled.

"Less than a mile as the crow flies. You walk more than that every day."

"But that's on concrete," she protested. "In the city. You're talking about trees and snakes and briars, aren't you?"

"It used to be an Indian trading path," Nauman coaxed, leading her out through the terrace gate. "It'll be like a walk through Central Park."

"I hate walking in Central Park," Sigrid muttered, but she followed him across a narrow meadow to a scrub forest. As Nauman disappeared behind a curtain of wild grapevines, she hesitated a moment, then took a deep breath and plunged in after him.

Ten minutes later, sweaty, her ankles whipped by thorns, a stinging scratch on her arm, she was ready for mutiny. "No Indians ever walked through this jungle."

"Not this part. We're taking a shortcut. The path is just past those tall oaks."

"If it isn't, I'm going back."

But it was; and once they were on it, the walk became more pleasant. Sigrid was used to covering twenty-five or thirty city blocks at a stretch, but she was deeply suspicious of nature in the raw. Still, it was cooler under the massive trees in this part of the forest. The path angled downward and was so broad that no branches caught at her clothing. She began to relax. They crossed a small stream on stepping stones and the path rose gently again.

As Nauman paused to re-tie his sneaker, a large black bird lazily flapped along overhead in their general direction.

"That crow of navigational fame, no doubt," said Sigrid.

Her smiles were so rare, thought Oscar, that one forgot they transformed her face. She was more than twenty-five years younger than he and nearly as tall and she photographed badly, but perhaps a painting? He hadn't attempted a portrait since his student days.

"Hi, Oscar!" came a little voice from the top of the path. "Welcome to Treasure Island."

To Sigrid, Jemima Bullock looked like a thoroughly nice child as she ran down to meet them in cut-off jeans. She was sturdily built, athletic rather than buxom, with short reddish-blonde hair, an abundance of freckles on every inch of visible skin, and an infectious grin as Nauman effected introductions.

"Jemima's the art world's contribution to oceanography."

"What Oscar means is that he's eternally grateful I didn't stay an art major at Vanderlyn," Jemima explained cheerfully. "My technical drawing was good, but I bombed in creativity."

"At least you had the native wit to admit it," Nauman said.

At the top of the path, they rounded a hummock of wisteria and honeysuckle vines to find an old cottage of undressed logs. A wide porch ran its length and gave good views of rolling woodlands and of Jemima's battered VW van, which was parked on the drive beneath an enormous oak.

"My uncle was caretaker for the Rawlings eatate," said Jemima, leading them up on the porch and pulling wicker chairs around a bamboo table. "The main house is farther down the drive, but no one's lived there for years. Uncle Jim mostly had the place to himself."

What looked like a small telescope on a tripod stood at the far end of the porch. "He called this Spyglass Hill but that's really a surveyor's transit."

"Nauman said his hobby was Robert Louis Stevenson," said Sigrid. "Is that why you welcomed us to Treasure Island?"

"Partly, but Uncle Jim was nutty about only one of Stevenson's books: *Treasure Island.* He was my mother's favorite uncle, see, and their name was Hawkins; so when he was a kid, he used to pretend he was Jim Hawkins in the book. Mom named me Jemima Hawkins Bullock after him, and, since he never married, we were pretty close. I used to spend a month up here every summer when I was growing up. He's the one who got me interested in oceanography, though it started off with treasure maps. Every summer he'd have a new one waiting for me."

She darted into the house and reappeared a moment later with a book and a large leather-bound portfolio of charts which she spread out on the porch table.

"This is a survey map of the area," she said. Her finger stabbed a small black square. "Here's this cottage." She traced a short route. "Here's Oscar's house and the path and stream you crossed. See the way the stream comes up and intersects the creek here? And then the creek runs back down and around where a second stream branches off and merges again with the first stream."

"So technically, we really are on an island," said Sigrid, obscurely pleased with that idea.

"A body of land surrounded by water," Nauman agreed. He pulled out his pipe and worked at getting it lit.

"The freaky thing is that it's actually shaped like the original Treasure Island," said Jemima. She flipped the book open to an illustration. To Sigrid's eyes, the two were only roughly similar, but she supposed that wishful thinking could rationalize the differences.

"Uncle Jim made all these treasure maps for me. So many paces to a certain tree while I was small; later he taught me how to use a sextant and I'd have to shoot the stars to get the proper bearing. He didn't make it easy, either. It usually took two or three days and several false starts to find the right place to dig. It was worth it, though."

Sigrid leafed through the sheaf of hand-drawn charts. Although identical in their outlines, each was exquisitely embellished with different colored inks: tiny sailing ships, mermaids, and dolphins sported in blue waters around elaborate multi-pointed compasses. Latitude and longitude lines had been carefully lettered in India ink, along with minute numbers and directions. Sigrid peered closely and read, "Bulk of treasure here."

"He never made much money as a caretaker," said Jemima, "but the treasures he used to hide! Chocolates wrapped in gold and purple foil, a pair of binoculars I still use, maps and drawing pads and compasses so I could draw my own." There was a wistful note in her voice as of a child describing never-to-come-again Christmas mornings.

"Tell her about the real treasure," Nauman prompted, bored with the preliminaries.

"I'm coming to it, Oscar. Be patient. She has to understand how Uncle Jim's mind worked first—the way he liked making a mystery of things. It wasn't only his maps," she told Sigrid. "He never talked freely about his life either. He'd trained as a surveyor but seldom held a steady job till after his leg was hurt—just bummed around the world till he was past thirty. I guess he might've seen or done some things he didn't want to tell a kid; but when he was feeling loose, he'd talk about a treasure he brought home from England during World War II. Nothing direct, just a brief mention. If you asked too many questions, he'd cut you off. I used to think it might be gold, then again it'd sound like jewels. Whatever it was, he got it in London. He was on leave there and the building he was in was hit by a buzz bomb. Crushed his left leg.

"That London hospital was where he really got into the *Treasure Island* thing. The nurses kept bringing him different editions of the book. Because of his name, you see. He'd always had a flair for precision drawing—from the surveying—and when he started mapping the wards on scrap paper, they brought him sketch pads and pens and he was off to the races. I think they made a pet out of him because they knew his leg would never heal properly. Anyhow, he let it slip once that if the nurses hadn't liked him, he never would have recognized the treasure when it appeared."

She looked at Sigrid doubtfully through stubby sandy lashes. "That doesn't sound much like gold or diamonds, does it?"

"He never revealed its nature?"

"Nope. Anyhow, Uncle Jim knew it takes an M.S. to get anywhere in oceanography. That means an expensive year or two at some school like Duke, and I just don't have the money. In fact, I haven't been able to get up here much these last four years because I've had to work summers and part time to stay at Vanderlyn. Uncle Jim said not to worry, that he was going to give me the treasure for graduation and I could sell it for enough to finance my postgraduate work.

"When he called three weeks ago to make sure I was coming, he said he was drawing up a new map. The heart attack must have hit him within the hour. I drove up the next morning and found him slumped over the table inside. He'd just finished sketching in the outline. It was going to be our best treasure hunt."

An unembarrassed tear slipped down her freckled cheek, and she brushed it away with the back of her hand.

"The trustees for the Rawlings estate have been very understanding, but they do need the cottage for the new caretaker. Uncle Jim left everything to me, so they've asked if I can clear out his things by the end of the month. You're my last hope, Lieutenant Harald. Oscar said you're good at solving puzzles. I hope you can figure out this one 'cause nobody else can."

Sigrid looked at Nauman. "But I don't know a thing about sextants or surveyor's transits, and anyhow, if he died before he finished the map—"

"Nobody's asking you to go tramping through hill and dale with a pickax," Nauman said, correctly interpreting her horrified expression. "Jemima doesn't think he'd buried it yet."

"Come inside and I'll show you," said the girl.

In essence, the cottage was one big room, with kitchen equipment at one end and two small sleeping alcoves at the other end separated by a tiny bath. A shabby couch and several comfortable-looking armchairs circled an enormous stone fireplace centered on the long rear wall. A bank of windows overlooked the porch, and underneath were shelves crammed with books of all shapes and sizes. Most were various editions of—"What else?" said Jemima—*Treasure Island.* In the middle of the room was a round wooden table flanked by six ladder-back chairs, one of which was draped in an old and worn woollen pea jacket with heavy brass buttons. A rusty metal picnic cooler sat beside one chair with its lid ajar to reveal a porcelain interior.

"Things are pretty much as Uncle Jim left them. That cooler was our treasure chest because it was watertight. As you can see, there was nothing in it."

Sigrid circled the table, carefully cataloguing its contents: an uncapped bottle of India ink, a fine-nibbed drawing pen, a compass, a ruler, four brushes, a twelve-by-eighteen-inch block of watercolor paper with the top half of the island sketched in, a set of neatly arranged water colors and a clean tray for mixing them. Across from these, a book was opened to a reproduction of the map Robert Louis Stevenson had drawn so many years ago, and several more books formed a prop for two framed charts. Sigrid scanned the cottage and found the light oblongs on the whitewashed walls where a chart had hung on either side of the stone chimney.

"Uncle Jim often used them as references when he was drawing a new map," explained Jemima. "The right one's a copy of the survey map. It's the first one he drew after he took the job here and realized that the stream and creek made this place an island almost like the real Treasure Island. The other one's the first copy he made when he was in the hospital. I guess he kept it for sentimental reasons even though the proportions aren't quite right."

Sigrid peered through the glass at the sheet of yellowed watercolor paper, which was frayed around the edges and showed deep crease lines where it had once been folded into quarters. It, too, was minutely detailed with hillocks, trees, sailing ships, and sounding depths although, as Jemima had noted, it wasn't an accurate copy.

She turned both frames over and saw that the paper tape that sealed the backings to the frames had been torn.

"We took them apart," Jemima acknowledged. "A friend of mine came over from the rare book library at Yale to help appraise the books, and he thought maybe the treasure was an autographed letter from Stevenson or something like that which Uncle Jim might've hidden inside the matting."

"None of the books is rare?" asked Sigrid. That had seemed the most likely possibility.

"He thought they might bring a few hundred dollars if I sold them as a collection," said the girl, "but individually, nothing's worth over forty dollars at the most. And we thumbed through every one of them in case there really was a letter or something. No luck."

Sigrid's slate gray eyes swept through the large, shabby room. Something jarred, but she couldn't quite put her finger on the source.

"Not as simple as a double-crostic, is it?" Nauman asked.

Sigrid shrugged, unnettled by his light gibe. "If a treasure's here, logic will uncover it."

"But we've *been* logical!" Jemima said despairingly. "Last week my mom and I and two cousins went over every square inch of this place. We looked behind knotholes, jiggled every stone in the fireplace, checked for loose floorboards, and examined mattress seams and cushion covers. Nothing. And my cousins are home ec majors," she added to buttress her statement.

"Mom even separated out all the things Uncle Jim might have brought from England." She gestured to a small heap of books stacked atop the window case. "Luckily he dated all his books. My Yale friend says none of those is worth more than a few dollars."

Sigrid lifted one. The blue cloth binding was familiar, and when she read the publication date – 1932 – she realized it was the same edition of *Treasure Island* as the one her father had owned as a boy and which she had read as a child herself. Memories of lying on her stomach on a window ledge, munching toasted cheese sandwiches while she read, came back to Sigrid as she paused over a well-remembered illustration of Jim Hawkins shooting Israel Hands. Inscribed on the flyleaf was *A very happy Christmas to our own Jim Hawkins from Nurse Fromyn and staff.* Underneath, a masculine hand had added *12/25/1944.*

The other four books in the heap carried dates which spanned the early months of 1945. "Mom said he was brought home in the summer of '45," said Jemima, peering around Sigrid's shoulder.

"What else did he bring?"

"That first map he drew," she answered promptly, "a shaving kit, that jacket on the chair, and Mom thinks that leather portfolio, too."

She fetched it in from the porch and carefully removed the charts it held before handing it over. It measured about eighteen by twenty inches.

The leather was worn by forty years of handling, but when Nauman turned it over, they could still read the tooled letters at the edge of the case. "Bartlelow's," he said. "They're still the best leather goods shop in London. And the most expensive."

Sigrid found a worn spot in the heavy taffeta lining. Carefully, she slipped her thin fingers inside and worked the fabric away from the leather. Had any slip of paper been concealed there, her search should have found it. Nothing.

The shaving kit and threadbare pea jacket were equally barren of anything remotely resembling treasure. "My cousins thought those heavy brass buttons might be worth five dollars apiece," Jemima said ruefully. She looked around the big shabby room and sighed. "If only Uncle Jim hadn't loved secrets so much."

"If he hadn't, your childhood would have been much duller," Oscar reminded her sensibly. He knocked his pipe out on the hearth. "You promised us lunch, and I for one am ready for it. Food first, ratiocination afterwards. Lead us to your galley, Jemima Hawkins, and if it's water biscuits and whale blubber, you'll walk the plank."

"It's cold chicken and fresh salad," Jemima giggled, "but we'll have to pick the greens ourselves. Uncle Jim's garden is just down the drive."

Sigrid looked dubious and Oscar grinned. "Don't worry. I know you can't distinguish lettuce and basil from poison oak and thistles. You stay and detect; we'll pick the salad."

Left alone, Sigrid circled the room again. Although spartan in its furnishings, the area itself was so large that another thorough search was impractical. One would have to trust the home ec cousins' expertise. As a homicide detective with her own expertise, she told Nauman that logic would uncover a treasure if it were there to be found, but perhaps she'd spoken too soon.

If there were a treasure...

She stared again at the forlorn table where Jemima's uncle had died so peacefully. At the drawing paraphernalia and the uncompleted map. At the empty chest on the floor, its lid ajar to receive a treasure as soon as old Jim Hawkins had mapped its burial site. She lingered over the two framed charts and a sudden thought made her measure the older one against the leather portfolio.

Jemima said this had been the very first *Treasure Island* map her uncle had attempted and that he'd kept it for sentimental reasons. But what if this were the map Robert Louis Stevenson had drawn himself? Wouldn't that be a real treasure? And what better place to hide it than in plain sight, passed off as Hawkins' own work?

She strode across the rough-planked floor and pulled two likely books from the shelves beneath the windows. One was a fairly recent biography of Stevenson, the other a facsimile copy of the first editon of *Treasure Island.* Both contained identical reproductions of the author's map, and the biography's version was labeled *Frontispiece of the first edition as drawn by RLS in his father's office in Edinburgh.*

She carried the books over to the table, but there was no denying the evidence of her eyes: the embellishments were different and the map Hawkins had brought home from London was misproportioned. The uncle's island had been drawn slightly longer and not quite as wide as Stevenson's original version.

Disappointed, Sigrid returned the books to their former slots and continued circling the room. Surely that expensive portfolio had something to do with the treasure. Or was it only a bon voyage gift from the nurses when Hawkins was shipped home?

She paused in the door of the tiny bath and inspected the battered shaving kit again. Had such a homely everyday pouch once held diamonds or gold?

Nothing about the cottage indicated a taste for luxury. Devising modest treasures and drawing exquisitely precise maps for his young namesake seemed to have been the caretaker's only extravagance. Otherwise, he had lived almost as a hermit, spare and ascetic, still making do with an ancient pea jacket whose eight brass buttons were probably worth more than everything else in his wardrobe.

She paused by the chair which held the jacket and again tried to make herself take each item on the table top separately and significantly.

And then she saw it.

When Jemima and Oscar reentered the cottage, hilarious with the outrageous combination of herbs and salad greens they had picked, they found Sigrid standing by the window with her finger marking a place in the blue clothbound book she'd read as a child. Jemima started to regale her with their collection, but Oscar took one look at Sigrid's thin face and said, "You found it."

Her wide gray eyes met his and a smile almost brushed her lips. "Can you phone your expert at Yale?" she asked Jemima.

"Sure, but he checked all the books before. Or did you find a hidden one?"

Sigrid shook her head. "Not a book. The map." She pointed to the older of the framed charts.

"What's special about Uncle Jim's map? It's not the original, if that's what you're thinking. Charlie told me that one was auctioned off in the forties and he's pretty sure the same person still owns it."

Nauman had found a reproduction of the original and silently compared it to the faded chart on the table. "Look, Siga, the proportions are wrong."

"I know," she said, and there was definite mischief in her eyes now. "That's precisely why you should call him, Jemima."

"You mean the books are all wrong?" asked the girl.

Sigrid opened the blue book to the forward. "Listen," she said. With one hand hooked into the pocket of her jeans, she leaned against the stone chimney and read in a cool clear voice Stevenson's own version of how he came to write *Treasure Island;* of how, in that rainy August of 1881, he and his stepson "with the aid of pen and ink and shilling box of water colours," had passed their afternoon drawing.

On one of these occasions, I made a map of an island. . . the shape of it took my fancy beyond expression. . . and I ticketed it ''Treasure Island''. . . the next thing I knew, I had some papers before me and was writing out a list of characters.

Sigrid turned the pages. "The next is familiar territory. The story was written, serialized in a magazine, and then was to be published in book form." She read again,

I sent in my manuscript, and the map along with it ... the proofs came, they were corrected, but I heard nothing of the map. I wrote and asked; was told it had never been received, and sat aghast. It is

one thing to draw a map at random, set a scale in one corner of it ... and write up a story to the measurements. It is quite another to have to examine a whole book, make an inventory of it, and, with a pair of compasses, painfully design a map to suit the data. I did it; and the map was drawn in my father's office ... but somehow it was never Treasure Island to me.

Sigrid closed the book. "If you'll look closely, Jemima, you'll see the handwriting on that map's a lot closer to Stevenson's than to your uncle's."

Oscar compared the maps with an artist's eye, then lifted the phone and wryly handed it to Jemima. "Call your friend."

It took several calls around New Haven and surrounding summer cottages to chase Jemima's expert to earth. While they waited, Oscar created an elaborate dressing for their salad and sliced the cold chicken. Lunch was spread on the porch and Sigrid was trying to decide if she really approved mixing basil and parsley together when Jemima danced through the open doorway.

"He's going to call Sotheby's in New York!" she caroled. "And he's coming out himself just to make sure; but if it's genuine, he says it'll bring thousands—enough to pay for at least two years in any M.S. program in the United States!"

Oscar removed an overlooked harlequin beetle from the salad bowl and filled Jemima's plate. "Admit it, though," he said to Sigrid. "It was the coincidence of remembering that passage from your childhood book that made you suspect the map, not logic."

"It was logic," she said firmly, forking through the salad carefully in case more beetles had been overlooked. She was not opposed to food foraged in a garden instead of in a grocery, but Nauman was entirely too casual about the wildlife.

"Show me the logic," Oscar challenged, and Jemima looked at her expectantly, too.

"All right," said Sigrid. "Why would your uncle acquire an expensive portfolio if not to bring home something special?"

"It didn't have to be that map."

"No? What else was the right size?"

"Even so," objected Oscar, "why not assume he was taking pains with it because it was the first copy he'd drawn himself?"

"Because it's been folded. You can still see the crease lines. If he'd ever folded it up himself, why buy a leather case to carry it flat? We'll probably never know exactly how the map disappeared in the 1880s and reappeared during the Blitz, but I'd guess one of the publisher's clerks misfiled it or maybe an office boy lifted it and then was afraid to own up."

"So that it rattled around in someone's junk room until it caught a nurse or corpsman's eye and they thought it would cheer up their Yank patient? Maybe," Oscar conceded. He cocked a skeptial eye at Sigrid. "So, on the basis of some old crease marks, you instantly deduced this was the original Stevenson-drawn *Treasure Island* map?"

"They helped. Made it seem as if that paper hadn't been carefully handled from the beginning." She peered at a suspicious dark fleck beneath a leaf of spinach. "Too, he'd told Jemima that if it hadn't been for the nurses, he wouldn't have recognized the treasure when it appeared. Lying there in bed, he would have read the book they'd given him from cover to cover, wouldn't he? Including the foreword about the missing map? I'm sure it would have interested him because of his own mapping skills. That's really what made me look twice: the map was all wrong.

"Jemima's uncle was far too skillful to have miscopied a map with the book right there in front of him. I don't care how sentimental he might later have been over a first attempt, I couldn't see him framing and hanging a misdrawn, ill-proportioned copy.

"And *that*," she concluded triumphantly as she presented Oscar with a potato beetle done in by his dressing, "is logic."

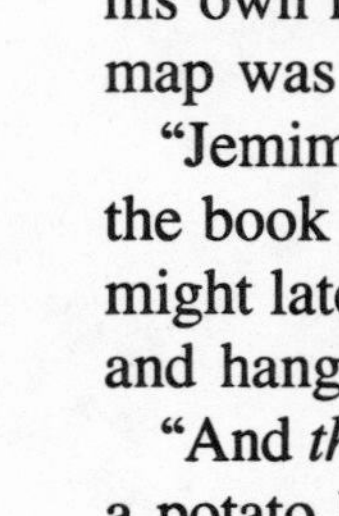

NICE, WELL-MEANING FOLK

by N. Scott Warner

N. Scott Warner, like Stanley Ellin, is an Ellery Queen's Mystery Magazine *"Department of First Stories" discovery. He lives on the Maine Coast, having moved there from an Air Force post in Washington, D.C. In the following story he considers the difference between a good neighbor and a bad neighbor.*

Lower down gives way to what has drifted up. The new Chevy police cruiser was driven by Sheriff Gagne because he was older, supposedly experienced, and, anyway, it was his county, right? Ezra Katz, the tall Maine deputy with sandy hair cropped close, was next in line and so drove a yellow rustbucket of a Bronco. The vehicle parked in the dusty driveway and its weary engine spluttered to a halt. Katz got out and walked to where the body lay in the grass.

The dead man was Roy Finney, a carpenter who took odd jobs. His tarpapered home wasn't far away. The chalky face pointed upward, the mouth slightly open and shriveled like a dead rose. Finney seemed to float in the bright grass, half swallowed by waves of hawkweed and mountain fern. His right temple was a dark mess, as if it had been sampled with a scoop. Beside him a cherry-red, new-looking Honda three-wheeler, a vehicle somewhere between a motorcycle and an oversized toy, was leaning crazily on its side. Oil, spilled from the crankcase, smeared the grass and rocks. The ignition key pointed to "on," but the engine was silent.

To the west, the field rose and melted into a gritty yard surrounding a farmhouse of unpainted granite fieldstone. Its metal roof, a protection against the harsh Maine winter, glittered in the sunlight like a battered medieval helmet. A peeling barn flanked and dwarfed the building, a mountain of grassy manure looming up behind it. This was Hatch property, next to the Finney land. It didn't go far, for Mildred Hatch had been selling bits and pieces, holding onto a few acres that were no longer farmed. It was Mildred who had phoned in, claiming a body lay outside.

In the tan driveway dirt, there were faint marks that the deputy tentatively identified as boot prints. A recent, sudden shower had smudged them.

Katz knocked softly, then hard, but there was no movement around the green window shades. He stepped aside and put his face close to a pane. His knuckles rapped, and a startled face appeared on the other side. Katz stepped back and turned toward the door again. The lady of the house, a short, oldish woman in a purple sack of a dress, beckoned him inside.

"Come in, Ezra," she rasped. Her tough amber face, like a dried apple, split into a grin.

A hot wind flew out from the large, undivided downstairs room. The Clarion wood stove roared, although it was at least sixty-five degrees outside. A dented tin kettle steamed on its hot black surface. Katz loosened his collar a little and shut the door behind him. Mildred slopped hot water on instant coffee in a mug without a handle.

"Have some?"

"Sure."

He took the mug gingerly, anxious not to burn his fingertips, and sat back in a chrome-trimmed chair heavily patched with silver tape. He noticed a large wooden baseball bat leaning against the table.

Katz sipped the bitter brew. "Out of sugar and milk again," Mildred said. "Food stamps ain't what they used to be. Don't go far nowadays."

"Yep," Katz said. It hadn't been long ago that his mother had gone off stamps. That had taken some doing. "Good coffee," he said brightly.

"Nice and polite, aren't you?" Mildred said, dragging a step stool roughly across speckled linoleum. She sat down briskly, pushing heavy eyeglasses up her short nose.

"Want to tell me what you saw?" Katz asked after a carefully measured sip.

Deep furrows lined Mildred's forehead. "Not much to tell. There was that damned noise again, and a bang—must have hit that rock. Drinking, no doubt. Always drinking, he was."

"Bashed his head, Mildred."

"Ayep," Mildred agreed. "Reckon he did."

"You go to look?"

"Just a bit," Mildred said. "Dead man doesn't need no ambulance, I figure, so I called the sheriff. Couldn't think of nothing else."

"Subject drove into your yard," Deputy Katz summed up, "made a short turn, hit that rock, fell over, and hit his head on another rock."

Mildred wasn't listening. Her beady eyes followed a cricket hopping on the well-worn floorboards along the edge of the linoleum. Her hand crept to the bat, there was a quick movement and a noisy grind, and the fat insect became a whorl in the cracked linoleum. Katz noticed a good many others.

"Lots of them about now," he said. "It's the wet weather brings them out."

Mildred cackled. "Get every single one of them. Unwholesome little buggers. They slip in the food."

Katz studied the bat. It was large and splintered slightly. There were no dirty fingerprints on it as on every other object he saw around. Mildred didn't waste time on cleanliness.

"You always get them with the bat?"

"Stamp on them, too," Mildred said. "Got to get them good."

Katz finished his coffee with one courageous gulp. "Finney hadn't had the machine too long?"

Mildred poked carefully at a remaining tooth. "Only last week. Didn't know how to handle it yet. Drinking didn't help."

"He come often to visit?"

"Nah." Mildred leered. "Don't encourage no bums around here. Keep to myself."

Katz remembered seeing a car in the barn. He had seen her in town, too. She was getting around and had some welfare, maybe savings from selling land.

"You ever worry about getting robbed?"

"Of what?" Mildred asked.

"But Finney came to visit."

"Once in a while," Mildred said. "Not too often. Not today. Just showing off and racing his dumb machine, making a racket."

"What time, Mildred?"

"Got no time here." She pointed at what was left of a clock. "Sun'd been up a while."

"You phoned in at ten."

"Maybe ten," she said. "It's Saturday, ain't it?"

"Yes, Mildred, " Katz said gently.

"Fridays he got drunker."

"Than what?"

"Than other days."

"Wonder where he got the money to buy that Honda," Katz said.

"Same here." Mildred waddled to the stove. "More coffee?"

"No thanks," Katz said quickly. "Bought it on time, cut the beer to make the down payment, maybe. Had he been working lately?"

"With that other bum, Levesque," Mildred said. "He lives in the other side of them alders. I've seen them go off in Levesque's car."

"Last night, too?"

Mildred nodded. "Plowing up my dooryard again, them bastards."

Katz got up. "I better get going. See you, Mildred. Take it easy."

"Always do." She opened the door for him.

Finney's shack showed some effort at design, with a pretty gable sloping smoothly to a side where a shed had been started and never finished. But Katz noted other details, too. Exposed timbers on the unfinished shed were weathered to a silver grey. A stack of shingles rotted in the tall grass and shreds of tarpaper, blotched with water stains, blew about in the breeze. The roof was covered in odd-sized sheets of corrugated iron, some rusted, and there were yellow drip stains on the siding. Katz investigated several junk cars. The closest, a Ford Galaxy, might have worked until recently—the registration was still valid, but bottles were heaped against its fenders. Blackberry shrubs grew over the other phantoms. Bags of garbage ripped and worried by animals spread their contents across the yard and path, the labels and torn packages mostly faded into a tired white by the sun and rain.

Katz fanned blackflies and mosquitos aside as he pushed the poorly hung door and stepped inside. Light streaked weakly through greasy windows. Dust settled in clouds onto the contents of the single room. A couch wrapped in dark, brittle burlap sagged under a collection of damp newspapers and discarded clothes. A low cot with a blackened, dimpled mattress stood under a staircase that seemed ready to slide away. A tower of magazines, some bound with yellowed twine, leaned into a thin shaft of light, obliterating a window. Fast-food packing littered the table and floor. An old console television set, its screen oily and dark, might still be in working order.

Katz left the shack and crossed Mildred's property, heading for alders thickly veiled in the gauze of tentworm colonies. It was raining again. Levesque's location was a lookalike of Finney's, but there was only one car, a badly rusted compact that probably started up all right. Katz noted it was overdue for an inspection. The Toyota made a brave effort to shine as it got washed by the rain.

Katz found his way between heaps of debris and approached the shack. A plastic flamingo, its eyes missing, had been stuck next to a cracked concrete slab that served as a step. "Anybody home?"

Levesque, a large, red-faced man with woolly sideburns, showed up at the door. He hadn't shaved for a while and his beergut ballooned over oily jeans, stretching the limits of a ribbed tee-shirt. A dirty hand, hanging limply, carried a beer bottle by its neck.

"The law," Levesque grunted, opening the door.

Katz followed Levesque inside.

"Someone notice my inspection is out of state?" Levesque asked. He put on a funny squeak. "Will see to it right away, officer—first thing Monday morning. Sorry about that, *sir.*"

The living room had a low ceiling the texture of cottage cheese and the carpet could have been made out of matted red hair. Levesque pointed at a chair and stumbled onto a vinyl recliner. He sat down clumsily. "Why did you put yourself out? I have a phone and I'm in the book. Could have saved yourself the trip." He tipped back a plastic baseball cap with the mouth of the bottle, revealing a red crease that bordered a bald patch in wet, thin hair.

Katz ignored the chair that was one leg short and sat down gingerly on a sofa that looked like it had slept in the green army blankets that partially covered its ungainly bulk. The cushions were hard as brick.

"Something else," Katz said. "Never mind the inspection for now."

"Like what?" Levesque asked brightly, slurring comfortably now.

"You went drinking with Finney last night?"

Levesque tried to sit up. "As a matter of fact, I did," he said pleasantly. "Yes, sir, we had a few—but never again, and that's right, too. Silly no-good bum."

"Finney's dead," Katz said.

"No," Levesque said, draining his bottle. "What's that?"

"Dead," Katz said softly. "Lying in Mildred's yard with his head bashed in."

Levesque thought. He closed one eye. "Good for him."

"You two didn't go home together?"

"Must have walked," Levesque said. "Kept punching me in the bar. I wasn't paying much attention so he got thrown out alone."

"You didn't mind?" Katz asked. "He wasn't your buddy?"

Levesque's forefinger wagged. "Bad influence, officer. Never drank this much until I started working with old Finney. So he's dead now, eh? Well, what do you know."

Katz looked around. There was a baseball bat near the door. The handle was sooty with dirt. He pointed it out. "Go in for a bit of sport?"

"Guns are expensive," Levesque said, studying his bottle with a fascinated, intense stare; shaking it as if hoping it might fill itself again. "Had all sorts once. Twelve-gauge shotgun, a good twenty-two, a couple of handguns. Sold them all. Now I've got to bash them."

"Bash who?"

"Them that bother me."

A cricket crawled by Katz's right foot. He stamped his boot, avoiding the insect.

"Got some bugs here," he observed.

Levesque looked. "What—them little fellows? Come to keep me company. They have pretty legs, too. Sure can hop."

"Don't they get into your food?"

"What?" Levesque tried to focus. "No, not that I notice." He burped heavily. "Out of beer again. Bah. So what do you reckon happened to old Finney?"

"Drunk?" Katz asked. "Fell off his bike?"

"Nah."

"You don't think so?"

"Stupid bastard didn't get drunk in the morning, and besides—"

"Besides what?"

"He rode pretty good."

"You didn't see him this morning?"

"No, sir," Levesque said. "Wish I had, though. Might have bashed him myself."

"Would you do that?"

"Me?" Levesque asked. "I'm a good guy. I've been to Viet Nam. I got a medal."

"Come and have a look at Finney," Katz suggested.

"Not right now," Levesque said. "I'll read about it in the paper come Monday . . . "

Nice people, Katz thought as he drove back in the heavy rain. Then: They aren't really bad. They all got lost somehow. This is a good place to get lost in. Water pelted the roadside hard, mottling the runny mud. Budding trees and evergreens with rust-colored needles beneath their umbrellas swayed with the wind. A grey sky sat on a seamless horizon as if determined to keep the sun out forever. The Bronco's tires slammed into potholes and ruts.

But, Katz thought on, I wish all these nice, well-meaning folk got lost somewhere else.

He parked the car in the new hospital's parking lot and pulled the emergency brake, noting smooth, recently laid pavement through a hole by the shift lever. The brake lever felt loose. He looked over his shoulder and saw a small tree. If the brake didn't hold, then perhaps the tree would for a bit.

He marched into the lobby, khaki uniform spotted in dark brown. He smiled at the switchboard operator, a middle-aged woman with protruding brown eyes and a pouty mouth. She folded her puffed arms on the counter and showed him her gums.

"Could you direct me to the morgue?" Katz asked. He shook the water from his hair.

"The morgue? You must be Deputy Katz."

He frowned. Should he be associated with corpses?

"The doctor is working on your client," the heavy woman said. "We got your call and the ambulance picked him up. The doctor won't know anything yet. Why don't you come back in an hour?"

The hospital had a coffee shop. Katz ordered some tea to wash his mouth with and there was some banana pie. The pie wasn't bad. He leafed through magazines.

The operator waddled in. "The doctor is ready for you now. Would you care to follow me?"

Katz shuddered as he got up. The elevator took him down to a corridor still smelling of fresh paint. The morgue was a tiny room that the doctor seemed to consider palatial. "Deputy Katz," the pathologist, still a young man but with a shock of white hair, said precisely, as if he were memorizing the title and name for future use. "Look what we have here. Everything in tip-top order. Much better than what we're used to in the city. Am I glad I got this job—unspoiled country, lots of space, a cottage instead of an apartment that gets burglarized twice a week, a garden. My wife just planted it. Broccoli! Leeks!"

"Glad to have you with us," Katz said obediently.

There were steel plates covering the concrete block of the far wall. In an alcove was a cabinet of blue-grey metal and glass containing surgical gowns and basins. To the left stood a deep porcelain sink with a long hose and spray nozzle curled around the wide drain. The center of the morgue contained a cutting table, a long metal altar with a beveled surface and a gutter on the side. Finney's belly had been slit open, the incision spreading at the breastbone to create a flap of skin that stretched back over Finney's face. A scale hung by Finney's feet. Organs in labeled plastic bags were neatly corralled between the knees.

"Bit of a boozer," the doctor said. "Or, rather, a confirmed and terminal alcoholic, as we can see by the liver. This in here is the liver." He indicated a zip-locked bag filled with clear liquid in which swam a large purple object, yellow and brittle-looking at the edges.

"But was he drunk when he died?" Katz asked.

"No," the doctor said. "Yes, I can say that with some degree of certaintly. No, Deputy Katz, this man was not drunk during the last few hours of his miserable life. I would say he had one hell of a hangover, but that's something else."

"And the wound, doctor?"

"A bad wound." The doctor rubbed his chin. "He got hit with something. Instantaneous death."

"Maybe he hit something?" Katz tried. "I mean he hit *it* rather than *it* hit him?"

"Yes," the doctor said. "That's police talk. You men think differently. Yes, I see. Well, perhaps, yes—why not? Hit a tree?"

"Why a tree?" Katz asked. "Why not a rock?"

The doctor brought a pair of tweezers. "This here is no rock, Deputy Katz. This is definitely a splinter."

"Pine," Katz said.

"Pine, do you think? I don't know about trees yet. They're all green to me. In summer, that is—maybe not in winter. I'll find out in due time. I'm looking forward to some hiking."

"Any trace of rock in the wound, doctor?"

"No. Dust, yes, bit of dirt. I'll have it analyzed. I can mail it out today."

"Ah," Deputy Katz said. "Thank you, doctor."

Lichen-smothered rocks shouldering spruce trees marked the entrance to the property, and this time Katz turned the wheel softly so as not to spin the tires in the soft dirt road. He cut power and the engine quieted with a sigh. He let the Bronco coast down the incline and winced when it rattled heavily over a deep rut. Once within sight of the small farmhouse, he turned the wheel and softly applied the brakes by a tight cluster of firs. Katz got out and walked soundlessly to the sand by the foundation of the house. There was a line of laundry suitable for cover. He got behind it and worked his way along the wall.

Now.

He yelled and kicked the door, then jumped back into a crouch. He waited only a little over a second. Mildred was out, swinging her bat.

"Mildred?" Katz asked.

She whirled around and the bat came down. Katz deflected the weapon with his raised arm but the blow still stung. He grabbed the handle and wrenched it free. Mildred staggered back and whimpered. "Let's go in," Katz said.

Mildred backed to the rear wall.

"You always do that when you're bothered?" Katz asked. "Let them have it, huh?"

Mildred cried.

"It's all right," Katz said.

"It's not all right!" Mildred screamed. "He bugged me, like them damn crickets. I've thrown him out before. But he kept coming on that damn machine, making noise, wanting beer and what not. I got nothing to give away."

"Could have called us," Katz said. "That's what we're for, Mildred, to protect you. So you hit Finney. Then what happened?"

"Nothing," Mildred said. "He wasn't dead. He rode away."

"And bashed his head on a rock when his three-wheeler tipped over?"

"Right," Mildred said. "Right."

"Not right," Katz said. "Maybe you better come with me."

"Chains?" Mildred asked. "I don't want no chains."

"No chains," Katz said.

"Can't have no-good bums tearing around my place," Mildred said in the Bronco. "I'll tell the judge. He don't want no bums around his place, either."

"You tell the judge, Mildred," Katz said, "and I'll tell him, too. Don't worry now, you'll be all right in jail."

Sheriff Gagne rested behind his desk, dapper in his starched uniform, studying his trimmed fingernails. He could see himself in the glass of the bookcase. He touched his hair that had started greying at the temples. He thought that looked nice. Katz stood on the other side of the mahogany desk.

"So Mildred bashed the fellow," the sheriff said. "Amazing. I would think it was Levesque. A pretty rowdy lot, Finney and Levesque, bound to start bashing each other."

"Levesque is kind of kindly," Katz said. "Wouldn't kill a fly." He coughed. "Well, a cricket, anyway. Seems to like the little varmints. He says they keep him company. Mildred squashes bugs."

"So I heard." The sheriff blinked at Katz. The deputy was framed in the background of the office – thin rosewood paneling, certificates, pictures of goats from county fairs, and drapes. "Well, we've got some good charges against our suspect."

"Lonely," Katz said, "for one. And crazy. Lonely folk are often out of it a bit."

"Extenuating circumstances?" the sheriff asked. He got up and marched around his desk, stopped in front of a picture of a framed billy goat, and turned around. "Nah. First she bashes him dead, then she picks him up, then she slams him on his machine, then she starts the damned thing, gets it into gear, and aims it at the rocks. First-degree murder, Katz. We won't go easy on her."

"I'll go easy on her," Katz said, "and I made the arrest."

"Yes," the sheriff said curtly. "Back to work for now. The day isn't over yet."

Katz marched out of the office and Gagne snapped the report folder with his fingers to the rhythm of the step. He studied the billy-goat photograph, his scowl weakening into a grin. Crickets, he mused to the goat. No crickets here. Just a smart deputy who likes odd people. Why not? Someone should.

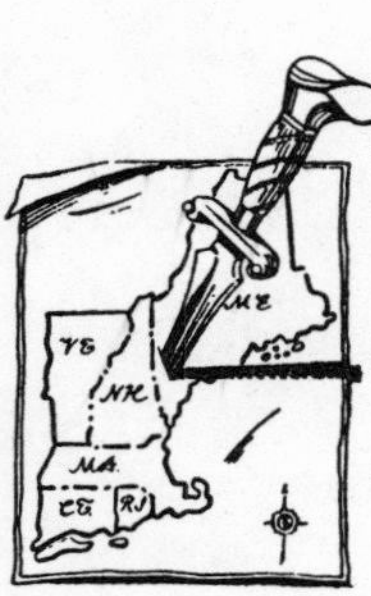

THE DAY THE CHILDREN VANISHED

by Hugh Pentecost

A highly prolific mystery writer, Hugh Pentecost is best known for such series characters as crusading artist John Jericho and hotel manager Pierre Chambrun. One of his less well-known series characters is really a series location: the town of Lakeview, a small New England spot never at a loss for mysterious goings-on. "The Day the Children Vanished" is thought by many to be not only the best of the Lakeview stories, but one of Pentecost's best stories, period. Certainly, the plot hook cannot be topped: the impossible disappearance of a station wagon full of children . . .

On a bright, clear winter's afternoon the nine children in the town of Clayton who traveled each day to the Regional School in Lakeview disappeared from the face of the earth, along with the bus in which they traveled and its driver, as completely as if they had been sucked up into outer space by some monstrous interplanetary vacuum cleaner.

Actually, in the time of hysteria which followed the disappearance, this theory was put forward by some distraught citizen of Clayton, and not a few people, completely stumped for an explanation, gave consideration to it.

There was, of course, nothing interplanetary or supernatural about the disappearance of nine children, one adult, and a special-bodied station wagon which was used as a school bus. It was the result of callous human villainy. But, because there was no possible explanation for it, it assumed all the aspects of black magic in the minds of tortured parents and a bewildered citizenry.

Clayton is seven miles from Lakeview. Clayton is a rapidly growing quarry town. Lakeview, considerably larger and with a long history of planning for growth, recently built a new school. It was agreed between the boards of education of the two towns that nine children living at the east end of Clayton should be sent to the Lakeview School where there was adequate space and teaching staff. It was to be just a temporary expedient.

Since there were only nine children, they did not send one of the big, forty-eight-passenger school buses to get them. A nine-passenger station wagon was acquired, properly painted and marked as a school bus, and Jerry Mahoney, a mechanic in the East Clayton Garage, was hired to make the two trips each day with the children.

Jerry Mahoney was well liked and respected. He had been a mechanic in the Air Force during his tour of duty in the armed services. He was a wizard with engines. He was engaged to be married to Elizabeth Deering, who worked in the Clayton Bank and was one of Clayton's choice picks. They were both nice people, responsible people.

The disappearance of the station wagon, the nine children, and Jerry Mahoney took place on a two-mile stretch of road where disappearance was impossible. It was called the "dugway," and it wound along the side of the lake. Heavy wire guard-rails protected the road from the lake for the full two miles. There was not a gap in it anywhere.

The ground on the other side of the road rose abruptly upward into thousands of acres of mountain woodlands, so thickly grown that not even a tractor could have made its way up any part of it except for a few yards of deserted road that led to an abandoned quarry. Even over this old road nothing could have passed without leaving a trail of torn brush and broken saplings.

At the Lakeview end of the dugway was a filling station owned by old Jake Nugent. On the afternoon of the disappearance the bus, with Jerry Mahoney at the wheel and his carload of kids laughing and shouting at each other, stopped at old man Nugent's. Jerry Mahoney had brought the old man a special delivery letter from the post office, thus saving the RFD driver from making a special trip. Jerry and old Jake exchanged greetings, the old man signed the receipt for his letter —which was from his son in Chicago asking for a loan of fifty dollars —and Jerry drove off into the dugway with his cargo of kids.

At the Clayton end of the dugway was Joe Gorman's Diner, and one of the children in Jerry's bus was Peter Gorman, Joe's son. The Diner was Jerry's first stop coming out of the dugway.

It was four thirty in the afternoon when Joe Gorman realized that the bus was nearly three-quarters of an hour late. Worried, he called the school in Lakeview and was told by Miss Bromfield, the principal, that the bus had left on schedule.

"He may have had a flat, or something," Miss Bromfield suggested.

This was one of seven calls Miss Bromfield was to get in the next half hour, all inquiring about the bus. Nine children; seven families.

Joe Gorman was the first to do anything about it seriously. He called Jake Nugent's filling station to ask about the bus, and old Jake told him it had gone through from his place on schedule. So something had happened to Jerry and his bus load of kids in the dugway. Joe got out his jeep and headed through the dugway toward Lakeview. He got all the way to Jake Nugent's without seeing the bus or passing anyone coming the other way.

Jake Nugent was a shrewd old gent, in complete possession of all his faculties. He didn't drink. When he said he had seen the bus—that it had stopped to deliver his letter—and that he had watched it drive off into the dugway, you had to believe it. Cold sweat broke out on Joe Gorman's face as he listened. The dugway had a tendency to be icy. He had noticed coming over that it hadn't been sanded. Joe hadn't been looking for a major tragedy. But if the bus had skidded, gone through the guard-rail . . .

He used Jake's phone to call the Dicklers in Clayton. The Dicklers' two children, Dorothy and Donald, were part of Jerry's load and they were the next stop after Joe's Diner. The Dicklers were already alarmed because their children hadn't come home.

Joe didn't offer any theories. He was scared, though. He called the trooper barracks in Lakeview and told them about the missing bus. They didn't take it too seriously, but said they'd send a man out.

Joe headed back for Clayton. This time his heart was a lump in his throat. He drove slowly, staring at every inch of the wire guard-rails. There was not a break anywhere, not a broken or bent post. The bus simply couldn't have skidded over the embankment into the lake without smashing through the wire guard-rail.

Joe Gorman felt better when he came out at his diner at the Clayton end. He felt better, but he felt dizzy. Five minutes later Trooper Teliski came whizzing through from Lakeview and stopped his car.

"What's the gag?" he asked Joe.

Joe tried to light a cigarette and his hands were shaking so badly he couldn't make it. Teliski snapped on his lighter and held it out. Joe dragged smoke deep into his lungs.

"Look," he said. "The bus started through the dugway at the regular time." He told about Jerry's stop at Nugent's. "It never came out this end."

A nerve twitched in Teliski's cheek. "The lake," he said.

Joe shook his head "I—I thought of that, right off. I just came through ahead of you—looking. Not a break in the guard-rail anywhere. Not a scratch. Not a bent post. The bus didn't go into the lake. I'll stake my life on that."

"Then what else?" Teliski asked. "It couldn't go up the mountain."

"I know," Joe said, and the two men stared at each other.

"It's some kind of a joke," Teliski said.

"What kind of a joke? It's no joke to me—or the Dicklers. I talked to them."

"Maybe they had permission to go to a special movie or something," Teliski said.

"Without notifying the parents? Miss Bromfield would have told me, anyway. I talked to her. Listen, Teliski. The bus went into the dugway and it didn't come out. It's not in the dugway now, and it didn't go into the lake."

Teliski was silent for a moment, and then he spoke with a solid attempt at common sense. "It didn't come out this end," he said. "We'll check back on that guard-rail, but let's say you're right. It didn't skid into the lake. It couldn't go up the mountain. So where does that leave us?"

"Going nuts!" Joe said.

"It leaves us with only one answer. The station wagon never went into the dugway."

Joe Gorman nodded. "That's logic," he said. "But why would Jake Nugent lie? Jerry's an hour and three-quarters late now. If he didn't go in the dugway, where is he? Where *could* he go? Why hasn't he telephoned if everything is okay?"

A car drove up and stopped. A man got out and came running toward them. It was Karl Dickler, father of two of the missing children. "Thank God you're here, Teliski. What's happened?"

"Some kind of a gag," Teliski said. "We can't figure it out. The bus never came through the dugway."

"But it did!" Karl Dickler said.

"It never came out this end," Joe Gorman said. "I was watching for Pete, naturally."

"But it did come through!" Dickler said. "I passed them myself on the way to Lakeview. They were about half a mile this way from Jake Nugent's. I saw them! I waved at my own kids!"

The three men stared at each other.

"It never came out this end," Joe Gorman said, in a choked voice.

Dickler swayed and reached out to the trooper to steady himself. "The lake!" he whispered.

But they were not in the lake. Joe Gorman's survey proved accurate; no broken wire, no bent post, not even a scratch . . .

It was nearly dark when the real search began. Troopers, the families of the children, the selectmen, the sheriff and twenty-five or thirty volunteer deputies, a hundred or more school friends of the missing children.

The lake was definitely out. Not only was the guard-rail intact, but the lake was frozen over with about an inch of ice. There wasn't a break in the smooth surface of the ice anywhere along the two miles of shore bordering the dugway.

Men and women and children swarmed through the woods on the other side of the road, knowing all the time it was useless. The road was called the "dugway" because it had been dug out of the side of the mountain. There was a gravel bank about seven feet high running almost unbrokenly along that side of the road. There was the one old abandoned trail leading to the quarry. It was clear, after walking the first ten yards of it, that no car had come that way. It couldn't.

A hundred phone calls were made to surrounding towns and villages. No one had seen the station wagon, the children, or Jerry Mahoney. The impossible had to be faced.

The bus had gone into the dugway and it hadn't come out. It hadn't skidded into the lake and it hadn't climbed the impenentrable brush of the mountain. It was just gone! Vanished into thin air!

Everyone was deeply concerned for and sympathetic with the Dicklers, and Joe Gorman, and the Williams, the Trents, the Ishams, the Nortons, and the Jennings, parents of the missing children. Nobody thought much about Jerry Mahoney's family, or his girl.

It wasn't reasonable, but as the evening wore on and not one speck of evidence was found or one acceptable theory advanced, people began to talk about Jerry Mahoney. He was the driver. The bus had to have been driven somewhere. It couldn't navigate without Jerry Mahoney at the wheel. Jerry was the only adult involved. However it had been worked—this disappearance—Jerry must have had a hand in it.

It didn't matter that, until an hour ago, Jerry had been respected, trusted, liked. Their children were gone and Jerry had taken them somewhere. Why? Ransom. They would all get ransom letters in the morning, they said. A mass kidnaping. Jerry had the kids somewhere. There weren't any rich kids in Clayton, so he was going to demand ransom from all seven families.

Thus Jerry Mahoney became a villain because there was no one else to suspect. Nobody stopped to think that Jerry's father and Jerry's girl might be as anxious about his absence as the others were about the missing children.

At nine thirty Sergeant Mason and Trooper Teliski of the State Police, George Peabody, the sheriff, and a dozen men of the community including Joe Gorman and Karl Dickler stormed into the living room of Jerry Mahoney's house where an old man with silvery white hair sat in an overstuffed armchair. Elizabeth Deering, Jerry's fiancée, was huddled on the floor beside him, her face buried on his knees, weeping.

The old man wore a rather sharply cut gray flannel suit, a bright scarlet vest with brass buttons, and a green necktie that must have been designed for a St. Patrick's Day parade. As he stroked the girl's blonde hair, the light from the lamp reflected glittering shafts from a square-cut diamond in a heavy gold setting he wore on his little finger. He looked up at Sergeant Mason and his small army of followers, and his blue eyes stopped twinkling as he saw the stern look on the Sergeant's face.

"All right, Pat," Sergeant Mason said. "What's Jerry done with those kids?" Pat Mahoney's pale-blue eyes met the Sergeant's stare steadily. Then crinkles of mirth appeared at the corners of his eyes and mouth.

"I'd like to ask you something before I try to answer that," Pat Mahoney said.

"Well?"

"Have you stopped beating your wife, Sergeant?" Pat Mahoney asked. His cackle of laughter was the only sound in the room . . .

There are those who are old enough to remember the days when Mahoney and Faye were listed about fourth on a bill of eight star acts all around the Keith-Orpheum vaudeville circuit. Pat Mahoney was an Irish comic with dancing feet, and Nora Faye—Mrs. Mahoney to you—could match him at dancing and had the soprano voice of an angel.

Like so many people in show business, Pat was a blusterer, a boaster, a name dropper, but with it all a solid professional who would practice for hours a day to perfect a new routine, never missed an entrance in forty years, and up to the day young Jerry was born in a cheap hotel in Grand Rapids, Michigan, had given away half what he earned to deadbeats and hopeless failures.

The diamond ring he wore today had been in and out of a hundred hock shops. It had been the basis of his and Nora's security for more years than he liked to remember.

If you were left alone with Pat for more than five minutes, he went back to the old days—to the people he had idolized, like Sophie Tucker, and Smith and Dale, and Williams and Wolfus, and Joe Jackson. He'd known them all, played on the same bills with them. "But," he would tell you, and a strange radiance would come into the pale-blue eyes, "the greatest of them all was Nora Faye—Mrs. Mahoney to you."

Once he was started on his Nora, there was no stopping Pat Mahoney. He told of her talents as a singer and dancer, but in the end it was a saga of endless patience, of kindness and understanding, of love for a fat-headed, vain little Irish comic, of tenderness as a mother, and finally of clear-eyed courage in the face of stark tragedy.

Mahoney and Faye had never played the Palace, the Broadway goal of all vaudevillians. Pat had worked on a dozen acts that would crack the ice and finally he'd made it.

"We'd come out in cowboy suits, all covered with jewels, and jeweled guns, and jeweled boots, and we'd do a little soft shoe routine, and then suddenly all the lights would go out and only the jewels would show—they were made special for that—and we'd go into a fast routine, pulling the guns, and twirling and juggling them, and the roof would fall in! Oh, we tried it out of town, and our agent finally got us the booking at the Palace we'd always dreamed of."

There'd be a long silence then, and Pat would take a gaudy handkerchief from his hip pocket and blow his nose with a kind of angry violence. "I can show you the costumes still. They're packed away in a trunk in the attic. Just the way we wore them—me and Nora—the last time we ever played. Atlantic City, it was. And she came off after the act with the cheers still ringing in our ears, and down she went on the floor of the dressing room, writhing in pain.

"Then she told me. It had been getting worse for months. She didn't want me to know. The doctor had told her straight out. She'd only a few months she could count on. She'd never said a word to me—working toward the Palace—knowing I'd dreamed of it. And only three weeks after that—she left us. Me and Jerry—she left us. We were standing by her bed when she left—and the last words she spoke were to Jerry. 'Take care of Pat,' she says to him. 'He'll be helpless without someone to take care of him.' And then she smiled at me, and all the years were in that smile."

And then, wherever he happened to be when he told the story, Pat Mahoney would wipe the back of his hand across his eyes and say, "If you'll excuse me, I think I'll be going home." . . .

Nobody laughed when Pat pulled the old courtroom wheeze on Sergeant Mason about "have you stopped beating your wife." Pat looked past the Sergeant at Trooper Teliski, and Joe Gorman, and Karl Dickler, and Mr. and Mrs. Jennings, whose two daughters were in the missing bus, and George Peabody, the fat, wheezing sheriff.

"The question I asked you, Sergeant," he said, "makes just as much sense as the one you asked me. You asked me what Nora's boy had done with those kids? There's no answer to that question. Do I hear you saying, 'I know what you must be feeling, Pat Mahoney, and you, Elizabeth Deering. And is there anything we can do for you in this hour of your terrible anxiety?' I don't hear you saying that, Sergeant."

"I'm sorry, Pat," Mason said. "Those kids are missing. Jerry had to take them somewhere."

"No!" Liz Deering cried. "You all know Jerry better than that!"

They didn't, it seemed, but they could be forgiven. You can't confront people with the inexplicable without frightening them and throwing them off balance. You can't endanger their children and expect a sane reaction. They muttered angrily, and old Pat saw the tortured faces of Joe Gorman and Karl Dickler and the swollen red eyes of Mrs. Jennings.

"Has he talked in any way queerly to you, Pat?" Mason asked. "Has he acted normal of late?"

"Nora's boy is the most normal boy you ever met," Pat Mahoney said. "You know that, Sergeant. Why, you've known him since he was a child."

Mrs. Jennings screamed out, "He'd protect his son. Naturally he'd protect his son. But he's stolen our children!"

"The Pied Piper rides again," Pat Mahoney said.

"Make him talk!" Mrs. Jennings cried, and the crowd around her muttered louder.

"When did you last see Jerry, Pat?"

"Breakfast," Pat said. "He has his lunch at Joe Gorman's Diner." The corner of his mouth twitched. "He should have been home for dinner long ago."

"Did he have a need for money?" Mason asked.

"Money? He was a man respected—until now—wasn't he? He was a man with a fine girl in love with him, wasn't he? What need would he have for money?"

"Make him answer sensibly!" Mrs. Jennings pleaded in a despairing voice.

Joe Gorman stepped forward. "Pat, maybe Jerry got sick all of a sudden. It's happened to men who saw action overseas. Maybe you saw signs of something and wouldn't want to tell of it. But my Pete was on that bus, and Karl's two, and Mrs. Jennings' two. We're nowhere, Pat—so if you can tell us anything! Our kids were on that bus!"

Pat Mahoney's eyes, as he listened to Joe Gorman, filled with pain. "My kid is on that bus, too, Joe," he said.

They all stared at him, some with hatred. And then, in the distance, they heard the wail of a siren. The troopers' car was coming from Lakeview, hell-bent.

"Maybe it's news!" someone shouted.

And they all went stumbling out of the house to meet the approaching car—all but Elizabeth Deering, who stayed behind, clinging to the old man.

"I don't understand it," she said, her voice shaken. "They think he's harmed their children, Pat! Why? Why would they think he'd do such a thing? Why?"

Old Pat's eyes had a faraway look in them. "Did I ever tell you about The Great Thurston?" he asked. "Greatest magic act I ever saw."

"Pat!" Elizabeth said, her eyes widening in horror.

"First time I ever caught his act was in Sioux City," Pat said. "He came out in a flowing cape, and a silk hat, and he . . ."

Dear God, he's losing his reason, Elizabeth Deering told herself. Let the news be good! Let them be found safe!

The police car with its wailing siren carried news, but it was not the sort the people of Clayton were hoping to hear.

It was reassuring to know that within a few hours of the tragedy the entire area was alerted, that the moment daylight came a fleet of army helicopters would cover the area for hundreds of miles around, that a five-state alarm was out for the missing station wagon and its passengers, and that the Attorney General had sent the best man on his staff to direct and coordinate the search.

Top officials, viewing the case coldly and untouched by the hysteria of personal involvement, had a theory. Of course there had to be a rational explanation of the disappearance of the bus, and Clyde Haviland, tall, stoop-shouldered, scholarly-looking investigator from the Attorney General's office, was ordered to produce that explanation as soon as possible upon his arrival in Clayton. But beyond that, officials had no doubt as to the reason for the disappearance: this was a mass kidnaping—something novel in the annals of crime.

Since none of the families involved had means, Haviland and his superiors were convinced the next move in this strange charade would be a demand on the community to pay ransom for the children. The F.B.I. was alerted to be ready to act the moment there was any indication of involvement across state lines.

While mothers wept and the menfolk grumbled angrily that Jerry Mahoney, the driver, was at the bottom of this, officialdom worked calmly and efficiently. The Air Force turned over its complete data on Technical Sergeant Jerry Mahoney to the F.B.I. Men who had known Jerry in the service were wakened from their sleep or pulled out of restaurants or theatres to be questioned. Had he ever said anything that would indicate he might move into a world of violence? Did his medical history contain any record of mental illness?

Sitting at a desk in the town hall, Clyde Haviland reported on some of this to George Peabody, the sheriff, the town's three selectmen, Sergeant Mason, and a couple of other troopers. Haviland, carefully polishing his shell-rimmed glasses, was a quiet, reassuring sort of man. He had a fine reputation in the state. He was not an unfamiliar figure to people in Clayton because he had solved a particularly brutal murder in the neighboring town of Johnsville, and his investigation had brought him in and out of Clayton for several weeks.

"So far," he said, with a faint smile, "The report on Jerry Mahoney is quite extraordinary."

"In what way?" Sergeant Mason asked, eager for the scent of blood.

"Model citizen," Haviland said. "No one has a bad word for him. No bad temper. Never held grudges. Never chiseled. Saves his money. His savings account in the Clayton bank would surprise some of you. On the face of it, he's the last person in the world to suspect."

"There has to be a first time for everything," Karl Dickler said. He was a selectman as well as one of the bereaved parents.

"It's going down toward zero tonight," George Peabody, the sheriff, said glumly. "If those kids are out anywhere—"

"They're one hell of a long way from here by now, if you ask me," Sergeant Mason said.

Haviland looked at him, his eyes unblinking behind the lenses of his glasses. "Except that they never came out of the dugway."

"Nobody saw them," Mason said. "But they're not there so they did come out."

"They didn't come out," Joe Gorman said. "I was watching for them from the window of my diner."

"There were the three seconds you were getting something out of the icebox in your pantry," Mason said.

"And I suppose everyone else along Main Street had his head in a closet at just that time!" Joe Gorman said.

"Or someone reached down out of the heavens and snatched that station wagon up into space," Haviland said. He was looking at Peabody's pudgy face as he spoke, and something he saw there made him add quickly, "I'm kidding, of course."

Peabody laughed nervously. "It's the only explanation we've had so far."

Karl Dickler put his hand up to his cheek. There was a nerve there that had started to twitch, regularly as the tick of a clock. "I like Jerry. I'd give you the same kind of report on him you've been getting, Mr. Haviland. But you can't pass up the facts. I'd have said he'd defend those kids with his life. But did he? And the old man–his father. He won't answer questions directly. There's something queer about him. Damn it, Mr. Haviland, my kids are–out there, somewhere!" He waved toward the frost-coated window panes.

"Every highway within two hundred miles of here is being patrolled, Mr. Dickler," Haviland said. "If they'd driven straight away from here in daylight–granting Mason is right and everybody was in a closet when the station wagon went through town–they'd have been seen a hundred times after they left Clayton. There isn't one report of anyone having seen the station wagon with the school-bus markings." Haviland paused to light a cigarette. His tapering fingers were nicotine-stained.

"If you'd ever investigated a crime, Mr. Dickler, you'd know we usually are swamped with calls from people who think they've seen the wanted man. A bus–a bus load of kids. Somebody *had* to see it! But there isn't even a crackpot report. If there was some place he could have stayed under cover–and don't tell me, I know there isn't–and started moving after dark, he might get some distance. But alarms are out everywhere. He couldn't travel five miles without being trapped."

"We've told ourselves all these things for hours!" Dickler said, pinching savagely at his twitching cheek. "What are you going to *do,* Haviland?"

"Unless we're all wrong," Haviland said, "we're going to hear from the kidnapers soon. Tonight–or maybe in the morning–by mail, or phone, or in some unexpected way. But we'll hear. They'll demand money. What other purpose can there be? Once we hear, we'll have to start to play it by ear. That's the way these cases are."

"Meanwhile you just sit here and wait!" Dickler said, a kind of despair rising in his voice. "What am I going to say to my wife?"

"I think all the parents of the children should go home. You may be the one the kidnapers contact. It may be your child they put on the phone to convince you the kids are safe," Haviland said. "As soon as it's daylight—"

"You think the kids *are* safe?" Dickler cried out.

Haviland stared at the distraught father for a minute. Then he spoke, gently. "What kind of assurance could I give you, Mr. Dickler? Even if I tried, you wouldn't believe me. People who play this kind of game are without feelings, not rational. When you fight them, you have to walk quietly. If you scare them, God knows what to expect. That's why I urge you all to go home and wait." He dropped his cigarette on the floor and heeled it out. "And pray," he said. . . .

Elizabeth Deering, Jerry Mahoney's girl, was sick with anxiety. Jerry was foremost in her mind; Jerry, missing with the children; Jerry, worse than that, suspected by his friends. But on top of that was old Pat Mahoney.

He hadn't made the slightest sense since the angry crowd had left his house. He had talked on endlessly about the old days in vaudeville. He seemed obsessed with the memory of the first time he had seen The Great Thurston in Sioux City. He remembered card tricks, and sawing the lady in half, and his wife Nora's childish delight in being completely bewildered. He seemed to remember everything he had seen the man do.

Elizabeth tried, but she could not bring Pat back to the present. The tragedy seemed to have tipped him right out of the world of reason. She was partly relieved when she heard firm steps on the front porch. The other part of her, when she saw Sergeant Mason and the tall stranger, was the fear that they had news—bad news about Jerry.

Mason was less aggressive than he had been on his first visit. He introduced Haviland and said they wanted to talk to Pat. Elizabeth took them back into the living room where old Pat still sat in the overstuffed armchair.

Mason introduced Haviland. "Mr. Haviland is a special investigator from the Attorney General's office, Pat."

Pat's eyes brightened. "Say, you're the fellow that solved that murder over in Johnsville, aren't you?" he said. "Smart piece of work."

"Thanks," Haviland said. He looked at Pat, astonished at his gaudyvest and tie and the glittering diamond on his finger. He had been prepared for Pat, but not adequately.

"Sit down," Pat said. "Maybe Liz would make us some coffee if we asked her pretty."

Mason nodded to Liz, who went out into the kitchen. He followed her to tell her there was no news. Haviland sat down on the couch next to Pat, stretched out his long legs, and offered Pat a cigarette.

"Don't smoke," Pat said. "never really liked anything but cigars. Nora hated the smell of 'em. So what was I to do? You go to vaudeville in the old days, Mr. Haviland?"

"When I was a kid," Haviland said, lighting a cigarette. "I never had the pleasure of seeing you, though, Mr. Mahoney."

"Call me Pat," Pat said. "Everyone does. I was nothing, Mr. Haviland. Just a third-rate song-and-dance man. But Nora—well, if you ever saw my Nora . . ."

Haviland waited for him to go on, but Pat seemed lost in his precious memories.

"You must be very worried about your son, Pat," he said.

For a fractional moment the mask of pleasant incompetence seemed to be stripped from Pat's face. "Wouldn't you be?" he asked, harshly. Then, almost instantly, the mask was fitted back into place, and old Pat gave his cackling laugh. "You got theories, Mr. Haviland? How're you going to handle this case?"

"I think," Haviland said conversationally, "that the children and your son have been kidnaped. I think we'll hear from the kidnapers soon. I think, in all probability, the whole town will be asked to get up a large ransom."

Pat nodded. "I'll chip in this diamond ring," he said. "It's got Jerry out of trouble more than once."

Haviland's eyes narrowed. "He's been in trouble before?"

"His main trouble was his Pop," Pat said. "Sometimes there wasn't enough to eat. But we could always raise eating money on this ring." He turned his bright, laughing eyes directly on Haviland. "You figured out how the bus disappeared?"

"No," Haviland said.

"Of course it doesn't really matter, does it?" Pat said.

"Well, if we knew—" Haviland said.

"It wouldn't really matter," Pat said. "It's what's going to happen now that matters."

"You mean the demand for money?"

"If that's what's going to happen," Pat said. The cackling laugh suddenly grated on Haviland's nerves. The old joker did know something!

"You have a different theory, Pat?" Haviland asked, keeping his exasperation out of his voice.

"You ever see The Great Thurston on the Keith-Orpheum circuit?" Pat asked.

"I'm afraid not," Haviland said.

"Greatest magic act I ever saw," Pat said. "Better than Houdini. Better than anyone. I first saw him in Sioux City—"

"About the case here, Pat," Haviland interrupted. "You have a theory?"

"I got no theory," Pat said. "But I know what's going to happen."

Haviland leaned forward. "What's going to happen?"

"One of two things," Pat said. "Everybody in this town is going to be looking. They're going to be looking for that station wagon in the lake, where they know it isn't, and they're going to be looking for it in the woods, where they know it isn't. That's one thing that may happen. The other thing is, they buy this theory of yours, Mr. Haviland—and it's a good theory, mind you—and they all stay home and wait to hear something. There's one same result from both things, isn't there?"

"Same result?"

"Sure. Nobody in Clayton goes to work. The quarries don't operate. The small businesses will shut down. People will be looking and people will be waiting . . ."

"So?"

"So what good will that do anyone?" Pat asked.

Haviland ground out his cigarette in an ashtray. "It won't do anyone any good. The quarry owners will lose some money. The small businesses will lose some."

"Not much point in it, is there?" Pat said, grinning.

Haviland rose. He'd had about enough. Mason and Elizabeth were coming back from the kitchen with coffee. "There isn't much point to anything you're saying, Mr. Mahoney."

Pat's eyes twinkled. "You said you never saw The Great Thurston, didn't you?"

"I never saw him," Haviland said.

"Well, we'll see. If they're supposed to stay home and wait, they'll stay home and wait. If they're supposed to be out searching, they'll be out searching. Ah, coffee! Smells real good. Pull up a chair, Sergeant. By the way, Mr. Haviland, I'll make you a bet," Pat said.

"I'm not a betting man," Haviland said.

"Oh, just a manner-of-speaking bet," Pat said. "I'll make you a bet that tomorrow morning they'll be out searching. I'll make you a bet that *even if you order them to stay home and wait,* they'll be out searching!"

"Look here, Pat, if you know something . . ."

A dreamy look came into Pat's eyes. "Nora was so taken with The Great Thurston that time in Sioux City I went around to see him afterwards. I thought maybe he'd show me how to do a few simple tricks. I pretended it was for Nora, but really I thought we might use 'em in our act. He wouldn't tell me anything—that is, not about any of his tricks. But he told me the whole principle of the business."

"Sugar?" Elizabeth asked Haviland. Poor old man, she thought.

"The principle is," Pat said, "to make your audience think only what you want them to think, and see only what you want them to see." Pat's eyes brightened. "Which reminds me, there's something I'd like to have you see, Mr. Haviland."

Haviland gulped his coffee. Somehow he felt mesmerized by the old man. Pat was at the foot of the stairs, beckoning. Haviland followed.

Elizabeth looked at Mason and there were tears in her eyes. "It's thrown him completely off base," she said. "You know what he's going to show Mr. Haviland?" Sergeant Mason shook his head.

"A cowboy suit!" Elizabeth said, and dropped down on the couch, crying softly. "He's going to show him a cowboy suit."

And she was right. Haviland found himself in the attic, his head bowed to keep from bumping into the sloping beams. Old Pat had opened a wardrobe trunk and with the gesture of a waiter taking the silver lid off a tomato surprise, revealed two cowboy suits, one hanging neatly on each side of the trunk—Nora's and his. Chaps, shirt, vest, boots, Stetsons, and gun belt—all studded with stage jewelry.

". . . and when the lights went out," Pat was saying, "all you could see was these gewgaws, sparkling. And we'd take out the guns . . ." And suddenly Pat had the two jeweled six-shooters in his hands, twirling and spinning them. "In the old days I could draw these guns and twirl 'em into position faster than Jesse James!"

The spell was broken for Haviland. The old guy was cuckoo. "I enjoyed seeing them, Mr. Mahoney," he said. "But now, I'm afraid I've got to get back . . ."

As soon as dawn broke, Haviland had Sergeant Mason and Sheriff George Peabody take him out to the scene of the disappearance. Everyone else was at home, waiting to hear from the kidnapers. It had been a terrible night for the whole town, a night filled with forebodings and dark imaginings. Haviland covered every inch of the two-mile stretch of the dugway. And he couldn't get away from the facts. There was no way for it to have happened—but it had happened.

About eight thirty he was back in Clayton in Joe's Diner, stamping his feet to warm them and waiting eagerly for eggs and toast to go with his steaming cup of black coffee. All the parents had been checked. There'd been no phone calls, no notes slipped under doors, nothing in the early-morning mail.

Haviland never got his breakfast. Trooper Teliski came charging into the diner just as Joe Gorman was taking the eggs off the grill. Teliski, a healthy young man, was white as parchment, and the words came out of him in a kind of choking sob. "We've found 'em," he said. "Or at least we know where they are. Helicopters spotted 'em. I just finished passing the word in town."

Joe Gorman dropped the plate of eggs on the floor behind the counter. Haviland spun around on his counter stool. Just looking at Teliski made the hair rise on the back of his neck.

"The old quarry off the dugway," Teliski said, and gulped for air. "No sign of the bus. It didn't drive up there. But the kids." Teliski steadied himself on the counter. "Schoolbooks," he said. "A couple of coats—lying on the edge of the quarry. And in the quarry—more of the same. A red beret belonging to one of the kids—"

"Peter!" Joe Gorman cried out.

Haviland headed for the door. The main street of Clayton was frightening to see. People were running out of houses, screaming at each other, heading crazily toward the dugway. Those who went for their cars scattered the people in front of them. There was no order—only blind panic.

Haviland stood on the curb outside the diner, ice in his veins. He looked down the street to where old Pat Mahoney lived, just in time to see a wildly weeping woman pick up a stone and throw it through the front window of Pat's house.

"Come on—what's the matter with you?" Teliski shouted from behind the wheel of the State Police car.

Haviland stood where he was, frozen, staring at the broken window of Pat Mahoney's house. The abandoned quarry, he knew, was sixty feet deep, full to within six feet of the top with icy water fed in by constantly bubbling springs.

A fire engine roared past. They were going to try to pump out the quarry. It would be like bailing out the Atlantic Ocean with a tea cup.

"Haviland!" Teliski called desperately.

Haviland still stared at Pat Mahoney's house. A cackling old voice rang in his ears. "I'll make you a bet, Mr. Haviland. I'll make you a bet that even if you order them to stay at home and wait, they'll be out searching."

Rage such as he had never known flooded the ice out of Haviland's veins. So Pat had known! The old codger had known *last night!*

Special Investigator Haviland had never witnessed anything like the scene at the quarry.

The old road, long since overgrown, which ran about two hundred yards in from the dugway to the quarry, had been trampled down as if by a herd of buffalo.

Within three-quarters of an hour of the news reaching town, it seemed as if everyone from Clayton and half the population of Lakeview had arrived at the quarry's edge.

One of the very first army helicopters, which had taken to the air at dawn, had spotted the clothes and books at the edge of the abandoned stone pit.

The pilot had dropped down close enough to identify the strange objects and radioed immediately to State Police. The stampede had followed.

Haviland was trained to be objective in the face of tragedy, but he found himself torn to pieces by what he saw. Women crowded forward, screaming, trying to examine the articles of clothing and the books. Maybe not all the children were in this icy grave. It was only the hope of desperation. No one really believed it. It seemed, as Trooper Teliski had said, to be the work of a maniac.

Haviland collected as many facts about the quarry as he could from a shaken Sheriff Peabody.

"Marble's always been Clayton's business," Peabody said. "Half the big buildings in New York have got their marble out of Clayton quarries. This was one of the first quarries opened up by the Clayton Marble Company nearly sixty years ago. When they started up new ones, this one was abandoned."

In spite of the cold, Peabody was sweating. He wiped the sleeve of his plaid hunting shirt across his face. "Sixty feet down, and sheer walls," he said. "They took the blocks out at ten-foot levels, so there is a little ledge about every ten feet going down. A kid couldn't climb out of it if it was empty."

Haviland glanced over at the fire engine which had started to pump water from the quarry. "Not much use in that," he said.

"The springs are feeding it faster than they can pump it out," Peabody said. "There's no use telling them. They got to feel they're doing something." The fat sheriff's mouth set in a grim slit. "Why would Jerry Mahoney do a thing like this? *Why?* I guess you can only say the old man is a little crazy, and the son has gone off his rocker, too."

"There are some things that don't fit," Haviland said. He noticed his own hands weren't steady as he lit a cigarette. The hysterical shrieking of one of the women near the edge of the quarry grated on his nerves. "Where is the station wagon?"

"He must have driven up here and—and done what he did to the kids," Peabody said. "Then he waited till after dark to make a getaway."

"But you searched this part of the woods before dark last night," Haviland said.

"We missed it somehow, that's all," Peabody said stubbornly.

"A nine-passenger station wagon is pretty hard to miss," Haviland said.

"So we missed it," Peabody said. "God only knows how, but we missed it." He shook his head. "I suppose the only thing that'll work here is grappling hooks. They're sending a crane over from one of the active quarries. Take an hour or more to get it here. Nobody'll leave here till the hooks have scraped the bottom of that place and they've brought up the kids."

Unless, Haviland thought to himself, the lynching spirit gets into them. He was thinking of an old man in a red vest and a green necktie and a diamond twinkling on his little finger. He was thinking of a broken window pane—and of the way he'd seen mobs act before in his time.

Someone gripped the sleeve of Haviland's coat and he looked down into the horror-struck face of Elizabeth Deering, Jerry Mahoney's girl.

"It's true, then," she whispered. She swayed on her feet, holding tight to Haviland for support.

"It's true they found some things belonging to the kids," he said. "That's all that's true at the moment, Miss Deering." He was a little astonished by his own words. He realized that, instinctively, he was not believing everything that he saw in front of him. "This whole area was searched last night before dark," he said. "No one found any schoolbooks or coats or berets then. No one saw the station wagon."

"What's the use of talking that way?" Peabody said. His eyes were narrowed, staring at Liz Deering. "I don't want to believe what I see either, Mr. Haviland. But I got to." The next words came out of the fat man with a bitterness that stung like a whiplash. "Maybe you're the only one in Clayton that's lucky, Liz. You found out he was a homicidal maniac in time—before you got married to him."

"Please, George!" the girl cried. "How can you believe—"

"What can anyone believe but that?" Peabody said, and turned away.

Liz Deering clung to Haviland, sobbing. The tall man stared over her head at the hundreds of people grouped around the quarry's edge. He was reminded of a mine disaster he had seen once in Pennsylvania: a whole town waiting at the head of the mine shaft for the dead to be brought to the surface.

"Let's get out of here," he said to Liz Deering, with sudden energy.

Clayton was a dead town. Stores were closed. Joe's Diner was closed. The railroad station agent was on the job, handling dozens of telegrams that were coming from friends and relatives of the parents of the missing children. The two girls in the telephone office, across the street from the bank, were at their posts.

Old Mr. Granger, a teller in the bank, and one of the stenographers were all of the bank staff that had stayed on the job. Old Mr. Granger was preparing the payroll for the Clayton Marble Company. He didn't know whether the truck from the company's offices with the two guards would show up for the money or not.

Nothing else was working on schedule today. Even the hotel down the street had closed. One or two salesmen had driven into town, heard the news, and gone off down the dugway toward the scene of the tragedy. A few very old people tottered in and out the front doors of houses, looking anxiously down Main Street toward the dugway. Even the clinic was closed. The town's doctors and nurses had all gone to the scene of the disaster.

Down the street a piece of newspaper had been taped over the hole in Pat Mahoney's front window. Pat Mahoney sat in the big overstuffed armchair in his living room. He rocked slowly back and forth, staring at an open scrapbook spread across his knees. A big black headline from a show-business paper was pasted across the top.

MAHONEY AND FAYE
BOFFO BUFFALO

Under it were pictures of Pat and Nora in their jeweled cowboy suits, their six-shooters drawn, pointing straight at the camera. There was a description of the act, the dance in the dark with only the jewels showing and the six-shooters spouting flame. "Most original number of its kind seen in years," a Buffalo critic had written. "The ever popular Mahoney and Faye have added something to their familiar routines that should please theater audiences from coast to coast. We are not surprised to hear that they have been booked into the Palace."

Pat closed the scrapbook and put it down on the floor beside him. From the inside pocket of his jacket he took a wallet. It bulged with papers and cards. He was an honorary Elk, honorary police chief of Wichita in 1927, a Friar, a Lamb.

Carefully protected by isinglass were some snapshots. They were faded now, but anyone could see they were pictures of Nora with little Jerry at various stages of his growth. There was Jerry at six months, Jerry at a year, Jerry at four years. And Nora, smiling gently at her son. The love seemed to shine right out of the pictures, Pat thought.

Pat replaced the pictures and put the wallet back in his pocket. He got up from his chair and moved toward the stairway. People who knew him would have been surprised. No one had ever seen Pat when his movements weren't brisk and youthful. He could still go into a tap routine at the drop of a hat, and he always gave the impression that he was on the verge of doing so. Now he moved slowly, almost painfully—a tired old man, with no need to hide it from anyone. There was no one to hide it from; Jerry was missing, Liz was gone.

He climbed to the second floor and turned to the attic door. He opened it, switched on the lights, and climbed up to the area under the eaves. There he opened the wardrobe trunk he'd shown to Haviland. From the left side he took out the cowboy outfit—the chaps, the boots, the vest and shirt and Stetson hat, and the gun belt with the two jeweled six-shooters. Slowly he carried them down to his bedroom on the second floor. There Pat Mahoney proceeded to get into costume.

He stood, at last, in front of the full-length mirror on the back of the bathroom door. The high-heeled boots made him a couple of inches taller than usual. The Stetson was set on his head at a rakish angle. The jeweled chaps and vest glittered in the sunlight from the window. Suddenly old Pat jumped into a flat-footed stance, and the guns were out of the holsters, spinning dizzily and then pointed straight at the mirror.

"Get 'em up, you lily-livered rats!" old Pat shouted. A bejeweled gunman stared back at him fiercely from the mirror.

Then, slowly, he turned away to a silver picture frame on his bureau. Nora, as a very young girl, looked out at him with her gentle smile.

"It'll be all right, honey," Pat said. "You'll see. It'll be another boffo, honey. Don't you worry about your boy. Don't you ever worry about him while I'm around."

It was a terrible day for Clayton, but Gertrude Naylor, the chief operator in the telephone office, said afterward that perhaps the worst moment for her was when she spotted old Pat Mahoney walking down the main street—right in the middle of the street—dressed in that crazy cowboy outfit. He walked slowly, looking from right to left, staying right on the white line that divided the street.

"I'd seen it a hundred times before in the movies," Gertrude Naylor said afterward. "A cowboy walking down the street of a deserted town, waiting for his enemy to appear—waiting for the moment to draw his guns. Old Pat's hands floated just above those crazy guns in his holster, and he kept rubbing the tips of his fingers against his thumb. I showed him to Millie, and we started to laugh, and then, somehow, it seemed about the most awful thing of all. Jerry Mahoney had murdered those kids and here was his old man, gone nutty as a fruitcake."

Old Mr. Granger, in the bank, had much the same reaction when the aged, bejeweled gun toter walked up to the teller's window.

"Good morning, Mr. Granger," Pat said, cheerfully.

"Good morning, Pat."

"You're not too busy this morning, I see," Pat said.

"N-no," Mr. Granger said. The killer's father—dressed up like a kid for the circus. He's ready for a padded cell, Mr. Granger thought.

"Since you're not so busy," Pat said, "I'd like to have a look at the detailed statement of my account for the last three months." As he spoke, he turned and leaned against the counter, staring out through the plate-glass bank window at the street. His hands stayed near the guns, and he kept rubbing his fingertips against the ball of his thumb.

"You get a statement each month, Pat," Mr. Granger said.

"Just the same, I'd like to see the detailed statement for the last three months," Pat said.

"I had to humor him, I thought," Mr. Granger said later. "So I went back in the vault to get his records out of the files. Well, I was just inside the vault door when he spoke again, in the most natural way, 'If I were you, Mr. Granger,' he said, 'I'd close that vault door, and I'd stay inside, and I'd set off all the alarms I could lay my hands on. You're about to be stuck up, Mr. Granger.'

"Well, I thought it was part of his craziness," Mr. Granger said, later. "I thought he meant *he* was going to stick up the bank. I thought that was why he'd got all dressed up in that cowboy outfit. Gone back to his childhood, I thought. I was scared, because I figured he was crazy. So I *did* close the vault door. And I *did* set off the alarm, only it didn't work. I didn't know then all the electric wires into the bank had been cut."

Gertrude and Millie, the telephone operators, had a box seat for the rest of it. They saw the black sedan draw up in front of the bank and they saw the four men in dark suits and hats get out of it and start up the steps of the bank. Two of them were carrying small suitcases and two of them were carrying guns.

Then suddenly the bank doors burst open and an ancient cowboy appeared, hands poised over his guns. He did a curious little jig step that brought him out in a solid square stance. The four men were so astonished at the sight of him they seemed to freeze.

"Stick 'em up, you lily-livered rats!" old Pat shouted. The guns were out of the holsters, twirling. Suddenly they belched flame, straight at the bandits.

The four men dived for safety, like men plunging off the deck of a sinking ship. One of them made the corner of the bank building. Two of them got to the safe side of the car. The fourth, trying to scramble back into the car, was caught in the line of fire.

"I shot over your heads that first time!" Pat shouted. "Move another inch and I'll blow you all to hell!" The guns twirled again and then suddenly aimed steadily at the exposed bandit. "All right, come forward and throw your guns down," Pat ordered.

The man in the direct line of fire obeyed at once. His gun bounced on the pavement a few feet from Pat and he raised his arms slowly. Pat inched his way toward the discarded gun.

The other men didn't move. And then Gertrude and Millie saw the one who had gotten around the corner of the bank slowly raise his gun and take deliberate aim at Pat. She and Millie both screamed, and it made old Pat jerk his head around. In that instant there was a roar of gunfire.

Old Pat went down, clutching at his shoulder. But so did the bandit who'd shot him and so did one of the men behind the car. Then Gertrude and Millie saw the tall figure of Mr. Haviland come around the corner of the hotel next door, a smoking gun in his hand. He must have spoken very quietly because Gertrude and Millie couldn't hear him, but whatever he said made the other bandits give up. Then they saw Liz Deering running across the street to where old Pat lay, blood dripping through the fingers that clutched at his shoulder.

Trooper Teliski's car went racing through the dugway at breakneck speed, siren shrieking. As he came to the turn-in to the old quarry, his tires screamed and he skidded in and up the ragged path, car bounding over stones, ripping through brush. Suddenly just ahead of him on the path loomed the crane from the new quarry, inching up the road on a caterpillar tractor. Trooper Teliski sprang out of his car and ran past the crane, shouting at the tractor driver.

"To hell with that!" Teliski shouted.

Stumbling and gasping for breath, he raced out into the clearing where hundreds of people waited in a grief-stricken silence for the grappling for bodies to begin.

"Everybody!" Teliski shouted. "Everybody! Listen!" He was half laughing, half strangling for breath. "Your kids aren't there! They're safe! They're all safe—the kids, Jerry Mahoney, everyone! They aren't here. They'll be home before you will! Your kids—" And then he fell forward on his face, sucking in the damp, loam-scented air.

Twenty minutes later Clayton was a madhouse. People running, people driving, people hanging onto the running boards of cars and clinging to bumpers. And in the middle of town, right opposite the bank, was a station wagon with a yellow school-bus sign on its roof, and children were spilling out of it, waving and shouting at their parents, who laughed and wept. And a handsome young Irishman with bright blue eyes was locked in a tight embrace with Elizabeth Deering.

Haviland's fingers shook slightly as he lit a cigarette. Not yet noon and he was on his second pack.

"You can't see him yet," he said to Jerry Mahoney. "The doctor's with him. In a few minutes."

"I still don't get it," Jerry said. "People thought *I* had harmed those kids?"

"You don't know what it's been like here," Liz Deering said, clinging tightly to his arm.

Jerry Mahoney turned and saw the newspaper taped over the broken front window, and his face hardened. "Try and tell me, plain and simple, about Pop," he said.

Haviland shook his head, smiling like a man still dazed. "Your Pop is an amazing man, Mr. Mahoney," he said. "His mind works in its own peculiar ways . . . The disappearance of the bus affected him differently from some others. He saw it as a magic trick, and he thought of it as a magic trick—or rather, as *part* of a magic trick. He said it to me and I wouldn't listen. He said it is a magician's job to get you to think what he wants you to think and see what he wants you to see. The disappearance of the children, the ghastly faking of their death in the quarry—it meant one thing to your Pop, Mr. Mahoney. Someone wanted all the people in Clayton to be out of town. Why?

"There was only one good reason that remarkable Pop of yours could think of. The quarry payroll. Nearly a hundred thousand dollars in cash, and not a soul in town to protect it. Everyone would be looking for the children, and all the bandits had to do was walk in the bank and take the money. No cops, no nothing to interfere with them."

"But why didn't Pop tell you his idea?" Jerry asked.

"You still don't know what it was like here, Mr. Mahoney," Haviland said. "People thought you had done something to those kids; they imagined your Pop knew something about it. If he'd told his story, even to me, I think I'd have thought he was either touched in the head or covering up. So he kept still—although he did throw me a couple of hints. And suddenly, he was, to all intents and purposes, alone in the town. So he went upstairs, got dressed in those cowboy clothes, and went, calm as you please, to the bank to meet the bandits he knew must be coming. And they came."

"But why the cowboy suit?" Liz Deering asked.

"A strange and wonderful mind," Haviland said. "He thought the sight of him would be screwy enough to throw the bandits off balance. He thought if he started blasting away with his guns they might panic. They almost did."

"What I don't understand," Liz said, "is how, when he fired straight at them, he never hit anybody!"

"Those were stage guns—prop guns," Jerry said. "They only fire blanks."

Haviland nodded. "He thought he could get them to drop their own guns and then he'd have a real weapon and have the drop on them. It almost worked. But the one man who'd ducked around the corner of the building got a clean shot at him. Fortunately, I arrived at exactly the same minute, and I had them from behind."

"But how did you happen to turn up?" Jerry asked.

"I couldn't get your father out of my mind," Haviland said. "He seemed to know what was going to happen. He said they'd be searching for the kids, whether I told them to wait at home or not. Suddenly I had to know why he'd said that."

"Thank God," Jerry said. "I gather you got them to tell you where we were?"

Haviland nodded. "I'm still not clear how it worked, Jerry."

"It was as simple as pie à la mode," Jerry said. "I was about a half mile into the dugway on the trip home with the kids. We'd just passed Karl Dickler headed the other way when a big trailer truck loomed up ahead of me on the road. It was stopped, and a couple of guys were standing around the tail end of it.

"Broken down, I thought. I pulled up. All of a sudden guns were pointed at me and the kids. They didn't talk much. They just said to do as I was told. They opened the back of the big truck and rolled out a ramp. Then I was ordered to drive the station wagon right up into the body of the truck. I might have tried to make a break for it except for the kids. I drove up into the truck, they closed up the rear end, and that was that. They drove off with us—right through the main street of town here!

"Not ten minutes later," Jerry went on, "they pulled into that big deserted barn on the Haskell place. We've been shut up there ever since. They were real decent to the kids—hot dogs, ice cream, soda.

"So we just waited there, not knowing why, but nobody hurt, and the kids not as scared as you might think," Jerry laughed. "Oh, we came out of the dugway all right—and right by everybody in town. But nobody saw us."

The doctor appeared in the doorway. "You can see him for a minute now, Jerry," he said. "I had to give him a pretty strong sedative. Dug the bullet out of his shoulder and it hurt a bit. He's sleepy—but he'll do better if he sees you, I think. Don't stay too long, though."

Jerry bounded up the stairs and into the bedroom where Pat Mahoney lay, his face very pale, his eyes half closed. Jerry knelt by the bed.

"Pop," he whispered. "You crazy old galoot!"

Pat opened his eyes. "You okay, Jerry?"

"Okay, Pop."

"And the kids?"

"Fine. Not a hair of their heads touched." Jerry reached out and covered Pat's hand with his. "Now look here, Two-Gun Mahoney . . ."

Pat grinned at him. "It was a boffo, Jerry. A real boffo."

"It sure was," Jerry said. He started to speak, but he saw that Pat was looking past him at the silver picture frame on the dresser.

"I told you it'd be all right, honey," Pat whispered. "I told you not to worry about your boy while I was around to take care of him." Then he grinned at Jerry, and his eyes closed and he was asleep.

Jerry tiptoed out of the room to find his own girl.

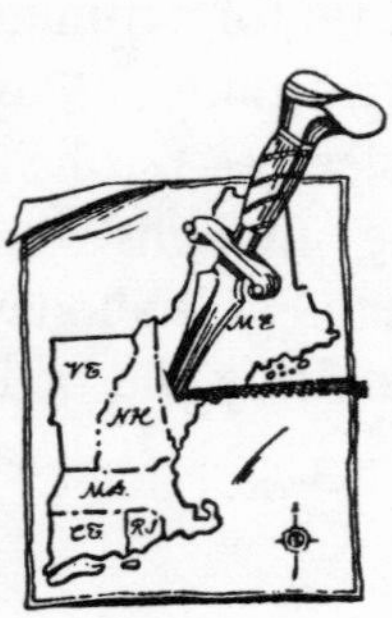

OLD KILLEEN'S PROMISE

by Thomas Walsh

Thomas Walsh received two Edgar Awards, one for Best Short Story and one for Best Novel (for the book on which the movie Union Station *was based). He is best known for his sensitive and realistic police procedurals, but he has also received praise for non-cop stories such as the following not-quite-realistic tale of just desserts.*

Henry Potter worked for forty-six years, the only job he ever had, as bookkeeper, and then in time as head bookkeeper, for the Bon Ton Department Store in his hometown of North Pequanset, New Hampshire. All that time he never received what could be called a princely salary, and on one or two occasions he might have bettered himself considerably. But he was New England born and bred, with a wary inward conviction that it was probably better to be safe than sorry, and only once did he broach the subject of leaving to old Mr. Killeen, whom he liked and respected very much, as old Mr. Killeen did Henry.

"Now, I'm sorry to hear that," old Mr. Killeen said, peering up at Henry over his spectacles. "Another offer, eh? Well, I don't know if you'd be doing the right thing or not. I've always thought of you as a very valued friend and employee, Henry. I've come to depend on you very much, and never once have you let me down. I have to admit to you right off that I can't match the offer you've got. As you know, business isn't too good at the moment. All I could do—how much more is it that these other people would offer you? $1500 a year, did you say?"

Henry had a long and Gothic New England face, and long and slender New England fingers. New the fingers clasped together the front of his worn alpaca coat, and he shifted an obviously distressed glance to the office window behind old Mr. Killeen. Henry never liked to push himself forward in any way, but for once his ingrained new England thriftiness—$1500 a year, after all—set up in him a certain stubborn determination.

"That's right, Mr. Killeen, sir. I'd hate to leave here too, but what I calc'late, in fairness to me and Abbie, is I just about have to. I'm very sorry, Mr. Killeen. A chance like this, though—"

"Sit down," old Mr. Killeen said, and removed his spectacles. "I think before you make any decision, you ought to look at this business all around, Henry. What about your pension benefits, for one thing? How old are you now?"

"Forty-seven," Henry said. "And you've always been very good to me, Mr. Killeen, sir. It isn't that. It's just—"

"Forty-seven," old Mr. Killeen said, stroking his white mustache thoughtfully. "Which means you have eighteen years to go before retirement, Henry. Now this isn't company policy, but when the time comes, and if you stay with us, I'd see to it that you went out of here on half pay. You'd better consider that, too. What would your pension be in this new job? In most cases, there has to be twenty-five or even thirty years' service before any retirement benefits at all are paid out. Checked on that part, have you?"

And Henry, who had not, found out the next day that old Mr. Killeen had known what he was talking about, and at home that night he went over the whole thing with his wife, Abbie, from start to finish. He had a dry and precise bookkeeper's mind, and drew up a balance sheet on the back page of Abbie's household-accounts book.

With the new people, receiving $1500 a year more, he would receive a total of $27,000 in eighteen years. Against that, no pension. With the Bon Ton, on the other hand, when he retired at sixty-five, and granted two or three small increases over the years, he would have an assured retirement income of about $4000, in addition to his Social Security.

"And we better calc'late," he told Abbie, "that the Potters are a mighty long-lived family, Mother. Look at Aunt Susan and Uncle Nathaniel, for instance. Both over eighty-five years old, and still sound as a dollar. No sensible reason why I shouldn't go along that far—and $4000 a year for twenty years makes a grand total of $80,000. Which means I'd do $53,000 better than with these other people, and our Social Security. So all in all, we could count on at least $8000 a year coming in, safe and secure."

"And without touching even a penny of our capital," Abbie marveled. She was New England also, and like Henry believed that anyone who spent as much as a dollar of capital was beyond the pale. "It seems too good to be true. Are you sure your figures are right?"

Henry rechecked even more carefully, while Abbie set out their usual bedtime treat of hot cocoa and homemade brownies. She was a slender, rather frail woman, with severe arthritis of the right hand and arm, and though she never complained about it, Henry knew only too well how she suffered.

"Yep, $8000 a year," he repeated, having finished the second go-round. "Right down there in black and white, Mother. Means we could live anywhere we wanted to live, even in Florida."

"Oh, Mr. Potter," Abbie breathed, that being invariably her one form of address for him. "Do you really mean it? Just think of sunshine every day of the year, and out own nice airy little place, and no more ice or snow or cold weather. Oh, Mr. Potter!"

At which Henry, with a rather audible sniff to show her how silly and emotional she was about Florida, nevertheless made up his mind. He had Abbie, anyway, if not much else in the world, and if she wanted Florida for them after all she had done for him in his life . . . Without saying a word to her he made up his mind then and there, and the next day he and old Mr. Killeen shook hands on it.

"I feel that you're doing the right thing," old Mr. Killeen encouraged him, "and I'm very glad to see that you are, Henry. Florida is going to be a grand place for you and Abbie. Just think of it. Nothing to do but sit around in the sun for the rest of your days, both of you. I'm very glad that we have it all settled. Half pay from us the day you turn sixty-five, Henry, and you have my word on it."

Which satisfied Henry, because in his whole life old Mr. Killeen's word had always been as good as his bond. It would be more sensible for anyone who knew him to question that the sun would come up again in the east than to doubt a promise made by old Mr. Killeen. So Henry stayed on at the Bon Ton, though thinking with a certain wistfulness now and again of all that extra $1500 a year would have meant to him. But in the end the Bon Ton would be the better choice, and after turning sixty-four he and Abbie began to spend many contented evenings around their little iron stove, examining pamphlets and descriptive folders from various Florida retirement communities. His last year at the Bon Ton seemed to go by in almost a flash, and every night he came home he could hear Abbie humming to herself "The Old Rugged Cross" or "Work, For the Night is Coming."

"How's the hand?" Henry would ask dourly. It would never do to let her think he was concerned about it. "Is it troubling you today, Mother?"

"Only a little," Abbie would say, which was her invariable answer to that question, also. "Dr. Barnes thinks it's mostly the climate we have up here. He says Florida should help me, the sunshine and all. Sometimes I can hardly wait, Mr. Potter. Just six months now. Oh, I know we're going to be so happy down there!"

"Now, now," Henry reproved. "No silly blather, Mother. Same as any place else, I reckon. Moderate your words. And we're not down there yet. Say nothing, and saw wood. We've six months to go still."

But Henry was very happy, too, particularly so as old Mr. Killeen reaffirmed the promise about the pension on what proved to be his deathbed. One day Henry went out to the house with some papers for Mr. Killeen to sign, and although he would never have had the bad manners to mention it under those circumstances, Mr. Killeen himself brought it up. Very worn now, very ill with a heart condition, he grasped Henry's hand in his thin shaking one, and spoke to young Mr. Killeen at the foot of the bed.

"Dear old Henry," he said. "Walter, I never knew a man I trusted more, or respected more. When do you retire, Henry?"

"In the fall," Henry told him. "The end of October, Mr. Killeen. Six months."

"Then don't think I've forgotten what I promised you," old Mr. Killeen said. "I want you and Abbie to enjoy Florida. You deserve it, Henry, and you're going to get it. I meant to talk to you about this before, Walter. Because if anything happens to me I want you to be sure that—"

"Now, Dad," young Mr. Killeen said. "None of that talk. You're going to be up and around in no time, so don't worry about Henry. There's no need."

"No need at all," Henry put in. "You've been very generous to me all my life, sir. Very good."

"As you've been to the Bon Ton," old Mr. Killeen said, gripping his hand feebly. "Thank you, Henry. And don't worry. I'll arrange everything with Walter here after my nap. Come back and see me next Monday. I'll have it all properly settled for you."

But he never woke up from the nap, and unfortunately young Mr. Killeen turned out to be a much different type of man from old

Mr. Killeen. After the funeral young Killeen went down to Boston for a week, and when he came back he brought along an elegant blonde secretary to replace Mrs. Bradford. She got twice the salary, as Henry discovered from the checks he sent out, and in her second week she charged a fur coat and a sports runabout to young Killeen's account. Henry tightened his lips at that, but loyalty to old Mr. Killeen kept him from telling anyone at all, even Abbie.

For himself, after the estate was probated, young Killeen sold off some of his father's utility stocks and bought himself a new Piper Cub, a $24,000 motorboat, and a ski chalet up around Mount Washington, where he began spending longer and longer weekends with Hazel Sampson, the new secretary. One day he rode up in the office elevator with Henry, but he failed to realize that he was not alone, even after Henry said good morning to him. He looked up blankly, as if at the wall, and then, humming to himself, adjusted his tie very carefully in the small mirror. So things were not in any respect as they had been with old Mr. Killeen, and Henry was very glad that his time at the Bon Ton was coming to an end very soon.

In late summer that year, having decided on their dream house, Henry and Abbie made a down payment on a small Florida home so that, come November, everything would be all ready for them. About that time, too, Henry, who was always very orderly and methodical in his habits, handed over the new Florida address to his brother-in-law, Russell Carpenter, the Bon Ton general manager. Russell, stout and jovial, had been a paratrooper in the Korean War, and Henry considered him, not quite approvingly, as a complete man of the world. Two or three times a month he had been observed going into one of the state liquor stores; he never really used up his automobiles, but traded them in every two years; and once a disreputable friend of his down in Boston, someone named Chips McGinty, whose life Russell had saved in Korea, had given him a tip on a horse race through which Russell had won $1300. He had wanted Henry to bet too, but Henry would not. He would as soon have agreed to spending his capital. Henry Potter a gambler?

"So it's off to Florida for you and Abbie, eh?" Russell asked cheerfully. "You're a sly old dog, Henry. Never thought you were that well fixed. But all the luck in the world to you. Hit a hundred down there, old boy, and let's hear from you once in a while."

"Oh, yes," Henry assured him. "Reckon a lot of people are a sight too careless about their mail, Russell. But every month, soon as you send me my pension check, I'll let you know that I got it safely. Only businesslike things to do. Then neither of us will have to worry about it."

"Your pension check?" Russell said, looking a bit startled at first, then uneasy. "You mean from the Bon Ton here? I don't know a thing about that, Henry. Perhaps you better go in and check it out this morning with young Mr. Killeen."

But the blonde secretary did not appear to know Henry, either, and was obviously much annoyed at having to interrupt buffing her nails.

"Some old man," she snapped into the intercom. "Parker or something. Want to see him, hon?"

And in old Mr. Killeen's office, which was all new and shiningly modernistic now, Walter was keenly absorbed in a copy of the *Wall Street Journal*, every inch the executive. He had also begun investing in stocks lately, and now put through at least eight or ten transactions a month, buy or sell.

"Yes?" he said, hardly glancing up from the paper. "What is it, Potter? What do you want?"

"It's about my pension," Henry told him, finding that he had to brace himself for some reason. "I just spoke to Russell about it, and he thought I should speak to you."

"Your what?" young Killeen said, running down another column of stocks, and then throwing the paper aside in some temper. "Look. We don't happen to be IBM around here, Potter. What are you talking about?"

Something jolted itself loose in Henry's chest, but the thought of Abbie flew through his mind, and it made him fight.

"I think you know," he declared a bit more loudly and tightly than he wanted to. "Years ago your father promised me that if I agreed to stay on here–"

"Agreed to stay on here?" young Killeen repeated as if incredulously. "Why, you damned silly old dodderer. I'd have got rid of you ten years ago. All Dad ever said that way was something about Florida. You know as well as I do that pensions to our employees was never company policy here. And now you come in to me and talk as if–Dad give you anything in writing?"

Suddenly the office seemed very small to Henry, suffocatingly small. It was necessary to grip the desk in order to steady himself.

"I thought that I had something better than writing," he said, his heart lurching a second time. "Your father's word, sir. Years ago, when I got an offer from those people over in Manchester, he told me that he couldn't match it, but that if I stayed here he'd see that I went out on half pay when the time came. A man like your father didn't have to put it in writing—but I expect you to honor his wishes, Mr. Killeen. I deserve it. I was promised it. And all these years I've been counting on it."

"Have you?" young Killeen said, getting up coolly. "Don't try the sympathy line on me, Potter. I won't go for it. I'm not a damned fool. Don't think you can maneuver me around the way you did Dad. He kept you on all these years because he felt sorry for you—and this is the way you try to repay him?"

Henry, long face bleakly set—oh, Abbie, Abbie—glanced numbly at him across the desk.

"No, no, no," young Killeen said, brushing it all aside with a great-man-of-affairs gesture. But then, it came to Henry, he was probably feeling the pinch a little. Hazel the secretary was quartered in the newest and most expensive highrise in town, while young Killeen's personal checks the last month, as Henry also knew from the bank statement, were running about $600 a week, even in North Pequanset. Very likely, it had become necessary to slow things down a little, and where better to start than Henry?

"So it won't work," young Killeen said, curling his lips openly. "You've either got something in writing, Potter, or else you haven't. If you have, show it to me. If you haven't, get out of here and stop wasting my time."

Henry, feeling a sudden rush of hot physical nausea, could only turn quickly, not to let young Killeen see any of that. But when he had closed the office door after him, he paused numbly for a minute or so, still holding the knob. Florida gone—and probably the deposit on the dream house also gone. All Abbie would have from now on were the bleak and everlasting New Hampshire winters, because there would be nothing for both of them but the monthly Social Security check. He rested his shoulders against the wall, felt a miserably helpless shiver go up his spine, and closed his eyes. How could he tell her? He had promised that he would give her the one thing she had ever asked from him, and now he could not. Oh, Mother!

Russell came along the hall.

"What's the matter?" he asked.

Henry rolled tormented gray eyes at him, and shook his head silently.

"Dirty rotten little cur," Russell gritted, glaring past Henry at the office door. "Don't bother telling me, Henry. I was afraid of this. Damn it to hell!"

"But it's not fair," Henry whispered distractedly. "It's not right. Old Mr. Killeen did promise me. Half pay, he said–when the time came. How can I explain it to Abbie, Russell?"

"Come on out to lunch," Russell said. "I'm going to buy you a drink, Henry. You look like you need one."

But even two unaccustomed martinis at lunch, altogether unique for Henry, failed to help. He told the whole story to Russell, who got a hard shiny glint in his eyes listening to it.

"Damned little welsher," he muttered. "But what can we do, Henry? He's living it up high, wide, and handsome–and the hell with the way you'll live."

"But how could he do it?" Henry whispered again. "Old Mr. Killeen told him that day. And still–it wouldn't even mean anything important to him. He's spending his capital, Russsell. Only last week he sold off some more utilities stock from his father's estate–$36,000. And he owes me that money. He owes it! The thing just isn't fair."

"The boy plunger of Wall Street," Russell sneered. "That's how he sees himself now. Buy and sell, buy and sell, because he thinks it makes him a big man–and losing his shirt every week. But I wouldn't tell Abbie just yet. Let me talk to him, Henry. It won't help, I suppose, but let me try, anyway. He does owe you that pension, by all that's fair, and the damn little cur knows it as well as we do."

But Russell could not help. Young Killeen dismissed him as curtly as he had dismissed Henry, and he had the law on his side. There was no written agreement–and so there would be no pension. Saturday afternoon Russell invited Henry to drive down to Boston with him, and broke the news. Then he glanced at Henry's averted face, and clenching and unclenching his hands, Russell compressed his lips. Later, after he had done his shopping in Boston, he took Henry to see Chips McGinty.

"Called that," he explained in the elevator, "because he was always in them, one way or another. Could bet you on cards, dice, or your own mother's maiden name—and always win. Used to be able to think up an angle on anything at all. Maybe he can on this too. Might as well ask."

"Eh?" Henry said, thoughts wandering wretchedly.

"Oh, nothing," Russell said, giving him a quick, sidewise look. Henry was about the most moral man he knew. "Talking to myself, I guess. Here's our floor, Henry."

And meeting with Chips McGinty was another new experience for Henry. Chips was a thin brisk man, very quick in movement, and snappily dressed. A wise, knowing grin marked his lips, even in repose, and he had a habit of giving you a nod and a wink, as though there was something understood and extremely confidential between you, with everything he said. He smoked cigarettes one after another, and addressed Henry from the first moment as Pal. A great many people trooped in and out of his office, and to Henry they all looked like extraordinary people.

There was a very stout man, referred to as Fat Joey, who spoke with an impressive Oxford accent, and wore a fur-trimmed impresario's overcoat. There was a wisp of a man, Spook, who sidled in, whispered hoarsely and mysteriously in Chip's ear, and sidled out again. Then there was another man to whom Chips tossed over three brand-new one-hundred-dollar bills as if they were so much waste paper, and when the man was putting away that money in his wallet Henry caught sight of what looked like a policeman's badge on the inner flap.

"So we're all set for Tuesday night now," Chips said, tipping him a wink this time. "You took care of the watchman?"

"No trouble," the policeman said, after studying Henry and Russell for a moment with guarded stolidity. "Dandy Donovan's first cousin, Chips. You got the truck ready?"

"Out in Dorchester," Chips nodded. "What do you figure we should ring up?"

"Somewhere around twenty big ones," the policeman said. "Guarantee it. All latest model sets, and all in color."

"Then drop by Wednesday morning," Chips said. "I'll hit you again if it works out that way."

The phone rang and rang, and once Chips went into a passionate rage with somebody about if-money, whatever that was. A tearful blonde girl, prettier even than Hazel Sampson, was advised to get in touch with Feeley the shyster, and after she left, the reception clerk ushered in a tiny and sad-faced old nun.

"Here's Drunken Flossie," he told Chips. "Wants to see you a minute."

"So how you making out?" Chips greeted her. "You do yourself any good at the ball game last night?"

"Could have," the nun said bitterly, lighting a cigarette for herself, pouring out half a glass of Chip's whiskey, and hiking her skirts up so high around the begging tray in her lap that Henry blushed and looked aside. "We win in the ninth, Chips, so everybody feels real good. I'd a made thirty, forty dollars, maybe, only that crud Jack O'Mara spots me over by Grandstand Admissions, and I had to get lost."

"Getting a lot of complaints about him," Chips sympathized. "Looks like I'll have to do something."

"I can tell you what I'd like to do," the nun said, and amazed Henry by declaring, in the bluntest possible terms, where Jack O'Mara ought to be kicked.

"Well, yeah," Chips said, "if he got any. He never learns, that guy. Okay, Flossie. I'll see if I can't have him put back pounding a beat again."

"Wish he was pounding a beat down in hell," the nun muttered, and again shocked Henry beyond words by adding something to the effect that Jack O'Mara was a divinely condemned, physically unclean, markedly malodorous descendant of unmarried parents. Henry had always been a bit wary of priests and brothers, but he would never have expected that kind of language even from a nun.

Then there was someone named Three-to-One O'Connor, who seemed furious as a mad hornet, all because he had met a friend of his last night and had invited the friend in for a drink at Pat Kehoe's place.

"Closing time," he said grimly, "so there he was totting up at the end of the bar. 'Evenin', Pat,' I says. 'The usual for me, I guess, and rye with a beer chaser for my friend, Mr. McCarthy.' He just keeps adding. 'Go back to wherever you got your load on tonight,' he tells me. 'I ain't serving you. You're both drunk already.' " Rage shook him. "The embarrassment of it," he said, appealing to Russell. "Inviting a friend to have a drink with me and gettin' that kind of treatment. I want his license suspended for thirty days, Chips. Who do I see?"

But at last they were left alone and Russell explained about Henry's pension.

"Yeah, yeah," Chips said, glancing at Henry. "Want this fellow chastised, do you? That it?"

"No, nothing like that," Russell put in hastily. "Thought maybe you could hit on an angle, Chips. Henry deserves that pension. He earned it, and he was promised it. But what can we do?"

"Tell you," Chips said, having heard enough, apparently. "When I got out of the service I did a job with old Louis Thatcher, who was the best front man you ever saw, next to Fat Joey. He knew this fellow in Wellesley Hills who had all the money in the world, but had never earned a nickel of it. So what we doped out, to kind of even things up a little–"

"Henry," Russell interrupted, "go down and check on the parking meter, will you? I can't remember whether I put in anything or not, and if I didn't, they might hook me for twenty-five dollars down here."

Which of course they would have, Henry told himself. City people for you. But the parking meter was still good for half an hour, and when he got back upstairs he could hear Russell laughing out in the hall. Inside, Chips had the tight grin on his face, and when he saw Henry, gave him the wink.

"But one thing," Russell said, as they were leaving. "Any time you open a bank account, Chips, they want your Social Security number. How do we get his?"

"Just write in using his name," Chips said. "Say that you lost yours, and ask for a duplicate. Nothing to it. They'll send one along in a couple of days. I keep half a dozen different ones at home myself, just in case. And if you have somebody right there to look over the mail before it's brought in to him, where's any problem?"

Russell gave Henry another quick glance.

"Then you'll get in touch with Fat Joey?" he asked.

"Owes me a favor," Chips said. "Let you hear, Russell. No trouble on this end. You just go back there and take care of yours the way I told you."

And as they drove back to North Pequanset, Russell had the same happy grin on his lips, and two or three times he laughed aloud. But Henry was quiet. Another four weeks now, no way out of it, and he would have to tell Abbie. His long fingers twined and twined, and it was small comfort when Russell again told him not to worry.

"Remember," he said, "that he can still change his mind. Maybe next time I'll catch him in a better mood, Henry. Let's hope."

But even when Henry's last month came, then his last week, things had not changed. Russell had always been a bit late getting into the office, and Henry was surprised when all of a sudden he became the first one in, and was personally checking over the mail when Henry arrived and before anyone else saw it. And he must have been keeping something secret from his wife, Prudence—another woman, Henry wondered uneasily—because several times he slipped letters out of the pile, and put them covertly into his pocket.

Then Henry's last day came, and young Killeen did not even bother to come and say goodbye. He and Hazel were getting married on Saturday, and then, everyone in the office knew, they were taking a two-week honeymoon trip to Hawaii. They left right after the ceremony, and a bit later Russell phoned Henry.

"Caught him just right," he exulted. "I guess he had more of his father in him than we thought, Henry. He agreed to let your pension go through, starting November first. Only he says he doesn't want it to go around the office or everybody else will be looking for the same thing. So it's been arranged with an insurance company, nice and quiet, and you'll get your $400 a month now as long as you live."

Henry felt a quick rush of tears to his eyes. It shamed him very much, and he could not even thank Russell.

"Is there anything wrong?" Abbie asked him, coming into the room as he was still standing by the phone and blowing his nose. "Who was that, Mr. Potter?"

"Russell," Henry said. "They want us to come over for dinner tonight, Mother. I think I'll bring along a bottle of wine."

"Well, our farewell to North Pequanset," Abbie conceded. "That's a very kind thought, Mr. Potter. First thing Monday morning now, you'll have to get in touch with the moving men. We don't have a worry in the world after that. It's just like a dream."

And a month later, down in Florida, Henry found that he did not have a worry in the world. His first pension check from the insurance company came through right on time, on a balmy and glorious Florida day, with Abbie as brisk and chipper again as a young girl, and lovingly waxing all the brand-new appliances they had. That night Henry took her to dinner in the best cafeteria around—the only one with both wall-to-wall carpeting and pine-scented air conditioning in all of south Florida—and afterward splurged on a very good quarter cigar.

Later they sat out on their screened porch, holding hands contentedly, and looking at all the brightly glowing Florida stars. It was only later on that Henry remembered the letter Russell had also sent on, and took it out of his coat pocket while Abbie was preparing the cocoa and cookies. It went:

"Dear Henry: All kinds of commotion up here. When our Walter got back from Hawaii with the blushing bride, it was discovered that some more of his utility stocks had been sold off for $58,000. The check was cashed at a bank down in Boston, but so far nobody has any idea as to who could have cashed it. Now we have all kinds of investigators on the job, but they're still running around in circles. They've been questioning everybody here down to old Mrs. Wiggins, the cleaning woman, but they haven't come up with a blessed thing, and I doubt if they ever will. So somebody did a job on our Walter all right, and it seems to have been done in this way.

"Walter P. Killeen might be a big name up in this neck of the woods, but of course down in Boston he's just another John Doe. Well, whoever did it opened a bank account down there last month under the name of Walter P. Killeen, and even showed a Social Security card in that name, which is all the identification a bank usually requires of anyone. After that the fellow made about fifty transactions a week, in and out, in and out, and every time he deposited a check it was perfectly good. Finally he had the account built up to $14,000, a pretty good amount of money, and then it appears he wrote in to the utility company—just a typed letter, with our Walter's usual scratch and scrawl at the bottom.

You know how he always loves to sign his letters the way Churchill or FDR did.

"What he said in the letter—and he even got hold of some Bon Ton stationery to write it on, however he did it—was that he had inadvertently burned up the stock certificates and wanted them replaced. Well, they naturally replaced them, only they must have been intercepted in the mail, because our Walter is screaming he never wrote such a letter. And never got the certificates. But it seems that the duplicate certificates were mailed to his broker in New York, right away, with instructions to sell at the market price, and of course, with the way he's been buying and selling ever since old Mr. Killeen died, the brokers did sell. Then they sent the check to Walter P. Killeen at the Bon Ton—and the Boston Walter P. Killeen walked into his bank that day and cashed it.

"Maybe they called New York first to see if it was good, but as soon as they found out that it was they couldn't do anything but hand over the money. And a week later—remember our Walter was in Hawaii all that time—the Boston WPK cleans out the rest of his account, telling them that he had a big deal going, and needed cash.

"But now, as I've told you, all hell's broken loose. Everybody's hiring lawyers, the bank, the stockbrokers, and our Walter—but I wouldn't be surprised if he finally gets stuck for the whole thing. The brokers argue they aren't responsible, because they got his letter on Bon Ton stationery ordering them to sell, and because they made out the check properly, and sent it on properly to Walter P. Killeen at his business address here, where they always sent his mail. And the bank says they aren't responsible, because he should have taken care of his Social Security card, and not let somebody else pass himself off as Walter P. Killeen by getting hold of it and using it as identification. Quite a mix-up, eh?

"And now a private detective agency has found out that Hazel's last good provider was a con man named Earl Harrington, and I guess they're trying to figure out whether our Walter was working a con game on the bank or the broker, or whether Earl and Hazel were working a con game on him. Hazel could have intercepted all the missing letters, of course, and I guess our Walter believes that she did. They have flaming fights every day now. Yesterday she hit him over the head with that big ashtray in his office, and he lost his voice screaming at her. Too bad you missed all the fun, old boy. It was really something!

"Saw our friend Chips McGinty last week—bought him and his sidekick Fat Joey a little present apiece for a certain favor they did—and they send along best wishes to you and Abbie. Enclosed is your pension policy, all legal and proper, which I had Chips arrange with one of the biggest insurance companies in Boston. So sit back and enjoy, enjoy, Henry. All blue skies for you and Abbie from now on. With much affection and respect to you both—Russ."

LIZZIE BORDEN IN THE P.M.

by Robert Henson

Robert Henson often blurs the lines between True Crime and crime fiction in his stories, such as the following tale, ostensibly a document of Lizzie Borden's sister's take on the famous killings. Mr. Henson received the prestigious O. Henry Prize for this story.

I read about her death in the local papers—it was news even here—"Lizzie Borden Again" for the last time, so to speak.

She entered the hospital under an assumed name. They knew who she was, of course, and she knew they knew. Pure Lizzie, the whole thing!

No other details—only a rehash of the murders and trial. I read just far enough to see if the dress was mentioned.

I wrote to Miss Jubb to say I'd heard. On the way home from the post office I fell and broke my hip. That same night, in the hospital, I dreamed Lizzie pushed me. I was lying on the sidewalk. "Why, Lizzie?"

She said what she had said thirty years before in Fall River jail: "You've given me away, Emma." Then she turned her face away, as she had done then, and said again: "Remember, Emma, I will never give in one inch—never!"

Well, Lizzie, you never did, I thought, waking. But neither did I, though for twelve years you kept after me.

I finally left her—moved clear away—first to Providence, then here. Miss Jubb sometimes smuggled in a bit of news—"After all, she is your sister!"—but I never saw her again.

I heard from her once, indirectly, when she threatened legal action to keep me from selling my share in the Borden Building. I knew she could have no sound business reasons, with mills closing and property values going down in Fall River. I sent word through my lawyer that I intended to proceed.

But then newspapers got wind of the suit. I made myself unavailable—Lizzie talked: Father had wanted the building to perpetuate his name—she could not conceive why I wanted to endanger family ownership—selling would be disloyal to his memory, etc.

I knew that holding onto a poor investment would be even more disloyal to Andrew J. Borden. However, I offered to sell my share to no one but her. I was even prepared to take a loss.

She refused: the building must be ours, not hers.

Ah, Lizzie, I thought, will you never give up?

Reporters became more numerous—the past began to exercise its fascination—I capitulated. I did not have her toleration for publicity. I knew how she would interpret my retreat, but I had never been able to prevent her misconstructions—I did not hope to now.

She dropped the suit but not all the reporters went away. A young man from the Providence *Journal* persisted. I could not evade him—my address had become too well known. Yet he was very courteous. He surprised me by asking through the screen door if the *Journal's* coverage of the trial was my reason for refusing to talk to him: "I've been reading our back files—I understand how you may feel . . ."

"No, that was before your time—I do not blame you."

"The *Journal,* I believe, was your father's favorite paper."

"Yes. Not that that helped when the time came."

"In one thing our coverage was like everyone else's—there was nothing but respect for you. Affection might be a better word," he said.

"I was not the consideration. Most papers—yours excepted—were also well disposed toward my sister."

"There was perhaps more admiration than affection for Miss Lizzie," he said, begging me not to be offended.

"Admiration for my sister is surely not something that could give offense," I said, "except perhaps to the *Journal.*"

"My erring employer!" he smiled.

I unlatched the screen. "Well, I will speak with you briefly if it will help you."

"At the time of her acquittal," he said, "it was predicted that the verdict wouldn't be acceptable to everyone—hasn't that proved true?"—"Yes, only too true."—"In all these years no one else has ever been arrested or accused or even suspected."—"Well, that is strange, but I do not blame Lizzie for that."—"It played no part in your decision to leave her?"—"I remained with her for twelve years!"—"You never had any reason yourself to find the verdict unacceptable?"—"My lips must remain sealed as to my precise reason for leaving—I remained with her," I heard myself saying, "until conditions became unbearable."

"Unbearable?"

"And now I deserve to be left in peace."

I paid for my indiscretion. Reporters again descended. For a second time I had to call upon Miss Jubb—"It will not die!" I said. She hurried over from Fall River and helped spirit me away. She is the only person who knows my present whereabouts.

She apologized for not coming in person to tell me about Lizzie's funeral. Poor soul! she's old as I am. But I understand what she meant: if she could just tell me she could make it seem less—Lizzie. As if I expected anything else!

She wrote that Lizzie had an operation about a year ago from which she never really recovered—in fact, she felt so strongly that she was going to die that she made plans for her own funeral and left them in a sealed envelope with Helen Leighton.

Miss Leighton was her latest close friend—a young woman—from Boston, not Fall River. According to Miss Jubb, people liked her but made fun of her a little after she took up with Lizzie. She became obsessed with the idea that Fall River had mistreated Lizzie, but would maintain in the same breath that Lizzie said and did nothing to influence her.

She faithfully carried out Lizzie's last wishes: the funeral to be held at home—someone to sing "My Ain Countree"—a select list of people to be invited. Miss Jubb was one.

When the mourners arrived there was no Lizzie—only Miss Leighton, pale as death. She had just learned that Lizzie had been buried the night before. Lizzie had left the undertaker instructions, too—and paid him well to keep them secret. She had not mentioned a funeral service to him. On the contrary, she specified that after the laying-out the coffin was to be closed, draped in black, and taken by night—it must be the same night—to Oak Grove cemetery. There it was to be lowered into the grave by Negroes—dressed in black. She specifically forbade any other attendants.

He had carried out her instructions to the letter, including the malicious timing.

Poor Miss Leighton! Most of the people on that select list came out of mere curiosity. She must have realized too late that Lizzie only wanted to spite them—and she would have to partly admit that they deserved it. I picture her standing in the parlor—she cannot quite condone Lizzie's action—cannot quite condemn it. People file past her in the awkward silence. She is just beginning to understand what was required of a friend to Lizzie Borden.

Lizzie did not exchange class rings with a friend when she graduated from high school. She gave hers to Father. We had just got home from the exercises. "I want you to wear it always."

Father was not sentimental but he was always solicitous of Lizzie's feelings. Perhaps he felt that she had been more disturbed by Mother's death than I was, though she was only two at the time, while I was twelve. And she was only four when he remarried—she found it natural to call Abby "Mother." I did not, and received permission to use her first name. A few years before the murders, we both changed to "Mrs. Borden."

Lizzie soon found that attempts to treat her as a mother only embarrassed and alarmed her. From the beginning, she could scarcely be prevailed upon to go out of the house or do anything in it except eat. She took to staying upstairs as much as possible—she would come down only for meals or between-meals foraging. Her weight, before many years passed, made even these descents laborious.

Lizzie turned back to me—she came to dislike Mrs. Borden intensely. I did not. I just could never grow fond of her—of her sloth, her physical grossness. I compared her to Mother and found her wanting. I did not, however, think of her as coming between Father and me. The older Lizzie grew, the more she behaved as if every token of affection for Mrs. Borden were stolen from her. She fought back.

Father said he would attach the ring to his watch chain. "No, you must wear it on your finger!"—he said it was too small—"Then wear it on your small finger!"—he started to put it on his right hand—"Not that hand, Father!" I remember how he hesitated—the least thing was liable to send her off into one of her peculiar spells—then, silently, he worked the ring onto the small finger of his left hand. It clashed unavoidably with his wedding band. Abby said never a word. I saw her a few minutes later groaning up the stairs with a mutton sandwich, a wedge of apple pie, and a pitcher of iced tea with half an inch of sugar boiling up from the bottom.

When Lizzie was excited her eyes seemed to grow larger and paler—color and expression would drain away—she would stare hard, but at something no one else could see. The effect was not pleasant, though reporters at the trial found it "incandescent," "hypnotizing," and so on—descriptions she cherished. No one found the mottling of her skin attractive. Even as a girl Lizzie did not blush in the usual sense—blood rising in her face would not blend with the pallor of her skin but fought an ugly battle all along her jaw and straggled out in her cheeks. Often when these signs of inner emotion were most evident her voice and manner would indicate total self-possession: "I have received Mr. Robinson's bill. Twenty-five thousand dollars. I will not pay it."

Noting the inner stress, I did not mention her new house on French Street nor any of the other extravagances that had followed her acquittal far more quickly than Mr. Robinson's fee.

"I thought he was my friend—he called me his little girl."

"He saved your life, Lizzie."

She stared. "I was innocent, was I not?"

"Mr. Robinson made the jury see it."

"You did not think it was self-evident?"

"It is not a matter of what I thought."

"Well, I won't pay it! I won't be robbed, I won't be blackmailed!"

"Blackmailed!"

"Don't you see the dilemma Mr. Robinson is trying to put me in? No innocent person would be charged such a fee. If I pay, it will be said that I bought an acquittal."

"And if you don't?"

"That I wasn't willing to pay for one."

I hardly knew where to begin. "Why would he create such a dilemma?"

"You can't guess?"

"No."

"Mr. Robinson doesn't believe me innocent," she said flatly. "This is his way of saying so. I will not pay it!"

Either then or later—for we went over and over every point—she said: "You look so downcast, Emma. If it will make you feel better, you may pay him."

"How could it make me feel better, unless you lacked the money?"

"True," she said. "And you've had enough expenses from the trial as it is."

"I? I have had no expenses."

"Yes," she said, staring hard, "it is common knowledge."

Either then or later, when I wearied of playing games, I asked bluntly: "Are you speaking of Bridget?"

"Yes—of the way she dressed at the trial—her ticket back to Ireland—the farm she bought there. She couldn't possibly have saved enough from the wages Father paid her."

"Servant-girls may believe she was bribed," I said sharply, "but no sensible person does."

"No sensible person believes that Bridget couldn't recall what dress I was wearing that morning, or whether I had changed from cotton to silk."

"If she remembered and chose not to tell, it was because she did not think the matter important. Her silence did not become an expense."

She opened her fan and looked at me over the edge. It was Mr. Robinson who persuaded her to carry a black fan during the trial. She had never used one before but so much attention was paid to it that she was never afterward without one. To my occasional annoyance: "Put that away. Coyness does not become either of us. I will tell you now that I made arrangements to help Bridget financially during the trial. She was, after all, unemployed for almost a year. She chose to spend the money on showy dresses—that was indiscreet, but I was not bribing her and therefore had no right to object. However it may have looked, my conscience was clear. When the trial was over she wanted to go home—that is natural—and Ireland is her home."

"It is all so easily explained, yet you have never explained it before."
"It was my own affair."
"Oh, Emma," she suddenly said in a tone of peculiar satisfaction, "you are not a good liar! You believe I changed from the cotton to the silk that morning! You believe Bridget lied when she said she couldn't remember!"
"Lizzie, Lizzie! if you say you wore the silk all morning, I believe you. If Bridget lied when she said she could not remember anything to the contrary, she lied upon her own motion. The money I gave her was not a bribe!"
"It was a reward."
"It was neither—it was a simple gift!"

She would not pay Mr. Robinson but I found her at work on a gift for Mr. Moody. I thought at first she was adding to her own scrapbook of clippings and memorabilia of the trial. Then I saw two police photographs mounted opposite each other—Father—half sliding off the couch—profile streaked with blood—Mrs. Borden—wedged between the bed and bureau—feet awkwardly splayed . . .
"Where—how—did you get these?"
"I asked for them. Oh, not for myself—" and she showed me the flyleaf: "For Mr. William Moody, as a memento of an interesting occasion."
"Lizzie, you cannot!"
"It's a duplicate of my own—except for those additions."
"Oh, Lizzie, at the very least this is not in good taste!" For some reason the remark made her laugh out loud. I persisted: "It is—inappropriate—it will seem that you are taunting him."
"Not at all," she replied, fetching string and wrapping paper. "Mr. Moody is a young man on the threshold of his career. Even though he lost this case, his connection with it cannot but help him. He will be grateful."
The assistant prosecuting attorney!

That time the house was broken into—in broad daylight—about a year before the murders—the police questioned and questioned Bridget. A little gold watch and some jewelry were missing from Mrs. Borden's dressing table. She discovered the theft when she returned from one of her rare outings, a drive with Father to Swansea. The rest of us had been home all day—none of us heard any suspicious noises. It was Lizzie who discovered how the thief got in: someone had left the cellar door unbolted—the lock had been picked with a nail—Lizzie pointed to it still hanging in the keyhole.

The police came back next day to question Bridget further. Maybe she had opened the cellar door for an accomplice . . . Lizzie had to be sent to her room—she could not stop talking and interfering. Father had already asked the police not to release news of the theft to the papers—now he asked them to drop the investigation altogether. "You will never catch the real thief . . ." The word "real" struck me as odd at the time, but I believe he was trying to let the police know that he had no suspicion at all of Bridget.

That night he locked and bolted the door between Lizzie's bedroom and the one he and Mrs. Borden used. It had never been locked before, it was never unlocked again.

I knew Lizzie would forgive Father anything—I braced myself for an attack on Mrs. Borden for that silent accusation. Instead she seemed to put the matter completely out of her mind.

But a few weeks later, while Alice Russell was paying a visit, Lizzie suddenly began a rambling account of the theft. Alice had not heard of it before—after a few questions she fell tactfully silent. Lizzie said Father had been right to call off the investigation. Robberies so bold yet limited in scope (nothing taken but what belonged to Mrs. Borden!) could seldom be solved. Even the police said so. All we could do was try to prevent a repetition—as she had done by putting a lock on her side of the door. If a thief came up the backstairs again, he would no longer be able to pass from Father's room into hers and so to the front of the house . . .

I heard this in startled silence. Later I checked. There indeed on Lizzie's side of the door was a shiny new lock.

Of the people who dropped away after the trial I missed Alice Russell most of all—she had been my best friend. Lizzie once made the astonishing suggestion that I exchange calls with her again.

"You know I cannot do that, Lizzie."

"Why not?—unless you have some quarrel I don't know about."

"We have not quarrelled, for we have not spoken since she testified against you."

She was toying with her fan. "She did not testify against me. She told what she saw. It could not hurt me."

I said wanly, "I wonder that you can put it out of your memory so easily."

"Well," she said negligently, "what did she have to tell except that she saw me tearing up an old dress? But you saw me, too—you knew the dress. When I told you I was going to burn it, you said, 'Yes, why don't you?' "

"In that," I said bitterly, "I had to contradict her."

"Is she angry about that? She can't be so petty!"

"I do not know how she feels."

"If she wanted her reputation for accuracy to go unchallenged, she shouldn't have waited three months before telling her story."

I could have wept. "Out of fondness for me, Lizzie! When she could bear it no longer she sent to beg my forgiveness!"

"Ah, now I understand a little better your desire not to see her again," Lizzie said on that note of satisfaction I was learning to dread. "She needn't have implicated you."

"She did not implicate me."

"Forced you to contradict her, then."

"You did that! I told about the dress-burning the way you remembered it."

She rose and walked about the room, opening and shutting her fan. "Why did you let me burn it, Emma, when you still believed I had changed?"

According to Alice I had tried—I had not said, "Why don't you?" but "I would not do that if I were you!" She was coming back from church—on Sunday after the murders on Thursday—I let her in the back door—followed her through the entry into the kitchen—Lizzie was standing between the stove and the coal closet—she had a blue dress in her hand—with brown stains on the skirt. I knew she had stained a blue dress with brown paint several months earlier—several times she had mentioned throwing it away. I also knew the police were looking for a blue dress with blood stains on it. I could have said either,

"I would not do that if I were you" or "Why don't you?" Either.

"Alice may resent my contradicting her testimony," I said, "but she would never misinterpret my reasons for doing so."

"Do you think that I do?"

I would not answer.

She was never satisfied if I said I did not remember, or had not been paying attention, or had lost my way in the technicalities, contradictions, details . . . Yet when Mr. Moody opened for the prosecution I remember thinking, So there it all is—so *that's* their side, just as if nine months had not gone by, with an inquest and preliminary investigation. Mr. Robinson could bring tears to my eyes but I could seldom apply what he was saying to the point at hand. Mr. Moody was mercilessly clear and orderly. Watching Lizzie during his presentation, I thought, Innocence alone can account for that detached expression.

Only when he came to the very end did her eyes and complexion show a change. The case against her, he said, had always had a weapon, a motive, and an opportunity. The real puzzle had been the absence of a blood-stained dress. He promised to clear up this mystery—the prosecution would present new testimony by a witness who had seen Lizzie burning a bloody garment!

I felt my blood turn to ice—Alice was going to testify. Lizzie opened her fan—shut it. In later years, sensational journalism had her swooning virtually every day. In fact she did so only once. Just as Mr. Moody finished and started for his table she fainted dead away.

Mr. Moody's triumph was short-lived. In the days following, so many rulings from the bench favored the defense that he was rumored to have urged the District Attorney to withdraw from the case—throw the responsibility for freeing Lizzie upon the Court. There was much ugly comment upon the fact that the presiding judge was one of Mr. Robinson's appointees when Mr. Robinson was governor of the state. The District Attorney, however, did not withdraw. Apparently he did not feel as strongly as Mr. Moody that the trial was a mockery of justice.

Still, it was not to him that Lizzie sent her "memento of an interesting occasion."

Eventually she paid Mr. Robinson but announced that her door would be closed to him. Not that he had ever made any attempt to call. Neither had Mr. Jennings, her other lawyer, our family lawyer. After we moved up on the hill, he simply dropped away.

The house seemed far too large to me, but Lizzie said she planned to entertain extensively and would need room. She was no longer content with one maid—she engaged a "staff"—a housekeeper, a second maid, a cook, a Negro coachman. What, I wondered silently, will I do with myself all day?

One afternoon I came back from shopping and found a workman carving the word "Maplecroft" on the front doorstep. I broke my silence.

"What is this?"—"The name I've given the house."—"What does it mean?"—"It doesn't mean anything, I simply like the sound of it."—"You are making a mistake."—"In what way?"—"Naming a house will be thought inappropriate, in bad taste."—"By whom?"—"Everyone, and especially those whom you would least like to think it."

"Dearest Emma," she said, "you can only mean yourself. And while I value your opinion, you're too close to me to realize that I can't be what I was before."

"No, you cannot. More is now expected."

"Well, that is my point," she said, and would discuss it no further.

But people who accuse Lizzie of "social climbing" because she bought the house on French Street do not understand that Father could have moved up on the hill at any time—he would only have been taking his place among his peers. But he was not concerned with external signs of his standing. Lizzie's hints and pleas fell on deaf ears.

It was the only thing he would not do for her—he sent her on the Grand Tour—paid dressmakers' bills without complaint—stretched her allowance with gifts of money . . . This generosity somewhat contradicted his basic nature but I never resented it. In such things as property and stocks he treated us equally, and he praised me where he could never have praised her—for wise management. He took both of us into his business confidence, however. I can recall only one time when he did not—and that was when he put a house in Mrs. Borden's name without telling us. We learned of it only by accident.

Lizzie was extraordinarily agitated: "She has persuaded him to go behind our backs! He would never have done this by himself!"

I agreed it was unlike him.

"What shall we do?"

I said we could do nothing except hope it would not happen again. That was not enough for Lizzie: "I shall let her know what I think of her!" She ceased to call her Mother. She went further—she would speak if they met but would not talk. Her silences were brooding—palpable—disquieting even to me. Mrs. Borden was clearly miserable, though her appetite was unaffected.

Father found a rental duplex and put it in our names. It was worth to each of us exactly what Mrs. Borden's house was worth. I was astounded by the crudeness of this attempt to atone for his secrecy and favoritism. Lizzie responded by refusing to take any more meals with him and Mrs. Borden. The house was heavy with tension.

He came to me for help. I had always had the room adjoining his and Mrs. Borden's. It was larger than Lizzie's, better furnished, and cheerier with two windows on the south. It fell to me when we first moved to Second Street only because I was the older. Now Father asked if I would exchange with Lizzie.

I said, "Yes, if you think it will raise her spirits."

But he would not directly admit his motive: "She has to go through your room to reach the hall closet. She shouldn't always be disturbing you."

True, eighteen or twenty of her dresses hung in the hall closet—her own would not hold them all. I said, "It is a considerate suggestion."

"I want you to offer it as your own," he said in his driest voice.

I thought for a moment. "She will not be deceived."

"Will you do it?"

"Well, I will say that the subject came up and that we agreed on the idea."

As I did. But he did not profit much from the exchange. Close on its heels came the daylight robbery. By then I was taking my meals with Lizzie and had ceased to call Mrs. Borden by her first name . . .

I had nothing to do the livelong day— I began to occupy myself at Central Congregational. Lizzie was scathing: "You've become a regular pew-warmer, Emma. You never were before. Why this sudden compulsion?"

"I am under no compulsion. I go freely."

"But you can't stay away freely, that's the point!"

I did not answer.

She leaned her cheek on her fan and gazed at me poignantly: "Perhaps Miss Jubb is your reason. If so, why not say it? I know you need someone besides me."

I ached to hold her in my arms at that moment, comfort her, as when she was a child and had no mother but Emma. I had never cultivated the people who rallied round her during her trouble—I did not feel neglected when they dropped away. She seethed as if from an injustice.

For ten months the people we now lived among but seldom saw had made her their special care. They extolled her in the press as a person of the highest character and most delicate sensibilities—charged that she was being sacrificed to inept police performance and indifferent law enforcement—called her a martyr to low-bred envy or political opportunism—the scapegoat periodically demanded by the moneyless and propertyless. Mrs. Holmes, Mrs. Brayton, Mrs. Almy, and their like kept her cell filled with fresh flowers. Only persons with influence obtained seats in the courtroom—and how many of them female! What a murmur of feminine admiration went up when she entered the first day in her dress of severest black but latest fashion—great leg-of-mutton sleeves—ruching of black lace—a black lace hat to set off the pallor of her face. And from one hand (the other lay on Reverend Buck's arm) drooped the quickly famous long black fan.

When the words "Not guilty" were at last pronounced these same admirers wept, fainted, sank to their knees in prayers of thanksgiving. Mrs. Holmes gave a splendid reception. All the people Lizzie had always admired were there to admire her. How could she escape the conclusion that she had done something for them?

We returned to Second Street next day. While we waited for the housekeeper to answer the bell, Lizzie kept glancing about. Only yesterday forty reporters or more were vying for her attention, people holding up children for her to kiss . . . Now the street was deserted.

We went in. I made a move toward the parlor but Lizzie walked straight ahead to the sitting room. She did not seem to notice the bare space along the wall—left by the couch where Father had been hacked to death. She was taking the pins out of her hat. "Do take another peek outside, Emma. Someone may be there."

I refused. "It is over," I said.

Gradually she saw that it was, though in more ways than the one

I meant. She did not ask why—she retaliated. Formerly she had been a mainstay of Central Congregational—now she said spitefully, "Let Mariana Holmes find someone else to cook and serve dinners for newsboys!"

Reverend Buck tried without much enthusiasm to reconcile her, then turned the task over to his assistant. Reverend Jubb was more solicitous, going so far as to bring his sister with him each time. But after two visits Lizzie refused to come downstairs. I was their only catch.

"Aren't you afraid someone will think you are trying to atone for something?" Lizzie asked with a disagreeable smile.

Her other guess, about Miss Jubb, was closer. If I helped with the Christmas dinner for newsboys or kept accounts for the Fruit-and-Flower Mission, the reason was Miss Jubb's friendship. That and the fact that I had nothing to do all day long—except think.

Their clothing lay in a heap in the cellar for three days, then the police gave me permission to bury it— behind the stable—with an officer watching. Then I scrubbed the blood off the doorjamb downstairs—the baseboard upstairs—thinking, So little here, so much on their clothes . . . Father's had spurted forward—only one splash hit the doorjamb by his head—the murderer might have entirely escaped being splattered. But he had straddled Mrs. Borden's body, they said, after felling her with the first blow—he could scarcely have avoided stains below the knees. Yet her blood shot forward, too—onto the baseboard—so possibly he could have walked along the street without attracting attention—once he got out of the house . . .

It was their clothing that was soaked—pools of blood had spread out on the floor. Lizzie's shoes and stockings were spotless—so was her blue silk dress. There had been no cries or sounds of struggle to alert her. Both had died with the very first blow, medical examiners said. The senseless hacking that followed was—just that.

I had been at the seashore. Alice met me at the station, all in tears. Lizzie was waiting at home, dry-eyed. I do not know why she sent for Alice instead of one of her own friends upon discovering Father's body. It was poor Alice who went upstairs and found Mrs. Borden.

In the carriage she said: "Lizzie came to see me last night—burst in, really. I felt quite concerned—she looked, well, distraught. She said she was depressed and wanted to talk to someone—she said she couldn't shake off the feeling that something terrible was going to happen—she felt as if she should sleep with her eyes open . . . Shall I mention all this, Emma?"

"It will come out."

I never asked, never hinted that Alice should either speak or be silent on any matter. She stayed with us the entire week following the murders. So much of what she told me before Lizzie was arrested is mixed up in my mind with what she told afterward in court. Was it when she met me at the station, or later, that she mentioned a bundle on the floor of my closet? Detectives had been searching for a murder weapon, she said, but they had been very considerate—they had not turned things completely upside down. In my room they had not even disturbed the bundled-up blanket in the closet . . . I could not think what she meant—I left no such bundle—I found none when I got home.

Mrs. Borden had received twenty blows, all from behind—Father ten. He had been taking a nap—one side of his face had been sliced away—the eye sliced in half. In the coffin, that side was pressed into the pillow. Lizzie bent down and kissed the upturned cheek. Her ring was still on his little finger.

Crowds lined the route to the cemetery. The hush was eerie. When Lizzie stepped out of the carriage at the gate it was possible to hear someone whisper, "She's not wearing black!"

It was like a portent of the future. I asked her if the printer had made an error when I saw "Lisbeth Borden" on her new calling cards. She had never been called anything but Lizzie.

"It's not an error. Lisbeth is my name now, and you must call me by it."—I cannot do that."—"You mean you will not."—"Is it a legal change?"—"You know it isn't."—"Then of what use is it?"—"Oh, *use!*"—"Very well, for what reason at all do you wish to take a different name?"

She was silent, then with a curious little smile she said, "I'll tell you—if you'll tell me why you've taken to wearing nothing but black."

"There is no mystery in that."

"Surely you're not still in mourning."

"Not mourning exactly. I have never cared much for clothes. You know that. These now seem appropriate."

"That is becoming your favorite word."

"I am a limited person."

"Then this is a permanent change in your dress?"

"I have not thought of it that way—it may be."

"Well, and I'm changing my name!"

"The two things are not the same."

"True—they aren't. You must take care that your black doesn't begin to look like penance," said Lisbeth of Maplecroft.

She purchased one of the first automobiles in Fall River. I had only Miss Jubb's description of it—"long, black, like the undertaker's limousine." The Negro who had been her coachman, or perhaps another, became her chauffeur. She could be seen every day going for a drive, looking neither left nor right but staring straight ahead. By then her ostracism was complete. All too appropriately had "Maplecroft" been carved on her doorstep by a man from the tombstone works.

I went to her coachman after the unpleasantness over the book and asked him bluntly if he had been a party to it. A certain journalist had compiled an account of the case from his daily reports, court transcripts, and so forth, and was giving it the sensational title *Fall River Tragedy.* It was supposed to clear up some "doubts" that Lizzie herself had stonily refused to clear up. Fall River was agog with anticipation—the outside world, too, it was said, though the printing was being done locally. Lizzie was several times observed entering and leaving the shop. It was assumed that she was threatening legal action. But on publication day the printer announced that Miss Borden had bought up the entire printing and had it carted away the night before.

"Did you help her?"—"She say I help her?"—"The printer said she came with some Negro assistants—he couldn't identify them."—"Miss Lisbeth know what she doin' if she get colored mens . . ."

I caught the note of admiration—it was Bridget all over again. "If she changed her dress you must tell Mr. Jennings," I said.

"Lizzie may be foolishly afraid that innocent stains will incriminate her," Mr. Jennings patiently explained. "But to a jury a perfectly clean dress may seem more suspicious."

"A silk dress, Bridget—heavy silk for house wear!—on the hottest day of the year!"

"If she changed from her cotton and don't want to tell, I daresay she has her reasons," Bridget said, addressing Mr. Jennings. " 'Twouldn't be foolishness—not her."

"A pool of blood had dripped from the sofa when she discovered her father," said Mr. Jennings, "yet not even her hem was stained. It might be *very* foolish to maintain that."

"I can't see how me backin' up her own statement can harm her," Bridget said stubbornly. "Besides, all I'm really sayin' is, I don't *remember* what she was wearin'."

Mr. Jennings was still not easy in his mind—he went to Lizzie and pleaded with her not to conceal anything that might damage her case later. He was explicit.

She retaliated by replacing him with Mr. Robinson—but blamed me for undermining his faith in her innocence. She was lying on a cot when the matron let me in after their interview. "You have given me away, Emma."—"I only told him what I thought he ought to know for your defense."—"Bridget's word wasn't enough?"—"Bridget did not say you hadn't changed, only that she could not remember."—"And you persuaded Mr. Jennings that that wasn't enough! Upon what grounds? Upon what grounds?"—"Upon grounds of common sense."

She turned her face to the wall: "I will never give in one inch—never!"

Nor did Bridget, though subjected to great pressure on the witness stand. Lizzie was wearing a blue dress but whether it was cotton or silk she did not remember. Her steadfastness deserved our gratitude, I thought, but as for bribing her, I might as well be accused of buying the coachman's silence! "Were the books destroyed?"—"Miss Lisbeth know best about that."—"Did any escape? were any saved back?" —"She know best about that."

After Alice testified that she saw Lizzie pulling a blue dress out of the coal closet that Sunday morning, Mr. Moody asked me if we usually kept our ragbag there. The question was excluded. I could easily have answered: no, we kept the ragbag in the pantry, for cleaning cloths and such. Lizzie probably got the dress out and tossed it into the coal closet, next to the stove, while she made a fire. Mr. Moody asked why Lizzie was burning the dress at all if we kept a ragbag. Excluded. I could have said: well, we didn't save every scrap! He asked if Lizzie usually disposed of old clothes by burning them in sweltering August heat. Excluded.

When I saw her there by the stove I didn't really think of *how* she was disposing of the dress, only of the fact that she was *doing* it, and that it might look suspicious. I might very well have said, "I wouldn't do that if I were you!" And yet I knew she had a blue cotton dress she had been planning to throw away. She was holding the dress so that the paint-stains didn't show, but it was the same one.

For all I knew it had been in the ragbag for weeks! I could just as easily have said, "Yes, why don't you?"

Under siege, as it were, we pulled the blinds and spoke to no one but each other.

"Where are the books? Have they been destroyed?"

"You needn't worry. I paid well."

"It was the worst thing you could have done!"

"Yes—to the hypocritical."

"How could the book have hurt you? It could only show your innocence."

"Oh," she said with an ugly smile, "people are no longer interested in that—if they ever were."

"Then this latest act will give them comfort."

"This *latest* act!" she mocked.

"Why do you torture yourself?"

"Why have you stopped sitting on the porch in the evening?"

I did not answer. She recited coldly:

"Lizzie Borden took an axe,
Gave her mother forty whacks,
When she saw what she had done
She gave her father forty-one."

I shuddered. "You have heard the singing from the shrubbery," she said with her peculiar relish. "You have heard the taunts."

"Urchins—from under the hill."

"All the hill listens."

"What has this to do with the book!" I cried.

Her eyes had gone pale. "The book—why, if they want that, they must come to me."—"You saved copies then?"—"They must admit they are fascinated . . ."

Over and over every point! Twelve years of it! What she would not tolerate from outsiders, she required of me: "Do you think Father really planned to give Swansea to her?"

"I do not know."

"He knew how much it meant to us—all the summers we spent there, from childhood on—until she came along and spoiled it."

"I should be surprised if he made the same mistake twice. He had already seen the consequences of one such secret transaction."

"If you *had* known, though, or even suspected, you'd have told me, wouldn't you? You wouldn't let me learn by accident?"

I would not answer. About two weeks before the murders I had heard some such rumor, but I was preparing to leave for the seaside and had no desire to upset her with anything so vague.

Either then or later (for she could not be satisfied) she said: "Suppose I had discovered such a plot—overheard them discussing it, say—if I had come to you, what would you have done?"

"Done?"

"Or suggested."

"I would have said what I said before: we can do nothing."

"Nothing—" she echoed restlessly.

"I mean, we could not undo Father's decision."

"We could have shown our displeasure again—more strongly! We could have moved away, left them—left *her,* with her everlasting gorging and grasping!"

"I had no wish to leave Father."

"He had driven the wedge."

"I did not blame him. He could not have foreseen her unsuitability."

"But dwelling with such an impasse! Surely there were times when you felt you could bear it no longer!"

"I was more content then than I am now."

Yes, I said to the young man from the *Journal,* the lack of motive is puzzling, but no one who really knew Lizzie would believe that money or property could be *her* motive if she were guilty. She was not acquisitive—that is a vulgar error.

How well I remember Mr. Moody's question after he had listened to an explanation of her break with Mrs. Borden.

"A house put in her name? Is that all? There was no more to it than that?"

Even he detected that property was insufficient as an explanation . . .

Perhaps it was unjust that a kind of obsession with Lizzie grew up right alongside the isolation of her. Perhaps she could not have prevented it. But from the day of her acquittal she adamantly refused to reassure her admirers. Questions they had been willing to suspend during her ordeal they must be willing to suspend forever. Of that, at least, she left them in no doubt. Not that anyone ever challenged her directly, she said irritably.

"Well, they are friends, not lawyers. They are waiting until you are ready."

"Ready? I should like to know one topic upon which you think I ought to set their minds at rest."

I had one on the tip of my tongue but suppressed it: "No, that is for you to decide."

And so the questions remained. "Where was your sister during the murders?" Thirty years later! The very question I had bitten back! The first one I asked when I returned from the seaside!

"Her whereabouts were established at the trial," I said to the reporter. I could still see Mr. Moody exhibiting his plan of the house and yard. The front door was locked—the intruder had to come in the back—pass to the front—go upstairs to kill Mrs. Borden—come down to kill Father—escape out the back again—all without being seen or heard by either Lizzie or Bridget. And between the two deaths, an hour and a half gone by . . .

He traced Bridget's movements with a pointer: working outside when Mrs. Borden died—taking a nap in her room in the garret when Father died. But where was Lizzie when Mrs. Borden died? Ironing in the kitchen? How did the murderer manage to slip past her? Somewhere else on the ground floor? How did he muffle the crash of a two-hundred-pound body overhead? Why did she hear no cries, no sounds of struggle? Where did the murderer hide during that hour and a half before Father came home and lay down for a nap? And where was

Lizzie when the second hacking to death took place? I could still hear Mr. Moody's relentless mockery of the defense: "Eating a pear—in the loft of the barn!—where she had gone to find a piece of screen-wire!—in a heavy silk dress!—in one-hundred-degree heat!"

"There were contradictions at the trial," said the reporter. "I mean, did she ever explain to *your* satisfaction where she was?"

"My satisfaction was not the question."

The dress was immaculate when the police arrived. No blood on the hem, no dust from the loft . . .

She had a telephone installed at "Maplecroft." It was of little use to her and proved a trap to me. She had begun to take short trips out of town, staying for a day, sometimes overnight, in Boston or Providence . . . On these occasions I would sometimes ring up Miss Jubb and invite her to bring her work over. One day while we were cozily occupied in my room, crocheting doilies for a church bazaar, Lizzie returned unexpectedly from Providence. I heard her speaking to the maid. I rose without haste and went to the head of the stairs. She had already started up. I remember her fur cape and her hat with the iridescent birds-wings. Her muff, oddly enough, was stuffed into her reticule.

"Miss Jubb is here, Lizzie," I said firmly. "Won't you come say hello?"

She brushed past me—she seemed distracted, breathless: "In a moment . . ."

"She is taking off her things," I told Miss Jubb, but my face betrayed me. She started to put away her work: "Perhaps she does not feel well . . ."

At that moment Lizzie swept into the room—color high—eyes luminous—both hands extended.

"Dear Miss Jubb, how very nice to see you! I've been hoping you'd call!" For the next five minutes she chattered torrentially. Miss Jubb sent me so many gratified glances that I was forced to bend my eyes upon my crocheting. "You came back early. Did you finish all your shopping?"

"Oh, yes—or rather, no. After Tilden's I let the rest go."

"Tilden's have such lovely things," sighed Miss Jubb, who could not afford any of them.

"Shall I show you what I bought there?" cried Lizzie. She hurried out and returned with two porcelain paintings. One was called "Love's

Dream," the other "Love's Awakening." Miss Jubb went into raptures over them. Lizzie said effusively: "I meant them for my wall but now I have a different plan. One will be yours, the other Emma's, as a reminder to you of your friendship. You shall not refuse me!"

Miss Jubb burst into tears. For some time she had been hinting that I kept her away from Lizzie unnecessarily. I was unpleasantly reminded of other times when Lizzie pressed gifts on people, but reproaching myself, I said that if Miss Jubb would accept her porcelain, I would accept mine. Blushing, she chose "Love's Dream" as more appropriate for herself. Lizzie laughed heartily: "Well, Emma, appropriate or not, that leaves 'Love's Awakening' to you!"

Not that it mattered. Miss Jubb broke hers while fastening it to the wall. Too embarassed to say anything, even to me, she made a trip to Providence to have it repaired. At Tilden's the manager was summoned. When had she purchased the painting? "It was a gift." From whom? "Why, Lizzie Borden . . ." Then she learned that the two porcelains had disappeared, unpaid-for, on the day of Lizzie's shopping trip.

Fall River woke to the headline "Lizzie Borden Again!"

Tilden's sent a detective with a warrant. Lizzie talked agitatedly with him, then came upstairs to me and said—so great was her confusion—"We must call Mr. Jennings right away!"

"An attorney is not necessary," I said. "Tilden's will not prosecute you if you go talk the matter over with them. You have been a good customer for many years."

"They have no grounds!" she began, then broke off. In a moment she said, "Well, then, I shall go to Providence. I couldn't have taken the paintings without paying for them, but who will believe me?"

"Are you certain you have no receipt?"

"Yes. I seldom pay cash at Tilden's—I forgot all about a receipt."

"The clerk will have a record, a duplicate."

"No," she said, staring, "if anything it was the clerk who perpetrated this fraud—by slipping the paintings into my reticule."

"But Lizzie, you remember paying for them!"

"I mean, he slipped them in to make me overlook the receipt."

He slipped them inside your muff, I thought, suddenly weary of trying to believe her.

Her jaw had mottled slightly: "And Miss Jubb played right into his hands."

"Miss Jubb is not to blame," I said angrily. "Miss Jubb has been greatly mortified!"

"I'm only saying that she gave the clerk his chance to raise a hue-and-cry against me."

"He would have done that the first day," I said with a cruelty I could not control, "if all he wanted was to have his name linked with that of Lizzie Borden."

She fell silent for a moment. "You're not coming with me, then? I must settle with Tilden's alone?"

"The purchase was yours alone."

"When I come back," she said, "the paintings will still be yours and Miss Jubb's."

As soon as she left the house I found a hammer—I broke "Love's Awakening" to bits.

In the spring before that terrible August, Father went out to the stable with a hatchet. Lizzie's pigeons had been attracting michievous boys. Tools—feed—pieces of harness had been disappearing. To discourage marauders, Father beheaded the pigeons.

I began to think of leaving her.

The nurse asked today if there was anyone I wanted to get in touch with—just for company, she said, now that the doctor has decided I must not leave the hospital—"not for a while."

I said there was no one but asked to see the doctor as soon as he was free. I knew what her question really meant.

And yet I procrastinated—for I knew that if I ever left Fall River I would not come back. Lizzie could not stay away. Her trips became more frequent, more prolonged—not only Boston and Providence but New York—Philadelphia—Washington. But after a week, or two weeks, or a month away, she would return—Lizzie Borden would be seen again in Fall River.

Playbills showed how she occupied herself when her shopping was done. She did not discuss this new interest with me—I learned about her friendship with Nance O'Neil from the newspaper—inexorably "Lizzie Borden Again" arrived.

A lawsuit against Miss O'Neil would have been news in any case, a popular actress sued by her manager to recover advances and loans. But add that Lizzie Borden appeared every day in court as her champion—that Lizzie Borden hired the lawyer who was defending her—that Lizzie Borden had given her the little gold watch that was pinned to her bosom!

She came home during a recess in the case. I had not seen her for a month. She had been at a resort hotel near Boston. According to the newspapers, she had met Miss O'Neil there, taking refuge from the cupidity of her manager. She warned me in provocative words not to tamper with Miss O'Neil's portrait of herself as a woman wronged, misunderstood, persecuted—just the kind of woman, in effect, that she was best known for portraying on the stage. "She is a gifted and sadly maligned young woman. The manager has used her ruthlessly. I will not desert her!"

"I have not suggested that you should. I know nothing about her, the case, or your friendship—except what anyone can know."

She opened and shut her fan.

"As for the newspapers, she is not ashamed to have her name linked with Lizzie Borden's."

"To which of you is that a compliment?"

"When we first met she knew me by the name I use at hotels for the sake of privacy. I merely presented myself as an admirer, someone who had seen all her plays. Later I had to tell her that the person who wished to befriend her was not Lisabeth Andrews but Lizzie Borden. She said, 'But, my dear, I've known that all along! It makes no difference to me.' "

I said nothing. She toyed with her fan. "The remark doesn't dispose you in her favor?"

"Why should it? Such professions cost her nothing but you a great deal."

"Oh, *cost!*" she said harshly. Then her tone softened: "Poor Emma! Some things are worth paying for, others aren't. You've never learned the difference."

"I have not had good teachers," I said.

After the suit was settled, Lizzie continued to rescue her from small debts and indulge her taste for trinkets and jewelry. Miss O'Neil repaid her by introducing her to "artistic" people and consulting her (or pretending to) on personal and professional matters. I accused myself of small-mindedness. I still had Miss Jubb, she had not deserted me—why should I begrudge Lizzie this friendship, sorely in need as she was?

So when she announced that Miss O'Neil's company had been engaged for a performance in Fall River and that she was entertaining them afterward, I said briskly, "Then I'm to meet Miss O'Neil at last!"

"There's time for you to make other plans," she said. "I know you don't approve of artists—"

"I do not know any artists," I interrupted. "If I did I would judge them on individual merits, not as a group."

"Dearest Emma," she said, "I've always been able to count on you . . ."

I felt a familiar dread . . .

Caterers, florists, musicians came and went. "Maplecroft" was finally going to serve its function. Only, from my window, there was not a soul to be seen on the street unless someone delivering ice—potted palms—a grand piano . . . Not even any children hanging around the front gate in a spirit of anticipation—their mothers had swept them out of sight.

I tried to help—once I went downstairs in time to collide with a delivery of wine. "Oh, don't look so stricken, Emma! It's champagne, not gin!" I thought of all those years she'd worked for the Temperance Union—how they had held prayer meetings for her during the trial. She read my mind. "Don't worry, I'm not going to break my pledge. Only my guests aren't used to lemonade and iced tea!"

Long before the guests arrived, I had decided to keep to my room. Anything, I thought, would be better than appearing with my feelings on my sleeve. I had prepared an excuse I hoped would placate Lizzie. I awaited her knock momentarily. But only the sounds of the party increasingly assaulted my door.

Shortly before eleven I crept down the back stairs and phoned Miss Jubb. She could hear the din in the background—the music, the strident laughter, the crashing of glass: "I'll be waiting in a carriage down the block."

I hurriedly began to pack an overnight bag, but now that I hoped to escape undetected there came a knock. I opened the door on Nance O'Neil.

She glided in, casting a glance all about as if to say, "What a charming room!"—then, turning, clasped her hands entreatingly: "It is Emma, isn't it? I've so wanted to meet you! I'm naughty to force myself on you this way, but Lisbeth told me the beautiful thing you said about artists—I knew you wouldn't turn me away!"

She was extraordinarily pretty—I could understand Lizzie's infatuation with her—that delicacy of face and figure did not run in the Borden family. But her effusiveness left me ill-at-ease. I thought at first that it was inspired by wine, but soon saw that it was only one of many poses she could summon up with instant ease. Her eyes fell on my traveling bag: "You're taking a trip? Lisbeth didn't say why you hadn't come down."

"Yes—I'm sorry I cannot spend time with you."

"But you're not leaving tonight surely!" she cried. "Won't you come downstairs for a while? Lisbeth would be so pleased—she's very proud of you!"

"No, I cannot. I am sorry she has sent you on a futile errand."

"No, no, no! I came of my own free will! Oh, I'm too impulsive—it's my greatest fault—you do think me naughty!" Here she pouted charmingly.

"You have not been naughty," I replied, "only misused. You may tell my sister I said so."

She ceased magically to convey childlike sincerity—her bearing and expression shed an atmosphere of injured pride and reproachful forgiveness. I returned to my packing, not wanting to furnish her with further opportunities to display her art.

Five minutes later I stood at the door with my bag. I turned out the light and listened. Just as I was ready to slip out, I heard voices hurrying along the hall—then a sharp rapping—then the door was flung open. I had just time to shrink into the darkness behind it.

"She's not here," Lizzie said.

"Her suitcase was on the bed . . ." A shaft of light fell where it had been.

"It's gone—she's gone."

"Perhaps you can overtake her," Miss O'Neil murmured plaintively.

"You don't know her," Lizzie said in a hoarse voice. She closed the door but they did not move away. "I wonder what you said to precipitate her flight?"

"I?" Miss O'Neil fairly shrieked. "I said nothing! Her flight, if that's what it was, was already planned!"

"She would never have left at this time of night—she dreads scandal too much."

"Perhaps *you* are the one who doesn't know her," Miss O'Neil wisely remarked.

"She is my sister!" Lizzie said harshly.

"But you've often said how different you are."

"We're two sides of the same coin."

"Don't let's stand here arguing," Miss O'Neil said placatingly. "She'll come back."

"Is that what you want?" Lizzie asked in a strange tone.

"Why, what do you mean?"

"It isn't what I want—I don't want her to come back."

"Well, then, neither do I!"

"I thought not," Lizzie said with satisfaction.

"I don't know what you're trying to prove," Miss O'Neil said in a disturbed voice. "I assure you I did nothing to cause her to leave—I came to her at your request . . . She said you had misused me," she ended with some heat. "I'm beginning to think she was right!"

Then Lizzie became placating: "I haven't misused you—Emma spoke out of jealousy—because I feel closer to you than I ever did to her—and because you understand me better."

"I don't like that kind of jealousy, Lizzie. You must go after her and explain. Why, what is the matter?"

"You called me *Lizzie.*"

"Did I? Well, talking to your sister—hearing her—you know how I simply absorb things—"

"It is not my name. But perhaps there are those who make jokes about it in private," Lizzie said grimly.

Poor Miss O'Neil! "This is beside the point! We were talking about your sister!"

"I cannot go after Emma, I cannot bring her back. She left me long before tonight. I've lived with her door locked against me for twelve years. I'll hardly know she's gone."

"Don't talk about it, Lisbeth dear!"

"No, I won't burden you," said Lizzie. "And yet—I can't help feeling that somehow you took my side when you were with her—perhaps not even knowing it."

Miss O'Neil's voice, already at a distance, faded rapidly: "Come now! Quickly! No, I won't listen to any more, . . ."

After the scandal at Tyngsboro, she apparently did not. Lizzie was sadly in error if she imagined that her connection with drunkenness and misconduct would go unnoticed simply because it did not occur in Fall River but in a house she rented for a week somewhere else. Miss Jubb learned a great deal more than I would allow her to tell me—"If you are fascinated with her," I said snappishly, "you must not use me as an excuse." There need not even have been the bitter climactic quarrel that Miss Jubb got wind of. Those butterfly wings could not in any case have supported the burden of Lizzie Borden for long.

The doctor came. I said, "I want my body taken to Fall River—we have a family plot in Oak Grove cemetery."

"I've already promised to see to that, Miss Borden, and your other requests will be honored, too."

His choice of words roused my attention: "I have asked before?" —"Yes."—"And made other requests?"—"Yes, but when you weren't quite yourself perhaps."—"What did I say?"—"You asked to be buried the same way your sister was."—"That is correct, I do not want a ceremony."—"I mean, you asked to be buried at night."—"Did I?" —"You asked for Negro pallbearers only . . ."

I fell to thinking. "Well, I will go halfway with you," I said. "I don't mind the Negro pallbearers but I don't want the other part."

"I'm not surprised," she said. "Do you remember the day you changed rooms with Alice Russell? It was Saturday, after the police told us not to leave the house."

"You asked if someone in the house was suspected—you demanded to know who it was!"

"That night you asked Alice to sleep in your room. You took the one she'd been using. Father's and Mrs. Borden's. You put their lock and bolt between us. We never again had rooms opening freely into each other."

"Yes, I knew what you meant, even if poor Miss O'Neil did not."

"You have given me away, Emma."

"If you changed your dress you must say so."

"I will never give in."

"*I have no reason to wish to be buried at night!*"

"Now that's more like it." The doctor's voice startled me. "Let's have less talk about dying and more about getting well. You have a long time to live!"

Well, that is not true. In the very course of nature I cannot live *much* longer. If I die quite soon, though—say within seven days of your death, or ten days, some such noticeable number—remember, I am seventy-seven!—it will be concidence! I hope you will not try to make any more of it than that.

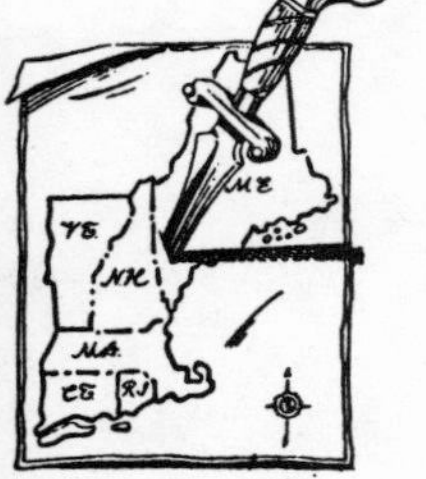

SOMETHING YOU HAVE TO LIVE WITH

by Patricia Highsmith

Patricia Highsmith is the author of Strangers On A Train, *the novel on which Alfred Hitchcock based his suspense masterpiece. Her short fiction and novels have been deservedly acclaimed for their picture of a world in which guilt and innocence are turned on their heads. Though she lives in Switzerland, Ms. Highsmith was born in the United States, and often sets her short stories in New England. The following story is an unsettling tale that will remind many readers of Katherine Anne Porter's ''Noon Wine.''*

"Don't forget to lock all the doors," Stan said. "Someone might think because the car's gone, nobody's home."

"All the doors? You mean two. You haven't asked me anything—aesthetic, such as how the place looks now."

Stan laughed. "I suppose the pictures are all hung and the books are on the shelves."

"Well, not quite, but your shirts and sweaters—and the kitchen. It looks—I'm happy, Stan. So is Cassie. She's walking all around the place purring. See you tomorrow morning then. Around eleven, you said?"

"Around eleven. I'll bring stuff for lunch, don't worry."

"Love to your mom. I'm glad she's better."

"Thanks, darling." Stan hung up.

Cassie, their ginger-and-white cat, aged four, sat looking at Ginnie as if she had never seen a telephone before. Purring again. Dazed by all the space, Ginnie thought. Cassie began kneading the rug in an ecstasy of contentment, and Ginnie laughed.

Ginnie and Stan Brixton had bought a house in Connecticut after six years of New York apartments. Their furniture had been here for a week while they wound things up in New York, and yesterday had been the final move of smaller things like silverware, some dishes, a few pictures, suitcases, kitchen items and the cat. Stan had taken their son Freddie this morning to spend the night in New Hope, Pennsylvania, where Stan's mother lived. His mother had had a second heart attack and was recuperating at home. "Every time I see her, I think it may be the last. You don't mind if I go, do you, Ginnie? It'll keep

Freddie out of the way while you're fiddling around." Ginnie hadn't minded.

Fiddling around was Stan's term for organizing and cleaning. Ginnie thought she had done a good job since Stan and Freddie had taken off this morning. The lovely French blue-and-white vase which reminded Ginnie of Monet's paintings stood on the living room bookcase now, even bearing red roses from the garden. Ginnie had made headway in the kitchen, installing things the way she wanted them. The way they would remain. Cassie had her litter pan ("What a euphemism, litter ought to mean a bed," Stan said) in the downstairs john corner. They now had an upstairs bathroom also. The house was on a hill with no other houses around it for nearly a mile, not that they owned all the land around, but the land around was farmland. When she and Stan had seen the place in June, sheep and goats had been grazing not far away. They had both fallen in love with the house.

Stanley Brixton was a novelist and fiction critic, and Ginnie wrote articles and was now half through her second novel. Her first had been published but had had only modest success. You couldn't expect a smash hit with a first novel, Stan said, unless the publicity was extraordinary. Water under the bridge. Ginnie was more interested in her novel-in-progress. They had a mortgage on the house, and with her and Stan's free-lance work they thought they could be independent of New York, at least independent of nine-to-five jobs. Stan had already published three books, adventure stories with a political slant. He was thirty-two and for three years had been overseas correspondent for a newspaper syndicate.

Ginnie picked up a piece of heavy twine from the living room rug, and realized that her back hurt a little from the day's exertions. She had thought of switching on the TV, but the news was just over, she saw from her watch, and it might be better to go straight to bed and get up earlyish in the morning.

"Cassie?"

Cassie replied with a courteous, sustained, "M-wah-h?"

"Hungry?" Cassie knew the word. "No, you've had enough. Do you know you're getting middle-aged spread? Come on. Going up to bed with me?" Ginnie went to the front door, which was already locked by its automatic lock, but she put the chain on also. Yawning, she turned out the downstairs lights and climbed the stairs. Cassie followed her.

Ginnie had a quick bath, second of the day, pulled on a nightgown, brushed her teeth and got into bed. She at once realized she was too tired to pick up one of the English weeklies, political and Stan's favorites, which she had dropped by the bed to look at. She put out the lamp. *Home.* She and Stan had spent one night here last weekend during the big move. This was the first night she had been alone in the house, which still had no name. *Something like White Elephant maybe,* Stan had said. *You think of something.* Ginnie tried to think, an activity which made her instantly sleepier.

She was awakened by a crunching sound, like that of car tires on gravel. She raised up a little in bed. Had she heard it? Their driveway hadn't any gravel to speak of, just unpaved earth. But—

Wasn't that a *click?* From somewhere. Front, back? Or had it been a twig falling on the roof?

She had locked the doors, hadn't she?

Ginnie suddenly realized that she had not locked the back door. For another minute, as Ginnie listened, everything was silent. What a bore to go downstairs again! But she thought she had better do it, so she could honestly tell Stan that she had. Ginnie found the lamp switch and got out of bed.

By now she was thinking that any noise she had heard had been imaginary, something out of a dream. But Cassie followed her in a brisk, anxious way, Ginnie noticed.

The glow from the staircase light enabled Ginnie to find her way to the kitchen, where she switched on the strong ceiling light. She went at once to the back door and turned the Yale bolt. Then she listened. All was silent. The big kitchen looked exactly the same with its half modern, half old-fashioned furnishings—electric stove, big white wooden cupboard with drawers below, shelves above, double sink, a huge new fridge.

Ginnie went back upstairs, Cassie still following. Cassie was short for Cassandra, a name Stan had given her when she had been a kitten, because she had looked gloomy, unshakeably pessimistic. Ginnie was drifting off to sleep again, when she heard a bump downstairs, as if someone had staggered slightly. She switched on the bedside lamp again, and a thrust of fear went through her when she saw Cassie rigidly crouched on the bed with her eyes fixed on the open bedroom door.

Now there was another bump from downstairs, and the unmistakable rustle of a drawer being slid out, and it could be only the dining room drawer where the silver was.

She had locked someone in with her!

Her first thought was to reach for the telephone and get the police, but the telephone was downstairs in the living room.

Go down and face it and threaten him with something—or them, she told herself. Maybe it was an adolescent kid, just a local kid who'd be glad to get off unreported, if she scared him a little. Ginnie jumped out of bed, put on Stan's bathrobe, a sturdy blue flannel thing, and tied the belt firmly. She descended the stairs. By now she heard more noises.

"Who's *there*?" she shouted boldly.

"Hum-hum. Just me, lady," said a rather deep voice.

The living room lights, the dining room lights were full on.

In the dining room Ginnie was confronted by a stocking-hooded figure in what she thought of as motorcycle gear: black trousers, black boots, black plastic jacket. The stocking had slits cut in it for the eyes. And the figure carried a dirty canvas bag like a railway mailbag, and plainly into this the silverware had already gone, because the dining room drawer gaped, empty. He must have been hiding in a corner of the dining room, Ginnie thought, when she had come down to lock the back door. The hooded figure shoved the drawer to carelessly, and it didn't quite close.

"Keep your mouth shut, and you won't get hurt. All right?" The voice sounded like that of a man of at least twenty-five.

Ginnie didn't see any gun or knife. "Just what do you think you're doing?"

"What does it look like I'm doing?" And the man got on with his business. The two candlesticks from the dining room table went into the bag. So did the silver table lighter.

Was there anyone else with him? Ginnie glanced towards the kitchen, but didn't see anyone, and no sound came from there. I'm going to call the police," she said, and started for the living room telephone.

"Phone's cut, lady. You better keep quiet, because no one can hear you around here, even if you scream."

Was that true? Unfortunately it was true. Ginnie for a few seconds concentrated on memorizing that man's appearance: about five feet eight, medium build, maybe a bit slender, broad hands—but since the hands were in blue rubber gloves, were they broad?—rather big feet. Blond or brunette she couldn't tell, because of the stocking mask. Robbers like this usually bound and gagged people. Ginnie wanted to avoid that, if she could.

"If you're looking for money, there's not much in the house just now," Ginnie said, "except what's in my handbag upstairs, about thirty dollars. Go ahead and take it."

"I'll get around to it," he said laughing, prowling the living room now. He took the letter-opener from the coffee table, then Freddie's photograph from the piano, because the photograph was in a silver frame.

Ginnie thought of banging him on the head with—with what? She saw nothing heavy enough, portable, except one of the dining room chairs. And if she failed to knock him out with the first swat? Was the telephone really cut? She moved towards the telephone in the corner.

"Don't go near the door. Stay in sight!"

"Ma-wow-wow-*wow!*" This from Cassie, a high-pitched wail that to Ginnie meant Cassie was on the brink of throwing up, but now the situation was different. Cassie looked ready to attack the man.

"Go back, Cassie, take it easy," Ginnie said.

"I don't like cats," the hooded man said over his shoulder.

There was not much else he could take from the living room, Ginnie thought. The pictures on the wall were too big. And what burglar was interested in pictures, at least pictures like these which were a few oils done by their painter friends, two or three watercolors—Was this really happening? Was a stranger picking up her mother's old sewing basket, looking inside, banging it down again? Taking the French vase, tossing the water and roses towards the fireplace? The vase went into the sack.

"What's upstairs?" The ugly head turned towards her. "Let's go upstairs."

"There's *nothing* upstairs!" Ginnie shrieked. She darted towards the telephone, knowing it would be cut, but wanting to see it with her own eyes—cut—though her hand was outstretched to use it. She saw the abruptly stopped wire on the floor, cut some four feet from the telephone.

The hood chuckled. "Told you."

A red flashlight stuck out of the back pocket of his trousers. He was going into the hall now, ready to take the stairs. The staircase light was on, but he pulled the flashlight from his pocket.

"Nothing *up* there, I tell you!" Ginnie found herself following him like a ninny, holding up the hem of Stan's dressing gown so she wouldn't trip on the stairs.

"Cosy little nook!" said the hood, entering the bedroom. "And what have we here? Anything of interest?"

The silver-backed brush and comb on the dresser were of interest, also the hand mirror, and these went into the bag, which was now dragging the floor.

"Aha! I like that thing!" He had spotted the heavy wooden box with brass corners which Stan used for cufflinks and handkerchiefs and a few white ties, but its size was apparently daunting the man in the hood, because he swayed in front of it and said, "Be back for that." He looked around for lighter objects, and in went Ginnie's black leather jewelry box, her Dunhill lighter from the bedside table. "Ought to be glad I'm not raping you. Haven't the time." The tone was jocular.

My God, Ginnie thought, you'd think Stan and I were rich! She had never considered herself and Stan rich, or thought that they had anything worth invading a house for. No doubt in New York they'd been lucky for six years—no robberies at all—because even a typewriter was valuable to a drug addict. No, they weren't rich, but he was taking all they had, all the *nice* things they'd tried over the years to accumulate. Ginnie watched him open her handbag, lift the dollar bills from her billfold. That was the least of it.

"If you think for one minute you're going to get away with this," Ginnie said. "In a small community like *this*? You haven't a prayer. If you don't leave those things here tonight, I'll report you so quick—"

"Oh, shut up, lady. Where's the other rooms here?"

Cassie snarled. She had followed them both up the stairs.

A black boot struck out sideways and caught the cat sharply in the ribs.

"Don't touch that cat!" Ginnie cried out.

Cassie sprang growling onto the man's boot top, at his knee.

Ginnie was astounded—and proud of Cassie—for a second.

"Pain in the ass!" said the hood, and with a gloved hand caught the cat by the loose skin on her back and flung her against the wall with a backhand swing. The cat dropped, panting, and the man stomped on her side and kicked her in the head.

"You *bastard!*" Ginnie screamed.

"So much for your stinking—yowlers!" said the beige hood, and kicked the cat once again. His voice had been husky with rage, and now he stalked with his flashlight into the hall, in quest of other rooms.

Dazed, stiff, Ginnie followed him.

The guest room had only a chest of drawers in it, empty, but the man slid out a couple of drawers anyway to have a look. Freddie's room had nothing but a bed and table. The hood wasted no time there.

From the hall, Ginnie looked into the bedroom at her cat. The cat twitched and was still. One foot had twitched. Ginnie stood rigid as a column of stone. She had just seen Cassie die, she realized.

"Back in a flash," said the hooded man, briskly descending the stairs with his sack which was now so heavy he had to carry it on one shoulder.

Ginnie moved at last, in jerks, like someone awakening from an anesthetic. Her body and mind seemed not to be connected. Her hand reached for the stair rail and missed it. She was no longer afraid at all, though she did not consciously realize this. She simply kept following the hooded figure, her enemy, and would have kept on, even if he had pointed a gun at her. By the time she reached the kitchen, he was out of sight. The kitchen door was open, and a cool breeze blew in. Ginnie continued across the kitchen, looked left into the driveway, and saw a flashlight's beam swing as the man heaved the bag into a car. She heard the hum of two male voices. So he had a pal waiting for him!

And here he came back.

With sudden swiftness, Ginnie picked up a kitchen stool which had a square formica top and chromium legs. As soon as the hooded figure stepped onto the threshold of the kitchen, Ginnie swung the stool and hit him full on the forehead with the edge of the stool's seat.

Momentum carried the man forward, but he stooped, staggering, and Ginnie cracked him again on the top of the head with all her strength. She held two legs of the stool in her hands. He fell with a great thump and clatter onto the linoleum floor. Another whack for good measure on the back of the stockinged head. She felt pleased and relieved to see blood coming through the beige material.

"Frankie?—You okay?—*Frankie!*"

The voice came from the car outside.

Poised now, not at all afraid, Ginnie stood braced for the next arrival. She held a leg of the stool in her right hand, and her left supported the seat. She awaited, barely two feet from the open door, the sound of boots in the driveway, another figure in the doorway.

Instead, she heard a car motor start, saw a glow of its lights through the door. The car was backing down the drive.

Finally Ginnie set the stool down. The house was silent again. The man on the floor was not moving. Was he dead?

I don't care. I simply don't give a damn, Ginnie said inside herself.

But she did care. What if he woke up? What if he needed a doctor, a hospital right away? And there was no telephone. The nearest house was nearly a mile away, the village a good mile. Ginnie would have to walk it with a flashlight. Of course if she encountered a car, a car might stop and ask what was the matter, and then she could tell someone to fetch a doctor or an ambulance. These thoughts went through Ginnie's head in seconds, and then she returned to the facts. The fact was, he *might* be dead. Killed by her.

So was Cassie dead. Ginnie turned towards the living room. Cassie's death was more real, more important than the body at her feet which only might be dead. Ginnie drew a glass of water for herself at the kitchen sink.

Everything was silent outside. Now Ginnie was calm enough to realize that the robber's chum had thought it best to make a getaway. He probably wasn't coming back, not even with reinforcements. After all, he had the loot in his car—silverware, her jewelry box, all the nice things.

Ginnie stared at the long black figure on her kitchen floor. He hadn't moved at all. The right hand lay under him, the left arm was outstretched, upward. The stockinged head was turned slightly towards her, one slit showing. She couldn't see what was going on behind that crazy slit.

"Are you *awake?*" Ginnie said, rather loudly.

She waited.

She knew she would have to face it. Best to feel the pulse in the wrist, she thought, and at once forced herself to do this. She pulled the rubber glove down a bit, and gripped a blondish-haired wrist which seemed to her of astonishing breadth, much wider than Stan's wrist, anyway. She couldn't feel any pulse. She altered the place where she had put her thumb, and tried again. There was no pulse.

So she had murdered someone. The fact did not sink in.

Two thoughts danced in her mind: she would have to remove Cassie, put a towel or something around her, and she was not going to be able to sleep or even remain in this house with a corpse lying on the kitchen floor.

Ginnie got a dishtowel, a folded clean one from a stack on a shelf, took a second one, went to the hall and climbed the stairs. Cassie was now bleeding. Rather, she had bled. The blood on the carpet looked dark. One of Cassie's eyes projected from the socket. Ginnie gathered her as gently as if she were still alive and only injured, gathered up some intestines which had been pushed out, and enfolded her in a towel, opened the second towel and put that around her too. Then she carried Cassie down to the living room, hesitated, then laid the cat's body to one side of the fireplace on the floor. By accident, a red rose lay beside Cassie.

Tackle the blood now, she told herself. She got a plastic bowl from the kitchen, drew some cold water and took a sponge. Upstairs, she went to work on hands and knees, changing the water in the bathroom. The task was soothing, as she had known it would be.

Next job: clothes on and find the nearest telephone. Ginnie kept moving, barely aware of what she was doing, and suddenly she was standing in the kitchen in blue jeans, sneakers, sweater and jacket with her billfold in a pocket. Empty billfold, she remembered. She had her house keys in her left hand. For no good reason, she decided to leave the kitchen light on. The front door was still locked, she realized. She found she had the flashlight in a jacket pocket too, and supposed she had taken it from the front hall table when she came down the stairs.

She went out, locked the kitchen door from the outside with a key, and made her way to the road.

No moon at all. She walked with the aid of the flashlight along the left side of the road towards the village, shone the torch once on her watch and saw that it was twenty past one. By starlight, by a bit of flashlight, she saw one house far to the left in a field, quite dark and so far away, Ginnie thought she might do better to keep on.

She kept on. Dark road. Trudging. Did *everybody* go to bed early around here?

In the distance she saw two or three white streetlights, the lights of the village. Surely there'd be a car before the village.

There wasn't a car. Ginnie was still trudging as she entered the village proper, whose boundary was marked by a neat white sign on either side of the road saying EAST KINDALE.

My God, Ginnie thought. *Is this true? Is this what I'm doing, what I'm going to say?*

Not a light showed in any of the neat, mostly white houses. There was not even a light at the Connecticut Yankee Inn, the only funtioning hostelry and bar in town, Stan had remarked once. Nevertheless, Ginnie marched up the steps and knocked on the door. Then with her flashlight, she saw a brass knocker on the white door, and availed herself of that.

Rap-rap-rap!

Minutes passed. *Be patient,* Ginnie told herself. *You're overwrought.*

But she felt compelled to rap again.

"Who's there?" a man's voice called.

"A neighbor! There's been an accident!"

Ginnie fairly collapsed against the figure who opened the door. It was a man in a plaid woollen bathrobe and pajamas. She might have collapsed also against a woman or a child.

Then she was sitting on a straight chair in a sort of living room. She had blurted out the story.

"We'll—we'll get the police right away, ma'am. Or an ambulance, as you say. But from what you say—" The man talking was in his sixties, and sleepy.

His wife, more efficient-looking, had joined him to listen. She wore a dressing gown and pink slippers. "Police, Jake. Man sounds dead from what the lady says. Even if he isn't, the police'll know what to do."

"Hello, Ethel! That you?" the man said into the telephone. "Listen, we need the police right away. You know the old Hardwick place? . . . Tell 'em to go there . . . No, *not* on fire. Can't explain now. But somebody'll be there to open the door in—in about five minutes."

The woman pushed a glass of something into Ginnie's hand. Ginnie realized that her teeth were chattering. She was cold, though it wasn't cold outside. It was early September, she remembered.

"They're going to want to speak with you." The man who had been in the plaid robe was now in trousers and a belted sports jacket. "You'll have to tell them the time it happened and all that."

Ginnie realized. She thanked the woman and went with the man to his car. It was an ordinary four-door, and Ginnie noticed a discarded Cracker Jack box on the floor of the passenger's seat as she got in.

A police car was in the drive. Someone was knocking on the back door, and Ginnie saw that she'd left the kitchen light on.

"Hiya, Jake! What's up?" called a second policeman, getting out of the black car in the driveway.

"Lady had a house robbery," the man with Ginnie explained. "She thinks—Well, you've got the keys, haven't you, Mrs. Brixton?"

"Oh yes, yes." Ginnie fumbled for them. She was gasping again, and reminded herself that it was a time to keep calm, to answer questions accurately. She opened the kitchen door.

A policeman stooped beside the prone figure. "Dead," he said.

"The—Mrs. Brixton said she hit him with the kitchen stool. That one, ma'am?" The man called Jake pointed to the yellow formica stool.

"Yes. He was coming *back,* you see. You see—" Ginnie choked and gave up, for the moment.

Jake cleared his throat and said, "Mrs. Brixton and her husband just moved in. Husband isn't here tonight. She'd left the kitchen door unlocked and two—well, one fellow came in, this one. He went out with a bag of stuff he'd taken, put it in a waiting car, then came back to get more, and that's when Mrs. Brixton hit him."

"Um-*hum,*" said the policeman, still stooped on his heels. "Can't touch the body till the detective gets here. Can I use your phone, Mrs. Brixton?"

"They cut the phone," Jake said. "That's why she had to walk to my place."

The other policeman went out to telephone from his car. The policeman who remained put on water for coffee (or had he said tea?), and chatted with Jake about tourists, about someone they both knew who had just got married—as if they had known each other for years. Ginnie was sitting on one of the dining room chairs. The policeman asked where the instant coffee was, if she had any, and Ginnie got up to show him the coffee jar which she had put on a cabinet shelf beside the stove.

"Terrible introduction to a new house," the policeman remarked, holding his steaming cup. "But we all sure hope—" Suddenly his words seemed to dry up. His eyes flickered and looked away from Ginnie's face.

A couple of men in plainclothes arrived. Photographs were taken of the dead man. Ginnie went over the house with one of the men, who made notes of the items Ginnie said were stolen. No, she hadn't seen the color of the car, much less the license plate. The body on the floor was wrapped and carried out on a stretcher. Ginnie had only a glimpse of that, from which the detective even tried to shield her. Ginnie was in the dining room then, reckoning up the missing silver.

"I didn't mean to kill him!" Ginnie cried out suddenly, interrupting the detective. "Not *kill* him, honestly!"

Stan arrived very early, about eight A.M., with Freddie, and went to the Inn to fetch Ginnie. Ginnie had spent the night there, and someone had telephoned Stan at the number Ginnie had given.

"She's had a shock," Jake said to Stan.

Stan looked bewildered. But at least he had heard what happened, and Ginnie didn't have to go over it.

"All the nice things we had," Ginnie said. "And the cat—"

"The police might get our stuff back, Ginnie. If not, we'll buy more. We're all safe, at least." Stan set his firm jaw, but he smiled. He glanced at Freddie who stood in the doorway, looking a little pale from lack of sleep. "Come on. We're going home."

He took Ginnie's hand. His hand felt warm, and she realized her own hands were cold again.

They tried to keep the identity of the dead man from her, Ginnie knew, but on the second day she happened to see it printed—on a folded newspaper which lay on the counter in the grocery store. There was a photograph of him too, a blondish fellow with curly hair and a rather defiant expression. *Frank Collins, 24, of Hartford*...

Stan felt that they ought to go on living in the house, gradually buy the "nice things" again that Ginnie kept talking about. Stan said she ought to get back to work on her novel.

"I don't want any nice things any more. Not again." That was true, but that was only part of it. The worst was that she had killed someone, stopped a life. She couldn't fully realize it, therefore couldn't believe it somehow, or understand it.

"At least we could get another cat."

"Not yet," she said.

People said to her (like Mrs. Durham, Gladys, who lived a mile or so out of East Kindale on the opposite side from the Brixtons), "You mustn't reproach yourself. You did it in defense of your house. Don't you think a lot of us wish we had the courage, if someone comes barging in intending to rob you..."

"I wouldn't hesitate—to do what you did!" That was from perky Georgia Hamilton, a young married woman with black curly hair, active in local politics, who lived in East Kindale proper. She came especially to call on Ginnie and to make acquaintance with her and Stan. "These hoodlums from miles away—Hartford!—they come to rob us, just because they think we still have some family silver and a few *nice* things..."

There was the phrase again, the *nice* things.

Stan came home one day with a pair of silver candlesticks for the dining room table. "Less than a hundred dollars, and we can afford them," Stan said.

To Ginnie they looked like bait for another robbery. They were pretty, yes. Georgian. Modern copy, but still beautiful. She could not take any aesthetic pleasure from them.

"Did you take a swat at your book this afternoon?" Stan asked cheerfully. He had been out of the house nearly three hours that afternoon. He had made sure the doors were locked, for Ginnie's sake, before he left. He had also bought a metal wheelbarrow for use in the garden, and it was still strapped to the roof of the car.

"No," Ginnie said. "But I suppose I'm making progress. I have to get back to a state of concentration, you know."

"Of course I know," Stan said. "I'm a writer too."

The police had never recovered the silverware, or Ginnie's leather box which had held her engagement ring (it had become too small and she hadn't got around to having it enlarged), and her grandmother's gold necklace and so forth. Stan told Ginnie they had checked all the known pals of the man who had invaded the house, but hadn't come up with anything. The police thought the dead man might have struck up acquaintance with his chum very recently, possibly the same night as the robbery.

"Darling," Stan said, "do you think we should *move* from this house? I'm willing—if it'd make you feel—less—"

Ginnie shook her head. It wasn't the house. She didn't any longer (after two months) even think of the corpse on the floor when she went into the kitchen. It was something inside her. "No," Ginnie said.

"Well—I think you ought to talk to a psychiatrist. Just one visit even," Stan added, interrupting a protest from Ginnie. "It isn't enough for neighbors to say you did the natural thing. Maybe you need a professional to tell you." Stan chuckled. He was in tennis shoes and old clothes, and had had a good day at the typewriter.

Ginnie agreed, to please Stan.

The psychiatrist was in Hartford, a man recommended to Stan by a local medical doctor. Stan drove Ginnie there, and waited for her in the car. It was to be an hour's session, but Ginnie reappeared after about forty minutes.

"He gave me some pills to take," Ginnie said.

"Is *that* all?—But what did he say?"

"Oh." Ginnie shrugged. "The same as they all say, that—nobody blames me, the police didn't make a fuss, so what—" She shrugged again, glanced at Stan and saw the terrible disappointment in his face as he looked from her into the distance through the windshield.

Ginnie knew he was thinking again about "guilt" and abandoning it, abandoning the word again. She had said no, she didn't feel guilty, that wasn't the trouble, that would have been too simple. She felt disturbed, she had said many times, and she couldn't do anything about it.

"You really ought to write a book about it, a novel," Stan said—this for at least the fourth time.

"And how can I, if I can't come to terms with it myself, if I can't even analyze it first?" This Ginnie said for at least the third time and possibly the fourth. It was as if she had an unsolvable mystery within her. "You can't write a book just stammering around on paper."

Stan then started the car.

The pills were mild sedatives combined with some kind of mild picker-uppers. They didn't make a change in Ginnie.

Two more months passed. Ginnie resisted buying any "nice things," so they had nothing but the nice candlesticks. They ate with stainless steel. Freddie pulled out of his period of tension and suppressed excitement (he knew quite well what had happened in the kitchen), and in Ginnie's eyes became quite normal again, whatever normal was. Ginnie got back to work on the book she had started before moving to the house. She didn't ever dream about the murder, or manslaughter, in fact she often thought it might be better if she did dream about it.

But among people—and it was a surprisingly friendly region, they had all the social life they could wish—she felt compelled to say sometimes, when there was a lull in the conversation:

"Did you know, by the way, I once killed a man?"

Everyone would look at her, except of course those who had heard her say this before, maybe three times before.

Stan would grow tense and blank-minded, having failed once more to spring in in time before Ginnie got launched. He was jittery at social gatherings, trying like a fencer to dart in with something, anything to say, before Ginnie made her big thrust. *It's just something they, he and Ginnie, had to live with,* Stan told himself.

And it probably would go on and on, even maybe when Freddie was twelve and even twenty. It had, in fact, half-ruined their marriage. But it was emphatically not worth divorcing for. He still loved Ginnie. She was still Ginnie after all. She was just somehow different. Even Ginnie had said that about herself.

"It's something I just have to live with," Stan murmured to himself.

"What?" It was Georgia Hamilton on his left, asking him what he had said. "Oh, I know, I know." She smiled understandingly. "But maybe it does her good."

Ginnie was in the middle of her story. At least she always made it short, and even managed to laugh in a couple of places.

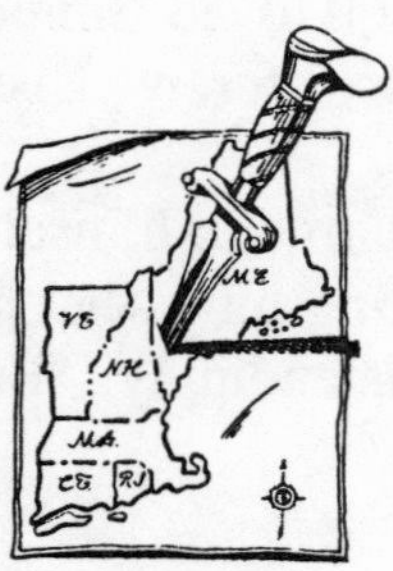

PAID IN FULL

by W. W. Fredericks

W. W. Fredericks is the pseudonym of a mystery writer who lives in Massachusetts. Though he keeps his identity carefully cloaked, the following story suggests a background in theater-reviewing or, at least, journalism. Or perhaps the author's imagination is such as to allow him to re-create an unfamiliar world with consummate confidence and elegance. Either way, his storytelling ability raises the following story to a special level. What other author could succeed at making theater critics sympathetic?

I remember the moment I became friends with Richard Devane. It was at a producer's party, the kind where the show's stars and pretty girls mingle with the financial backers, media types, and all the hangers-on who could scrounge invitations. Devane, short and round, always affected a white scarf and dark jacket which emphasized the black-white contrast of his ebony eyebrows and pure white hair.

As critics for rival Boston newspapers, we knew each other's work intimately and each other not at all. He had been writing about the theater for forty years. I had been doing the job for eighteen months, since moving over from news.

Devane's wit was evident in both his writing that I admired so much and his conversation, which I had briefly shared on a few occasions. His pleasure in his cleverness was obvious and had earned him the nickname "Richard the Vain." Until that night, I had assumed he took himself seriously. I was standing among a circle of six listening to Devane's quips, stories, and word plays when he realized the others would laugh at anything he said, funny or not. He dismissed them with a wave of his hand, saying, "Now leave us, I wish to tell the competition how to do his job."

I was smiling at a slim blonde who was sliding away when Devane's low rumble of a voice said, "She is, shall we say, an intimate of our hosts, the wonderful Garrio brothers. Her job is to provide a little glamor, flirt with the bylines and moneybags, but always go home with a Garrio."

Devane's lips were pressed together as he shook his head, his eyes following the doxy.

"Her name's Lea Harling," he said. "She was a good actress, a good singer too. Not too smart, but she had the right instincts. She was just about to make the jump from ingenue to second billing when the parts started drying up. The rumor is that her morals were never a problem—for her or anyone else—and she was given a leading role in the Garrios' private lives." He paused, then added, "I don't think she ever knew that the parts stopped coming because the two Garrios declared her off-limits."

"Another uplifting tale of backstage life," I said.

"That's why they act," replied Devane.

I turned to face him and said, "Your monologue to the group was very amusing. But, if I counted correctly, you stole three quotes from Churchill, two from Disraeli, and one from Saki."

Devane began to smile.

"And," I continued, "you knew you weren't going to be discovered by any of the bunch: each theft was from one of the Englishmen's speeches or a lesser-known writing. Richard Devane, I believe your strength is in your memory, not your wit."

His amusement grew into laughter, and he held his drink with both hands to prevent its spilling.

"Oh, Stephens, I knew you were going to be trouble. That first month, when you referred to the original set design of *The Price,* I thought, Oh, hell, he knows his theater. And when you dismembered Galsworthy on your way to picking apart Joyce, I decided you weren't the idiot-reporter-turned-critic I had hoped for."

"Sorry to disappoint."

"Well, now I have some intelligent reviews to read—besides my own. And," he sighed with mock pomposity, "the life of a king is boring, except for challenges to his throne."

"Should we just start throwing Oscar Wilde's epigrams at each other?" I asked. "We seem to be heading that way."

"No, Stephens, we both know them all anyway. It wouldn't impress either one of us. Care to try a real conversation?"

"Don't mind if I do," I said, and we began an alternately highbrow, lowbrow discussion of Arthur Miller's work and his marriage to Marilyn Monroe. Devane's recall of productions and performances was faultless, his memory prodigious and exact. Maneuvering him into the areas of musical comedy, Shakespeare, light comedy, and the heavy-handed proletarian dramas of the Depression, I could find no cracks in his knowledge.

"Does the professor pass the student's test?" Devane chided, mockingly.

"With full honors," I said. And from then on we were excellent friends.

Later I understood that Devane's flamboyant image was clever PR. For a critic, the basic equation is taste plus fame equals power, and everyone knew Richard Devane. From a distance, he was a hard man to understand. Although married, he was frequently photographed with young women at his side and he never mentioned his wife, who was not seen in public. Under the gossips' eyes, Devane enjoyed the attention of beautiful women, which led to constant speculation. The rumormongers were always disappointed by the lack of proof; they failed to realize that Devane flirted with the old women too, out of kindness, while playing on the younger ones out of duty.

I met Virginia Devane at their house, where she was lying in the bed she had occupied for the past four years after her kidneys began to malfunction and a stroke made her left side useless. I often had dinner at their house. It was bad form for rival critics to be good friends, so we only exchanged polite greetings in public. Devane suggested once that it would be more fitting if we just growled at each other.

I had considered myself well versed in the theater, but then my education truly began. In theatrical discussions, I was a poor match for Devane. I would read heavily on one or two subjects before each dinner and steer the talk into my staked-out territory. I felt like a general with too few troops, forced to depend upon tactical skirmishes until my army was strong enough for honest battle. Devane's greatest advantage was his four decades of experience, so I spent dozens of hours in the microfilm room of the city library, studying his early reviews and articles. He was sixty-four now and had covered everything from Albee to *Gigi* and *Sweeney Todd* to Shaffer.

Devane and I used to sit in Virginia's room and argue our points across her bed. The stroke had permanently depleted her energy, but her mind and personality were left intact. She rarely spoke and usually kept her eyes closed, but a half-smile or raised eyebrow proved her attention. Each night I left the two of them upstairs, Devane in his chair, holding her hand and reading aloud until she fell asleep. As I left the house on summer nights, I could hear the soothing steadiness of his voice drifting down from the open window.

Two years after that first party, we were at the Barrymore Theater for the opening of yet another Garrio brothers production. The lobby was packed, the crowd able to move only in a tight shuffle-step. With difficulty, an arm could be raised to brush the February snow from a shoulder or lapel. Devane was in his usual place, halfway up the left staircase, looking down at the crowd, smiling and nodding to those who waved or called his name. The white scarf and hair and the dark eyebrows made him recognizable even to those whose vanity kept their glasses in a pocket until the house lights went down.

The opening was of a musical held over in Philadelphia for a month while show doctors tried to breathe some life into it. According to rumor, the songs were instantly forgettable, the humor was sit-com quality, and the female lead was eating garlic twice a day to spite the male lead, her former husband. To cover the absence of good writing, good acting, or good music, the Garrios had added a high-priced comic, a nude love scene performed in silhouette behind a scrim, and plenty of double-entendres. That the setting had been switched from Brooklyn 1950s to New Orleans 1930s to Maine 1900 did not bode well. While interviewing a veteran understudy the week before, I was told—off the record—that the cast of *Hope for Love* was calling the show *Hope for a Miracle.*

The Barrymore is majestic, with its neoclassical friezes, its intricately carved arches, and the murals on the vaulted ceiling painted by an obvious admirer of Michelangelo. Seating capacity was twenty-seven hundred and, by tradition, the top critics were placed on the aisle so that as the final curtain came down, they could get out quickly to make their deadlines.

I was always pleased to have Devane in the seat in front of me, as he was tonight, for he was short enough that my view was never blocked. The lobby lights had dimmed twice, and most people were in their seats when the orchestra did its best with an unpromising overture. The show's first act was as bad as I'd feared or, to be honest, as terrible as I had hoped. The male lead/former husband went flat three times on his first song, and the cast's accents were a free-wheeling melange of Brooklyn, Southern, and Down East.

If it's true, as most actors believe, that the number of coughs indicate a show's appeal, this one was either a bomb or being played before an outpatient ward. One man in my row was hacking so badly he left, coughing, wheezing, and whispering apologies as he moved through the darkness during a scene change.

To a critic, a bad show can be a joy. A scathing review usually makes better reading than words of praise, for the same reason, I suspect, that villains are inherently more interesting than heroes. I was waiting to see the slow shake of Devane's head as he started to scribble his scorn, but he was still watching.

As the first-act curtain fell to barely perfunctory applause, I leaned forward to ask Devane whether he intended to be bombastic or smoothly devastating. Instead, I found myself staring at a single red-edged hole in the back of his head. Disbelieving, I pulled myself upright and leaned over his left shoulder. His eyes were still, locked in a frozen stare.

Time slowed with my adrenaline rush and I remembered a train wreck I'd covered. The survivors had been stunned, unable to fit sudden death into their ordinary lives. Now I understood them. My chest felt tight and I tried for a deep breath. My lungs hesitated, as if they had forgotten how, then pulled in new air and my mind began to clear. I realized that many people in the audience were standing now and moving towards the lobby. Nothing I did would save Richard Devane, but I could act with the discipline he would expect.

I pulled out a handkerchief and folded it across Devane's forehead as I tilted his head back against the seat. His eyelids I brushed closed as I took my hand from the handkerchief. With his face up, the bullet hole couldn't be seen. His heart must have stopped pumping immediately because only a little blood had oozed out and trickled down his collar.

The aisle was on the left and the seat on Devane's right was empty. I didn't know the man on the other side of it. I leaned toward him and in a half-whisper said, “Hey,” with an unpleasant sharpness that made him look up.

“My friend’s not well. I want you to make sure no one comes through this way and that no one bothers him.”

The man’s expression was uncertain behind his tortoise-shell glasses. He stammered for an answer, then looked at the hefty woman beside him. She leaned forward and in a take-charge voice said, “Don’t worry. I’ll make sure nobody goes through here.” I nodded and turned away, certain that no one would challenge her.

The aisle was jammed and I wouldn’t be able to work my way up to the lobby for several minutes. I moved down the six rows to the orchestra pit, saw the small ladder in the far left corner, and used it. A few musicians were still in their small folding chairs, and I reconized one of the surprised faces.

“Hello, Margaret,” I said to the oboist, forcing my voice to be casual. “Where’s that phone you all get in trouble for using?”

Taken aback by my invasion of stagehouse territory, she just pointed.

The conductor was on the phone and a second man was waiting to use it. I pulled a roll of bills out of my pocket, and holding a twenty in each hand, gestured towards each of them at eye level. Almost in unison they nodded, the conductor saying, “Must run,” as he hung up and the other man stepping back with a flourish. When I handed them the money, I said it was a personal call, and they willingly walked away, admiring their quick profit.

What I was doing would seem callous, almost ghoulish, to a normal person. Perhaps detachment is a reporter’s way of resisting shock —using objectivity to seal off the cave of emotions.

The operator at the paper put me through to Frank, the front page editor. I told him what had happened, and he told someone next to him to slow down the first edition run; everything above the fold would be rebuilt.

“Okay, ready,” he said to me and I dictated about seven hundred words off the top of my head, heavy on setting and circumstances, Devane’s prominence and the show itself. I made him repeat Devane’s age.

“And don’t let some idiot change it,” I said. “I don’t care what source he gets it from. Also, lay out the story, then call the police. Send a photographer over here now so he's in position when things start happening. Another reporter should work the lobby as the audience leaves. And, Frank, play it straight. Don't even think of using 'Death on the Aisle' as a subhead. Leave me a lot of room on the jump page for a long add and a second story."

Frank was good. In his early fifties, he had never missed a typo and had covered so many stories as a reporter or editor that nothing excited him any more. That's the kind of person you want handling the front page.

I went back to my seat as the lights were dimming again. The police arrived twenty minutes into the second act. A cop in uniform and the theater manager came down the aisle and knelt next to Devane. Using the manager's penlight, the cop first looked at Devane, then flicked the light into my face. He shut it off as he told the manager, "Stop the show."

The whole cast was on stage for a song and dance number. The manager, deferentially hunched over to avoid blocking anyone's view, hurried to the back of the loge seating. The order was relayed by a technician on the lighting board, and the curtain was brought down at the song's end. The cop's arrival had started the audience murmuring, and they craned their necks to see what was happening. Five more policemen came down the aisle as the lights went up, and a voice on the loudspeaker said that due to "extraordinary circumstances" the rest of the show had been cancelled and patrons were to keep their ticket stubs for reimbursement or use at another performance. The audience was requested to leave the theater, but police told the approximately thirty people in seats near Devane to remain. The rest departed reluctantly, looking over their shoulders while being herded out.

"Are you Stephens?" one cop asked me.

I nodded.

"Your paper called us. Why the hell didn't you call us when this happened?"

"Can you bring dead men back to life?" I asked.

He didn't like my attitude and switched tactics.

"Because of you we'll probably never catch the guy who killed him."

"Tell me what you would have done differently thirty minutes ago."

His response was to narrow his eyes and give me an "I'm remembering your face for the next time" look. I didn't care.

A Lieutentant Featherstone arrived to take charge. Photos were taken, the coroner came and left, and the remaining audience members whispered among themselves as they watched the police. No one had seen anything exceptional. The timid man and his big wife told of my wanting to make sure Devane wasn't disturbed–which, I pointed out, also served to avoid a panic and preserve the evidence. After names and addresses were taken, everyone else was allowed to leave. Featherstone began quizzing me. A nasty look sprang into the first cop's eyes when Featherstone noted I had the best seat for killing Devane. But the lieutenant neatly reversed field by commenting that only an idiot would consider it for long.

"You're a possibility, Stephens, but not a good one. And a conspiracy among the group of you sitting near Devane is ridiculous. A long-range shot is out–too many variables and probably the wrong kind of bullet. My other problem is 'Why here?' No plan is foolproof, and the logistics are dangerous. It's a lot safer to have an 'accidental' death some other place, by shredding the electric wiring at his house or slipping an air bubble into an artery. Also, we can forget mistaken identity. Devane was too well-known, and even in the dark that white hair stands out."

Featherstone explained that either a zipgun or a pistol with a silencer must have been used, but I was sure no one could have reached behind Devane's head without my seeing him. Then I realized who the killer was.

"The coughing man," I said.

"Who's he?" asked Featherstone.

"The only person who stepped between Devane and me during the first act. He's the only person who could have done it," I said, then related the little I had noticed of the man. "But I do remember that his loudest cough was as he stepped in front of me. His hands were hidden, I think he was holding his overcoat in front of him."

"And under that was the gun," said Featherstone. "My guess is that the shot went in just where he wanted–three or four inches above the collar. The killer needs a minute to get out of the building–if there's a lot of blood, he gets caught. So he aims for the brain stem because a bullet there shuts down the whole body and the only bleeding would be from the scalp. If he uses a small-caliber gun, the entrance hole is small and there's no exit wound. The killer thought everything out. We can find out what seat he was in and whether anyone remembers what he looked like, but that won't help us."

"In other words," I said, "we are going to find that the ticket was paid for in cash and that he arrived just after the lights went down. And if he wore a fake beard or mustache, that's the only feature anyone will remember."

Featherstone gave a discouraged nod.

"In answer to your question 'Why here?' I'd say the purpose was to make a point—in a very public way."

"Seems so," said Featherstone. "But who is the lesson meant for?"

Neither of us had an answer. He wrote a few more notes and I could see he had run out of questions for me. After taking down my home telephone number, he gave me permission to leave, then stopped me.

"You seem a little dispassionate about all this," Featherstone observed.

"My first newpaper job was working the police beat," I said. "I know this will all get to me later, when I start thinking about it. I'm trying not to—until I'm alone. Make sense?" I asked.

The lieutenant said it did and turned away.

Two minutes later I was back on the orchestra pit telephone.

"Any problems, Frank?"

"Nope, great shape. Each of the television stations quoted our story, and Jimmy got a good photo of Devane being wheeled through the lobby, past a lot of rich types. Rachel interviewed about a dozen people from the audience and got two actors as they came out the stage door. Both wire services picked up our story, giving us full credit, and the new publisher saw it on TV in Chicago. He called with congratulations."

I took no pleasure in the compliments. I just said, "Good, glad they're using our name," and asked for someone who could type fast and spell correctly. A woman came on the line, said she had read everything I sent in before and was ready for the add. I dictated another six hundred words for the bottom of the main story, then gave her five hundred words for a sidebar about Devane's life. I didn't need any notes. She spelled back all the names and checked the times and numbers before we hung up.

Once before I had to tell a wife she was a widow. I remember the hateful duty exactly. The second time was no easier. A nurse always sat with Virginia when Devane was away, and I motioned for her to leave the room. As the door closed, Virginia said, "Richard's not alive, is he?" Her voice was slow and matter-of-fact.

"Did you hear it on TV or did someone call?"

"Neither," she said. "From the first year we were together, I could always feel Richard's moods, even when we were apart. There was always a presence I could feel and read. A few hours ago, when I woke up," her voice began to break, "I couldn't feel him there any more. He was gone."

She closed her eyes and was silent for more than five minutes.

"Life isn't very forgiving, is it," she said. It wasn't a question.

"No," I agreed, aware that I didn't fully understand her meaning. "Basically, it's cruel."

"You can't make any mistakes," she said softly, her eyes still closed, but their lashes wet. "My mistake was one of judgment, Richard's mistake was one of faith." She lay still, but her right hand was clenched in a small fist so tight that the knuckles were a row of white mounds.

"Come back tomorrow morning," she said.

"I will," I promised, and as I left I heard her slight exhalation and the single word "Damn."

I slept for four hours that night. Only my body seemed to shut down, to get the rest it needed. I woke up fully alert at six A.M. and that's when the loss of Richard Devane hit me. Men of principle are hard to find, and my friend with the small round hole in the back of his head had been one of them. I know that grief is a self-centered emotion, that only the living can regret their losses. For the dead, well, maybe it's better for someone like Devane if there is nothing on the other side; then he would never know he had been robbed of his life. Neither life nor death was fair.

Fair. And yet Virginia, by saying Richard had paid, was implying there was a balance sheet—an unforgiving ledger kept somewhere. Devane had done something wrong, and Virginia knew what it was.

I do not remember getting up, showering, or eating. These are the times when habits are helpful, when the hands, arms, and legs do their appointed tasks without request while the mind works on, apart and distant.

I could not guess what mistake Devane's death answered for. His values, in life and work, had been the highest. Wealth had no allure for him. The man who said the word "theater" with the reverence that others reserved for the word "church" had already attained the status and position he most wanted. As a critic, Devane's standards were impeccable. Repeatedly he had told me I must adhere to what I thought was right. "Keep the standards fair and high and they'll respect you," he said. "If you want to be loved, find another job.

"The shows will come and go, but you and the standards remain. If you send the public to wretched productions or keep them from the great ones, you deserve to lose your seat on the aisle," he had told me. "You must be a fair Roman: thumbs up and the show should live, thumbs down and it deserves to die."

At ten o'clock I was standing next to Virginia's bed. She was dozing, and I softly called her name. Her face twitched, then lost its concentration as she came out of her dream. She opened her eyes and blearily tried to focus on me.

"I was dreaming of my honeymoon with Richard," she said slowly, her voice still mired in sleep. "I was young again, reliving everything, but I knew how Richard was going to die. I wanted to tell him, so he could avoid it, but I couldn't say the words."

She paused and I stayed silent.

"I'm sorry," she said. "I guess I'm not making much sense." She pushed herself up into a half-sitting position and I saw she had put on one of Devane's old button-down shirts.

"I'll try to explain, but it's hard to put into words. I never would have told anyone if it hadn't finally killed Richard. Four years ago is when it started, when I first became sick." She stopped for a moment to compose herself, then continued.

"Richard and I never could have children. Somehow, that pulled us closer together, rather than pushing us apart like it does to most couples. We developed that special sense of being a twosome. Richard was the kindest of men and he trusted me completely. He had a need to trust, to believe absolutely in someone, and I was lucky enough to be that someone.

"Richard never told me about his life when he was growing up, about what happened to his parents. His father left Richard and his mother when he was only seven—one afternoon his father went to the store and never came home. Two years later, his mother abandoned him. She took a few things but left no note. Richard waited in that apartment at the age of nine for two weeks, waited for his mother to come home. She never did.

"There was no other family. A neighbor with three children took him in. I believe they loved him like one of their own, but the damage had been done. To Richard's mind, it was his fault that his parents left. He felt that their leaving somehow meant he wasn't good enough. About twenty years ago, I met the woman who took him in, and she said it broke her heart that Richard always expected his second family to leave him, too. She said that some days, when he came home from school, he looked almost surprised to see she was still there. He never got his hopes up and he tried to protect himself by always being prepared for the worst."

Virginia stopped to get her breath again, then continued.

"He immersed himself in books—his own emotions were safe when he was in someone else's make-believe world. I always thought he loved the theater because it was the closest thing to life where he could still be safe, where no part of him was at stake.

"When I started to feel sick, I didn't tell him about the tests and the doctors' appointments. That was my mistake in judgment. And I didn't realize I was becoming distant and preoccupied with the medical problems. For one test, I had to stay overnight at the hospital. I scheduled it for a night Richard would be in New York. I waited until after his usual evening call, at about six o'clock, then I went to the hospital.

"Much later, I learned that he had called the house at ten o'clock and then every hour after that until four A.M. The next day, when he got back, he didn't tell me he had tried to call again, just asked what I had done that night, and I said I'd stayed home. Richard had noticed all my silences, felt my distance from him, and with that last lie, he concluded I was having an affair. Emotionally, I think he always expected it. He was braced for it because that would be the first step for the final abandoning—by me."

The talking was visibly tiring her and she stopped to sip from the water glass on the bedside table before proceeding.

"Richard's self-defense was to find someone else, another woman, so that when I left him he wouldn't be alone again. The woman was in her early forties, not part of the theater world, and very discreet. There was no scandal though it lasted several months.

"One night, I blacked out and Richard took me to the hospital. There he learned how long I had been sick. My doctor said that Richard turned a terrible white and began to shake, for he realized what had happened and what he had done. He refused to leave my hospital room, he was there when I woke up and every day after. I remember him sitting next to the bed, not saying a word, tears running down his face. Not until three years later did I know he was crying for his lack of trust, his lack of faith in me.

"He didn't tell me about the affair, not even when the other woman's maid saw the chance to make some fast money. Her brother was a stagehand and he went to the Garrios. They paid the maid ten thousand dollars for a written statement, including dates and times, about Richard's affair. They knew I was sick, and that's when they began to blackmail Richard. What they wanted were good reviews for their shows."

I had never heard of its being done, but it was so logical it seemed inevitable. At least a half million dollars was needed to mount even an average sized production. Paying salaries of cast and crew; renting a theater, costumes and props; hiring an orchestra if necessary; and buying the rights to a property or an option amounted to an expensive gamble on the critical tastebuds of a few men making reporters' salaries. If the praise of the most important man was assured, then it was no gamble at all—and better than a million-dollar ad campaign.

Virginia continued, "Richard decided he would compromise all his standards as a critic rather than let me know about the affair. He wrote four reviews he didn't believe in, and I knew it each time. The Garrios covered themselves by using front men as the producers on three of the four shows so they wouldn't be the common link between the inconsistent reviews. Two shows were comedies, two were musicals, and Richard was depressed for nearly a week after writing each false review.

"A year ago, I begged him to tell me what was going on, and he finally told me everything. It was hard, thinking of him with another woman, but I understood, and after a time the hurt was less. The other result was that it ended the Garrios' hold on him. For the past year he had looked forward to this show because the Garrios had invested so heavily in it. They were relying on the ticket sales that Richard's review would generate. He waited until two days before the opening; then he told them they didn't own him any more."

"In just two days, the Garrios decided to hire a killer and go from blackmail to murder," I said.

"When you came back from the opening, instead of Richard, I knew what had happened, and why," she said. "And the Garrios have gotten away with it. A killer like that is untraceable, and he is the only tie between the Garrios and what happened to Richard. And that means they're safe."

We talked for nearly two hours more. She wanted no words of comfort, I didn't offer any. We talked about Devane, about the quality of his work, and even laughed again at things he had done or said.

It was a wake for a party of two.

Driving from the house, I thought how the Garrios had misjudged Devane. They had killed him to keep him quiet, but he never would have gone public with a story about the blackmail—the personal shame would have been too great.

I stopped at a pay phone and called the office. I asked the top business writer to gather what he could about the Garrios from safe sources, people who wouldn't pass along the fact that questions were being asked. My second call was to Featherstone, but I was told he was out, possibly at the Barrymore. For several minutes I considered going there but decided to try a long shot, to give a tug on one of the few threads leading into the Garrios' world. The phone directory was ripped and water-curled, the page I wanted was missing, but information had the number.

The telephone line changed its hum three times before ringing on the other end. The receiver was picked up and I heard the sound of a vacuum's dying roar before I heard a voice.

"Hello, this is Miss Harling's house," said a woman with an Asian accent.

"Is Miss Harling there?" I asked.

"I am sorry, sir," she said, articulating each word. "She has gone to Detroit for the day. She will be home tonight."

I thought for a moment, then asked, "Do you know what time her plane left?"

"Yes, sir. She said it would be at about one o'clock."

My watch showed 12:25.

"Did she mention what airline?"

"Yes, sir, but I do not remember the name. I think it is the one with the rhyme, the one that says, 'We bring Chicago to you and Detroit too.' "

I thanked her and hung up.

Twenty minutes later, I was running through the door of the airline terminal. On the overhead TV screen, "Final Call" blinked next to the 12:55 to Chicago and Detroit. I took the stairs two at a time and hoped my story would get me past the guards at the "Passengers Must Show Ticket" sign. As I came up to the glass partition, I saw Lea Harling step from the waiting area onto the gangway leading to the plane. It would do no good now to claim she was my wife and had both our tickets.

I sprinted back down the stairs to the ticket counters and found an agent just opening a window. I bought a round-trip ticket for the flight and within four minutes was back up the stairs past the guards and metal detector, and was the last passenger to board the plane. As I stepped into the cabin, I saw Lea Harling sitting alone. The sunlight from the window she was gazing out made her blonde hair glow as if it had a light of its own. I sat down next to her and was putting on my seat belt when she turned to look at me. Where she had expected to find a stranger was instead a familiar face, though it took her a few moments to place it.

"You're the other critic," she said. "I remember you." She paused while her mind kept working. "And you're the one who wrote the stories about Devane in today's paper."

The first half-hour of our flight to Chicago was spent talking about the murder, and then I moved the conversation where I wanted it.

"Where are you going to?"

"Back to Boston, really. This plane makes two stops and then turns around and heads back. I'm delivering a script for the Garrios," she touched a corner of the large brown envelope in her lap. "There is this writer in Detroit, I never heard of him, but he has to read this tonight. The Garrios are deciding whether to produce the show and their option on it expires tomorrow."

I thought that someone had taken the time to prepare a plausible story for the innocent messenger.

We talked about the Garrios' shows, their successes, and how they had stayed with light entertainment, avoiding the heavy dramas. Financially, revivals, musicals, and comedies were the best bets, she said.

"Isn't that what you were best at, Lea? Comedy?"

"You remember!" she said happily. "It's been five years since I was on a stage, and I think that's about fifty years in show business time. I haven't been in a show since I did that revival of *Boy Crazy.*"

"I got all good reviews and a great one. I had two songs, one was just for laughs but I could pull it off and the other was a slow, sad ballad. Some people were surprised I had the voice for it, but I do. One night I knew I did it just right, before the right kind of audience. I finished it and walked off and no one clapped. I know it sounds strange, and it scared me at first, because I thought no one liked it. Then they began to applaud, louder and louder, until I had to go back out and take a bow because they wouldn't let the show go on. You see," she said, "nobody clapped because they didn't want to break the spell of the song. That's the best it ever was for me."

She closed her eyes and leaned back in her seat, feeling again her glorious moment.

"Why was that your last show?" I asked.

"I don't know," she said, her eyes opening with a troubled look. "I've thought about it a lot. I guess people just have streaks of bad luck in life. For two years I got turned down for parts. After that, people just forgot about me. I wasn't even called for readings any more."

"Did you ever wonder if you'd been blacklisted?"

"That's just what it seemed like," she said, "but I didn't have any enemies. I'd never had any fights with anyone."

"What do you think about the idea you were blacklisted—not because someone hated you but because they liked you?"

She was quiet for a few moments before slowly saying, "I don't understand."

"Have you ever thought that the people who blacklisted you were the Garrios?"

Her look was incredulous and the meaning of my words silenced her. She looked out the window and, while combing through the past five years, thought of evidence to fit the new idea. The bright sunlight at thirty thousand feet showed the small lines that age had brought to her eyes and mouth.

"I don't want to believe it," she said. I can't believe they . . . that they would take that away from me. But it fits. They always say they get what they want. I guess I'm no different from anything else.

"Who else could tell me that's what happened?" she asked.

"Who are the critics around the country you respect the most?"

"In New York there are Dorrance and Briggs, and Ramos in L.A."

I pulled a small address book out of my jacket pocket and said, "We have thirty minutes during the stopover in Chicago. Pick a name and we'll call him."

After a rough landing, we walked off the plane together, Lea still carrying the brown envelope. At a nearby bank of telephones, she took the address book out of my hands and studied Dorrance's number. She watched as I punched it in, then added my calling card number. I was relieved to hear Dorrance's voice. I told him I was with Lea and that she wanted to confirm my story about what ended her career. I handed her the receiver. She said hello, listened for several minutes, and the pain in her face gave way to a hard anger. She said, "Thank you," hung up, and then surprised me.

"Our meeting on the plane wasn't by chance, was it?"

"No, not at all," I admitted.

"Then you must want this," she replied, handing me the brown envelope. "It must be quite a script."

"It's no script."

She pulled the envelope back and ripped it open. Her expression told me I had guessed right. "This is all money," she said in disbelief. "It's all hundred-dollar bills."

A lot of new ideas had hit her in the last hour, and she was having trouble adapting to them all. She stared into the envelope, bewildered.

"You need to deliver it," I told her. "Take the money to the man you're supposed to meet. But this is your chance to get back at the Garrios."

She looked up at me and cocked her head to the side. "Will it be worth five years?"

"It might be worth even more," I replied, and asked her for the envelope.

She handed it to me without a word. Before we reboarded, I bought an identical envelope and a notepad at the airport gift shop.

Lea didn't talk during the short hop to Detroit. Oblivious to me and everything else, she stared dully out the window into the darkening sky. I prepared the new envelope and wrote a single sentence on a sheet of notepaper.

I tried to coach Lea a little, to get her out of the robotlike trance she was caught in. I made her realize she had to play the role of dutiful messenger, and she nodded her understanding. She had to make the delivery alone because I might be recognized by the coughing man. The killer would have looked down the aisle to see who sat behind Devane. My plan was based on an assumption: any doubts would kill it, along with Lea and me.

She walked off the plane in Detroit carrying the envelope in both hands and returned within five minutes. A white man of "average height with an average-looking face" waved to her, took the envelope out of her hands, and walked away. Whether it was the killer or someone else made no difference.

As the plane pulled out of the gate and taxied to the runway, Lea asked, "How dangerous was what I just did?"

"Very, if I guessed wrong. If I guessed right, it will be the best thing you ever did."

"That payoff," she said, "was it for the man who shot Devane?"

I nodded. "I can almost guarantee it. The killer is the kind who only works away from his home city, who flies in, does the job, and leaves. The very good ones, like this one must be, set their own prices and their own conditions. For example, a hand-carried cash payment the next day."

"Do they care who they kill?"

"Most of them don't, though I've heard of a few who won't take a job if a child is the target. The important thing is the pride in being a real pro, never making mistakes and planning every detail. Every clean job adds to the reputation, which adds to the price. The client gets full value for his money.

"And," I said, "he is not the kind of person who would want a messenger to talk about her trip."

"It could be fatal?" she asked.

"If he ever thinks you were anything but a good little errand girl,we can write your obit now. And mine, too, because before he killed you, he would ask a lot of questions in a very forceful way."

She nodded and was quiet for most of the trip back to Boston.

As the plane began its descent, I asked if anyone was likely to meet her at the airport.

"Maybe," she answered. "The Garrios are unpredictable. I'm supposed to call in and tell them I'm back."

"Good, do that, but stay away from them for the next week or so," I said. "If you have a good friend somewhere, out of New England, now's the time to pay a visit. In case anyone is here to meet you, get off early and walk away from the gate. I'll try to be the last one off."

As the plane pulled to a stop, Lea gave me the name of a friend on Long Island she might stay with. She stood up and slipped down the aisle without saying goodbye, but just before she moved out of sight, she looked over her shoulder and gave me a smile with only a hint of the actress in it.

Devane's funeral the following day became a media event because of the celebrities in attendance. Some came because of their feelings for Devane, others for their love of free publicity. There were some great performances on the church steps. Virginia avoided the circus and the cameras. She was wheeled into the church through a side door after everyone was seated and left the moment the eulogy was over. The burial was private. Virginia stayed in the car parked on a side road thirty feet away.

For the next two days there was no news on the murder, and the daily "police are continuing their investigation" stories were shorter and moved deeper into the paper. A special matinee of *Hope for Love* was given for the opening-night crowd and the critics. Every review was a hatchet job.

One night later, I got the telephone call I was hoping for. At two A.M I was asleep but picked up the receiver after the first ring.

"Stephens?" said the familiar voice.

"Hi, Frank. What's happened?"

"The Garrios aren't being original, but they are big news. A half hour ago they were found downtown in their office, each with a bullet in the back of the head."

"Any sign of their being tortured?" I asked.

Frank's hesitation reflected his surprise at my question.

"No, the guy we've got over there said they were each sitting at a desk, wearing an expensive suit. No sign of a struggle, their hands weren't tied."

"No clues?"

"One, but it was intentional so it's no clue at all."

"What was it?"

Frank read me the note.

"I don't know what it means," I lied. "Do you need any background on the Garrios?"

"No, we looked in your files and took out the clips you had on them. I'll make sure the folder's put back."

"I appreciate the call," I said and hung up.

Forty minutes later, I was standing next to Virginia's bed. The night nurse had been sent downstairs.

"The Garrios had a visitor tonight," I began and told her most of what Frank had said.

"And what do you know about it?" she asked, watching my face.

I told her about my trip to Chicago and Detroit, Lea's call to Dorrance, and the delivery of the envelope.

"How much was Richard's life worth?"

"Sixty thousand dollars was the price."

"What was it you did with the envelope?"

"I took out forty thousand and added a short note from the Garrios."

"Which said . . ."

"Just the words, 'We have decided this is what the job was worth.' "

"I don't think the man in Detroit would have liked that," she said softly.

"No," I agreed. "He couldn't let anyone short him like that. I bet that it would be a matter of pride and reputation. If word got out, other customers would do the same thing. My worry was that the killer might have had some doubts about the note's being from the Garrios. Then he would have interrogated them first. But they had a reputation for arrogance, so it fit that they would try something like that. No interrogation means that Mr. Detroit didn't suspect Lea. I made sure she was away from the Garrios when the killer came back. If she had been around, he would probably have killed her too, just to be thorough. And he left a note, so I'm sure he won't go after her."

"Or you," Virginia said.

"Or me," I agreed. "But I knew the risk. Lea was just a pawn. I didn't tell her beforehand because I didn't want her to look nervous and give anything away when she delivered the money. She's an actress, but acting for your life is too hard for anyone.

"I think I know now why Richard's death was done so publicly, so obviously that it would be big news. That was the purpose—for two reasons. First, think of the public as having a complex personality. The same people who give money for earthquake victims or to end a famine can yell 'Jump!' or 'Coward!' to a man standing on a building ledge. The Garrios knew how to market a show, and murder was their ultimate gimmick."

"They killed Richard just to have a hit?" Virginia asked, her voice shaking.

"No, I think he was going to be killed anyway. But the right circumstances would be worth millions to the Garrios, and they were right. Despite all the reviews, *Hope for Love* is a sellout for the next four weeks here, and the advance sale in New York is two million dollars—every ticket going to someone who wants to see the show a critic was murdered at."

"God, it's ghoulish," she said.

"Yes, it is. And the irony is that the Garrios' murders will hype the sales even more."

Virginia was quiet for a while before asking, "And the second reason for its being done at the theater?"

"I'm not sure, but I'll bet Richard wasn't the only critic the Garrios had a hold on. If that's true, his murder was the best possible threat to keep all the other critics in line. By proving they were willing to kill, the Garrios could prevent any revolt. When Richard was killed, those critics would have guessed what happened. Now that the Garrios are dead, the same critics are breathing a lot easier."

"What about the evidence the Garrios used to blackmail each of them? Someone else could start using it."

"I called Featherstone. He said he'll look for whatever photos or letters the Garrios might have been holding. There's a safe in the Garrios' office, and Featherstone will be there when the police open it tomorrow. He'll personally mail the evidence back to each critic. For Lea, I'll send her the forty thousand, spread out over two years. It will be money to live on while she rebuilds her career. I'll do it anonymously, with a warning to keep quiet about the money, but I think she'll eventually figure out where it came from."

"And the note the killer left at the Garrios', what did it say?"

"Simply, *Paid in full.*"

Virginia nodded slowly, then said, "By everyone."

She was crying as I left the room.

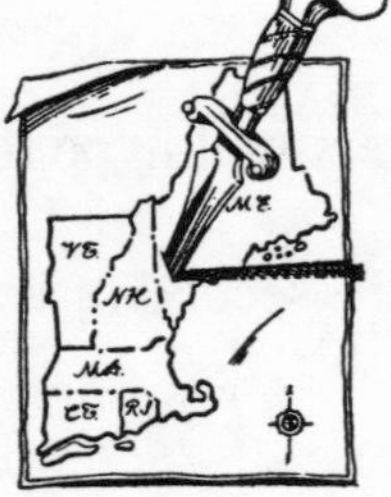

THE LIBRARY OF CRIME CLASSICS®

CHARLOTTE ARMSTRONG
The Balloon Man
The Chocolate Cobweb
A Dram of Poison
Lemon in the Basket
A Little Less Than Kind
Mischief
The Unsuspected
The Witch's House

JACQUELINE BABBIN
Bloody Soaps
Bloody Special

GEORGE BAXT
The Affair at Royalties
The Alfred Hitchcock Murder Case
The Dorothy Parker Murder Case
I! Said the Demon
The Neon Graveyard
A Parade of Cockeyed Creatures
A Queer Kind of Death
Satan Is a Woman
Swing Low Sweet Harriet
The Talullah Bankhead Murder Case
Topsy and Evil
Who's Next?

KYRIL BONFIGLIOLI
After You With the Pistol
Don't Point That Thing At Me
Something Nasty in the Woodshed

ANTHONY BOUCHER
Nine Times Nine
Rocket to the Morgue

CARYL BRAHMS & S.J. SIMON
A Bullet in the Ballet
Murder a la Stroganoff
Six Curtains for Stroganova

CHRISTIANNA BRAND
Cat and Mouse

MAX BRAND
The Night Flower

HERBERT BREAN
The Traces of Brillhart
Wilders Walk Away

JOHN DICKSON CARR
Below Suspicion
The Burning Court
Death Turns the Tables
The Door to Doom
Fell and Foul Play
Hag's Nook
He Who Whispers
The House at Satan's Elbow
Merrivale, March and Murder
The Murder of Sir Edmund Godfrey
The Problem of the Green Capsule
The Sleeping Sphinx
The Three Coffins
Till Death Do Us Part
Writing as Carter Dickson
Death In Five Boxes
The Gilded Man
He Wouldn't Kill Patience
The Judas Window
Nine—and Death Makes Ten
The Peacock Feather Murders
The Plague Court Murders
The Punch and Judy Murders
The Reader Is Warned
The Red Widow Murders

The Skeleton In the Clock
The Unicorn Murders
The White Priory Murders

HENRY CECIL
Daughter's In Law
Settled Out of Court
Without Fear or Favour

LESLIE CHARTERIS
Angels Of Doom
The First Saint Omnibus
Getaway
Knight Templar
The Last Hero
The Saint In New York

EDMUND CRISPIN
The Case of the Gilded Fly
Holy Disorders

CARROLL JOHN DALY
Murder from the East

LILLIAN DE LA TORRE
Dr. Sam: Johnson, Detector
The Detections of Dr. Sam: Johnson
The Return of Dr. Sam: Johnson, Detector
The Exploits of Dr. Sam: Johnson, Detector

PETER DICKINSON
Perfect Gallows
The Glass Sided Ants' Nest
Lizard In the Cup
The Sinful Stones

PAUL GALLICO
The Abandoned
Love of Seven Dolls
Mrs.'Arris Goes To Paris
Farewell To Sport

Too Many Ghosts
Thomasina

J. H. H. GAUTE AND ROBIN ODELL
The New Murderers Who's Who

JAMES GOLLIN
Eliza's Galliardo
The Philomel Foundation

DOUGLAS GREENE & ROBERT ADEY
Death Locked In

JONATHAN GOODMAN
The Passing of Starr Faithfull

DASHIELL HAMMETT & ALEX RAYMOND
Secret Agent X-9

A.P. HERBERT
Uncommon Law

REGINALD HILL
A Killing Kindness

RICHARD HULL
The Murder of My Aunt

E. RICHARD JOHNSON
Cage 5 Is Going To Break
Case Load Maximum
Dead Flowers
The God Keepers
The Inside Man
The Judas
Mongo's Back in Town
Silver Street

JONATHAN LATIMER
The Dead Don't Care
Headed for a Hearse

The Lady in the Morgue
Murder In the Madhouse
The Search for My Great Uncle's Head
Red Gardenias
Solomon's Vineyard

VICTORIA LINCOLN
A Private Disgrace—Lizzie Borden by Daylight

BARRY MALZBERG
Underlay

CYNTHIA MANSON & CHARLES ARDAI
New England Crime Chowder

NGAIO MARSH
The Collected Short Fiction of Ngaio Marsh

MARGARET MILLAR
An Air That Kills
Ask for Me Tomorrow
Banshee
Beast in View
Beyond This Point Are Monsters
The Cannibal Heart
The Fiend
Fire Will Freeze
How Like An Angel
The Iron Gates
The Listening Walls
Mermaid
The Murder of Miranda
Rose's Last Summer
Spider Webs
A Stranger in My Grave
Vanish In An Instant
Wall of Eyes

WILLIAM F. NOLAN
Look Out for Space
Space for Hire

WILLIAM O'FARRELL
Repeat Performance

STUART PALMER
The Penguin Pool Murder
Murder On The Blackboard
Murder On Wheels

STUART PALMER & CRAIG RICE
People VS Withers and Malone

BARBARA PAUL
Liars & Tyrants & People Who Turn Blue
Your Eyelids Are Growing Heavy

ELLERY QUEEN
Cat of Many Tails
Drury Lane's Last Case
The Ellery Queen Omnibus
The Tragedy of X
The Tragedy of Y
The Tragedy of Z

PATRICK QUENTIN
Black Widow
Puzzle for Players
Puzzle for Puppets
Puzzle for Wantons
Run To Death

S.S. RAFFERTY
Cork of the Colonies
Die Laughing

CLAYTON RAWSON
Death from a Top Hat
Footprints on the Ceiling
The Headless Lady
No Coffin for the Corpse